The
Medici
Guns

The
Medici
Guns

MARTIN WOODHOUSE

ROBERT ROSS

BOOK CLUB ASSOCIATES
London

This edition published 1975 by
Book Club Associates
by arrangement with J. M. Dent & Sons Ltd

© Windward Ltd, 1974

Printed in Great Britain by
Richard Clay (The Chaucer Press) Ltd
Bungay, Suffolk

To Penny again
and Ranette always

CHAPTER ONE

Science is the study of things possible.

Leonardo da Vinci

All day long, under a yellow and smoking Tuscan sky, the two huge guns vomited fire.

For seven weeks they had done so, and the weeks were lost in futility, in the wash and thunder of monstrous strength against the greater strength of granite ten feet thick which, cracking an inch here and dribbling a soft fall of dust there, still stood against the onslaught of hundred-pound iron shot.

Each gun fired three rounds in every hour. Thus, from one side or the other of Roderigo Leone, Captain-Gunner to the army of Florence and the Medici, the deep roar surged at intervals of ten minutes or so, pounding upon his cotton-stuffed eardrums as his lieutenants laid their slow-matches to the cannons' bellies. The powder-trains hissed and sparked, died into a half-second of silence while fire crept like a serpent down the touch-holes; power gathered, growling for an infinite moment of time inside an eight-inch thickness and more of Milanese bronze, and then flamed into incandescence and erupted, rocking four tons of barrel and five more of oak and ebony carriage, of leather strapping over greased axles, of beech-spoked wheels the height of a standing man, before driving the great weapons back into the piled earth of their redoubts; and woe betide the powder-boy who, fascinated by the titanic power he served or deafened into stupidity after eight hours of fetching and carrying, allowed a careless foot to linger in the trenched groove of their recoil.

In that long moment of stillness before eruption, Rigo's head would turn, away from Scudo upon his left or Agnolo Fulvio at his right (leaping nimbly backward, match in hand) and towards the massive wall he sought to breach, half a mile away across the valley. Sometimes his gunner's eye would pick out the nine-inch ball in flight; sometimes he would imagine that it had done so;

7

often he would miss the hurtling shot until its impact against the grey, implacable breastwork of the citadel of Castelmonte.

Watching the spurt of shattered rock-fragments he would know, before the ball fell to the sloping earth at the wall's foot and rolled into the muddy river, what effect it had made. Longing always for the spreading fissure, the tumble of stones from above which would announce that this blow—*this*—had brought about the beginning of the end, he measured his success meanwhile in ounces, in hand-spans of flaking surface or gouged crater, like a sculptor carving his will into a block of marble chip by slow chip, now attacking with a chisel-blow, now standing back to assess its worth. 'Patience,' he would tell his guns, reaching out to them with his mind: and, from right and left, the blackened muzzles replied in turn, saying 'Patience; what can withstand us? Given time, all must fall; only wait.'

It had been, thus far, a long and idle war, fought through a sun-lit autumn. Only the gunners sweated, their skins tattooed with ingrained powder at finger and wrist and neck. Forty strong, they slaved, ate and slept upon a ridge-top overlooking that small tributary of the Arno river which formed the perimeter defence of the hill-fort of Castelmonte. Relieved in groups of six for perhaps half a day in every ten, they walked to Pistrola, the nearest village, and drank in silence at the tavern.

It was unwise (so many an infantryman had found) to provoke a gunner. It was also difficult, since it was necessary to shout in order to do so—gunners being hard of hearing after the age of twenty. A gunner, however, was liable to take offence at the effortful opening and shutting of your mouth before he heard what you were saying, unless you were gesturing plainly with a tankard in an open and friendly fashion.

Moreover, gunners were immensely strong; they started at fourteen by hurling powder-kegs as apprentices, graduated (where they survived) to carrying shot as loaders and (by the time they were adequately bearded) to shifting, levering, cajoling and shoulder-heaving eighteen thousand pounds weight of weapon hither and yon in the pursuit of accuracy.

This training gave to each and every gunner three qualities, for good or ill: item, breadth of back; item, intemperance; item, a strong—some would say excessive—self-opinion. Thus when, in September, a certain ill-starred Florentine man-at-arms had observed, loudly and after several vain attempts to obtain attention, that Rigo Leone was a bare two-thirds of a man tall and resembled a pig both in the shape of his features and by reason of the centuries of dirt which blackened those parts of him which were visible, the latter had straight-armed him above his head and pitched him through the tavern window, breaking his skull upon the pump of a horse-trough at the other side of the street.

This incident being observed and its lesson passed on, the gunners (whose normal conversation could be heard from a mile away as they approached Pistrola) often found the inn deserted, or occupied only by those of obvious goodwill and respectfully silent habit. They therefore drank, agreed for the space of an afternoon that siege-guns were whores and the daughters of bitches, and returned to them with heavy pleasure and a perverse and ramrod pride.

That the wall of Castelmonte had survived for seven weeks they took as a personal affront, few of them having developed the tolerance of their Captain. Yet survived it had, and seemed likely to survive longer. If his guns spoke to Rigo of patience, none the less patience was not all. For in a week or two would arrive Castelmonte's strongest ally; winter.

*

On this late afternoon in October, A.D. 1477, two men on horseback watched the siege of Castelmonte from a rise above the road that ran through the upper valley of the Arno and connected Florence with Rome. Below them, in the basin between guns and city, the foot-soldiers of the *condottiero* Guido Toscanelli, mercenary in the employment of Florence, milled aimlessly between rows of tents and along the willow-lined banks of a stream which fed the small river beneath the citadel wall. Few approached the river itself; it ran a bare ten paces from the battlements and hence within easy bowshot of the besieged.

Between the river and the gunners' ridge the hooves of the Medici cavalry struck plumes of dust from the ancient road, the horses sidestepping in ragged and nervous unison with each bellow of the cannon. Smoke drifted from the ridge-top, sinking in the still autumn air and pooling in the bowl of brown and trampled grass below, seeping acridly into the lungs of the men who moved about their evening domestic tasks.

9

The man on the big roan patted his fretting mount and pointed to where, a hundred paces away, the flap of a scarlet pavilion had opened and a figure in dulled campaign-mail was emerging.

'Ha,' the man on the roan said. 'Our good Toscanelli takes the sun. An idle man.' He laughed, waving a white-gloved hand. The man in the tent mouth gestured in returned greeting. 'An idle man,' Giuliano de' Medici repeated, 'yet a good soldier for all that.'

'Why idle?' asked the rider on the piebald horse beside him. He was holding his reins in his right hand; with his left he drew upon the top page of a notebook resting on his thigh, tied in place by a narrow thong and chained to the waist of his tunic for security.

Both men were in their twenties. Except that the harness of the piebald was of merely serviceable leather, and that of Giuliano's roan glittered with gold and silver chasing, both were equally well-attired, equally handsome, equally flamboyant in appearance and temper; they might have passed at a distance for brothers. True, the rider of the roan smiled easily and often, while his companion tended towards a more serious mien; but such things are not easily seen from afar.

The man on the piebald dropped his stub of charcoal deliberately to the ground beside him, let go his reins, and dusted his fingertips together.

'Why call him idle?' he asked again. 'He has little to do. Until your Captain-Gunner rips yonder wall apart, a circumstance for which we may all wait yet awhile, how should he occupy himself? In knocking upon the main gate for admittance, or challenging Montefeltro to single combat?'

'There speaks the artist,' Giuliano said mockingly. 'Stick to your easel, my perceptive friend. Here we be soldiers, Guido and I. Where you see flowing wreaths of smoke, I smell brimstone. Where you see figures in a landscape—'

'How do you know what I see?'

'I imagine it, Leonardo; I imagine it. When I was ten, or perhaps twelve, as I recall, my tutors encouraged me to dabble paint on canvas, play the lute, and indulge in other sorts of foolery. I told them that my fingers would not answer my soul, which was none the less that of an artist, and made the canvas into a kite.'

'Which never left Mother Earth,' said the man on the piebald horse with good humour.

'I allow that. I insist, however, upon my artistic soul.'

'Continue, then. Where I see figures in a landscape—with the eye of a ten-year-old lad, I make no doubt—what do you perceive, Giuliano?'

'Idle soldiers. Look for yourself. They have set their tents on low ground, in order to be near the water—being too idle to carry their pitchers more than ten steps—and therefore they are choked by Rigo's brimstone; whereas, Leonardo, had they but the industry to hoist their water a mere thirty paces uphill they could breathe easily. Do not ask me, by the by, why guns should smell of brimstone. They do. I—'

His words were drowned in the boom of one of the siege-guns from the ridge to their left. By the time the echoes of its roll had died away, Giuliano had lost his advantage in dialogue; the man on the piebald was speaking.

'I have no need to ask you,' said Leonardo da Vinci. 'Guns smell of brimstone for the excellent reason that gunpowder contains brimstone, along with saltpetre and charcoal. Therefore, ride with me and learn; all friendship brings profit, the more so to the thick-headed. Tomorrow, if fortune smiles, I may teach you to fly kites.'

*

A short ride away, upon their ridge, the gunners of Florence still tended their massive charges between shot and shot, levering them forward from the recoil-banks with baulks of timber and with shoulders that strained against wheel-rim and carriage. While the staveman thrust his fifteen-foot ash pole, tipped with bound and oil-soaked rags, down the muzzle of Agnolo Fulvio's gun to scour the bore, Rigo Leone stood, fingering a smooth pebble and estimating what daylight he had left to him. The setting sun announced the close of the day's bombardment; it remained for Rigo to announce it too. He cast the pebble from him.

'Enough,' he said.

Agnolo Fulvio waved his powder-boys down. His men stood away from the spokes of the four great wheels, their grimy foreheads streaked with sweat. He spat casually upon the cannon's breech, and the spittle hissed gently; the axles creaked, settling. Agnolo raised a finger at his approaching Captain.

One more,' he said. 'One, Rigo.'

'No,' Rigo said.

'Give me my thirty. One is all I lack.'

'And is there some magic in thirty, then?'

'No magic. A mere satisfaction of the spirit,' said Agnolo, showing his teeth. 'The number twenty-nine, lacking form and fullness, offends me. Yonder the Duke of Urbino stands, whittling notches into a stick and making his reckoning of the gifts we deliver him. Having reached twenty-nine, his knife is doubtless still poised. Who am I to disappoint him? It would disturb my sleep, Rigo.'

The Captain-Gunner kicked at the turf.

'I have more to consider than Montefeltro's tally and your nightmares,' he pronounced. 'Lay your hand on the breech.'

Agnolo rested a horny palm briefly on the sweltering metal, withdrawing it again in suspicious haste. As though to contradict the clear evidence of his senses, he then leaned his leather-clad back against the gun.

'She'll fire from now until Doomsday,' he said.

'Not while I stand here,' said Rigo.

There was a certain formality about the shape of this exchange between the Captain-Gunner and his lieutenant, owing to the fact that it was performed (with variations) every evening and, indeed, served as a signal to the entire corps of gunners that the day's work was done. The crew of the second cannon trooped across, with the exception of those apprentices whose duty it was to clean the barrel and fittings against the morrow and Rigo's ill-tempered early morning inspection.

'Thirty,' announced Scudo innocently, upon arriving behind his commander. 'A good day. God grant us more of them. Though I think,' he went on, squinting against the sky, 'that I smell snow.'

'Leave your snow,' Agnolo said. 'Tell us how this thirty of yours is reached. Did we not fire the first shot this morning?'

'That is possible,' Scudo admitted.

'Then doubtless I must have fallen asleep during the day, thus allowing you to get off two rounds to my one. Three, in fact, since I was also the last to fire this evening.'

'That, too, is possible,' agreed Scudo. 'And your jacket is smoking, friend Agnolo, which means that you have, as ever, allowed your weapon to overheat.'

Agnolo pushed himself off the gun's breech with his elbows, feeling the small of his back hurriedly to disprove this piece of slander. Scudo laughed. Meanwhile Tesoro di Veluti—at seventeen, the youngest fully fledged gunner of the force—had sidled around the rear of the carriage and now tapped Agnolo's shoulder.

'I have counted the shot, Agnolo,' he said cautiously. 'We began with fifty, and now have but nineteen left. Therefore . . .'

'Therefore you have swallowed one, I dare say, and Agnolo another,' said Rigo testily, 'and therefore perhaps we may call a halt to this monkey-chatter, since I have better things to do than to stand here listening to it. Scudo, you smell snow, you say?'

'No,' Scudo said. 'It was a jest.'

'Then keep such jests from my hearing, Scudo. Snow is a serious matter.' He kicked again at the earth in front of his boot-tips, then turned away from the cannon to greet the arrival of the two horsemen who had just ridden up the reverse slope of the ridge. 'Welcome to the cavalry,' he said.

Leonardo da Vinci and Giuliano dismounted, looping the reins of the piebald and the roan around one of the upright posts of the rudely thatched hut which served as field magazine to the siege guns. Leaving Leonardo at the hut, sketch-book once more in hand, Giuliano strode forward.

'How goes the day?' he asked.

'Badly,' said Rigo. 'Yet there is always tomorrow.'

'And the day after,' said Giuliano. 'Well . . .' He looked across the valley at the city of Castelmonte. 'A strong wall, then,' he went on. 'I begin to think this a fruitless exercise—by which I intend no reproof whatever to yourself, Captain. What is your opinion?'

'A gunner's opinion, as always,' Rigo said. 'It is a strong wall indeed, but I shall bring it down.'

Giuliano de' Medici looked at the Captain-Gunner closely.

'Come, Rigo,' he said coaxingly. 'You speak to me alone, not to my brother Lorenzo; nor are you some half-witted knight who must give me phrases and flourishes. Therefore tell me. Five days? Or ten? Twenty?'

'Ten,' Rigo said. 'Ten; but the ground softens. I have heard it said that horses catch the scent of bad weather before men do. What does your horse say? Give me rain, as in September, and I am in difficulty. Give me snow, and I am lost. Do you see?'

'I do indeed. Bones of God, but Federigo da Montefeltro must be laughing at us, over there,' Giuliano said. 'He sacked Volterra for us, and Forli. Now he holds Castelmonte against us, and with more success than ever Forli or Volterra achieved.'

'He is a fox,' Rigo said. 'None the less, God willing, I will dig him out for you.' He broke off. 'Look,' he said. 'Is that Montefeltro himself, do you think?'

From the wall of Castelmonte a trumpet sounded a single, drawn-out note. There was a moment's silence and then, softly, the slow beat of a drum arose, deliberate and menacing. All the men on the ridge turned their faces towards the city. The last rim of the setting sun at theis backs picked out the battlements in glowing red; and, to the left of that portion of the wall's summit where Rigo Leone's flying shot had reduced its granite teeth to intermittent and ragged stumps, figures were gathering.

'Not Montefeltro,' Agnolo Fulvio announced. 'I count eleven, but the Duke is not among them.'

'I trust your eyesight,' Rigo said. 'Who are they, then?'

'Give me time. The light is poor, but Montefeltro I would know by his gait, were he there. I have studied him often enough.'

'One, at least, is Giovio della Rovere,' said a quiet voice from behind them. They turned. Leonardo da Vinci had come forward from his vantage-point beside the thatched powder-magazine, his right hand inside the breast-fold of his tunic. 'Also his wife, I judge,' the artist continued. 'A woman large with child? Am I right?'

'Aye,' growled Rigo. 'That would be della Rovere's sweet Contessa. A bitch from the hound-pack of hell itself. It seems you have sharp eyes too, sir. Who else?'

'Six soldiers, and a prisoner,' Leonardo replied. 'A tall man, fair-haired and with no beard. He wears a hacketon, from which I deduce him to be a cavalryman. Giuliano, what do you say?'

'Tedesco Giasone,' said Giuliano. 'They took him in a sortie four nights ago.'

'Pray for his soul, then,' said Leonardo grimly. 'For they have their executioner with them. The eleventh man . . . you see him there, in the shadow of the turret? I do not recognize him. He is a man of medium height, and armoured.'

'Armoured?' Giuliano frowned.

'In light mail, fluted, after the fashion of some of the Saxon knights I have seen. The breastplate is flexible, its seams picked out in black. Towards his left shoulder he wears a golden cross.'

'You can see all this, Leonardo? I cannot, and I have a keen eye for hawking, so they tell me.'

'He is as I describe him,' Leonardo da Vinci said. 'Shall I draw him for you?'

'No need for that,' replied Giuliano. 'I know well enough who he is. The Count of Imola.'

Beside him, several among the gunners crossed themselves. Rigo Leone thumped the cannon's oaken carriage with his fist.

'Yes,' said Giuliano. 'Pray, indeed, for the soul of Tedesco Giasone. You are sure, Leonardo? A black-haired man?' Leonardo nodded assent, and Giuliano pulled off a glove, slapping it against the palm of his other hand. 'Riario, then,' he went on. 'Riario. Yet how did he come there? He has not shown himself before now. No matter. Blood of the saints, but a man with such a treaty with Satan as Girolamo must long since have signed could doubtless ride through our lines invisible, or in the guise of some wild beast. Or so my knights would tell me.'

*

Upon the ramparts of Castelmonte Girolamo Riario, Count and Protector of Bosco and Imola, bastard son of Pope Sixtus IV and Captain-General to the Armies of the Church of Rome, watched impassively the preparation for the death of Tedesco Giasone. Had he been able to hear the words being spoken by Giuliano de' Medici upon the distant ridge, he would have approved of them, as showing an attitude in his enemies that he wished to foster. Indeed, the fostering of such an attitude was the purpose of the scene being enacted before him, since he bore no particular animosity towards the man who was now being trussed in an embrasure, his head downward and half-hanging outside the wall, his legs spread wide apart and strapped to the short pillars of stone at either side of him.

Count Girolamo's face, then, was neutral. Not so the faces of his natural half-brother Count Giovio della Rovere, and of Bona

15

della Rovere, the woman who gripped her husband's arm with animal ferocity and glee. Under the green and fur-trimmed cloak she wore, her belly was swollen with the seventh month of her pregnancy; her eyes, like those of Count Giovio, glinted with a hideous and sickly anticipation.

Within the turret in whose doorway Girolamo Riario stood and fingered the neck of his mail-jacket, the unseen drummer ceased his slow tattoo. The hooded axeman stood forward, testing his blade with broad thumb as della Rovere raised his hand; and Tedesco Giasone uttered a single, cut-off, weasel's scream, his head falling back limply in the instant that the swinging and razor-sharp edge clove him from groin to breastbone, spilling blood and entrails in a slaughterhouse gush that fouled the stone notch of the embrasure and dripped crimson fingers down the wall's outer surface.

The executioner stepped away, looking towards his lord for approval; Bona della Rovere, her fingernails tearing at the skin of her cheek, buried her face in her husband's sleeve. Count Girolamo Riario turned his back on the ruined and stinking puppet that still jerked lifelessly a dozen feet from him, passed through the turret doorway, and disappeared from the sight both of those assembled on the wall and of the far watchers upon the ridge beyond the river.

*

'Tomorrow,' said Agnolo Fulvio in the darkness. 'Tomorrow, by God's justice. Give me four shots in every hour, Rigo. My men can do it, as we did at Conselice. Impress me a score of fellows from Pistrola—I need them but as mules—and I can deliver you five to the hour.'

'You can,' Rigo said mildly. 'Your gun cannot.'

'Then impress me a water-cart also, to cool her.'

'No.' Rigo Leone was sitting, as he often did, on the axle of the siege-gun, between the wheel-spokes and the barrel; in one hand he held the remains of half a chicken, and with the other he stroked the metal. His men swore that he talked to the cannon as one might speak to horses, gentling and encouraging them; in reality, he used both sense and experience to tell him when—and for how long—he must allow each gun to rest. The searing heat of each discharge was, for the most part, quickly dispersed between one shot and the next. Yet, over ten rounds or twenty, the remainder slowly accumulated, expanding and distorting the bronze so that an over-impatient master-gunner might eventually find himself with a split barrel and surrounded by dead and wounded men. Among such impatient master-gunners, notoriously, were those who cooled their weapons with water, thus stressing the outer metal by shrinkage while leaving the interior hot. Even now—four hours after firing the last round of the day— the great gun beside him breathed out a meagre warmth; she would not be fully cold until dawn.

'And the Count of Imola?' demanded Agnolo.

'A foul man,' Rigo said. 'What of it, then? Della Rovere is another.'

'Della Rovere sits under the thumb of Montefeltro,' said Andrea di Veluti, brother to the youngest gunner, 'and Montefeltro is a soldier as we are, understanding matters as we do. If Montefeltro makes a sortie from his city and attacks us here, then we fight as all men fight, which is one thing. To die foully, as Giasone died, is something else.'

'Even so,' said Rigo. 'Yet if I allow Count Girolamo to provoke me into bursting my cannon, then he profits by his methods, foul or not. What would you do, Andrea? Scale the wall single-handed and cut him down?'

'No,' said Andrea.

'Then have patience. You are a gunner, not an infantryman. If you have the itch to wave a sword and shout battle-cries, join Toscanelli's infantry and do so.'

'And much may it profit you,' Scudo added, 'while yon wall stands.'

'And there speaks wisdom,' Rigo said. 'To be a gunner is to become a philosopher.' He laughed. 'Well, boy?'

'Yet I would give much to see that wall,' Andrea said. 'Fighting only at a thousand paces is wearisome, whether or not it breeds philosophers. Have we so much as cracked it?'

'In seven weeks? I hope so.'

'By how much, then? A hand-span?'

'Ask Agnolo,' said Rigo. 'Or better still, ask that artist-fellow who was here with my lord Giuliano; his eyesight is sharper even than Agnolo's. How do I know? If you are set on measuring progress, in God's name, then go down there and check matters for yourself. The wall will tumble no sooner—or later—for your doing so, but one cannot be a philosopher at twenty; therefore go with my blessing, by all means.'

'I think I will do so,' Andrea said, rising from his position by the fire that served to warm the gunners at night. 'Gunnery is poor exercise for the legs, though it strengthens the shoulders. I need to walk.'

'And I too,' said Tesoro di Veluti.

'Infant, you will remain here,' Rigo told him firmly. 'Being younger even than your brother, the knotty balance of philosophy versus exercise cannot yet be your concern. Because I permit one man to cool his fevered mind, it does not follow that I shall countenance general mutiny. If your legs need employment, use them in fetching me that wineskin.'

'But . . .' Tesoro said.

'And do me the favour, in future,' Rigo added, 'of speaking only when you are spoken to. Enough.'

*

The midnight moon hung in a clear, cold sky, spilling its silver light from the slanted sides of the tents below. Giuliano, with Leonardo da Vinci to keep him company, had completed his round of the guard-posts, exchanging their quiet challenges for his own password and some small-talk. The two men sat astride their horses now, on a lower ridge to the right of that upon whose summit the great guns rested, and directly overlooking the postern-gate of Castelmonte.

'The Count of Imola, then, is a monster,' Leonardo was saying. 'But what of it? More to the point, what will happen tomorrow? Roderigo Leone will hurl some sixty more shot at Castelmonte, and another sixty the next day, and the day after that; and then it will snow; and Count Girolamo will split or skewer another captive or so; and Christmas will come; and your guns lie idle.'

'As you would not,' Giuliano said irritably.

'Not I. I would consider a mine.'

Giuliano turned to him. 'A mine?' he said. 'Castelmonte's walls are bedded in rock. How would you drive your shaft, and how long would it take you?'

'Not eight weeks and more. That is certain.'

'We should have consulted you earlier, I can see,' said Giuliano ironically. 'We had need of your suggestions in August. You talk with hindsight, which all men can do.'

'Did you consider a mine, then?'

'No.'

'Then that is all my argument,' Leonardo said. 'I do not insist upon a mine; there are other methods. But had you spent three of the last seven weeks in thought, you might by now be inside Castelmonte.'

Giuliano patted his horse. 'Well,' he said. 'No doubt there is some truth in what you say; but show me the soldier who will spend three weeks in thought when he might be setting up his guns, and I will account you a wizard. For myself, I would sooner hawk than think, believing that thought is better left to monks, who have no time to spend upon war. Or women. In which connection . . .'

'Aha.'

'Tell me, Leonardo, what you think of Constanza d'Avalos.'

'You seek my opinion as a painter?'

'As what you wish.'

'A most gracious and fair lady, then.'

'Well said indeed. Also virtuous.'

'Aha.'

'I pray you to spare me your "ahas", Leonardo, or we shall fall out with one another before the night is much older.' He sighed. 'All Medici campaigns are unsuccessful this autumn, it seems. My brother has his fortress, which is Castelmonte, and I have mine, which is Constanza d'Avalos. Now here, Leonardo, is a campaign in which I might even welcome your instruction.'

'I perceive no campaign,' said Leonardo. 'You are betrothed to her.'

'Not yet.'

'But you will be. Do you love her?'

'As to that . . .' Giuliano began cautiously; but his companion was already pressing on.

'And in two years' time, when she is eighteen, you will marry her. Where, then, is your campaign? If there is one, it is certain of success.'

'By God,' Giuliano broke out, 'and what conquest is that? To bed by political convenience? Do I need a parade of bloodless nuncios and chamberlains to sound me a victory by contract? A plague on that! I want her now, not when she is told to come to me.'

'So speaks the child when the toy is taken,' said Leonardo. 'Constanza is wise here. Consider this—'

'I am not interested in her wisdom,' Giuliano interrupted. 'Shall her mind give me pleasure? No.'

'Possibly she thinks it might do so, were you to notice its existence inside her body.'

'And doubtless, therefore, you would have me lay out matters like a geometrician. Is that your advice? By all the saints, Leonardo, where is your romance? What of her breasts?'

'They are charming, and will serve admirably to feed her children.'

'More romance. I thank God I am a simple cavalryman.'

'Or so you delude yourself,' said Leonardo calmly.

'Meaning that you know me better than I do myself? I doubt it. However, friend artist, let me reward you for your advice, poor though it may be. I shall introduce you to a girl who is bound to take your fancy; Sforza's cousin, Bianca Maria Visconti. Have you seen her?'

'No.'

'A little narrow in the bosom for my taste, though this may cure itself, she being but fourteen,' said Giuliano. 'Fra Sigismondo insists that she is too clever for her own good; therefore she should suit you very well. Also she has a sharp tongue, and so may eventually distract you from your admiration of thought—or wisdom—in women. How say you?'

'I thank you for your courtesy,' said Leonardo gravely. 'Burdened as you are with two campaigns of your own, it is noble indeed of you to find another and press it upon myself. However . . .'

He stopped.

'What is it?' Giuliano demanded. The artist was staring fixedly towards the battlements at the far side of the river.

'Who is that?' he asked. 'There . . . at this side of the turret to our left. You see him?'

Giuliano looked where he was pointing.

'Andrea di Veluti,' he said. 'The pickets knew he was passing through our lines. It seems that he had some notion of examining the effect of Rigo's gunnery upon the wall, I am bound to say . . .'

He broke off in his turn. The man they were both straining their eyes to watch was all but hidden in the deep shadow beneath the wall; but now, immediately above his position, the light of a torch was gleaming.

'Trouble,' Giuliano said. 'I—' but his companion had already set spurs to his horse. The cavalryman at once did likewise, and both of them began the descent of the ridge-face, sliding in a welter of loose pebbles. At their right, and some three hundred paces south of the gunner's figure, the postern-gate had swung inwards, and a detachment of foot-soldiers was emerging from it. At almost the same instant the gunner collapsed, and his body began to roll downwards towards the far bank of the river.

'Stones,' said Giuliano, catching up with Leonardo as they reached the level expanse of meadow at the bottom of the ridge. 'They have dropped stones upon him from above!' He reined in his horse. Leonardo, who was already turning to ride along the river-bank, found himself blocked, and tried to force his way past his friend. 'No,' Giuliano said. 'You are not thinking as a soldier. We cannot hope to reach him before they do; therefore we must cut off their retreat.'

Leonardo seemed inclined to disagree with this strategy, but was urged to his right by Giuliano's insistent manoeuvres, and gave way. Instead, they rode for the ford immediately below and opposite the postern-gate and plunged into the water, which foamed around the bellies of their horses as they breasted the current. The soldiers upon the farther bank were now strung out in a line, and their vanguard had almost reached the motionless gunner; at the party's rear, five or six pikemen were forming up where the slope of the ford rose from the river's surface.

Their own disadvantage was clear to both Leonardo and Giuliano before they were half way across. The climb from the far bank to the postern was steep, and the halberdiers who opposed them could easily prevent them from leaving the river at all, let alone from forcing a passage to any higher ground. Leonardo stood in his stirrups for a brief moment, and dived from his horse. Surfacing ten yards away, he saw that his partner had perceived his intention—together with the futility of setting horse against ranged pikes—and had done likewise.

They reached the shore almost together, Leonardo being upstream from the now confused pikemen and Giuliano below them.

Pulling himself out of the water, Leonardo gained a purchase on the turf with one knee, stood upright, and headed for the defenders' rear. The latter, in some disarray, abandoned their bristling and effective outward formation and began to make a loose semicircle in order to protect their flanks.

Giuliano, with drawn sword, fell upon the nearest man to him, slipping under his point and hacking at his ribs; the halberdier fell, shouting imprecations, and hampered his neighbour's riposte in doing so. Leonardo, choosing not to unsheath his weapon, gripped the shaft of the pike which was swinging towards him, wrenched it bodily from its holder's grasp and, using it as a quarter-staff, charged the remaining group with it. Off-balance and badly placed to counter this unexpected form of assault, they strove to set their pikes in two directions at once, staggered, and toppled backwards into the river under the combined onslaught of their two assailants.

Finding themselves in command of the bank, therefore, Giuliano and Leonardo grinned at each other. Behind Giuliano and downstream from the ford, indistinct shapes could be seen around the prostrate Andrea, while more were beginning to return along the sloping grass in order to combat the counter-attack they had observed to be developing in their rear.

'Good,' said Giuliano. He looked across the river; in Toscanelli's camp, shouts and the clash of weapons being buckled on told of imminent reinforcement for their hard-won, but precarious position.

'Nothing of the kind,' said Leonardo shortly. 'Look behind you again.'

Giuliano did so, and saw the nature of his miscalculation.

The gunner's captors, wisely, had never intended to retrace their path to the postern across poor terrain and burdened with an unconscious man. A line had already snaked downward from the wall-top, and they were engaged in fastening this about Andrea's body; even as Giuliano watched, the tightening cord dragged him to the foot of the battlements. His feet left the ground, and he began a jerking ascent, hauled upward by invisible hands overhead.

'God rot their entrails,' said Giuliano. 'I had not thought of that.'

Leonardo took his arm and pointed towards the postern at their right.

'Then let us not stand here and consider it now,' he suggested, 'since there is nothing we can do to prevent it.'

From beneath the arch of the doorway, more pikemen were appearing. Moreover, the defenders they had knocked into the river were also retrieving their weapons and were preparing, furiously, to regain the shore, while from the guardhouse above the gate a crossbow-bolt hissed unseen and then buried itself at Giuliano's feet.

Giuliano sheathed his sword, rapidly if with some reluctance.

'I agree,' he said. 'And since we are already wet . . .'

They turned as one, ran the few necessary steps, and launched themselves once more into the dark waters of the river.

CHAPTER TWO

Piled high—preposterously high—with a load of rough-hewn barrel staves, the little cart trundled slowly across the Ponte Carraia, along the Via dei Fossi and into the piazza that spread like a tiled lawn around the steps of the Church of Santa Maria Novella. The bells of Florence chimed eleven times to mark the morning hour as it negotiated the entry to the street which passed the front of the studios and workshops of Andrea del Verrocchio, and pulled to a sudden halt at the emergence from a nearby alley of two dogs, growling and snapping in a furore of combat. The noise of their quarrel was too much for the horse, which reared in panic and tumbled the overladen vehicle onto its side, spilling staves in a hundred directions.

The snarling of the dogs, the crash of the falling wagon, and the hoarse maledictions of its owner all filtered through the casements of the upper-storey studio, lifting heads and hands from wood and canvas, brush and palette; work stopped, and the two north-facing front windows were crowded in an instant with the artisans and students who called Verrocchio their master.

Two men paid no attention to the commotion.

Leonardo worked on, skimming quick lines of charcoal across the whitewashed surface of a wooden board. Behind his shoulder stood Verrocchio himself, watching intently as these lines flowed together to form the delicate shape of a young man's head. Scarcely pausing, the artist pulled his thumb confidently over the soft carbon outlines, maturing the features and adding years with a few more rapid strokes; a crease here and there, a furrowed brow. The young man aged, to thirty, forty, and then, magically, the head seemed to wither and a grasping, tired old man's face took form; the cheeks sunken, the lips pulled and puckered over toothless gums. Da Vinci paused, changing his charcoal for the final thrusts; and the ancient face itself dissolved to reappear as a skull, with polished planes and eye-sockets as dark as death.

Verrocchio had been so absorbed in these transformations that

24

when he expelled his long-held breath Leonardo turned, grinning cheerfully.

'Look well, Messer Andrea,' he said. 'Consider the power you have given us, to create a lifetime in a moment. Even thus, sometimes, must the Almighty feel.' He returned to the drawing, now holding two charcoal pieces, one in his left hand, one in his right. Both hands moved over the death's head, working together as though they plucked the strings of a harp; and from the skull emerged again the face of a young man, laughing with the joy of life.

Verrocchio shook his head.

'To work thus is a conjuror's trick, Messer Leonardo,' he said. 'Better to do the work I set you with one hand well, and save your conjuring for the fêtes and fairs.'

In mock chagrin Leonardo spun on his stool and rose, dusting his darkened fingers on the sides of his smock. 'And does my work displease you, then, Master Andrea—rapid or slow? No matter. It was, as you say, a jester's trick. I will come back this evening and work on the head of my little angel there . . .' he pointed to a panel at the other side of the room, 'and it shall be exactly as you wish it done, I promise you.' He turned again, and began to gather a random array of papers and sketches, dropping them swiftly into a capacious portfolio.

'This evening?' inquired Verrocchio ominously.

'God sparing me, yes,' said Leonardo.

'You come in late this morning, and leave before noon? No, Leonardo, I fear not. I need you here, to work on your angel while there remains some light to see by.' The master-craftsman's body assumed a stance much like a barrier. 'No more holidays, I pray you, Leonardo. Not today.'

'No holiday at all, good Master Verrocchio,' said Leonardo, continuing his preparations unperturbed. 'I'll return after sundown and work until midnight, if need be. The candlelight serves me well. Do I cheat you, sir? You know I do not. Have you not crept in here of nights many times to assure yourself of the fact?'

'And what is it you wish to do with the daylight?' Verrocchio demanded acidly. 'More riding through the countryside—for the purpose of sketching, I doubt not—with our young Medici prince?'

'Not this time,' Leonardo said. 'Though I am sure you would not grudge me such pleasures, seeing that each time I ride with Giuliano there arises another commission for you. Even the Medici hounds must by now be eating from platters of your engraving, Messer Andrea. I have been considering charging you a fee for my services as agent.'

Unwillingly, his employer broke into a smile.

'True,' he admitted. 'Yet I cannot allow even the best of my artists to overthrow what discipline I manage to achieve here.' He broke off, noticing for the first time a matter upon which he could vent his disciplinary irritation. He called the watchers at the windows back to work with a few choice oaths, and turned back to da Vinci. 'Another experiment, then?' he inquired. 'The third this week, Leonardo, which is three times the licence I would extend to any of my other workers.' Curiosity now tempting him, he added, 'And what are these experiments that drag you from my studio so often? What do you seek from them?'

Leonardo lifted his head and stared briefly at a gable beyond one of the now-vacated windows.

'What is it I seek?' he asked thoughtfully. He shook his head lightly, as though to clear it. 'Why, it is but a light matter, Master Andrea. I seek to know everything there is to know.'

'Indeed,' said Verrocchio, his voice mildly sarcastic. 'I see. You wish merely to achieve the sum of all knowledge. Well, well. There being a full seven hours of daylight remaining today for your search, let us devoutly pray that it will prove time enough to make some headway. And you will work tonight, though how any man can lay down a true tint by candlelight is another thing I have to argue with you.'

'Why, as to that,' Leonardo said, 'there is no argument. Your own teaching suffices. When I came to you as a green journeyman, did you not tell me always to seek out the manner in which light varied, and both form and colour with it?'

'I was speaking of the light of day,' replied Verrocchio testily, 'and not of peering about in the gloom as an owl does.'

'Then, as a good student should, I have advanced upon your wisdom,' said Leonardo. 'For the light of a candle, or of a fire, brings its own tones and shadows, which belong to the technique we call *sfumato*—a technique I have not yet studied deeply enough. This is what I hope to capture, and therefore must work at night

—and therefore, with your permission, may I use the sunlight for other purposes, good Master Andrea?'

'Aye, go,' the craftsman grumbled. 'I would sooner have you gone than contest matters with you.'

'I thank you, again and always, for your kind consent,' Leonardo da Vinci said. Verrocchio watched as his tall figure moved easily down the centre of the room, through the narrow aisle that separated the work-tables upon either side. He scratched his head.

From the whitewashed board the face of the young man—smiling, he imagined, with the same faint mockery as its creator—looked out at him serenely. Verrocchio caught the drawing by its edges and carried it away, between the hastily lowered heads of his work force, to a far corner.

*

A quarter of a mile away, his boots, hose and doublet spattered with mire, Captain Roderigo Leone stood beneath the marble colonnade of the Medici palace courtyard and argued briefly with the tall and gorgeously arrayed page who sought to detain him. About the central fountain, courtiers drifted like peacocks, posturing in trivial discussion and casting occasional and somewhat disdainful glances at the gunner's drab hawk-figure before returning to their daily business of seeing and being seen. The page was querulous.

'Sir,' he said. 'Your dress . . .'

'Is muddy. I am aware of it, I thank you,' Rigo said.

'If you would care to change your attire, sir.'

'I would not.'

'Il Magnifico, sir, may feel . . .'

'Lorenzo de' Medici will know—as you do not—that I come from work and return to work. His work. Stand aside, boy.'

The page sighed in infinite weariness. 'I will conduct you then, sir, to the library.'

'I did not ask you to,' said Rigo. 'I requested you to stand aside, and permit me to find the library for myself. Now move—and do not try my patience.' He pushed the blue-and-silver-clad chest in front of him gently—as a battering-ram nudges a gate before trying its strength in earnest—and proceeded on his way in the shadow of the cloister, the page fluttering in his wake.

The library was on the upper floor, and was reached by a

wooden stairway from the gardens in the rear of the palace; Rigo attained its twin doors some fifty paces ahead of his feebly insistent guide, and went in.

Two women, he saw, stood in the arch of a window to his right, their gowns bright against the oak wainscoting between the shelves of leather-bound volumes. The younger, Bianca Maria Visconti, slender and fair, waved to him in silent gaiety and then turned back to her companion. Acknowledging the greeting with a bow (and with a frown) Rigo went across the room to the three men who sat at a table in gilt-lined chairs beneath the gaze of two sculptures by Mino da Fiesole. Guido Toscanelli and Giuliano de' Medici made room for him, while at the table-head Lorenzo de' Medici, Ruler of the Republic of Florence, looked up from a parchment map.

'You come late, Roderigo,' he said, 'though doubtless with good reason. We excuse you.'

'Of your kindness, sir,' said Rigo. 'I had already mounted my horse when there arrived a cartload of powder from Ser Nencio, and I was forced to see to its stowage.'

'And hence—as ever—you must return tonight,' Lorenzo said.

'I fear so, sir.'

'And have you eaten?'

'No.'

'Then do so, before you leave. For now, if you please, state us your case.'

Lorenzo de' Medici—The Magnificent—was a man of twenty-eight, though few who saw him would have guessed him to be younger than either his Captain-Gunner or the *condottiero* he employed. Dressed always in sober brown, his only concession to personal adornment a rough piece of amber hung about his neck on a silver chain, he gave those who surrounded him an impression of rock-like strength, being somewhat squat and ugly of face —a face impassive save for his eyes, which roved slowly yet continuously as though in restless search or in assessment of this man's worth and that. He had appeared the same at twenty-one, when the people had come to him at his father Piero's death and had begged him to assume responsibility for the City and State of Florence; looking at him, you might imagine he would appear the same in middle age; changeless, formidable, untiring.

Beside him, his brother Giuliano seemed a light and dashing

jewel of a man. Had it not been impolitic (besides untrue) to do so, there were those who could have suggested that the two had different sires. Yet, differing as extremely in both appearance and temper as they did, Lorenzo and his brother had reached an accord which few in their position achieved; they loved each other, respected each other, and went their own ways. Imprudent factions arose from time to time, proposing that Giuliano supplant his elder brother; Giuliano laughed, and took hawk to fist. Similar (but opposite) factions had proposed to Lorenzo that the presence of his popular younger brother at court might lead to danger and unrest; Lorenzo did not laugh, but banished one such proposer and hanged another. Thereafter, no more suggestions of a like nature were voiced. Giuliano managed horses, and women; Lorenzo handled money, and men; a division under which Florence prospered mightily in both pleasure and commerce.

'My case,' Rigo Leone said. 'My case, sir, is swiftly put. My guns sink in mud. Two weeks ago they placed nine shots in every ten within an area of Castelmonte's wall no bigger than the doorway of your library here. Last week the rain came, though mercifully at night only. Yesterday I had to shore my wheels with timber, and my spread at impact is twenty paces from side to side. My chance of breaching the wall is small, and lessens day by day. When the snows come, I must stop. One of my gunners is captive, as a result of a foolish escapade by moonlight which I blame myself for permitting.'

'His name?' Lorenzo asked.

'Andrea di Veluti, sir. An impatient youth, but competent.'

'And valued?'

'Yes. As are all my men, in your service.'

'By which you imply that I should value him too. I do. What price must I pay Montefeltro for an impetuous but competent gunner? A thousand florins, I dare say. It shall be paid.'

'I thank you.'

Lorenzo de' Medici gestured impatiently. 'Would that I might purchase time so easily,' he said. 'Your opinion is that I shall be forced to raise my siege, then?'

'Save by God's grace, sir, that is so.'

'Very well. Toscanelli?'

'Long sieges are always unsatisfactory, my lord,' said Guido Toscanelli. Booted, as was the Master-Gunner opposite him, he wore a cloak in dull blue, thrown back from the shoulders of an azure tunic; a swarthy man, angular of face and with greying hair. 'I have some two hundred hard soldiers, Magnifico,' he went on, 'these being men who understand the need to wait out a bombardment. For the rest of my *condotta*, I collect such as are willing to serve me for the duration of any campaign upon which I may be engaged. I collected them, in this instance, after harvest. Your Lordship will therefore rightly comprehend them to be peasants.'

'There are no lordships in this room, Guido,' Lorenzo said brusquely. 'What of your peasants, then?'

'They are, on the whole, stupid,' Toscanelli replied. 'Good men in a fight, it may be, but while your guns batter at Castelmonte's wall they swill, fornicate, and grow fat. Were it possible so to arrange matters, I would have gathered the bulk of my force after the wall had been breached, not before. Yet such a course would be impossible. Therefore I dislike sieges.'

'And if we make no breach, then I have wasted your hire, and theirs,' Lorenzo said.

'It is not entirely wasted,' Toscanelli pointed out. 'We have enforced your blockade; someone must do so, else your siege cannot exist. None the less it is unsatisfactory.'

Lorenzo grunted.

'Giuliano,' he said. 'Your cavalry?'

'In like case to Guido's infantry and pikemen,' Giuliano replied. 'What have I done these past months? I ride bravely from Florence to the upper Arno; I wave greetings upon every hand; where I can do so, I encourage my horsemen. Some few arrows and bolts, it may happen, are fired on me from the city's walls. I take wine with your Captain-Gunner here, and return gloriously to Florence. A healthful way to spend the autumn, but—as Guido says—unsatisfactory.' He paused in recollection. 'So also says Leonardo da Vinci, when he rides with me,' he added. 'I am forced to tell you, Rigo, that nobody loves your cannon.'

'Leonardo da Vinci?' said Lorenzo. 'The artist who painted the frescoes in my belvedere?'

'The same,' Giuliano said. 'An artist, and a notable singer of bawdy songs, though no drinker. He proposed a mine, in preference to your cannon. I disagreed; yet he is a man of surprising mind, for all that.'

'Evidently,' said Lorenzo. 'And what of the Count of Imola?'

'As to him,' Giuliano said, 'he has done nothing but to kill Giasone in a foul and cowardly fashion. As a demonstration of scorn, I take it, since he gained nothing by it.'

'Yet he is Captain-General of Rome,' remarked Lorenzo. 'Why is he at Castelmonte?'

Giuliano shrugged. 'Who knows? He is a vulture, as all men know. Which puts me to mind . . . by your leave, brother?'

He rose from the table at Lorenzo's nod, and crossed the room to where the two women now sat, sewing and murmuring quietly.

'A pretty picture you make, my ladies,' Giuliano said. He smiled confidently, bowing minutely and detaching a grape from a rose crystal dish that lay on the sill between them.

'Or is it the thought of the grapes that drew you here, I wonder?' Bianca Maria Visconti tipped her head at him pertly. 'Men think first and most often of food, so I have been told.' Her companion, dark-haired, raised her eyes briefly towards Giuliano and then returned to her embroidery.

'You do me wrong,' Giuliano said. 'I came here to feast my eyes upon your grace and beauty, my ladies. From across the room, could you but see it, the sun strikes glints from the hair of my lady Constanza here, as from the wing of a raven. Did I say a pretty picture? A glorious one, rather, that dazzles me as I draw closer!' He bowed again.

'My lord,' said Constanza d'Avalos dryly, 'I pray you take several more of these grapes.' She laid her sewing aside and, detaching a generous cluster, offered it to him.

'I thank you. Since they come from your hand, each shall taste the sweeter,' Giuliano said. 'Yet so many at once? I had rather eat them one by one and slowly, thereby remaining with you the longer.'

'And we,' Bianca told him, 'had rather you ate them all at once, Giuliano, since the more you eat the less will you talk, and thus we shall finish our work the faster. Besides, for the making of such long and courtly speeches you need sustenance, surely—even though these speeches say little.'

'Cousin, you overwhelm me,' Giuliano said. 'I am abashed.' He spoke blandly, but with a faint edge to his voice. This disconcerted Bianca not in the slightest, though it brought a blush to Constanza's cheek as she bent her head swiftly to her sewing. 'Directly to my purpose, then,' Giuliano continued. 'Constanza, does not your sister, Carla d'Avalos, journey to our court from Arezzo?'

'She does,' Constanza said.

'And when does she arrive, Madonna?'

'Tomorrow, Giuliano. Why?'

'It is no great matter. With your permission, I propose to ride out and escort her party. The Republic is no longer as safe as it once was.'

'You alarm me, sir,' said Constanza.

'There is no need for alarm,' Giuliano replied. 'Merely for sensible precaution. Ladies, I thank you for your courtesy.'

'It is I who should thank you for your concern, Giuliano,' said Constanza d'Avalos, 'and I do so.'

'Then, by your leave,' Giuliano said, and, bowing, left them. He sauntered easily back to the table at the far end of the room.

Bianca laughed. 'He takes the last word, after all,' she said. 'It is an uphill task to teach him to speak plainly, but I shall succeed.'

'Have a care that he takes no offence at your sharp tongue, then,' Constanza said crossly.

'Have a care?' Bianca demanded. 'What do I care? I am a Visconti. Nor do I gaze at him with your round and adoring eyes, cousin. Is this the fashion in which you speak at night in the gardens? Somehow I cannot believe it. Will this mountain of "by your leaves" and "of your sweet permissions" persuade you to his bed, Constanza? It would not persuade me.'

'Since you are barely fourteen and therefore a child,' Constanza said, 'I am glad to hear it. Have you been spying on us?' Anger flickered in her eyes. 'You go too far, Bianca.'

Bianca laughed gaily. 'We Visconti learn early the lessons that others learn too late,' she said. 'Of course I have watched you. In Milan, cousin, we survey the field before we fight upon it, and how else should I learn the tactics of love save from those who— being sixteen—are older and wiser than I am?'

'You have too much wisdom, child,' said Constanza crushingly, 'and insufficient sense. Get on with your work.'

*

Lorenzo de' Medici passed his hand across the map before him, smoothing its edges.

'Assume that I am forced to raise my siege,' he said. 'What then,

32

Toscanelli? Would you have us conclude a formal truce for the winter?'

The *condottiero* brooded, stroking the side of his face. 'That is hardly my decision to make, sir,' he said finally. 'It lies between yourself and the Count of Castelmonte, Giovio della Rovere, as principals in the matter. As between myself and Montefeltro—who represent you and the Count as professionals—such would be my choice, and his, I believe. Truce or no, the result will be the same. Your war will stop until next spring; nature, God, and snow will stop it. There remains the question of Count Girolamo, Rome's general; what his attitude may be, and what power over della Rovere he may have to enforce it, I know not.'

'But you would recommend a truce.'

'I would, sir.'

'A truce during which they will repair Castelmonte's wall.'

'That would be unavoidable,' Toscanelli admitted.

Lorenzo leaned back in his chair and closed his eyes in concentration.

'Let me lay out the facts of this campaign,' he said. 'I must take Castelmonte; not for itself, but because it controls—by reason of its commanding position—the road from Rome.' He opened his eyes again, resting his glance upon the mercenary. 'You agree?'

'Most surely,' Toscanelli said.

'The road along which—some time next year—Sixtus will march against Florence with an army twenty thousand strong. More, it may be.'

'With respect,' Toscanelli said, 'that is a question of military and political strategy. I am merely a tactician, and accepted the case to be as you stated it, when you came to me in July. Failure now stares us in the face, and I must ask you again what I asked you then. Do you not here deal in guesses? Can you be sure what His Holiness intends?'

Lorenzo considered.

'Not guesses,' he said. 'Calculation.' Then, appearing to digress for the moment, he went on: "Tell me, Guido. The Count of Imola; of what family is he?'

Toscanelli smiled, almost invisibly. 'He is the son, sir, of His Holiness's sister.'

'Is he so? Is it not whispered, discreetly, that His Holiness bears a closer relationship, shall we say, to the Count?'

'Girolamo is a della Rovere bastard,' said Rigo forthrightly, 'and the Count of Castelmonte another, so let us spare ourselves discretion.'

'Spoken like a gunner,' laughed Giuliano de' Medici.

'I thank you, Rigo,' Lorenzo said. 'Papal bastards both. Well then? Pietro Riario was made Cardinal, and died of his excesses in that holy office. Giovio della Rovere holds Castelmonte for Rome. Girolamo Riario is greater, both in ability and in evil, than either, and is Captain-General of the Armies of the Church; and he is in Castelmonte too.'

'And where does this lead us?' the *condottiero* asked.

'It leads us, good Toscanelli, to this question again; why is he there? If the Captain-General of Rome's army thinks it worth his while to join a beleaguered garrison, then it follows that he places the same value upon that garrison as I do. If I must take Castelmonte because it guards the upper Arno, he must hold it for the same reason. Therefore Rome intends to march. But my case does not rest on this alone.' Lorenzo raised his fingers in turn as he went on: 'One. Sixtus has denied us Imola, by purchasing it four years ago from Milan; thereby, he intends to deny us the Adriatic Sea. Two. He has removed Rome's banking affairs from our uncle, Giovanni Tornabuoni, and transferred them to the Pazzi family in Rome; thereby, he denies us profit. Three. He has appointed Francesco Salviati to be Archbishop of Pisa in our domain, against our wishes and against formal agreement; thereby, he seeks deliberately to provoke us.'

'And has succeeded,' Giuliano said.

'Admirably indeed,' said Lorenzo. 'Four. He holds Castelmonte against us, and has armed and provisioned it from his own purse. Five. He has sent Girolamo Riario there. Therefore the question I ask myself is not whether he intends to proceed to open warfare with us, but when? Girolamo's presence tells me the answer: early next year. Do you find fault with my reasoning?'

'Not I,' Rigo said. 'You state the case adequately enough.'

'Guido?'

'You persuade me, sir,' Toscanelli said, 'I agree.'

'Giuliano?'

'I agree also,' his brother said.

'And therefore,' Lorenzo drove the point home, 'Castelmonte

must be in our hands no later than two weeks after the start of campaigning weather next spring. Does this follow?'

'It does,' said Rigo.

'And if you begin your bombardment again as soon as the ground will hold your guns—in April, let us say—how long will it take you to reduce the wall, Roderigo?'

'You know the answer to that as well as I, sir. It must take me the eight weeks I have already spent this year, since they will by then have repaired what harm I have achieved. Unless Toscanelli is prepared to sit out the winter before the city, and prevent them from doing so.'

'Impossible,' Toscanelli said. 'Spend four months in tents, brush-fighting with repair parties? It cannot be done. In any case, they have only to build themselves a second redoubt behind the damaged portion. In four months they can do so with ease, and keep warm into the bargain; I cannot stop them.'

'Eight weeks and more, then,' Rigo said. 'Moreover . . .'

'Yes?' Lorenzo prompted.

'Sir, I have no wish to add to your troubles.'

'You do not do so, Roderigo, by pointing them out to me: Speak.'

'Then,' Rigo said, 'so soon as I have made my breach next spring—say summer, rather—and Toscanelli has taken the city through it, you will at once become the defender rather than the attacker. Rome will be upon the march. Thus the wall which I shall, at great pains, have knocked down for you will have at once to be repaired yet again, by yourself; and will His Holiness grant you the time in which to do so?'

Lorenzo de' Medici drummed his fingers upon the map awhile.

'Guido,' he said, 'what chance of taking the wall of Castelmonte without breaching it?'

'Small,' Toscanelli said. 'It can be done, but not with the troops I have; they are good enough for a blockade, but not for storm-attack. The Swiss, perhaps, could do it for you.'

'At enormous expense.'

'Most certainly. And, again, not until next spring. Furthermore, for such an enterprise you will need siege-engines; towers, bridges, rolling ladders, ballistae, rams. These are mechanical matters, and I have little skill in them.'

'But there exist men who have such skills.'

'Assuredly. Your best military engineer is Francesco di Giorgio Martini, the Sienese. His fee would be some twelve thousand florins per month, which is a full third of what you now pay myself and my *condotta*—and still does not include the engines themselves. Your good siege-engineer is a rare man, and an expensive one.'

*

'Gold,' the Supreme Pontiff said. 'This, then, is what it comes to, as always. Gold, Borgia.'

'An excellent and necessary tool,' the Cardinal agreed.

'You speak truly,' said Sixtus. 'A tool. And yet I perceive it also as a rock, Borgia; a rock upon which our work, our love, our grand design *in excelsis*, my old friend, may founder.'

Francesco della Rovere, Pope Sixtus IV by Almighty Grace and the expressed will of the College of Cardinals at Rome, former General of the Franciscan Order, past professor in Padua, Bologna, Pavia, Siena, Florence, Perugia, Venice, and now Vicar of God's Kingdom upon earth, raised jewelled hand to chin and shifted impatiently in his chair of rosewood inlaid with ivory.

About him, the walls of his chamber rose thirty feet and more into shadowed magnificence, above silken hangings and carved architraves, above the portraits of his predecessors since the great schism—Nicholas V, Callistus III, Pius II, Paul II—that seemed, looking down, to radiate their spiritual blessing upon his driven purpose; above panelling in cedar and olive, and pilasters in ebony and bronze.

Gross, dissolute, shrewd, and hypocritical, Sixtus drew strength both from his surroundings and from the webs of policy woven at his accession; advanced his family, repaid his supporters, and bought time from his opponents. The world, it had been revealed to him by the light of reason, was the Mediterranean; the Mediterranean—despite the Turks—was Italy; Italy was Rome, and Rome himself. Hence, reason and revelation both demanding it, the grand design of which he now spoke to Cardinal Rodrigo Borgia. The design was there, and the purpose. It was purpose that twisted the Pontiff's face into mobile and wrenching grimace as he talked, and forced his pace when he strode the corridors of the Papal Palace; purpose that led him into smoothly dissembled impatience with legate and nuncio.

It was something of this purpose, perhaps, which those who supported his election had seen in him, and for which they had lent him the weight of their favour. His grand design they had not perceived so readily, or they might have had second thoughts. Paul II, an ascetic, had left Rome with few friends, being as parsimonious with others as he had been with himself; Sixtus, they hoped, would retrieve the situation, with purpose but also with moderation, restoring to Rome her power through the judicious distribution of money, the golden pollen of power.

Francesco della Rovere, upon his election, overrode their hopes of moderation like a pious and flabby juggernaut. He had, it transpired, larger aims for Rome, and for himself.

'Florence,' said Pope Sixtus IV. 'Florence, Siena, Ferrara, Mantua, Venice, Milan. You see it, Borgia? Rome cannot be squeezed like a nut between south and north. She must extend, Borgia; extend and consolidate.'

'I see it indeed, Your Holiness,' Cardinal Rodrigo Borgia replied, 'and approve. Yet this is a large meal for Rome to digest.'

'Your metaphor,' said Sixtus, fluttering pudgy fingers, 'is inept. Digestion implies a crudity of which we are incapable. Let us rather think of Rome as a swan spreading her wings in protection over the City-States of our torn and misguided Italy.'

'By all means,' said the Cardinal equably. 'I accept the correction of Your Holiness happily, since Milan and Venice would, as morsels, strain the mouth of Gargantua. Adopting your more delicate phrase, then, it remains my feeling that Rome's wingspread may be too short to accommodate them.'

'It must do so.'

'Eventually, perhaps,' Borgia said, 'since Rome must control the Adriatic no less than the west. Moreover, through Venice—if I understand the thoughts of Your Holiness correctly—pours incalculable wealth.'

'You understand me, Borgia, as always.'

'Then let Rome proceed slowly.'

'Slowly?' Sixtus shifted in his chair again, his mouth working. 'Slowly?'

'With circumspection, then.'

'Better. We are not, I hope, to be thought of as rash.'

'Certainly not,' Cardinal Borgia replied. 'What of Naples, then?'

'Barbarians,' said Sixtus. 'Let Ferrante brew his own soup, and his dung-stained brats with him. We have given the Abbey of Monte Casino to one of those same brats, thus diverting to Naples revenue which should be ours. Beyond such gestures, nothing to our south is worthy of our consideration.'

'Very well. Let us fix our eyes upon Venice and her river of gold—but circumspectly.'

'Her river of gold,' Sixtus fluted. He clasped his hands across his ample stomach and looked towards the ceiling. 'Admirable. A trifle worldly, but admirable none the less. Bringing our gaze nearer home, however . . . Ferrara we may leave, since if we achieve Venice, Ferrara is surrounded and must fall to us by treaty. The same applies in the case of Siena, to my mind.'

'If Florence be overcome,' Cardinal Borgia accepted, 'Siena cannot stand. Now Milan—'

'Is powerful,' Sixtus interrupted him. 'There is no doubt of that. Were the Duke Galeazzo still alive, our problems with Milan would not exist; but they murdered him, Borgia, murdered him most foully.' He sighed. 'And the Duke Lodovico Sforza has not the same love for Rome that Galeazzo bore us. Ingratitude, my friend; it is sharper than a serpent's tooth. Sforza and Medici now walk hand in hand. Of our great love, Borgia, we must have them both.'

Cardinal Borgia stood up, a handsome and striking figure. Well-knit and robust, he was attired more sumptuously even than the Pontiff. His pleasant and yet noble bearing had been extolled by Geronimo di Porzio and Gaspare da Verona in their writings, and his attraction for women was the subject of a lightly indelicate tale by Masuccio Salernitano, set in Mantua. This fable had not incurred Rodrigo Borgia's displeasure; his Spanish ancestry encouraged him to take a certain pride in such stories. As a young man he had fought bravely for his uncle, the Borgia Pope Callistus III. Now, in his prime, he was a politician of both charm and presence.

'We return, it seems, to Florence,' he said.

'Florence,' agreed Pope Sixtus IV, sighing mellifluously once more. 'Ah, Borgia! If Rome be a swan, must she not yearn to enfold rebellious Florence as a swan does her cygnet? A city of such beauty, so near to God and yet so far! If we lend them not our care and guidance, may not her people slip into heresy? And is it not our holy duty, then, to care for Florence? It must be, Borgia.'

'Your Holiness is too kind, as befits your Office,' said the Cardinal. 'Florence is a city of free-thinkers, and damned thereby.'

'Nay, my dear friend, be not too harsh. She could be the flower of Italy, and a jewel in our crown.'

'Not while a Medici rules her,' said Borgia.

'The Medici,' Sixtus said irritably. 'What are the Medici but usurers, that have hoodwinked Florence these many years into accepting their rule? Our first kindness to that city, Borgia, should be to open her eyes to the stiff-necked greed of the Medici; but enough of that. Next year, Borgia . . . next year, we shall address ourselves, in love and goodwill, to Florence.'

Cardinal Borgia pinched the bridge of his nose in thought.

'If Castelmonte holds,' he said.

'It will. Our most excellent son Girolamo Riario will assist Count Giovio in this.'

'I had rather trust in Montefeltro,' Cardinal Borgia said, 'if Your Holiness wishes my frank views on the subject. The Counts of Imola and of Castelmonte are sometimes over-given to excesses.'

'To our sorrow,' said the Pontiff gently. 'It grieves us continually. Yet they are effective.'

'I admit that. The Count Girolamo strikes terror into the hearts of your enemies wherever he goes.'

'Terror, Borgia?' The Pontiff's voice was filled with tender reproach. 'How can that be, since he strives only to extend our benevolence to the lost and blind? Say rather, awe.'

'As Your Holiness pleases. As for the matter of the Medici themselves, I gather that certain notions have been put forward concerning them, for the greater comfort of Rome and of yourself.'

'They have not,' said Sixtus quickly. 'Understand this, Borgia; they have not. Rumours—wild rumours—have reached our ears; infamous suggestions, to put it bluntly. Our ears are closed to them.'

'I understand perfectly, Your Holiness,' Cardinal Borgia said. 'Perfectly.'

CHAPTER THREE

Before proceeding further I make a certain experiment, because my aim is first to present the experiment itself and then, by reasoning, to show why that experiment must give the results that it did. And this is the true rule according to which speculations upon natural effects must proceed; since Nature begins with reason and ends in experience, we must follow the opposite course, beginning with experiences and, upon their basis, investigating the reason.

Leonardo da Vinci

'Again?' protested Matteo Barletta, the archer. 'I am a wounded man, Leonardo.'

'So you have been at pains to tell me,' Leonardo da Vinci said, 'some fifty times or more. Again, if you please, since your wound is a trifle, and of no concern whatever to me. Science is merciless, Matteo. We must all suffer in her cause.'

'So I see. Your own suffering moves me to tears,' said the archer caustically. 'And furthermore there is no science in bowmanship. It is an art, and it will take more than your continual foolery with sticks to persuade me otherwise.' He took his stance once more, feet apart, his left shoulder towards the target seventy paces away at the far end of the field. The nock of the arrow rode back between his fingers as he drew the bow; the string thrummed, and a moment later the shaft thudded into the gold alongside four of its fellows, their heads buried deeply into the coiled straw behind the canvas.

Leonardo lowered the two pieces of wood he was holding in front of his eyes. They were hinged together at one end to form a rough protractor, with which he was measuring the angle made by the arrow's shaft with the level ground in the instant before Matteo Barletta loosed it. He entered the result in the notebook which, as ever, swung at his hip, using for the purpose a small quill recharged from a stoppered ink-horn that dangled alongside the notebook's spine.

It was four in the afternoon, and they had repeated this procedure one hundred and forty times since noon on this, the first biting day of winter. Each time Matteo Barletta would raise his five-foot bow of laminated ash and staghorn, bend it, pause for an instant with the king-feather to his lips, and loose. Each time, in the brief pause before he released the bowstring, Leonardo would rapidly set the arms of the wooden measuring device he had built, and which was in essence an oversized pair of calipers; the lower arm was laid at the horizontal by means of a plumb-bob and scribed line, while the upper one he adjusted to match the angle made by the arrow's shaft, and so measured its elevation.

Between groups of a dozen or so shots Leonardo (who was more concerned with his assistant's thigh-wound than his conversation implied) walked the length of the field to collect the arrows while Matteo rested.

So far, nine days had been spent upon this exercise, in a small water-meadow that lay some three hundred paces from the rear of the Medici palace and about the same distance—as it happened—from Verrocchio's workshop. A shallow stream divided the meadow, and beyond this the ground rose upward to the base of the high stone wall that surrounded the lawns and formal terraces of the *palazzo* itself. Occasionally the figure of one watcher or another had appeared at the wicket-gate in this wall, surveying the two experimenters; but nobody had approached them either in curiosity or in protest at their undoubted trespass. From noon until sunset, therefore, they had been able to follow their unusual pursuit without interruption; and Matteo Barletta was beginning to tire of it. He was also becoming impatient of the continual stream of questions directed at him by Leonardo da Vinci—the more so since he was, in the main, unable to understand their drift.

'I have told you,' he said, resting the foot of his weapon against his instep, 'that I do not know how it is done. It is a question of skill, and of practice by those who have the skill to start with.'

Leonardo eyed him. 'Do not unstring your bow, friend Matteo, if that is what you intend,' he said. 'We are not finished yet.'

The archer sighed gustily and replaced the loop of the bowstring in its notch.

'No?' he said. 'I had hoped that by now you might be as weary of writing figures as I am of this child's work. Enough, Leonardo.'

'Rest awhile. However, we still have'—the artist scanned his notebook rapidly, counting—'some sixty shots to complete the day's tale. Therefore, keep your bow strung. Now, as to this question of skill: tell me, at what point do you aim the tip of your arrow when shooting thus?'

'At this distance?' the archer said. 'A man's height above the target's centre.'

'And how do you know that this is the true point of aim?'

'I know it,' Matteo Barletta said tartly, 'because I have shot in some hundreds of tournaments since you and I were lads together in Anchiano, and have even taken a few modest prizes for this skill of mine. That is how.'

'And if we move the target to a hundred paces distant?'

'Then my point of aim is so much the higher. Every fool knows this. I have called this child's work, Leonardo, and I find your questions more childish still.'

'I approach these matters as a child does,' Leonardo said imperturbably, 'this being the only way to enlightenment. Moreover, I do so because to get a direct answer from you is like trying to squeeze juice from a dried fig. At a hundred paces, to continue, by how much higher is your aim?'

'That depends.'

'Upon what?'

'Upon the wind, for one thing.'

Leonardo closed his eyes in brief exasperation.

'With no wind, then?' he suggested.

Barletta considered this problem for several seconds. 'I cannot say,' he announced. 'Set the target up at a hundred paces, and I will tell you. We are not in a schoolroom.'

'God give me patience,' Leonardo said. 'I will do better than that. Stay here.'

He walked away from where the archer stood, heading to the left of the target and in the direction of the stream. Crossing this, he reached a group of willows. He tore a sheet from his notebook, pried up a wedge of bark from the nearest of the trees with the point of a knife, and wedged the piece of paper behind it. Then, splashing through the water once more, he returned to Barletta.

'Spit me yonder mark, winner of tournaments,' he said.

'With pleasure,' Barletta reached behind him for an arrow protruding from the turf, fitted it smoothly to his bow, and fired across the stream. The shaft transfixed the white rectangle towards one of its upper corners. 'A creditable shot,' Barletta said, 'though not perfect.'

'Most surely,' replied Leonardo. 'Tell me, therefore; how far distant is that tree?'

The archer rubbed the nape of his neck in thought. 'About ninety paces,' he said finally.

'Ninety-eight, by my count.'

'A close estimate, then.'

'Quite close. How did you arrive at it?'

'Why, it was but a guess, I suppose,' said Barletta. 'It does not seem to me to be quite a hundred paces; therefore I estimated ninety. And your pace may not have been even, Leonardo, since you had to cross the stream over there.'

'True, but not to the point,' Leonardo rejoined.

'And what is the point?'

'That you made your guess not as an archer, but as all men make such guesses. If I understood you aright, you asked yourself how many strides it would take you to reach the mark, and told me the result; which is what I would have done in your place.'

'Well?'

'Yet,' pursued Leonardo, 'there was another way in which you could have performed your calculation. For you know, as an archer, by how much above your target you must aim for any given distance; therefore, you could have observed by how much you needed to aim above my piece of paper in order to hit it as you did; and from that you could have deduced how far away it was, without any counting of paces inside your head. Do you not see this?'

Matteo Barletta scratched his neck more vigorously still, frowning.

'It is beyond me,' he said. 'I am no mathematician. I perform no calculations, as you put it. I am an archer. Do you think I have time to reckon this and compute that when I stand in front of a charging knight-at-arms and must bring him down before he rides me beneath his hooves? Blast and burn my bones, but a wondrous sight I should make, sharpening the end of my quill and scratching away at some tablet, begging my enemy the while to hold off while I worked out how far away from me he sat! I take aim and loose, and there's an end of it, Leonardo. If I miss with my first shaft, Providence may grant me a second. If I miss with that also, then I am a dead man—yet not so surely dead as if I were to stand like a stockfish and count upon my fingers.'

'All this is well argued,' said Leonardo. 'And yet . . . you are weary of shooting, did you say?'

'Exceedingly weary.'

'And your wound is troubling you.'

'My wound, as you call it, is a scratch, as you well know, and therefore I suspect your sudden concern for it. Are we done here or are we not?'

'We are not. But you may sit on the ground awhile and rest, prince of archers, while I walk to the house of Piero Novara and beg some timber from him,' said Leonardo.

'Timber? In God's name, what now?'

'Timber and nails. Wait for my return.'

'If we are going to set our hands to carpentry,' said Barletta ominously, 'it will not be today. I have a wife and family.'

'And there remains a full hour of daylight,' said Leonardo, 'so take your ease, and wait.'

The archer sat down, resting his bow across his knees.

'Then bring some wine with your timber and nails,' he said. 'I have no wish to catch an ague in your service. Wine I understand. Science—or whatever it pleases you to call this idiocy of yours—I do not.'

'And nor do you wish to.'

'Exactly. Nor do I wish to. At least,' Matteo Barletta said with feeling, 'we have reached some small measure of agreement. I await your return with impatience.' He lay back, placing his quiver beneath his head, and shut his eyes firmly.

*

At this moment in time, in the studio of Andrea del Verrocchio, heads were bent over work-tables and benches in silent industry, real or simulated. Now and again, however, one apprentice or another stole a glance from his appointed task towards the small group of persons in a far corner of the room, clustered round a whitewashed board.

The light was failing. Had this been a normal evening, subtle moves would have been taking place here and there, suggesting with the ease of practice that the day's labour was all but finished;

44

tidy pyramids of wood-shavings or of gold and silver swarf would have been brushed together, workpieces covered with protective cloth, briefly muttered conversations begun to the accompaniment of smiles betokening imminent release.

In the presence of Lorenzo de' Medici, the artisans' lord and chief patron, such gestures were considered injudicious. Cleaning-up could be done, if need be, by candle-light when he had gone, and an over-loud comment might draw embarrassing attention to its author. The one man—apart from Verrocchio—who would have cared little whether or not attention were directed at him was, at this juncture, somewhere else.

Lorenzo de' Medici laid down the drawing he had been examining. The portrayed face smiled out at him from the board's surface, as it had done at Verrocchio on the day of its execution, now a week past and more.

'And where is Messer Leonardo himself?' inquired the ruler of Florence mildly.

'He is not here, sir,' Verrocchio replied.

'So much I observe. Were he present, I doubt that he would have escaped our notice. None the less, since it was chiefly to speak with him that I came here, it would be convenient to know his whereabouts. Has he gone upon some errand?'

The master-craftsman hesitated.

'Why, not exactly, sir,' he answered. 'That is ... I am not certain, but I believe him to be in the field which adjoins your *palazzo*, though to be truthful I have never asked him where it is that he goes.'

'Have you not, Andrea? But he is absent with your consent, I take it?' Lorenzo smiled, and Verrocchio permitted himself a tentative answering grin.

'Unwillingly given, perhaps,' he said. 'But he has it.'

'Playing truant, I'll wager,' put in the young man who stood beside Lorenzo. 'Is it not always so with artists, good Verrocchio?'

The speaker was tall and supercilious of manner, with a handsomely flared nose down which he gave the appearance of looking constantly at the world around him; an appearance which was amply confirmed by everything he did, said, and implied. He was Silvio Grimiani di Torino, Prince of Savoy. Colourfully dressed in a slashed doublet of purple with gold embroidery, he sniffed delicately at a scented kerchief, the better to keep at bay the smells of paint, turpentine and heated chasing-irons. This delicacy of breeding had earned him the admiration of many ladies at court and the amused tolerance of a few, including Bianca Maria Visconti, who now stood at Lorenzo's other side.

'I imagine, Lorenzo,' he continued, 'that he will be found riding with your brother. Upon a borrowed horse, I make no doubt.'

'Then you are in this case mistaken, my lord,' said Lorenzo, 'or so I believe.' He turned back to Verrocchio. 'There have been two men in my meadow these last nine days, practising archery, as I am informed,' he said. 'Do you mean that one of them is Messer Leonardo? Curious. Why is he doing it?'

'You must ask him that yourself, sir. I have no idea, nor indeed do I swear that he is there at all.'

'He is.' Bianca Visconti spoke up, pulling the sleeve of Lorenzo's cloak gently. 'I saw him there not two hours ago, from the roof of the belvedere.'

'Did you, child? Then you could have saved me my journey hither.'

'If you had told me why you were making it, sir, perhaps I might have done. Since you did not—'

'And in any case it is no longer dignified for you to go scrambling about the walls and roof of my belvedere,' interrupted Lorenzo, 'as I have repeatedly asked Fra Sigismondo to impress upon you. Without effect, it seems. How do you know it was Leonardo da Vinci you saw from this unsuitable position of yours?'

'By the book at his waist,' replied Bianca promptly. 'Is this not so, Messer Andrea? On a chain, thus?'

'Indeed,' said Verrocchio. 'Leonardo beyond a doubt.'

'There you are, you see,' said Bianca triumphantly.

Her guardian surveyed her with a certain grim fondness.

'Very perceptive of you,' he said. To the master-craftsman he continued, 'Whether you grant your employees freedom from their labours to practise archery or not is your affair, Messer Andrea, though I am bound to say I find it somewhat odd.' He tapped the drawing. 'May I see some further examples of his work? The decorations he undertook for me in the belvedere of which the lady Bianca speaks pleased me well—as does this trifle here.'

'With pleasure, sir. His portfolio lies on the table yonder.'

Verrocchio led the way to the spot he had indicated. There, Lorenzo de' Medici turned over a wide leather cover and began to thumb through the collection of sheets and tattered scraps of paper that lay beneath it, turning them this way and that.

'A study for the Incredulity of St Thomas, sir,' Verrocchio commented. 'And what you hold in your hand now is a cherub in the style of Desiderio da Settignano, I believe; a poor thing, in my judgement. As you see, I cannot prevent him from borrowing my competitors' techniques when it suits him, many of which are unsound. But he has a good eye; one cannot deny it. He is, of course, too free in his sense of composition, far too free. I have often told him so, but he is impatient of instruction. He insists that he paints things as he sees them; in which case, as I have often been at pains to point out to him, his perception must be vastly different from my own. He is, sir, a hard man to dispute with, and needs discipline badly. When he is ready to accept it, his eye for movement may be turned to good account.'

Lorenzo nodded in abstraction.

'And then again,' Verrocchio continued, 'he has no appreciation of allegory.'

'Has he not, indeed?' said Lorenzo. 'How reprehensible of him. How old was Messer Leonardo when he first came to you?'

'Twenty-one, I believe, sir. Before that he was under Ser Antonio Pollajuolo.'

'Well, well, Master Andrea,' Lorenzo said, 'when I was twenty-one, I too was somewhat impatient of instruction, as I recall it. As for our good Leonardo, my guess is that he will shortly be thinking of setting up on his own account. Which, I imagine, is one of the reasons for your permitting him . . . certain liberties. Do I guess aright?'

'You do, sir. When all is said and done, he remains my best workman.'

Lorenzo grunted and took up a torn and triangular-shaped piece of paper from the portfolio in front of him. After scanning it closely in the fading light from the nearest window, he passed it without comment to the Prince of Savoy, who accepted it with an air of surprise. Lines creased his noble forehead. He turned it end for end once or twice, and handed it back.

'I can make neither head nor tail of it,' he confessed loftily, 'one

47

thing being drawn on top of another. What is the writing scrawled there? 'Tis Greek, I fancy.'

'I had not thought your lordship capable of Greek,' said Lorenzo, 'though I am sure you are right in your analysis. What think you, Bianca?'

Bianca Visconti took the proffered scrap.

'Nay,' she said at once. 'Here is no Greek.'

'Do you say so? You hear that, Silvio? Not Greek. Tell us further, little one. What is it?'

'I think it is written backwards,' Bianca announced. 'As in a mirror. Yes, I am sure of it. See, here is an *s*, and here an *e*.'

Verrocchio spoke up. 'Your ladyship is quite correct,' he said. 'He often writes thus, though for what reason I do not know.'

'For the mystification of others, perhaps?' Lorenzo suggested.

'I hardly think so,' said the craftsman. 'It has, after all, failed to mystify the lady Bianca for very long.'

'But then her perception is very acute,' Lorenzo said, 'as must be evident to all of us. Messer Leonardo begins to intrigue me. Have you a mirror anywhere?'

'Not here, sir. I could send next door for one, if you wish me to.'

'No matter. I see a piece of polished metalwork yonder.' Lorenzo pointed. 'Bring it to me, if you please; and a candle, perhaps. It grows dark.'

Verrocchio removed the silver dish which his patron had indicated from under the nose of one of his apprentices, and fetched it to the table on which the portfolio lay. He lit a candle-stub from a spirit lamp and carried it, with flaring wick, to set it beside the platter.

'Bianca,' said Lorenzo de' Medici, 'decipher it for us, if you can. Here; let me hold our makeshift looking-glass for you, so.'

After several false attempts, his ward succeeded in placing the torn leaf so that she could read its reflected script. 'It makes little sense,' she said in a disappointed voice. 'For all our trouble, it is but half a sentence upon . . . upon gunpowder, it seems. Do you wish to hear it?'

'By all means.'

'It says'—Bianca squinted at the distorted image in the silver surface—'*that force contained within gunpowder being like to the force of a man's arm.*' She stopped.

'That is all?'

'Yes.'

The Prince of Savoy lowered his kerchief. 'Very enlightening,' he said sarcastically. 'My lord Lorenzo, these nursery excursions are fascinating, but if you have finished here might I suggest we return home? Night draws in, and besides'—he flourished the silken square—'it is somewhat airless in here, I find.'

Lorenzo straightened up, laying the plate down upon the table-top. 'Then we must have you under the open sky before you are quite overcome, Silvio,' he responded briskly. 'Which being so, Master Verrocchio, I thank you for your courtesy in indulging our childish curiosity, and we shall now leave you in peace.'

'You are always welcome, sir,' Verrocchio said. 'And what of Messer Leonardo? Shall I instruct him to attend you tomorrow?'

'No need for that. If he is indeed in our meadow then we shall meet with him shortly, since I propose to return by way of it now.'

The Prince of Savoy opened his eyes wide in protest. 'Nay,' he said. 'This is an over-long walk for my liking, and damp besides. I do not care to plod through mud and wet grass—'

'And perhaps step on a toad, my lord,' laughed Bianca. 'Our meadow is full of toads of nights. Great ugly ones, that squash underfoot.' She studied the expression on his face closely. 'Some say,' she continued innocently, 'that they are venomous, I believe.'

'And your manners, Bianca,' interrupted Lorenzo coldly, 'leave much to be desired, as always. Be not so pert, or I shall have you confined all tomorrow with your tutors. Come, Silvio. The walk will clear your head.'

*

Leonardo da Vinci spat the remaining nail from between his teeth into his hand and took a purposeful grip on the hammer he held.

'Hold firm, Matteo,' he commanded. 'Have you got it?'

'I have, blast and plague it. And strike your own fingers if you must, not mine,' said the archer.

'I am somewhat unhandy at this work, I concede. I should have given more study to the framing of my canvases when I was an apprentice. But it will serve, I dare say.'

Leonardo drove the nail home into the structure of planks he had built with his colleague's unwilling aid, and stood back.

49

'There,' he said. 'A most excellent machine. Does it not appear devilish like a ballista to you?'

'Somewhat,' Matteo Barletta admitted grudgingly. 'Somewhat. Is that what it is intended to be? Where is your string?'

'That will be provided, tomorrow, by your bow.'

'Will it so? Having missed my supper tonight, I had hoped to spend tomorrow in resting.' The archer hacked at the frame moodily with his foot. Two lanterns rested on the ground beside it, casting a flickering but necessary light upon the scene—there being neither moon nor stars visible—which made the darkness a mere ten paces away seem impenetrable. A thin and cutting night breeze had arisen, and Matteo Barletta hunched his shoulders against it inside his leather jerkin. Absorbed in their work, neither man was aware of the approaching group of people who had, ten minutes earlier, left the workshops of Andrea del Verrocchio.

'Then lend me your bow, and stay at home,' said Leonardo.

'By no means. Where my bow travels, there do I travel also. Without it, I feel like a tortoise without its shell. I shall bring bread and cheese, and watch you at your labours; it will be a new sensation for both of us.'

'As an alternative,' Leonardo suggested after a minute's thought, 'you could borrow me a crossbow. It would serve as well, and might be more convenient to handle.'

'A crossbow,' snorted Barletta in derision. 'The crossbow is a contrivance of the Father of Lies himself, and both ungainly and ineffective withal. I can loose me ten shafts in the time it will take your crossbowman to handle his winch or goats-foot lever alone. I do not understand what it is you intend to do tomorrow, but I can promise you that with a crossbow it will take you from dawn to sunset to fire ten shots.'

'This smacks of prejudice, Matteo,' Leonardo said. 'But I will be advised by you, and use your bow. The effect is the same with either weapon.'

'Not so,' said Barletta stoutly. 'The arch of your crossbow is of steel, and therefore unnatural.'

'But the principle, friend Matteo, is the same. It is similar for all missiles, however launched; by crossbow, catapult, mangonel, or cannon.'

The archer sat down heavily on one side of the sloping wooden framework they had completed. It creaked, but held his weight.

'What nonsense is this?' he said. 'I will allow, if you like, that both bow and crossbow use—in some sort—the same force, which is that of the string. But there is no such force in your cannon.'

'Yet force there must be,' argued Leonardo, 'else the ball would not fly.'

'It is the noise of the powder which propels the ball,' said Barletta confidently, 'as all men know; and it does so but feebly, at that. Which is why the cannon is an invention still more useless than the crossbow, and fit only to frighten horses. I would not give you a soldo for all the cannon in the world. Rigo Leone's guns have been roaring at the wall of Castelmonte all autumn, and to what effect? None whatever. Whereas I, Matteo Barletta, have killed six men there, and been wounded in the leg by a man who—though doubtless a black, thieving and misbegotten son of a Roman whore—was none the less a bowman like myself.'

'Well spoken, archer,' said a dry voice behind them.

They turned. Lorenzo de' Medici stood just inside the circle of light thrown by the two lanterns. He had a wing of his cloak around Bianca Maria Visconti, whose fair head shone in the yellow radiance, and beside him was the Prince of Savoy. Matteo Barletta jumped up from his sitting posture in confusion.

'My lord,' he said, 'I did not see you.'

'Be easy,' Lorenzo said. 'There is nothing wrong with a man's expressing his opinions upon his own trade. Messer Leonardo da Vinci, I believe?'

'At your service,' the artist said.

'And what deep undertaking is this, Messer Leonardo, that you must drag a wounded bowman of mine from his sickbed in the middle of the night? To say nothing of using my meadow in the pursuit of it, without seeking permission to do so.'

'I had not thought, sir,' Leonardo said easily, 'that you would object.'

'I have not said that I do object. It is an explanation I seek, not an apology.'

'I am undertaking experiments.'

'Of what kind?'

'Upon the flight of missiles.'

'And for what purpose?'

'For the gathering, sir, of knowledge.'

'Very praiseworthy,' said Lorenzo. 'Let me reshape my question: to what immediate and practical end?'

'To no immediate end. The gathering of knowledge is sufficient end in itself.'

'Is it? I am far from certain that I agree with you, Messer Leonardo, though it may rest upon opinion. What harvest of knowledge do you wish to garner by the use of this contrivance I see?'

'I hope, sir,' said Leonardo courteously, 'to determine at what upward angle an arrow must be discharged to achieve a certain length of flight, and whether—as I suspect—this angle remains constant for any such given length; and to what height the arrow may rise in its path between bow and target; and whether there be any simple mathematical relationship between either the angle at which it is discharged, or the height to which it rises, and the distance it flies; and a few other such matters.'

If this polite but lengthy catalogue was intended to discourage any further questioning, the intention failed.

'What other matters?' asked Lorenzo relentlessly.

Observing the two men—artist and ruler—with their eyes fixed upon each other, Matteo Barletta began to feel uncomfortably as though he were watching a pair of stags with interlocked horns. Nothing, it was true, had been said that would confirm this view, but he was aware of it none the less. He also had an equally uncomfortable desire to be somewhere else.

'If your lordship would permit me . . .' he said. '. . . It is late, and my supper, sir . . .'

'We will not keep you from it, Barletta,' said Lorenzo, never lifting his gaze from the artist's. 'Eat well, and a swift recovery to you, bowman.'

'Thank you, sir.' The archer melted inconspicuously into the night.

'What other matters?' persisted Lorenzo de' Medici.

'There is the further question,' Leonardo said, 'of whether any such mathematical relationship as I may discover between the angle of discharge and the distance flown by the arrow also holds good for other types of missile—as I believe may also turn out to be the case—or whether the size, weight, or shape of the missile affects the relationship. And also, whether the amount of force used to propel the missile can be deduced from the curve and distance of its travel; an important matter, since it would lead to speculations upon the nature of gunpowder.'

'I see. A brave harvest, Messer Leonardo,' said Lorenzo. 'Is that the sum of it?'

'By no means. Gleaning knowledge—to use your metaphor—is like gleaning barley; for in the act of picking up one straw, the eye strays farther and perceives others to be garnered, and in reaching for these still more appear within reach. The harvest, sir, is endless.'

Lorenzo de' Medici lifted his hand and rested it idly upon the golden head of his ward.

'Yet the mind,' he said, 'is finite.'

'Save for the mind of God, that is true.'

'Hum. Well, Messer Leonardo, I suppose that a start to such a harvest may be made as well in my meadow as elsewhere. I hope your contrivance here may withstand the onslaughts of the urchins of Florence, who avail themselves as freely of my streams and pastures as you seem to do.'

'I confess, sir, that the same thought had occurred to me. Nor can I spend all day here, as I would wish.'

'No indeed. Master Andrea has some small need of your services.' Lorenzo surveyed the machine thoughtfully. 'What work are you engaged upon, at his studio?'

'For the present,' Leonardo replied, 'I am painting him an angel or two for an altarpiece.'

'And is this important?'

'That depends, sir, upon one's point of view. Di Credi could paint them as well as I, it is true; but a man must earn his wage, else he is a poor thing indeed.'

'So he is,' Lorenzo agreed. 'Nevertheless I will make you an offer, if you care to hear it. You may move your contrivance into my archery range, and work with it for as many days as it may take you to gather—shall we say—the first two or three straws of your harvest. I will approach Messer Andrea on your behalf, and perhaps free you from the painting of angels awhile. How does that strike you?'

'As being exceedingly generous,' Leonardo said. 'I offer you my thanks for it, since a few undisturbed days at this time would be more precious to me than gold. But a bargain has two sides to it. What might I give you in exchange?'

53

Lorenzo smiled fleetingly.

'Allow my doctors and mathematicians to pester you with such questions as their learned minds may produce upon the subject of the flight of missiles,' he said. 'Nor could I guarantee you that you will not be similarly plagued by my courtiers, I regret to say, though they will not damage your contrivances as others might, were you to continue working in this field. Whether the questions of my learned men will be more foolish than those of my courtiers I cannot say. You will have to find that out for yourself, if you accept. Well?'

'I accept with pleasure,' Leonardo said.

'Then present yourself to me early tomorrow, Messer Leonardo. And now good night.'

Lorenzo nodded affably and made as if to move on.

'Will you not take one of my lanterns?' Leonardo asked. 'The night is dark.'

'A kindly thought. Bianca, will you carry it for us? Come, Silvio.' Lorenzo turned back to the artist, still with a faint smile on his lips. 'We are,' he said, 'something afraid of toads.'

'There are none here,' said Leonardo. 'Toads, sir, croak, and thereby make their presence known.'

'So they do,' said Lorenzo de' Medici. 'So they do.'

CHAPTER FOUR

Many will believe they can fairly reprove me, saying that my experiments go against the authority of men whom their inexperienced judgements hold in great reverence; not conceding that what I do is the fruit of simple experience, the only true teacher.   *Leonardo da Vinci*

. . . for the archer exerts control over his missile by innate and unconscious skill; the gunner controls his through trial and error.

. . . and these rules of flight will be general in their application, I believe, because the power which causes all objects to move is itself general.

We must also inquire, whether the power of a great lord partakes of this like nature; for by reason that he commands the labour of many men and animals, his power is the sum of their powers.

What, then, of the power of the mind? For consider that, unless it be confined, gunpowder burns with light and smoke but without detonation; but when confined it explodes, hurling great stones or iron balls for a thousand paces. But confining the gunpowder is the idea of the mind; and therefore the mind has power.

. . . and herein is another similarity between the power of men and the power contained within gunpowder. For strong men being angry and confined by circumstance produce wars, even as the confining of powder makes it explode . . .

And we must ask, how does the force of the gunpowder exist inside it in the beginning?

. . . if an ounce of shot requires an ounce of powder, how much will two ounces of shot require? It must be believed that this depends upon the diameters of the shot, that is, according to the diameters multiplied by themselves, so that the proportion of powder to powder, I say, is as the square to the square . . .

And it must be asked whether greater forms of gunpowder exist . . .

And if these greater powders are discovered, how will they be used, or will men use them to destroy themselves utterly? For princes are princes, and seldom wise. Therefore one man (now) kills another by the sword or by fire, but with greater force one man may kill many men, or even destroy cities or realms, and this by the pressing of a lever as the crossbow-man does when he fires a bolt. And if a man finds such a lever under his hand, will he not use it?

By mid morning the scattering of frost on the lawn had melted, though the sun had not yet drawn the remaining beads of mois-ture from the short turf. Water still gathered, trickling, on the beaten-copper roof of the belvedere, and dripped unevenly to the cobbles beneath its eaves. Around the long, narrow enclosure the high stone walls, glowing with patches of golden lichen, threw back reflected glints of an icy fire where the cold of the night still lingered in shadowed angles.

It was three days since Leonardo's first meeting with Lorenzo in the field beyond the wicket-gate, and his first experiments with the framed bow that now stood at one end of the archery range were almost completed. He sat on a wooden bench in the sunlight and surveyed his untidy columns of figures, his breath steaming in the crisp air.

As before, his helper was Matteo Barletta. Since he now had less to do than in the meadow, his arguments with Leonardo about the purpose of their labours were as long-winded as they were obtuse, though he regarded the apparatus they were using with the proprietary air of a watchdog, barring the approach of those who showed signs of wanting to lay hands on it with a fero-city in no wise diminished by deference.

As for Leonardo himself, if he had spent but eight hours out of the past seventy-two in sleeping, he showed no sign of it. From dusk until midnight he performed calculations on the previous day's results, and he rose before three to prepare the next day's trials; but his smile was always ready and his willingness for discussion—whether informed or otherwise—unfailing. He was dressed colourfully, but far from gaudily, in orange and russet; and both his eye and his mind were clear.

After some discussion, he had reached a compromise with the archer upon the nature of their equipment. Their missiles were still arrows, chosen with care from among Barletta's finest, rather than crossbow bolts; but the device he had rebuilt—in a form somewhat more refined than his original roughly nailed framework—was none the less a crossbow in essence, since its drawn string was held taut by a filed and polished metal sear and was released by a trigger. The bow itself lay horizontally, clamped to an independent wooden mounting whose angle of elevation could be altered by raising or lowering it within the main body of the framework itself. The shaft of the arrow rested in a groove, in which it slid forward during the first foot or so of its flight towards the distant target.

Thus far, their onlookers had been only the more curious among the ladies and gentlemen of the court. Lorenzo de' Medici they had not seen, such arrangements as Leonardo deemed necessary having been delegated to a chamberlain who, in his turn, had referred them disdainfully to a head gardener. Nor, up till now, had any of the mathematicians attached to the Medici court put in an appearance.

This, as it happened, suited Leonardo very well, since on balance he preferred the company of courtiers to that of savants. The questions of the noblemen and their companions, while often delivered in a somewhat condescending fashion, obliged him only to give the barest outline of what he was attempting to do; he therefore answered them cheerfully and in words which they could understand, and they chattered like jays and passed on. Since they knew him by sight as Giuliano de' Medici's constant riding-companion, they were in their turn prepared to accord him a certain acceptance as one of themselves, their condescension thus springing more from defensive ignorance than from snobbery. A painter, they reasoned, was a tradesman; but a painter who rode at hawk with the brother of Il Magnifico, and thus showed an amiable disregard for his trade might be socially admissible—pen, inkhorn, and notebook notwithstanding—unless his manners proved to be those of a tradesman, which they did not. Besides this, life at court was often tedious, and to be able to take a turn through the gardens and comment upon the strange contraption which had been set up—for what purpose, Providence alone knew —in the practice butts gave a conversational edge to the day which it had formerly lacked.

A shadow fell across the page he was studying, and Leonardo looked up from it.

'And how goes it, artist?' asked Giuliano de' Medici.

'Well indeed, I thank you.'

'What have you discovered?'

'Poetry.'

'Have you? I am uncertain what you may mean by that.'

'A certain symmetry in nature, then,' Leonardo said, 'which has a poetical air, and pleases me thereby. Giuliano, you have a face like a thundercloud. Sit down.'

'Not for long,' said Giuliano, taking his seat on the bench beside the artist. 'I had hoped that you might have discovered some means of taking Castelmonte tomorrow, not the poetical aspect of nature.'

'Not tomorrow, or the day after. Why?'

'For good reason indeed, my friend,' said Giuliano. 'Constanza's sister, Carla d'Avalos, lies prisoner within its walls.'

Leonardo closed his notebook with a snap and turned to face the man beside him.

'How came she so?' he asked.

'How? Through the stupidity of that damnable popinjay, the Prince of Savoy,' Giuliano said bitterly. 'Had I not restrained myself, I could have killed him on the spot. They took her in a *camisado* two nights ago, and I was too late to do anything save clatter about, shouting curses.'

'You had better tell me what happened, Giuliano. A *camisado*? I would have thought the defenders of Castelmonte had better things to do than ride about the countryside at night with shirts over their armour.'

'It was but a chance piece of blockade-running, I think,' said Giuliano, 'though it turned out more profitable for them than they had intended. Very well, then. As you know, I had arranged to ride out and escort Carla d'Avalos and her party from Pistrola to Florence, since they had been ill-advised enough to travel close to Castelmonte rather than taking a harder path through the hills to the north. I sent word to the inn there, telling them to await my arrival. They did not do so; and why? Because our Prince of Savoy, if you please, took it upon himself to ride to Pistrola before me, with the foolish suggestion that the easiest way to pass Castelmonte would be under cover of darkness and that very night. He found one Corsario de Soto, a cousin to Carla and as stupid as himself, in agreement; whereupon what must they do but ride out under a good half-moon with but five men as escort—and one of these a friar, see you. Toscanelli heard them coming a mile away. He let them by, thinking that they were accompanied by myself and therefore secure. I told Toscanelli that if he supposed I would have less than a quarter-squadron of cavalry with me upon such an errand he must be nearly as dull-witted as Silvio, but no matter for that. As for me, I arrived at Pistrola shortly after midnight, to find them gone, and straightway rode after them. A mile beyond Castelmonte they were attacked in a defile by some thirty fellows from the citadel wearing tabards over their mail; I found de Soto wounded, the friar picking at his beads in prayer, one man dead, and Silvio engaging their rearguard, who fled at my approach. I wished him in like case to de Soto, and shouted so, at which he took great offence. Blundering fool! There was nothing I could do except ride in pursuit, which proved futile. I came back, damned his princely soul again heartily, and that was the end of it. A bad business.'

'Doubtless, however, he meant well.'

'I am sure he did. Who in the devil's name asked him to interfere? He is no soldier; he is a blowfly who prances about thrusting with a rapier after the fashion his French fencing-masters teach up there in the north. Having killed a few men at *duello* with his effeminate mincing and prodding, he probably conceived himself excellently suited as a ladies' escort. Well, it is done now, and we shall pay the price of his conceit. If della Rovere is prepared to release us Carla d'Avalos for a lesser sum than fifty thousand florins I shall be greatly surprised, and they may try to use her capture to advantage in arguing a truce. And unless matters move faster than I dare hope, I shall have to break the news to Constanza.'

'You will have to do that in any case,' said Leonardo.

'But not necessarily now. There is a chance, though a small one, of sparing her some anxiety.'

Leonardo shook his head. 'I do not see how.'

59

'Some, I said. Not all. But I would rather leave it until a ransom has been demanded and agreed by my brother, which may be today or tomorrow, for all I know. They are not likely to let the chance slip while they have it, and both Rigo and Toscanelli agree that a winter truce must be declared within the next few days. It will now cost us more than if the Prince of Savoy had not decided to give us a show of his addle-headed gallantry, that is all. You look thoughtful, Leonardo.'

'Unpleasantly so,' Leonardo rejoined, 'though for no good reason, it may be. Tell me, when did you arrive here in Florence?'

'An hour since.'

'Then take my advice, Giuliano, and seek out Constanza. She has as much right to know of her sister's plight as I have.'

'You do not think it would be better to wait?'

'No. Your reasoning is good-hearted, but wrong. Have I not already pointed out to you that she has a mind, even as you and I have minds? Therefore tell her, now.'

'Well,' said Giuliano, rising, 'I will consider it. And I have kept you from your work, and your archer friend yonder, long enough; though I see someone coming who will keep you from it still longer.' He pointed to the pillared archway which led from the range to its neighbouring inner courtyard. Framed in the arch there stood an imposing man with a forked grey beard, wearing a flowing robe of brown and a velvet cap to match it.

'And who is he?' Leonardo inquired.

'That, my dear Leonardo, is Dr Cino di Lapo Mazzone, scholar extraordinary to my brother, the Magnificent. I wish you joy of him; as for myself, I shall bid you farewell before I am forced to share your conversation.'

Giuliano crossed the stretch of level grass between bench and archway, bowed to the doctor, and hastened out of sight. Dr Mazzone, having inclined his head gravely in answer to this greeting, thrust out his chin and strode towards Leonardo, pausing in the centre of the range to examine the framed bow briefly and to receive a paralysing glare of discouragement from Matteo Barletta, who was testing its string for wear. Leonardo got up as he approached.

'Your servant, sir,' Dr Mazzone announced, insincerely.

'As I am yours, sir.'

'They tell me,' Dr Mazzone said, 'that you are presently

engaged here in mechanical pursuits. I had meant to come and offer you mathematical advice and assistance long before now, but it is hard, sir, very hard—as you may appreciate—to leave one's own labours and one's books. I seldom stray far from my suite these days, being engaged upon three separate proofs of a theorem by Anaximenes, my third especially being one of considerable refinement. You are familiar with the tenets of Anaximenes, I dare say?'

'To a degree,' Leonardo said.

'How, sir, to a degree? One is surely either familiar with Anaximenes or one is not. His reason shines upon us like a beacon; his philosophy is limpid; his mathematics superb; and his theory of the universe far superior, as I believe, to those of either Xenophanes or Anaxagoras. He is, sir, the greatest of the ancients.'

'It may be as you say,' Leonardo replied. 'Yet I find he has a singular disregard for facts.'

Dr Cino di Lapo Mazzone seemed taken aback, though not for long. He rallied.

'Facts?' he said. 'We do not know the facts. Until we do, we must rely upon hypotheses and systems, accepting or rejecting them as our intellects dictate. When, as in the case of Anaximenes, we come across a system of thought which is both harmonious and consistent, then you may depend upon it, sir, that the facts will eventually be found to agree with it. Such is the nature of philosophy. May I hazard a guess that you are a Pythagorean?'

'Sir, I am nothing of the kind.'

'What school, then, do you follow, may one ask?'

'I follow no school. Nor any man. If there is one among the Greeks whom I admire, it would be Eupalinos the Samian.'

'Eupalinos,' said Dr Mazzone slowly. 'I believe, sir, that I am unfamiliar with his work. Remind me of it, if you will.'

'He bored a double tunnel one hundred and fifty fathoms long beneath a mountain, so Herodotus tells us, for the supply of water to the city of Samos.'

'Ah,' said Dr Mazzone, relieved. 'Then, sir, he was no philosopher, but a mere engineer?'

'Even as I am,' replied Leonardo in amusement. 'Naturally I am aware that the intellect of an engineer must in all respects be inferior to that of a philosopher. Does not Plato tell us so? In *Georgias*, does he not point out that a man of sensibility will use the very title as a taunt, and that he will refuse to allow his daughter to marry an engineer's son? An ignoble calling indeed, then, we may be sure; but we must all follow that road in life along which God beckons us.'

'I perceive, young sir, that you are at least well read.'

'Thank you.'

In choosing to ignore any possible irony in Leonardo's argument, Dr Mazzone had reassured himself that his position of superiority was no longer under attack. He was, therefore, prepared to be gracious. 'This device of yours,' he went on. 'What is it, pray tell me?'

'It is a snare,' Leonardo said.

'Indeed? I do not quite understand you, I fear. What is it designed to catch?'

'Why, sir,' said Leonardo, 'facts.'

Dr Mazzone grew frosty again. 'I think that you attempt to reprove me,' he said.

'By no means. I speak but the truth. Facts are elusive, as Anaximenes might tell you were he alive; yet by means of my machine I entrap them, caging them upon this paper.' Leonardo held out his notebook. 'When I have caught a sufficient number, I may then proceed to theories; or again, I may not. Such, sir, is the nature of engineering.'

'Is it? It sounds, if I may say so, a rather mole-like approach to knowledge.'

'Excellently put. Would it interest you to see a demonstration?'

'It was for that express purpose that I came here,' said Dr Mazzone, 'upon the instructions of Lorenzo de' Medici himself, I may say, who has requested me to ... ahem ... evaluate the work you are doing under his protection. I have been but awaiting the arrival of a colleague—but I see him now.'

Hurrying towards them was a tall and thin-lipped man in Franciscan robes, who peered about him with bird-like darts of suspicion as he walked. Leonardo went with Dr Mazzone to meet him.

'May I present Fra Sigismondo Carregi,' Dr Mazzone announced. Leonardo bowed, and introduced his learned guests to the bowman, who uncrossed his arms and nodded to them silently.

'Proceed,' said Dr Mazzone.

While Matteo Barletta drew back the string of the bow and

hitched it over the protruding brass sear at the back of the frame-work, Leonardo consulted his notebook.

'If you would care to select any particular distance from where we stand to the target,' he said, 'please do so. At the moment it lies seventy paces distant.'

'Is this a matter of importance?' inquired the mathematician.

'None whatever, save as part of our demonstration.'

'Ninety paces, then.'

'Very well,' Leonardo said. He walked the length of the range, picked up the little straw disc and its tripod, and moved them twenty paces farther from the bow. Returning, he fitted an arrow into the groove on the top of the frame, engaging its nock with the half-inch of bowstring that lay between the two prongs of the sear, and adjusted the angle of the swivelling segment according to the written figures he had accumulated over the past three days. He then inclined his head at Matteo, who stepped forward and knelt behind the framework, reaching for the trigger. As it had done upon a thousand previous occasions, the scar slid downwards fractionally and released the string; as a thousand times before, the bent arms of the bow straightened with a whirr and a click, and the arrow flashed briefly in the pale sunlight before burying half its length in the target's centre. Matteo, his grin of relief hidden from the three men who stood behind him, got to his feet again.

'And is that all?' asked the friar.

'I am afraid so,' Leonardo rejoined. 'We can, of course, repeat the procedure as many times as you wish. The result will be the same, within an inch or two.'

Fra Sigismondo circled the contrivance warily and with evident disdain, stooping once or twice to touch one part of it or another. Having done so, he pronounced judgement.

'It does not seem to me,' he said, 'that there is overmuch of a mystery here. The bow being once fixed—as you have it here—one would expect the arrow to strike in the same place, would one not?'

Dr Mazzone, pursing his lips and parting his beard with his fingers, agreed.

Leonardo bowed once more, his face open and cheerful.

'Sirs,' he said, 'this also is the nature of engineering; that a thing being once achieved, all men readily perceive it as obvious.

I imagine that our remote ancestor who invented the wheel discovered this to be the case—doubtless to his chagrin. Well, it is a good thing that I do not deal in mysteries, but in science, and that I have wasted but three days upon this study of mine; and it has cost Lorenzo de' Medici little or nothing. I wish you good morning.'

CHAPTER FIVE

The following day dawned peacock-blue, and bitter.

Matteo Barletta, returning thankfully to the arms of his long-suffering wife, had taken his bow with him upon the dismantling of their experimental arbalest the previous evening, and Leonardo had been forced to borrow another for the casual practice he had been engaged upon since daybreak. He had also, as many unskilled archers do, skinned two of his knuckles and burned his wrist with the string; but was none the less whistling blithely, there being nobody about at this early hour to observe him making a fool of himself.

In theory he was still working with angles, distances, and suchlike scholarly matters, though less rigorously than before. In fact, he was merely enjoying the air, the morning, and his own high spirits. It may therefore have been the study of ballistics which made it necessary for him to raise the bow—as now—above his head and loose an arrow vertically upwards into the sky; on the other hand, it may not.

It may even have been predestination.

Watching the shaft climb against the glare of the ice-ringed sun, Leonardo shaded his eyes, counting. The time of its trajectory was an aspect of flight which he had not, until now, considered; he wondered if its fall would take exactly as long as its ascent, as seemed logical. If so, then it would follow . . . what would follow? That its speed upon striking the ground at the end of its descent must be the same as the speed with which it left the bow? Would this, of necessity, be true? He lost his count, and laughed; but in any case he was not fated to discover any such truth, derived or essential, on this occasion. For, at its zenith, the wind caught the arrow, drifting it sideways as it turned end for end and began to tumble, and it vanished, plunging, beyond the stone wall of the archery range to his right.

Laying the bow on the bench beside the dismantled sections of his framework, Leonardo walked to the wicket-gate that gave onto the meadow beyond the palace confines, and pushed it open.

The lie of the land outside was discouraging; the sloping bank down which a poorly trodden path led from the gateway to the edge of the brook below was tangled with briar and myrtle, and he was now at a level with the tops of the stunted willows that canted over the glinting water a bare score of paces away. It was unpromising terrain, then, in which to search for a lost arrow, unless it had been carried over the stream and into the long grass of the field beyond it.

He made his way downward, his feet sliding on the loose and granular soil. Arriving with a rush at the crumbling margin of the stream and clutching at a branch to halt his untidy plunge, he was at once rewarded by the sight of striped feathers and a good handsbreadth of varnished shaft protruding above the water's surface in midstream, and sat down to remove his boots.

Having done so, he slipped cautiously into the icy flood, wincing involuntarily, and waded out. The brook was here no more than twelve feet from side to side and, though fast-running, was everywhere shallow. Searching for footholds on its gravel bed, he reached the arrow and bent to pluck it out, but then stayed his hand. Instead, his eye caught by the precise and narrow pattern of the ripples that streamed out from around its shaft and the tiny, perfect vortices which coiled against it where it broke the water's swirling surface, he reached for the quill and notebook at his waist and began to draw these designs of nature, oblivious to the growing numbness of his feet and whistling softly once more.

He had been thus engaged for five minutes when he was startled by a girl's voice behind him.

'And is the water, then, warm?' it said.

Leonardo straightened up, his head turning. Standing on the bank by his discarded boots was the slight, beautiful and fair-haired figure of Bianca Visconti. She wore a flowing dress of apple-green silk, stained at the hem and bodice with mud, and a stray twig had grazed her face, leaving a smudged line across one cheek. Neither these small accidents of her descent to the river's brim nor the unsuitability of her clothing seemed to trouble her, since she was laughing merrily.

Leonardo closed his notebook, but remained where he was in midstream.

'My lady,' he said.

'You know me?' she asked, brushing a strand of hair away from

66

her forehead. 'I know who you are, of course; you are Messer Leonardo da Vinci, a painter of summer-houses and an indifferent archer, from what I have seen. But who am I?'

'The Countess Bianca Maria Visconti of Abbiategrasso, cousin to Duke Lodovico Sforza, Regent of Milan, I believe,' said Leonardo.

'So you do know me. How is that?'

Leonardo grinned at her in his turn. 'Nay, my lady, it was but a bow at a venture,' he said, 'and I am not such a poor archer in matters of the mind as elsewhere. Giuliano de' Medici pictured you to me—both in temper and in appearance—and it was, I thought, impossible for there to exist two women to answer his description. For the rest, have I not seen you peeping like a mouse from beneath Lorenzo de' Medici's cloak? Your guardian, I believe. It is very simple, as you see.'

'Good. Though I like not your mouse-like peeping,' said the Countess. 'I am no mouse.'

'It was dark at the time. I acknowledge my error, and repent of it.'

'That's as well. And how, may I ask, did Giuliano describe me?'

Leonardo, having drawn the arrow from the bed of the stream, began to wade towards the bank where she stood.

'Why,' he said, 'as impudent, my lady, and small-breasted, as I recall.' He stopped, knee-deep in the water still, in front of her. 'At least,' he went on, 'I think he said "impudent". He may have used the term "sharp-tongued". I am not sure.'

'Let us forget my temperament for the moment, if you please,' said Bianca sternly, looking down at him. 'I am more enraged by these loose comments of Giuliano's upon my ... my personal appearance. How dare he? And I am still further enraged that you should dare to repeat them to me.'

'I am afraid that men, when riding together, have the vulgar habit of making comments of the kind,' said Leonardo. 'But since you asked me a plain question, it would have been unworthy of me to withhold the truth from you, however vulgar.'

'I could have you horsewhipped. Do not think that I cannot arrange it.'

'I am sure you can, if you wish to terrify me, however, you must learn to control your laughter better than I see, from your eyes, that you are doing now. And if you will meanwhile grasp that willow-branch beside you with one hand, and extend me the other, I shall be grateful.'

The Countess obeyed him, with some loss of dignity. Leonardo sat down on the grass beside her, drawing on his boots.

'Now,' she said. 'Tell me why you were standing in the middle of the river, making pictures of . . . I know not what. Let me see.'

He obligingly unfastened the notebook from its chain and held it out to her. She examined its top sheet critically.

'What are these?' she asked.

'What do they look like?'

'Like lines in the water, and curls.'

'Admirable.'

'But what for?'

'That,' said Leonardo, 'is hard to explain.'

'I do not see why. It is as plain a question as any, and we know —do we not—that you are capable of giving plain replies.'

'Well, then,' said Leonardo, standing up, 'you should understand that I have, for some days past, been studying the flight of arrows—'

'I know that,' said Bianca impatiently. 'I have been watching you do so.'

'Is that so? I did not observe you.'

'I doubt that you are capable of observing anything more than a span from the end of your nose when you are working, if one may call it work,' said Bianca crisply. 'You did not even hear me approaching just now.'

'True.'

'Continue, then. What has the flight of arrows to do with ripples in water?'

'Perhaps nothing. The connection in my mind was made by the arrow itself. The ripples you see, and which I have set down there, prove that water resists motion, and is resisted by it. It occurred to me a few minutes ago that the air may resist the arrow's flight in the same way. If it does so, then I must take this into account when I study the motion of an arrow through the air. Do you understand me?'

Bianca frowned.

'Hold up the arrow, then,' she commanded. Leonardo did so. 'Where are the ripples in the air?' she asked him. 'I see none.'

'They are invisible.'

68

'Or they do not exist. If they are invisible, how do you know they are there at all?'

'Because,' Leonardo replied, 'I can see them elsewhere.'

'And where?'

'Had you a mirror, my lady, and could you therefore see your own hair blowing in this self-same air, you would perceive them too,' said Leonardo. 'Also, you would perceive that your face is smudged with grime; but that is by the way.'

'There was no need to spoil your compliment.'

'That is the difficulty with the eye of an artist,' said Leonardo in apology. 'Blowing hair and grime are all one to him.'

'I see. To return to this matter of the air, then,' Bianca said, eyeing him with some humour, 'it seems to me that you are mistaken. Water is heavy. Air is not. Air is . . . nothing.'

'Not so. Look over there.' He pointed to where some few remaining leaves drifted in the errant breeze, to rest lightly upon the surface of the brook and be swept downstream. 'The air sustains the gliding leaf,' he said. 'If this were not so, then the leaf would fall directly downwards, as a stone does. Hence the air has substance, even as the water.'

'But the leaves fall,' she objected. 'Slowly or swiftly, they still fall. This proves nothing.'

'You are hard to convince.'

'I am not. Ships do not fall through water. They float upon it.'

'As the clouds float in the sky, and fall not.'

'Clouds have no weight. Can a cloud bear a cargo? No. You will have to do better than this.'

'Say, then, as a kite floats,' argued Leonardo. 'You will agree with me that a kite has weight? Or a bird?'

She rubbed her cheek, still watching him.

'Yes,' she said slowly. 'I will admit that. Perhaps you are right after all, though it seems a peculiar notion. I must think upon it.' Then, swiftly, she changed her point of attack. 'Do you know what my aunt Francesca would say of you, sir? That you are a dreamer.'

Leonardo threw back his head, laughing. 'I cry mercy,' he said. 'I cannot withstand both your aunt and yourself, and survive. Yet I am no dreamer, Bianca, I promise you. Far otherwise. I do but deal with what I perceive, and cannot prevent myself from doing so; but this is not dreaming. Painters, it may be, see things more clearly than other men; and some, having seen clearly, draw lessons from what they see.'

'Lessons,' said the Countess. 'I have no liking for lessons. Indeed, I came down here to escape them; so keep your lessons to yourself, I pray you.'

'I wondered why you were dressed as you are. Silk and thorns hardly go well together. Who gives you your lessons?'

'A friar with the air of a Pisan hound,' said Bianca. 'He bores me. His name is Fra Sigismondo Carregi. Doubtless he is storming about the palace courtyards even now, looking for me, and will lock me in my room this afternoon. Much I care! I would sooner read books than listen to his droning. That is why I said that I have no liking for lessons.'

'You have not objected to this one,' Leonardo pointed out to her.

'Nay, sir,' she protested. 'This has been no lesson.'

'You are once more mistaken, little Contessa. Lessons are not always given by friars, nor even drawn from books. My own tutors are more congenial than either.'

'Your tutors? And where, then, are they?'

'All about us,' he replied. 'For this morning, at least, they have included arrows, leaves, water and'—he reached forward gently—'perhaps even blowing hair. Consider this when you are locked in your rooms this afternoon, my lady. It is a matter of even more importance than the relative weights of clouds and kites.'

*

Chin in hand, Lorenzo de' Medici sat behind a table of pinewood in a small room which much resembled a monastic cell, being bare of all decoration save for a map by the cartographer Petrus Vesconte upon one of its whitewashed walls. Its window, though large, was barred; from it could be seen a pleasant and commanding view of the *palazzo* gardens and the distant Florentine countryside.

It was a room used often by the ruler of the Republic. To it he retreated for private consideration of state problems, or to escape the conversation of the idle. Apart from himself, few entered it— and none without express invitation.

'Your experiments are satisfactorily concluded?' he asked.

'They are, sir.'

'Good. I must tell you that neither Dr Mazzone nor the worthy Fra Sigismondo Carregi have given me encouraging reports of them; but this you may have guessed already.'

Leonardo, seated on a low wooden stool at the other side of the table, crossed one leg over his other knee and held his ankle, comfortably at ease.

'I confess to no surprise,' he said. 'Neither of them understood what I was doing, though I gave them a fair and honest demonstration of my purpose. They seemed to believe that I was concerned with accuracy, and of course I was not; but they stayed far too short a time for me to be able to enlighten them.' He would have continued, but Lorenzo raised a discouraging hand.

'Spare me your science,' he said. 'I deal in men, a subject of which I have some little knowledge. What the good doctor and Fra Sigismondo may have said to me is of little importance. I offer you a position with me as military engineer. I propose to pay you but little until you have proved your worth to me, but on the other hand you may have such freedom to continue with your experiments as your duties may allow. What say you?'

'Your terms are fair. I accept them, as before, with gratitude. When do you wish me to start?'

'Now.'

'Now?' said Leonardo in surprise. 'Very well.'

'I will procure your release from contract with Messer Andrea del Verrocchio at no expense to yourself. You will lodge here with us, as a condition of your employment.'

'And my horse?'

'We will stable him for you. But not tonight. This evening,' Lorenzo said, 'you will ride to Castelmonte, where I still have a difficulty or two to clear up, as you will no doubt recall. You will carry my personal warrant to Captain Roderigo Leone, and assist him in reducing the wall of that city.' Seeing Leonardo about to speak, he raised his hand again, his eyes hard. 'Do not trouble to point out that you are no miracle-worker. I am aware of it. I expect no miracles; yet, even at this late hour, it may be that something will occur to you that others have missed. You know that the Lady Carla d'Avalos is prisoner within Castelmonte?'

'So your brother told me, sir.'

'We have as yet received no demand for her ransom. That we shall receive one, I am sure. I will be frank with you; my aim at this moment is to save my exchequer a matter of some fifty or one hundred thousand florins—which sum it will certainly cost Florence to obtain her release if the Count della Rovere can hold his citadel intact until the day after tomorrow. If it must be paid I do not grudge it, naturally, but those are the facts. Do I make myself clear to you?'

'Abundantly,' Leonardo said. 'I shall do my utmost, sir, as I trust always to do in your service.'

'Then good fortune go with you,' said Lorenzo de' Medici.

CHAPTER SIX

Allowing his sword-point to rest briefly upon the packed earth at his feet, his back hard against a side-column of Castelmonte's postern-gate, Guido Toscanelli took stock of his situation and found it desperate.

For the moment he was protected from above by the overhang of the archway, since his right shoulder was pressed against the studded timber of the door he sought to shatter; but the men who, under his blasphemous urging, were swinging a steel-shod ram against the planks an arm's-length away from him were not so fortunate. Of an assault force of thirty, five had been killed already, and as many wounded, by enfilading crossbow-fire or by rocks hurled down upon them from the slotted embrasures of the guardhouse above the gate.

His attack, made at a run from the summit of a low ridge on the opposite side of the river, had lasted a mere quarter of an hour, which was long enough to show that it had failed. He cursed himself silently for having allowed impatience to overcome good sense in making it at all. His hope had been to force an entry within a few minutes at most. In this he had been unsuccessful, and only stubbornness kept him from retreat; a stubbornness which bid fair to cost him another man for every blow of the battering-ram.

For one thing, his team of rammers was at a disadvantage owing to the lie of the ground. From the river's edge to the postern was a scant fifteen paces, and every pace lay uphill. Hence it was impossible for his men to put much energy behind the heavy ram, since they could not back off with it and charge, but could only swing it back and forth at arms' stretch. For another, the short time it had taken to ford the river had been long enough to allow the defenders to gather in strength above the postern and along the walls at either side, thus opposing him with a deadly hail of missiles. Even at forty paces from his flanks a crossbow-bolt could punch through a chain-mail corselet with lethal effect, as the groans of his wounded eloquently testified.

Penned in between river and wall and decimated by withering

73

crossfire, he was helpless. As for the door itself, it might as well have been built of solid stone for all the damage his ram was doing it.

He stepped out from beneath the archway and looked back across the river to where, sheltered in a tumble of boulders, his own arbalestiers crouched and gave his party what covering fire they could. Their bolts rattled off the parapet above him; as he turned his head to gauge their effect a defending bowman, his neck skewered, clutched feebly and fell outward. His body, dead before it touched the ground, rolled heavily down the steep embankment and splashed into the water, trailing twin streamers of blood across the ripples of its entry. A rapid survey, however, showed him that this was the only casualty his supporters had to their credit; and even in the instant it took to make this judgement, the rearmost of the men who swung the battering-ram grunted hoarsely and slid on his back, arms outflung, to rest at Toscanelli's feet with the reddening vanes of the short iron quarrel in his brain staring upward like a third and malignantly sightless eye.

A useless enterprise, Toscanelli reflected. It was no part of a *condottiero*'s task to waste lives in fruitless battles, even if—as now—only a quarter of his attacking force consisted of his own regulars, the remainder being Florentine volunteers eager for death or glory in the service of their city and of Lorenzo de' Medici. Would-be heroes, in Toscanelli's estimation, were fools; but on this occasion, he again reflected, no more foolish than himself.

The call for retreat was almost on his lips. Before he could utter it, however, he saw the postern-door swing inwards under the impact of the ram. Dropping it, his vanguard swept through the mouth of the archway, urged onward by the cheers of those behind them. After a moment of surprise and disbelief, he followed them.

Fortunately, and through no choice of his own, he was almost the last man to jostle through the open doorway. To this fact, as things turned out, he owed his life.

*

History does not reveal to us the names of the men who built and fortified the hill-citadel of Castelmonte. Indirect reference may be found in the *Annals* of Guidobaldo Canestrini to a certain Piero

Casale, a brigand of the *trecento*, and his two sons, who used the redoubt as a base for pillaging the surrounding Tuscan countryside; but Castelmonte must have been old when they did so. Surrounded on nearly three sides by sheer precipices, only its three-quarter-mile western and north-western aspect gave any hope of approaching its summit from the river-valley below it; and for the full length of this, its only natural weakness, ran the vast and forbidding wall which had defied two months and more of bombardment by Rigo Leone's siege-cannon.

Towards the northern end of this massive arc lay the main gateway, reached by a covered bridge from across the river which formed its outer line of defence. Thirty feet high and weighing eight tons each, the twin oaken doors which barred this entry were bound with wrought-iron strapping and secured from inside by a single pivoted beam so heavy that it could be raised only by four men working a windlass inside one of its flanking towers. Moreover, since this gateway had been designed to face north-west rather than directly across the valley, it could not be fired upon by the guns to the west of the river and the Roman road, being protected from them by the turn of the wall.

Along the entire length of the wall-top itself, three men could walk abreast in comfort and shielded by the battlements, curving southward as they walked and passing through its series of regularly spaced turrets until they reached the smaller bastions and guardhouse of the postern-gate. In times of peace this narrow gateway gave passage to washerwomen and to such as wished to draw water from the river. Under siege it was as impregnable—in its own subtle fashion—as were the main gate and walls of the city.

Its defenders called it, in grim jest, the Serpent's Mouth.

Above it, at this moment, stood Federigo da Montefeltro, Duke of Urbino and nominal commander of Castelmonte. Sardonic and competent, of military rather than of noble bearing—since he held his title through knowledge of arms rather than by inheritance—he was looking downwards through a slot between the timbers of the gatehouse floor at the milling Florentine attackers who surged through the passage beneath his feet, their weapons scraping against its stone walls. He heard the first faint note of uncertainty creep into their cries of battle, and smiled to himself.

75

'Wait,' he said softly to the men who stood about him. 'Not yet.'

Expecting to meet hand-to-hand opposition beyond the postern-door they had just forced, Toscanelli's men had found none. The more calculating of those in their forefront were beginning to suspect the truth; that the gate had not yielded before the blows of their ram, but had been deliberately opened in order to lure them into a snare, the nature of which they could not as yet discover.

Certainly Guido Toscanelli had thus concluded. He was, as we have seen, among the last of his force to enter the long defile in which they now found themselves. As he did so, he took rapid note of the unbroken bolt and socket, and of the similarly undamaged hinges at the opposite side of the door. He stopped, allowing the remaining hotheads behind him to elbow him aside.

The defile itself, he saw at once, was readily defensible. It ran for twenty-five paces through the solid outcrop of rock which was the foundation for the gatehouse, and then emerged into what appeared to be the edge of a vineyard, though from here he could see but little of the terrain at its farther end.

Where, he wondered, were the men who could so easily have held such an entry against him?

Ten paces ahead of him, rough-hewn doorways gaped darkly in the flanks of the passage upon either hand. These must, he knew, lead upwards by stairways to the guardhouse overhead. Three men, descending from either side by means of these stairways, could now be holding the passageway in the face of his twenty. Why were they not doing so? More simply still, a detachment of crossbowmen at the far end of the tunnel could by now have dropped a dozen of his soldiers before they could win through—as their vanguard was even now doing—into the open; yet his opponent in command, whoever he might be, had not seen fit to undertake this precaution either.

He turned and looked behind him once more. On the other side of the river another hundred of his troops were massed upon the the ridge-top, having appeared from concealment behind it. They but awaited his signal before charging across the stream to his support; he had only to raise his hand and beckon to them, and they would at once reinforce him in strength, as he had planned. Why, then, did he scent defeat?

Six feet above his head, Federigo da Montefeltro also observed these reinforcements. He was undisturbed by their presence. His mind ran on similar lines to Toscanelli's, and he would indeed have been surprised not to see them waiting there, this being how he would have arranged matters himself in Toscanelli's place.

Almost conversationally, he gave his orders to the captain of the gatehouse and to the archers outside on the battlements, who now crossed to the rear of the parapet and aimed their weapons downwards at the Florentines who were swarming, like bees, from the inner mouth of the tunnel. Four men in the small room with him were heaving a portcullis of forged-iron gridwork into place, its lower edge fitting into the slot by his feet. The top of this portcullis—the door of the trap he was about to close upon his victims below—was supported by cords and pulleys from the roof-beams; four more men held these cords, awaiting his command to release them.

'Wait,' he said again, softly.

Three or four heartbeats passed in unnatural stillness. A stray bolt from one of Toscanelli's crossbowmen, still hidden in the rocks beyond the river, clattered through an embrasure and rebounded harmlessly from the walls of the room to the seat of a bench, and thence to the floor, its square metal shaft ringing; and then Montefeltro's own archers began, methodically and with deadly accuracy, to shoot down the Florentines who had emerged into the small vineyard beyond the Serpent's Mouth.

Toscanelli, making his decision, raced down the passageway—now clear of his men—and cast a brief glance about him at its far end. Intuition had told him that his assault force was about to be killed to a man; reason suggested that the loss of thirty lives must at least be justified by some reconnaissance, however swift.

He saw at once that his intuition had been correct. The defile he had been allowed to capture gave onto a sloping, stony field, across which he would now have to advance. Any such advance would be useless, since the field, planted in regular rows with stunted vines, was itself totally surrounded by the citadel wall, which divided to enclose it; and beyond it, he perceived with anger and dismay, lay another gateway, the twin of the postern he had taken. Only a view from above the city could have shown him in advance that this was so, and no such view was, of course, possible. This the builders of Castelmonte had foreseen. If the

77

outer postern was the Serpent's Mouth, here lay its belly, ready to digest its prey.

Hemmed in on all sides by steep walls and with no enemy they could reach, his men were stumbling in all directions, fruitlessly seeking to escape the rain of arrows directed at them from all about. One or two, quicker to sense defeat than the rest, were already running back towards him down the slope they had so heedlessly begun to climb. There was nothing he could do to save the situation, except shout. He did so, and then ran back along the passage. He gained its outer end a narrow half-second before the portcullis, dropped by Montefeltro from above, sealed the tunnel with a clang of doom at his heels and condemned all those behind him to inescapable death. Plunging down the river-bank, he dived into the water and swam, cursing with what breath he could spare, for the far side and an inglorious safety.

*

On the summit of the higher ridge a quarter of a mile to the north of the spot from which Toscanelli's bloodily unprofitable assault had been launched, a light and penetrating rain was driving into the faces of Rigo Leone and his gunners. Leonardo da Vinci, his horse once more tethered by the powder-magazine, stood with flapping cloak by the master-gunner and tapped his arm, pointing.

'One man only,' he said. 'It is Toscanelli himself, I think.'

Rigo turned a streaming and irritable face to him.

'I have little time for Toscanelli's troubles,' he said tersely. 'The more so since he brought them upon himself. It was an ill-conceived and foolhardy attack, and he has paid for it.'

'I agree. But he may, at least, have brought back some information.'

'None in which I have any interest. The postern-gate is no concern of mine,' Rigo said. 'What concerns me is the accuracy of my guns, which at present is pitiful, as you observe. Since that warrant of yours from Lorenzo describes you as an engineer, perhaps you have some advice to offer me upon the question of working them waist-deep in mud. Have you?'

'No,' said Leonardo, 'except, it may be, to stop doing so.'

'I thank you. In which case, do not distract me with Guido's misfortunes. I have enough of my own. Out of my way, engineer.'

He stepped down from his small hillock, thrusting Leonardo

aside, as the right-hand of his two cannon roared. Leonardo, who had not yet accustomed himself to keeping his mouth open in order to avoid being deafened by the blast, shook his head to clear it and knelt, pushing his fingers into the sodden turf. To his left he could see Agnolo Fulvio's crew, who strained feverishly at their enormous charge, levering its carriage sideways by means of twenty-foot timbers, five men to each lever. Plastered to the eyes with reddish clay, the men were barely recognizable as human; Rigo might have been exaggerating his difficulties, thought Leonardo with amusement, but not by much. The gun slewed sideways, canted, and settled at an angle; it would take them half an hour to shore the sunken wheels again with wooden baulks, which would in their turn sink into the softened and trampled ground with the next recoil. He stood upright again, to find Rigo at his side.

'You are right, of course,' Rigo announced. 'A man with more sense than myself would have quit this task days ago. I cannot. Were I to stop now, I would be telling myself for the rest of the winter that one more shot might have been enough to tumble that damned wall.' He coughed and spat, sulphur thick at the back of his tongue. 'Well,' he continued, 'after tomorrow it will not matter.'

Leonardo grunted non-committally in acceptance of this, the closest to an apology Rigo would ever achieve.

'Given firm ground,' he asked, 'how accurate are your guns?'

Rigo grimaced. 'It has been so long since I saw firm ground that I can hardly remember,' he said. 'At this range? Ten feet upon either side of my aiming point, with good powder. Sometimes they will do better. Often they do worse.'

Leonardo walked away from him to where three of the great iron shot lay side by side. Crouching, he lifted one of these, two-handed but without strain; he straightened, hefting it at shoulder-level.

'How heavy?' he asked.

'A hundred pounds. Your build is deceptive, engineer. I should employ you as one of my loaders.'

Leonardo lowered the ball gently into place again.

'How many more rounds will you fire today?'

'As many as God grants. Perhaps eight before sunset.'

'In that case,' Leonardo said, 'I had better be on my way.'

'Where to?'

'Down to the wall over there. I have a fancy for observing the flight of your cannon-balls from either end.'

'Then you take your life in your hands,' said Rigo, 'my present accuracy being not ten feet at either side, but forty. This is folly.'

'Perhaps. I trust in God, and in your competence. Have you never wished to watch the fall of your own shot?'

'Me? Never. Why should I do that? A gunner's job is to stand behind his guns, not in front of them, and you would do well to follow my example. I had not thought engineering to be a dangerous calling.'

*

The lesson was going badly.

Fra Sigismondo Carregi sat primly upon the edge of the one comfortable chair, his pallid and scholarly finger marking a page of his book, and awaited Bianca's reply. The silence lengthened in the room so that, even through closed windows, the cry of a street urchin could be heard. Bianca heaved a sigh.

'I am sorry, Fra Sigismondo. I truly am. But I have forgotten your question.'

Her tutor's smug nod suggested that he had been expecting just such an answer. 'We were speaking, my child, of St Agatha,' he said. 'Perhaps you now recall her? St Agatha. Why was she sainted? When was she sainted? Let us grant St Eusabius to be difficult, and St Felicitas; but except for St Francis of Assisi, who is known to every babe in arms, all our blessed saints appear to be a mystery to you.'

'St Agatha,' said Bianca. 'No, I do not think I have heard of her. I'm sorry.'

The friar wet his narrow lips. 'Attend, then, if you please. Her intercession stopped an eruption of Mount Etna, madam, in Sicily. She was martyred in the year of Our Lord two hundred and fifty.'

Bianca laughed.

'She stopped Mount Etna from erupting? A volcano? Do you truly believe this, or is it a legend?'

Fra Sigismondo arose and drew his habit about him in anger and agitation.

'How much more of this must I listen to?' he demanded. 'Let

us hope that Il Magnifico, your guardian, never hears you speak thus. That you ignore your lessons is bad enough, in all conscience. That you challenge them is far worse.' He stood over her. 'Listen carefully to what I tell you, my lady. Whether you choose to pay attention to me or not may be your affair. But when you mock my teachings you do not mock me. You mock our Mother the Church; and that is heresy.'

'I do not mock you, nor the Holy Church,' said Bianca with some spirit. 'I but asked you a question because Messer Leonardo da Vinci has told me that it is only through questions that we learn. Am I not here to learn? I think you fear questions, sir, unless you already know the answers to them; yet Messer Leonardo says that it is such questions that—'

'Messer Leonardo, Messer Leonardo,' said Fra Sigismondo dangerously. 'It seems you now have two tutors, my child; one who would lead you towards grace and one, so it appears, who would do otherwise.'

He turned his back on her and looked out of the window. Bianca studied him with distaste.

'I am sorry if my questions offend you,' she said with deceptive meekness, 'yet may I ask you another? One more churchly, I think. Do angels have wings?'

Somewhat mollified by her tone, her tutor faced her again.

'Why, yes, child, they do,' he replied. 'Each of them, as we know, is a messenger from God, and therefore winged. Have we not seen them depicted thus, in paintings?'

Bianca nodded. 'I have seen such pictures,' she agreed. 'But I would ask you why?'

'Why?'

'Why do they have wings?'

'So that they can fly, of course,' said the friar indulgently. 'A foolish question.'

Bianca adopted a tone of intelligent interest. 'Are angels, then, heavy?' she went on.

'Heavy? I do not understand you, madam. They are spirits.'

'And hence weigh nothing.'

'Doubtless. Only things material have weight.'

'Then why,' she asked, 'do they have wings? For I have also talked with Messer Leonardo about birds, and wings, and the air, and he has shown me that wings are needed to lift the weight of the bird so that it may not fall to earth. If, therefore, an angel has no weight to lift, why should it need wings?'

Fra Sigismondo considered her for a long minute. 'I will not be angry with you, child,' he said piously. 'You provoke me, but it is not, I think, entirely your fault. This Messer Leonardo has poisoned your mind so that you can no longer distinguish wisdom from mere cleverness. Evening draws in, and perhaps it is time your lesson for today ended. You may go. And I, for one, shall pray devoutly for your guidance.'

*

Leonardo stood somewhat precariously beneath the wall of Castel-monte, his heels dug into the steep and treacherous slope of the river-bank and his back turned to the ramparts which soared above him. His footing was the less secure on account of the many loose fragments of rock which lay about him, together with the occasional deformed cannon-ball which had not tumbled down into the water to join its fellows.

He was staring alertly in the direction of the far ridge, his view of it uncertain because of the drifting rain and vapour. He had already learned that by the time the sound of one or the other of Rigo's cannon reached him its shot had passed the half-way mark in its trajectory; the muzzle-flash gave him earlier warning, allowing him a full count of six in which to pick out the hurtling sphere in flight, though it was still all but impossible to predict whether it would strike to his right or to his left. He had calcu-lated, however, that his chance of direct annihilation was small. His chief concern was to avoid being knocked from his perch by a rebounding ball as it fell and rolled.

Having been forced to swim the river to gain his present van-tage-point, he was also extremely cold. Hunching his shoulders and shivering, therefore, he waited.

Scudo's cannon spat flame and smoke, to vanish almost instant-ly as a rain-squall swept across the intervening valley. Leonardo swore softly. Whatever his calculations might have been, it was still unnerving to think of the compact, deadly, and now invisible power rushing towards him. In the swirling mist he heard its low-pitched, murmuring hiss overhead, and ducked in nervous reflex; the wall and ground shook to the crash of its impact, and chips of stone spattered about his ears as the shot thundered to earth a short three paces away from him, its energy spent. He scrambled upwards at once and stood below the spot where he had seen it strike the breastwork, an arm's-reach high and close to the angle made between the wall itself and the forward bulge of a turret.

Over an area many yards across, the wall's surface had here been gouged into a crater, at whose edges several clinging masses of stone seemed ready to fall away. At either side of this, smaller scars showed that while a creditable majority of Rigo's shots had fallen close together enough to make—given time—a single breach, many had flown wide and to little effect. He felt the raw margin of the wall's major wound thoughtfully, and edged across towards the angle where the turret curved outwards.

Here, he saw, was the rampart's weakness. A crack wide enough to admit his hand had developed in the recess, proving that however thick and massive the wall might be, it had nevertheless been pushed back fractionally under the pounding of successive balls, allowing the stonework to spring apart and shed mortar. He raked lime out of the crevice with his fingertips and tried to crumble it; it was hard, but not impossibly so.

Above him, Count Girolamo Riario withdrew his head from a window in the turret and beckoned to a man-at-arms.

'You serve under the Duke of Urbino, do you not?' he asked.

'Sir, I do.'

'Were you in his service for Florence, a year or two since?'

'I was, sir.'

'And are you, therefore, acquainted with that city?'

'Sir,' said the man, growing uneasy, 'I am in fact a Florentine by birth, though . . .'

Riario cut him short with a gesture. 'Excellent,' he said. 'Excellent. Be at peace, man. I care not if your mother were kitchenmaid to Lorenzo's own household, so you tell me what I wish to know. Look down from that window, and tell me what you see.'

The man obeyed him. 'I see a man, sir, standing at the foot of our wall and looking upward. I fear he caught sight of me.'

'I care nothing for that either,' said Riario. 'Do you know him?'

'I will not swear to it, sir, but I believe him an artist who used to work in the goldsmiths' quarter by the Ponte Carraia. His name is Leonardo da Vinci.'

Count Girolamo scratched his neck. 'Good,' he said, after a moment's consideration. 'What is your weapon?'

'I am a pikeman, sir.'

'A pity. Still, it is perhaps of little importance. Go and find me a crossbowman from among your fellows, and send him here to me. Hasten, man.'

Leonardo da Vinci, however, while unaware of the Count's casual plans for dispatching him as an impudent nuisance, had indeed seen the halberdier's face at the turret window, and decided upon prudence as his best course. Of the several bolts that were fired at him as he swam back across the river and into the protective mist, none came close enough to trouble him, and he reached the gunners' evening fire in safety some twenty minutes later. Wrapped in a horse-blanket, he accepted Rigo's wineskin gratefully.

'Well, Sir Scholar?' said the latter with amusement. 'What did you find?'

Leonardo lowered the skin. 'That, on the whole, you are wasting your time,' he replied. 'In another month or so, perhaps you will have made a worthwhile dent in Castelmonte's wall, but that is the best of it. You would do better to move both your guns over there'—he pointed to the southern ridge—'and concentrate your fire upon the side of the turret rather than upon the wall itself. The turret would fall within a week; the wall behind it might remain undamaged, but a determined force of infantry could easily scale the ruins of the tower. Shall I draw it for you?'

'No. And save your breath to warm yourself. Tomorrow I move my guns, but not to your ridge. We go to winter quarters in Pistrola. In the morning Toscanelli will parley with Montefeltro; his herald is at the main gate even now. Since all of us, no matter what side we fight upon, have known the cost of my failure to breach their wall for some time now, I can assure you they will reach agreement by early afternoon. How much the lady Carla d'Avalos, my young gunner, and the Count della Rovere's other prisoners will cost Il Magnifico to ransom I cannot tell. That is a matter for haggling. But, until next spring, this war is ended.'

CHAPTER SEVEN

By noon on the following day the weather had worsened, the rain becoming sleet. None the less, among the gunners who sat beneath the shelter of their magazine, their backs resting against powder-kegs, there was an air of cheerful relief and even of festivity. Leonardo, who had been admitted to their society after what all of them regarded as a piece of pure bravado undertaken the previous evening (it was no matter that he himself did not see it this way), had won their further approval by virtue of the fact that he was now lying at full stretch atop the rearmost stack of barrels, sketching his companions amicably and with that disregard for the explosive power of gunpowder which few except gunners ever achieved.

Giuliano de' Medici, in maroon riding-habit, stood by his horse and stroked it with concealed impatience. He had ridden from Florence overnight in order to negotiate, on his brother's behalf, the financial aspects of their truce with Castelmonte, and would not be needed until Toscanelli and Federigo da Montefeltro, as soldiers, had finished their discussion of military matters.

Of the assembled company, only Rigo seemed dispirited.

'Where is Guido?' he demanded, of nobody in particular. 'God's blood, he has been inside their damned citadel long enough, and we have work to do.'

'And why should he hurry?' asked Agnolo Fulvio. 'Doubtless they still have a skin or two of good wine left, even after so long a siege. We have been at war for three months; let them take the whole day to bring it to a conclusion, if they wish. My gun is not yet cold, and a few hours the less of polishing it between now and next year will make little difference to it.'

'It would not have taken me this long,' Rigo said, sourly.

'True,' his lieutenant agreed. 'That is because, being no politician, you would at once admit that Florence has been the loser, and pay the price for it. Toscanelli is somewhat more subtle. Give him time.'

'I mistrust politicians,' was all that Rigo would say. He stood in the open, looking across the valley and trying to penetrate the day's gloom.

An hour passed.

Then, from beyond the river, a trumpet sounded. Giuliano mounted, saluting them, and set off down the face of the ridge. The sleet had now thickened and turned to snow; he checked his horse as its hooves slid, and was hidden by the falling flakes before he had reached level ground below. Rigo removed his fur-lined cap, slapped it against his knee, and rejoined his men under the thatched roof of the powder-hut in silence.

Giuliano reached the river-bank and reined his mount to the left, intending to follow the line of the stream until he gained the unseen bridge by means of which he must cross and so arrive at the main gate of the city. From beyond the blanketing snow and mist he could hear, as though at a great distance, the sounds of Toscanelli's troops and his own cavalry going about their daily tasks as best they could in the foul weather; yet here, with the sullen water before him and the grey backdrop of the looming wall upon its farther side, he felt closed in and solitary, cut off from his fellow-men by accident of nature. He shivered, as much through premonition as from cold.

'Welcome, prince,' a harsh voice said.

He pulled in his reins, startled, and looked across the river to where, above him, dark figures were grouped upon the wall's crest. In one of its machicolations stood Count Girolamo Riario, the gilded cross between breastplate and shoulder of his mail-suit glinting dimly as he leaned a negligent elbow on the parapet and gazed down at the horseman.

'Welcome,' he repeated. 'And whither do you ride, Giuliano?'

'To speak with the Count Giovio della Rovere, as agreed, Captain-General. Where is he?'

'At the gate,' said Girolamo. 'But save yourself the journey; he is with the Duke of Urbino, engaged in farewell courtesies with our worthy and stupid friend Guido Toscanelli. Your business, prince, is not with them, but with me.'

'That I doubt,' Giuliano said. 'I have little to discuss with Rome's vulture for the present, being not yet formally at war with her.'

'Spoken with spirit, if discourteously,' Riario said. 'I shall not detain you long. I have something to show you.'

Impatiently Giuliano loosed his rein to move onward, but then stopped. A horrible suspicion was forming in his mind, and he could not gainsay it. He looked upward again. Four soldiers, he now saw, were lifting a wide plank to the top of the parapet, with a body bound to it. For an instant Giuliano thought they bore a corpse, but then the bound man's head moved and he saw that it was Andrea di Veluti, strapped on his back by encircling strips of leather.

'Your gunner,' Riario said. 'I believe you have come to ransom him, among others. Well?' He moved across from the embrasure to seize the young gunner's jaw, rocking his face back and forth casually as if inspecting a carcase. 'He is healthy,' Riario continued, 'despite some small discomforts he has undergone. A valuable specimen, one might say, if foolish. Come; what do you bid for him? A thousand florins? Two thousand?'

'Do not mock me, Girolamo,' said Giuliano between his teeth. 'Set the boy free, and we will talk it over.'

'Indeed? A moment ago you were not so eager for discussion. We must, accordingly, teach you manners.'

He signed to a man behind him, who now stepped forward and into view. This was, Giuliano saw, the hooded executioner who had once before committed public murder at the Count's behest, and he held in his left hand a pouch of deerskin. Horrified, although as yet uncomprehending, Giuliano could do nothing but watch him as he raised this object.

'Your gunner has not proved talkative, I regret to say, despite our persuasions,' Riario continued in an offhand manner. 'Since he has thereby angered us somewhat, we shall now silence him permanently, and in a fashion which befits his calling.'

Deliberately, the executioner took a short iron bar in his other hand and forced it between the gunner's teeth, prising his jaws apart. The boy screamed, but his cries were cut off as the hooded man above him trickled a black and grainy powder into his mouth from the pouch, choking him as it filled his throat. It overflowed his lips, spilling down the side of his face, and Giuliano could see the veins bulge in his neck as he tried to fight against his bonds in animal desperation. The executioner thrust a short length of stiff fuse into his packed mouth and lit its end from a slow-match. In the long instant of quiet while the cord sputtered the young gunner's eyes rolled, half-unconscious, yet staring with the terrible

87

knowledge of what was about to happen to him. Then there was a monstrous and repellent hiss of smoke and a noise like the bursting of a rotten melon as the gunpowder which packed his mouth and windpipe flared into a rending, muffled explosion.

Giuliano leaned to one side and retched. When he was able to sit erect again in the saddle, the gunner's body was already falling to earth at the foot of the wall, still bound to its plank. It rolled down the slope, mercifully hiding the charred ruin of what had once been its head in the rolling and discoloured water, and he lifted his eyes from it to the wall-top and to the man who stood there, wreathed in smoke and mist.

The curse he was about to utter died unspoken. In the embrasure which the Count had vacated now stood Carla d'Avalos, supported by two men and with her hands tied in front of her.

'I see that I still have your attention,' Riario said softly, fingering his collar. 'Therefore tell your Captain-Gunner that a similar welcome awaits him or any other of his men, should they be unfortunate enough to fall into my hands. And now to other matters. You know the Lady Carla d'Avalos, I take it?'

Giuliano steadied himself in his stirrups.

'Hear me, Count,' he said, with death in his voice. 'Spill one drop of her blood, and I will hunt you down and kill you, though I perish in the doing of it.'

Riario ignored this as though it had remained unsaid. He held out his hand, and the executioner put into it a soft and heavy cloth of black velvet.

'I have a message also for your brother, Lorenzo,' he said, 'and for Florence. Let him not imagine that he can play at war with me. The Medici have laid siege to me here, as they have to others in the past; as in the past, they have seemed to believe that success or failure in such things is a matter for settlement as one settles for an evening's gaming, with money and a few knowing smiles between winner and loser. You had better know me, prince, and Florence had better know me also. I am Girolamo Riario, Count of Bosco and Imola and Rome's Captain-General, and I do not play at war.'

Taking the velvet cloth, he advanced upon the trembling girl, who remained in the stunned and helpless silence of terror. Delicately, he placed the cloth over the lower half of her face, and held it there. The men who supported her gripped her arms more fiercely as her body arched and her forehead grew livid; pinching her nostrils through the material and pressing it into her mouth, the Count waited until her struggles had ceased with her suffocation, and then stood away.

Her figure, released by those who had been holding her upright, collapsed in the embrasure. Riario pushed at the body with the toe of his boot, urging it towards the edge of the wall until it tumbled loosely to join that of Andrea di Veluti in the waters at the foot of the bank.

'Take, then, the Lady Carla d'Avalos,' he said. 'I give her to you freely and at no expense. And when, in due course, Rome calls upon you to submit, remember this day—and comply.'

*

'Unnecessary,' said Sixtus IV in reproof, his eyes fixed upon the gorgeously illuminated ceiling above him. 'Completely unnecessary, and thus reprehensible. Have I not cautioned you many times before this, my son, to control yourself?'

'A lesson which I have taken to heart, Most Holy Father,' said the Count of Imola. 'I assure you of this with all the sincerity at my command; and it follows, therefore, that I must disagree with you. The example was needed, and I supplied it.'

'Needed?'

'Certainly. Demonstrations of will, however brutal they may appear, are tools of war no less than are Montefeltro's soldiers or the cannon of Florence. I need hardly add, Holiness, that my tools are the more effective. If Rome considers war essential, it is not for me to disagree.'

'And do you disagree?' asked Sixtus mildly.

'Not in the least,' Girolamo replied. 'But if I did, I would not say so. I am Captain-General, and Rome's servant; but the means of my service are mine to consider, and to select in Rome's cause.'

The Supreme Pontiff rubbed the arm of his chair uneasily.

'But a woman, my son?' he said. 'The gunner, perhaps, though even there I cannot condone your . . . severity. The Countess d'Avalos . . .' his voice trailed off.

'Which reminds me,' Riario said. He reached into his doublet, beneath the fluted breastplate of the armour he still wore, and produced a small piece of jewellery. He held it out to the Pontiff. 'Your Holiness will recognize this, I am sure. I removed it from the finger of the Countess before her most regrettable death.'

Resting in his palm was a ring of chased gold, bearing a single emerald. Sixtus recoiled from the sight of it, as though stung.

'I see that the memory of Your Holiness is as keen as ever,' continued Riario. 'This is the ring which you gave to the Countess on the occasion of her betrothal to the eldest son of the Duke of Ferrara. Since the alliance cannot, in the nature of things, now take place, I return it to you.'

They were alone in the audience chamber, from whose gilded walls their voices, muted, seemed to echo and press inward upon them, locking them into a complicity which neither of them desired. The Pontiff's shoulders moved uncomfortably beneath his embroidered robes of Barbary silk; Riario smiled thinly, like a polecat.

'Why?' demanded Sixtus. 'I have no need for it.'

'As you wish. It was merely that I believed that to see it might remind Your Holiness of the further fact that an alliance between Ferrara and Florence is something which, upon reflection, neither of us would consider to be in Rome's interest.'

'True. We would have prevented it politically at the time if we could have done so without provoking offence,' Sixtus said. 'I think I begin to understand your intentions.'

'Quite so. It would have been unbecoming in Rome's Father to offend in a matter of such seeming triviality. Rome's General, however, has a duty to offend. I take no pleasure in doing so, but if I may say so without arrogance, I am Rome's right arm just as surely as you are her head and her heart.'

'A mailed arm, then, my son? Is that what you seek to tell me?'

'Precisely. As for the gunner, I beg you to trouble yourself no further over him. The Medici cannon inconvenienced me. I put it no higher than that. I do not permit things to inconvenience me for long, as Your Holiness knows, and therefore used the man—whose soul, we must pray, is now in heaven when all is said and done—to impress upon the Medici the wisdom of submitting to Rome next year. A like reasoning applies in the case of the Countess d'Avalos. If I was severe, I regret it; but my conscience remains clear.'

He stood easily, looking into the eyes of Sixtus IV, his own eyes innocent of any particular challenge. Repelled and yet fascinated by this man, so closely tied to himself both by blood and by what he saw as Rome's need, the Pontiff found his emotions to be compounded of fear and distaste. He had summoned a monster to his service, as had others in legend, and began to wish he had not done so. He gathered himself.

'A mailed arm,' he said softly. 'Even so. I notice, my son, that you wear your armour now, as always. Rumour tells us that you have been known to sleep in it.' Suddenly and surprisingly, he uttered a falsetto laugh. 'Well. His Eminence the Cardinal Borgia has often pointed out that you feel yourself safe from a stiletto in the back; no doubt your wisdom and your conscience go hand in hand. We are pleased with your defence of Castelmonte, and you may convey our similar approval to the Duke of Urbino and the Count Giovio della Rovere, who are also among our beloved sons. You may leave us.'

*

In the privacy of his chamber Girolamo Riario paced the floor, animal-like and restless. With wrenching fingers he gripped the neck of his corselet, dragging at it continually as though desperate for air, an involuntary gesture which he had all but succeeded in controlling when in public but which, here and now, threatened to overwhelm him.

Raging inwardly, he recalled the Pontiff's last delicate gibe before dismissing him. Sixtus had no doubt recalled—as few were in a position to recall—Girolamo's childhood; how, in nursery play which had even then been vicious, his brothers and cousins would force cushions over his face, laughing at his struggles and hoping to provoke in him, as they often did, a fit of berserk and terrified fury. Malicious and clerkly by disposition, he had withdrawn—after stabbing his brother Pietro with a shard from a broken mirror, and being punished severely for it—into a private world in which all outsiders were seen as enemies, thus training himself unwittingly over the years of boyhood for that precise station in life he now occupied.

He relaxed slightly, showing his teeth in what might have passed for a grin. Well, he had overtaken his tormentors now. Or perhaps it was fortune which had defeated them, leaving him, because of his caution, unscathed. Pietro Riario, made Cardinal in 1471, had died three years later, and Girolamo had watched his decline with interest. Outwardly jovial while inwardly perverted, Pietro had squandered three hundred thousand florins on his way to the grave, upon orgies, routs, and sexual conquests. At twenty-eight and on his deathbed, he had been a slobbering and burned-out husk, his mind distorted by his own insensate cruelties and his body broken by excess. In cautioning Girolamo against just such excesses, Sixtus IV was wasting his breath. The Count of Imola had drawn his own conclusions from his elder brother's slide into perdition and had made up his mind to avoid the same fate.

When he now watched—as he sometimes did—the torture of a prisoner or the debauching of some hapless woman, he did so as a compulsive but reformed drinker watches others carouse, in order to test his own strength. Knowing the possible sources of his weakness, he determined, coldly, not to give way to them.

One such subject for Girolamo's study was his cousin Giovio, nominal ruler of Castelmonte. Girolamo considered that both Giovio della Rovere and his wife, equally vicious, were making the same descent into slavering impotence that Pietro had followed, and he was interested in seeing how long it took them. His private smile broadened somewhat, and then flickered out as he remembered his irritation with their most recent piece of folly.

The reason he had given the Pontiff for his execution of Carla d'Avalos, while valid, had not altogether been the true one. In fact, his hand had been forced. Following a drunken evening on the part of Giovio della Rovere, the Countess d'Avalos had been left in no physical condition to be returned to Lorenzo de' Medici; nor had the gunner, though this was of little importance. Andrea di Veluti, permanently crippled through having his feet and ankles crushed by wedges in the course of questioning him, was in any case expendable. The Countess was a different case. Enraged by her evident contempt for him, Giovio had ordered her removal to a cell beneath the castle, where he had first raped her and then flogged the skin from her back with a rawhide whip. Annoyed, Girolamo had remonstrated with della Rovere, pointing out that his evening's entertainment had cost them a considerable sum in ransom-money, there being now little to be done but to kill the girl; he had made the best he could of the situation, but to have had his own policy dictated by Giovio's lack of self-control was still vexing, to say the least.

Girolamo Riario sighed and stopped pacing. After testing the bolts on his door and the firmness of the window-bars, he began, slowly, to remove his armour.

CHAPTER EIGHT

'We have received,' said Cardinal Roderigo Borgia, 'a somewhat interesting letter. To be precise, His Holiness's secretary has passed it to me *sub rosa*; I am in turn to give it into the safe keeping of the Apostolic Chancery, where my good friend Cardinal Domenico della Palla will proceed to copy it, file it, cross-index it, and finally bury it irretrievably in one of the many ways he has devised since he took over the office of Chancellor. I took the liberty of asking you to visit me before it vanishes for ever.'

Cardinal Borgia, handsomely dressed for riding, sat on the balcony of his apartments in the December sunshine with a plate of figs and a flask of wine before him. Hospitably, he pushed these in the direction of his guest, his Spanish ancestry and manners concealing the fact that his opinion of the latter bordered on contempt.

The Count of Imola refused them.

'The Apostolic Chancery . . .' he began irascibly.

'Is the bane of our lives, my dear Count,' the Cardinal said. 'It was far more useful to those of us who thrive upon information in the days when it consisted largely of several cellars full of bundled documents, gathering soot. At least one could get at what one needed in private and without fuss; one cannot do so nowadays. However, that is neither here nor there. This letter—my clerk will show it to you if you wish—is from an artist. It requests permission to consult the libraries of the Church upon what its writer calls "the highest of all arts". Observe the curious phrase. His Holiness is uncertain what action to take in replying to it, but that too is by the way. My own interest in it arises from the name of its author.'

'Well?' Riario said.

'The letter comes from Florence. It is written by a man called Leonardo da Vinci.'

He paused, as though expectant. Riario did not gratify him.

'And so?' he suggested.

Cardinal Borgia raised the wine-flask and held it to the light.

'I find that the cold weather makes our northern vintages

cloudy,' he remarked. 'Perhaps you are wise to decline it. Well, now. Messer Leonardo describes himself as an artist, and indeed we have heard of him even here in Rome; I am informed that he is a brilliant young man. I am also informed that he has recently added a new dimension to his career, since he is now military engineer to our cousin Lorenzo de' Medici . . . my dear Count, if you do not remove that expression of feigned ignorance from your face I shall begin to fear for your sanity. You have your informant at the Medici court, as I have mine. I can hardly be amazing you by these revelations.'

'Occasional news does reach me from Florence,' Riario admitted. The Cardinal smiled in delight.

'But of course it does. I would scarcely be enjoying your company now if it did not; therefore let us be frank with one another. Your informant there, by the way,' he added casually, 'is seriously annoyed with you at present. I have not found out why, but there it is. Money, I dare say. However. One wonders, then, exactly what Messer Leonardo means by "the highest of all arts". To those of us with a classical bent, sculpture would spring to mind, as no doubt it is intended to. But then again . . . you don't by chance know this young man, I suppose?'

The Count of Imola, changing his mind suddenly, thrust a crystal goblet across the surface of the table. Borgia filled it for him.

'Very well,' Riario said. 'I have, as it happens, seen him.'

'Ah.'

'I confess I had not heard that he was Florence's engineer.'

'Perhaps my informant has been in Florence longer than yours,' said the Cardinal graciously. 'It takes time to build these'—he dabbled his fingers in the air—'these networks. I am delighted to have been able to assist you. What, then, do you know of Leonardo da Vinci?'

'That he was undertaking a study of this high art of his, beneath my wall at Castelmonte,' said Riario.

'The art of war? Yes. Excellent. We may infer a sense of subtlety in him, then. Rome's enemy wishes to tap Rome's springs of knowledge; I like that. I really am most pleased that you could join me this morning; we make progress, dear Count. Would you imagine him dangerous, all things considered?'

'Possibly.'

'Then I am sure I can prevail upon His Holiness to welcome him to Rome. It is always better to know what one is dealing with in cases like this, is it not?'

The Count of Imola lifted his goblet and drank.

'By all means,' he said. 'Invite him here, and I will have him killed.'

'But you would perhaps like to talk with him first?' asked the Cardinal. 'We all admire your sense of priorities, of course, but let us not crush the grape untasted. He will be conferring for the most part with His Eminence Cardinal della Palla, as librarian, but I see no reason why you should not assess him before having him disposed of. Though I am sure your instincts are sound, as always.'

'As you wish,' said the Count indifferently. 'My assessment of him at this moment, putting your information together with mine, is that he is likely to prove a nuisance, which is sufficient cause for removing him. Should I find no reason to change my mind, I will at least defer to Your Eminence to the extent of killing him on his way out of Rome rather than the moment he arrives. Unless, that is, you have some reason of your own for wishing him to stay alive?'

'I have none,' said Cardinal Borgia, 'except for a mistrust in over-hastiness. No matter. In the meanwhile, do prod that fellow of yours in Florence. It is always annoying to receive one's news at third-hand, and a lazy informant is worse than useless. I speak from long experience, and I trust you will not resent my advice.'

*

In Florence the Advent bells pealed merrily. The season of goodwill was at hand, and men were at peace with each other; or, if not precisely at peace, they at least ostensibly refrained from stabbing one another in the back. Under the ringing bells, then, friends, neutrals and undeclared enemies gathered together in harmony amid the appetizing scents of roasting meats; Christmas hymns were sung in cathedral and church, wine-barrels were broached, and rich and poor alike rejoiced.

In the courtyards and the Great Chamber of the Medici palace a swallow-throng of visitors assembled, to wheel, eddy, and settle or disperse as fancy took them. Earnest discourse and idle conversation flourished among legates, ambassadors, nuncios, arch-

bishops, guildsmen, minor nobles, poor scholars, wise men, virtuous women, whores, wits, jesters, priests, learned counsellors and
fools; in costumes plain and colourful, in linens, silks, furs and
fustian, adorned with pewter and gold, with trinkets of Venetian
glass and clustered diamonds, with emeralds from Nubia and the
Indus, Circassian tin, ivory, opal, lapis lazuli, pebbles, bezoars,
pyrites and pearls. Old alliances were warmly confirmed or
quietly severed, as prudence might demand; new ones were
forged with money and power and arrangements for marriage.
The common business of the City-States of Italy was carried on,
publicly and in private corners; and Lorenzo de' Medici moved
among his guests like a courteous shadow, listening to its hum.

*

Lodovico Sforza, the great and powerful Regent of Milan, *Il
Moro*, surveyed his young cousin with an iron-clad fondness,
looming over her as she sat demurely beneath the pergola that
formed the eastern wall of the archery range. It was evening, and
brief flurries of snow winked in the light of bracketed torches set
at intervals along the covered walks. A pavilion of green and
orange silk had been erected in the corner by the belvedere, which
itself served as stage for a group of Flemish lutanists; beside them
a miniature fountain bubbled a gentle stream of Calabrian wine
into an alabaster bowl decorated with floating peaches and artifi-
cial water-lilies.

'They tell me you are becoming quite a Florentine, madam,'
the Regent said.

'Indeed, sir? I do not know what they may mean by that. Is it
intended as a compliment?'

'What others may mean by it, I am not sure. My impression is
that it implies your having become both disputatious and unruly,
as the ladies of Florence have been for as long as I can remember.'

'Then you disapprove, my lord?' said Bianca.

'I did not say so. I am not sure of that either. I admire indepen-
dence of thought, even in womankind. But I must tell you that it
will not do in Milan, little cousin, however admirable it may be
here; we are less given to affairs of the mind, and prefer a decent
reticence in the fair sex. Nor,' he added, 'will it be welcome in
Savoy.'

Bianca coloured angrily. 'In Savoy?' she said. 'I had hoped

97

that you might by now have dismissed Savoy from among your plans for my future. Must I defy you again?'

'It would be unwise.'

'None the less I do so. My grandfather would not have wished me bartered with Savoy like a prize heifer for the political benefit of the house of Sforza. I am a Visconti, as your mother was, my lord; and you are my guardian, not my owner.'

Lodovico Sforza laughed in admiration, his teeth luminous in his darkly handsome face.

'Child, child,' he said, 'I shall do with you as I see fit. Your grandfather is dead, and the Visconti are scattered through France and Lorraine; your father gave you into my charge before he was murdered, relying upon me to seek the advantage neither of the Visconti nor of the Sforzas, but of Milan. Besides, what are your objections to the Prince of Savoy? Your grandmother was of their house. I do not understand you.'

'He is stupid, boorish, and vain. I detest him, as you well know. If you have any love for me—'

'And do you doubt it?'

'Sir, I . . . I do not know. Perhaps I presume too much. There is no reason why I should expect you to feel affection towards me; we are cousins, but God knows that means little enough in these times. Yet I trust you as a man of honour. Moreover . . .'

'Yes?' prompted her guardian.

'My lord, it seems to me that your purpose in wishing me to marry the Prince of Savoy cannot be altogether firm, else you would have us betrothed by now. I shall be fifteen next year.'

'And hence old enough for any man's bed? Is that your meaning?'

'Old enough,' said Bianca, looking at him straightforwardly, 'though, as yet, unwilling. And is Milan so feeble that you must bed me with a fool against my will?'

The Regent laughed again, this time so loudly that several passing couples stopped to look curiously in their direction.

'Little cousin, you delight me,' he said. 'Rightly despairing of my good nature, you appeal to my honour, my presumed subtlety, and Milan's pride. By the saints, they have taught you somewhat, these Medici! I shall begin to regret sending you here. Well. I make you no promises, and I insist upon your obedience; but it may be that my plans for you will change. If they do, be sure that

I will so inform you. If they do not, may I remind you that many women have gone to the marriage-beds of men they detested.'

'Many women, no doubt,' rejoined Bianca. 'But not I.'

'You will be no exception,' Lodovico said, 'and do not over-reach yourself, cousin.'

By a laden trestle-table in the Great Chamber, Paolo and Ippo-lito Pazzi chewed on capons' legs while their brother Francesco drank from a silver cup. Beside him old Jacopo Pazzi, their family head, stood with folded arms. Though they were surrounded by a swirling and multicoloured throng of people, the noise was such that they were effectively in private. This was as well.

'Nothing passes my lips here,' announced Jacopo Pazzi. 'I do not eat in the house of my enemy.'

'Then I wonder, my father,' said Paolo, 'that you came here at all.'

'Do not think I take any pleasure in it. Our absence would be remarked upon; that is all. But the food you are devouring so shamelessly would choke me, and I marvel that you can touch it.'

'Were I to allow hatred to interfere with my appetite,' Paolo said negligently, 'I should have starved long since. This fowl is excellent, though expensive when set against the loss of Cardinal Borromeo's lands to our bank, I grant you.'

'You speak as though it were a matter for jest,' said Jacopo, 'although it is but a tithe of the wrongs these upstarts have done us.'

'I agree, my father. Yet do not mistake me. I am not here as a gesture, but in order to speak with certain people whom I might otherwise be forced to meet in some inconvenient back-alley.' He pointed across the room with the bone he held. 'Grimiani, for instance.'

'A clown,' said his father.

'Again, I agree. Let us think of him, for the moment, as a go-between, which is a function admirably performed by clowns. We cannot move without Rome's agreement; and Rome's agreement may be hard to come by.'

'Rome will support us,' Francesco Pazzi said confidently, 'since His Holiness loves the Medici no more than we do. Did he not remove the assets of the Church in Rome from the Medici bank there and transfer them to ourselves?'

'It does not follow that he will wink at violence,' said Paolo. 'But we may hope that you are right.' He turned back to his father. 'If so,' he continued, 'then you will admit that a mere seven or eight hundred thousand florins stolen from us by an infamous piece of Medici legislation can safely be forgotten. We may regard it as . . . how shall I put it? An enforced loan, to be called at our leisure and at a high rate of interest.'

*

At the far end of the room, Leonardo was remonstrating with Florence's Captain-Gunner.

'In the name of St Barbara—who is, so I believe, your patroness —can you not forget your cannon for the space of a day and enjoy yourself?' he asked. 'Here we have music, wine, food, lovely ladies and well-dressed gentlemen. All are wasted upon you, since you do nothing but stand there scowling.'

Rigo Leone rested a foot on the edge of the vast open hearth and looked around him.

'There is nothing the matter with the food, or with the wine for that matter,' he said, 'but I find your well-dressed gentlemen effeminate. I invite you to inhale their scent, my friend. This place reminds me of nothing so much as a whorehouse in Rabat. As for your music, we have better in the taverns of Pistrola, and with less of this pestilent twanging; moreover, a man may break wind there without some damned overbred jackanapes looking as though the sky had fallen in. I shall return to my cannon as soon as I may, and I would suggest you join me.'

'Nay,' laughed the artist, 'that I cannot do. I am commanded to build fountains here, devise tableaux, and in general make myself useful. You see me now in the role of kitchen-knave.'

'I wondered why you were standing in the midst of the ashes. What are you doing?'

'Designing a turn-spit. I can see no reason why one should not turn a roast mechanically, by means of the rising draught in the chimney above a fire such as this. There are several advantages in doing so; first, since the strength of the draught depends upon the fire's heat, it follows that the brisker the fire, the faster would the spit rotate. Second—'

'I wish you joy of it,' said Rigo hastily. 'And after Christmas?'

'After Christmas I travel to Rome.'

'To Rome?' said the gunner, startled. 'In God's name, why?'
'To read books.'

'We have plenty of books here in Florence. Why stick your head in the lion's mouth?'

Leonardo, who was trying to look up the chimney-stack without getting singed by the heat of the embers, extricated himself and shot a look of innocence at his companion.

'What is this talk of lions?' he demanded. '*I* am not yet at war with Rome—or if I am, then Rome does not know it yet. I am a poor artist with a head full of curiosity. That is all.'

'A head full of misplaced optimism would be nearer the mark,' said Rigo. 'What of your forays underneath the walls of Castelmonte?'

'I can hardly have been recognized. Who would know me? And even were I known, what threat am I to Rome, since I shall travel there alone? In the spring matters may be different; for now, I am safe enough.'

*

Lodovico Sforza, Regent of Milan, having left his unruly young cousin to her own devices, was now sitting opposite the half-Moorish Ferrante of Naples in an alcove decorated with cherubim by Gozzoli. Their conversation, though seemingly casual and interrupted by waves of greeting dismissively bestowed upon all and sundry, was to the point.

'I am untroubled,' Lodovico pointed out. 'Have I not Genoa, Modesta and Lucca between myself and Florence? And is not Rome's hold on the Apennines tenuous, at best? Rome does not frighten me; her arm must grow long before it reaches out to Milan. All the same, I am by no means against an alliance.'

'Nor I,' King Ferrante said, 'though our good Sixtus is unlikely to look covetously southward towards me. Does Lorenzo press you?'

If the Regent noticed this over-familiar reference to His Holiness, he let it pass. Naples, Milan, Venice and Florence dealt with the Papal States as equals, as all men knew, and the easy flattery of smaller states found no place in their discourse.

'Not exactly,' he admitted. 'But then, he would be unlikely to concede his need of us, however strong it might be.'

'But his need exists. We accept that?'

'Certainly.'

'Then let Lorenzo force the pace in argument,' Ferrante said. 'To come to grips with the Medici is like trying to grasp a handful of mist at the best of times; therefore if he needs us, let him say so.'

Lodovico cracked a filbert with the handle of a jewelled dagger and pulled the shell apart delicately. 'Much will depend,' he said, 'upon the outcome of the Castelmonte affair. Do you not agree?'

'I do. Perfectly. If Rome can hold Castelmonte and the upper Arno valley, then we have the Medici at a disadvantage, to say the least. Since there is little doubt in my mind that Rome can do so, we may be better placed if we leave discussion of any alliance with Florence until next summer. If Lorenzo needs us now, he will need us the more desperately then.'

*

It was nearly midnight when Giuliano de' Medici nudged open the door to the upstairs library, holding in one hand a candelabrum and in the other a ring from which dangled several keys. He was humming a tune, oblivious for the moment both to the sounds of revelry that filtered upwards from hall and garden and to the echoes of gaiety outside in the streets of the city.

Resting the candles on the table, he crossed to where, between two rows of books, the triple-locked iron door of a strong box was set into the wall at floor level. He knelt, and was about to fit a key to the uppermost lock when his attention was caught by a still figure silhouetted against the dim light of a window at the opposite side of the shadowed room.

'Constanza?' he called softly. 'Is it you?'

'It is, my lord.'

'Almost you startled me. I had thought you in your chamber and asleep.' Dropping the keys to the boards beside him he rose and walked to her, brushing at his knees in abstraction. 'What are you doing here, my lady? Alone, and in a darkened room?'

'Sleep did not come to me, Giuliano,' she said, 'as it has not done these many nights. Therefore I dressed and came here to . . . to watch happier people pass.' She pointed. Lanterns gleamed in the alley beneath the palace wall, and snatches of song were rising from within a house on the corner of a small square to their right.

Her voice faltered and she added, whispering, 'It is good to see happy people, my lord.'

He nodded and held out his hands to her, taking her own and cupping them protectively. 'All of us mourn for Carla,' he said. 'Yet she was your sister, and the loss is yours. It is well enough to be a man, and hence to be able to drown grief in thoughts of vengeance; but yours is the harder part by far.'

She turned and looked out of the window again, her voice still soft.

'I am dry of tears, Giuliano,' she said. 'I have done little else these past weeks but weep.' He moved closer, and she leaned against his chest.

'And yet,' he said, 'though yours is the greater grief, I feel it too; and for reasons which are mine alone. For I rode to Florence behind her, Constanza, and laid her in our chapel; and as I rode, the thought came to me unbidden that had it been you, I would no longer have wished to live.'

He tightened his arm around her, and she moved to look into his eyes as though in search.

'You love me this much?'

'I do. I have loved you longer than I knew, being foolish and light-hearted. But so it is. When Carla died, I saw that I must not lose you.'

'So much did Leonardo tell me this very morning,' Constanza said, half to herself. 'Death is but a long journey, he said, and all of us meet again; and therefore, while we must weep, it should be as we weep when a loved one leaves us for many years, not for ever. And he also said that mourning must cease with the arrival of new joy, and that my new joy lay in your love for me.'

'A wise man. And did you believe him, Constanza?'

'I wanted to. But I wished to hear you say it too. Was that perverse of me?'

He shook his head. 'No,' he said. 'God knows that I, too, hunger to hear you say that you love me. How could it be otherwise?'

'I love you, Giuliano. I had not thought to find you so kind, so gentle, so quick to help me ease my pain at Carla's death. I loved you before that, but'—she smiled fleetingly—'in a different fashion, my lord, and one which I do not seek to have you understand.'

103

They stood in silence, looking out over the white city and the falling snow. A draught from the open doorway bent the candle-flames and made the shadows dance. Giuliano stirred.

'We might forget the world thus,' he said, 'but I cannot do so. I came here to find some small coin with which to reward a troupe of tumblers downstairs, and Lorenzo will believe me lost. He will not be far from the truth. But I must return.'

Constanza released herself from his arms, her face glowing. 'Then leave me,' she said. 'I am happy now, and will sit here a while longer.'

'No,' Giuliano said. 'Enough of darkness. Will you not come with me?'

'Is that what you wish me to do?'

'It is. Shall I find my good friend Leonardo and have him offer you advice on the subject?'

Constanza laughed. 'There will be no need to trouble him,' she said. 'I will come with you.'

'Then give me your hand,' Giuliano said.

*

The middle garden, serving chiefly as a means of passage between the halls and courtyard of the palace and the archery range for such as were willing to brave the wintry air, was deserted save for a group of five men who stood in shadow some thirty paces from the lighted causeway that crossed it. From beyond the wall at their backs the plangent notes of a *strambotto* sounded, drowning their muttered discourse in the soft cadences of lute and viol.

'The Count of Imola is for us,' said Silvio Grimiani. 'I received a letter from him yesterday.'

'It is not Riario's position which concerns us,' Ippolito Pazzi said, 'since we already assume his support. What we must know is the attitude of His Holiness.'

'I cannot speak for His Holiness,' said Silvio, 'and nor can any man. What would you have me do? Request an audience with him? Ask him whether or not he will give us his blessing if we commit murder on his behalf?' He brushed snowflakes from his hair, petulantly. 'Rome has always said one thing and meant another,' he went on, 'and His Holiness has refined Rome's ambiguity to the point where it is impossible to tell what his views are on any matter at all, least of all a question of massacre. I cannot even tell what Rome wishes me to do about this damned artist.'

'Leonardo da Vinci?' said Paolo Pazzi. He grinned in the darkness. 'Is he giving Rome the itch, as he gives it to you, noble prince?'

'Watch your words!' snarled Silvio. 'I have spitted better men than you, and upon less provocation.'

'If you feel so heated,' said Francesco Pazzi, 'over a small matter of his paying too much attention to the lady Bianca Visconti, then I suggest you use your sword upon Messer Leonardo forthwith, and cease from inflicting your annoyance upon ourselves, who have no interest in it. Eh, Bernardo?' He dug an elbow into the side of the man who stood next to him.

'Oh, by all means,' Bernardo Bandini said. 'By all means.' He was a well-set man with reddish hair, whose chief employment was the casual running-through of inconvenient persons on behalf of one patron or another. 'I dislike his superior airs myself, and should be happy to support you.'

'Too hasty,' said Silvio. 'I do not know whether Rome . . .'

'Of course. If you are uncertain of Rome's wishes, then there is no more to be said.' Francesco Pazzi prodded Bandini in the ribs again, laughing. 'It is always wise to consult Rome, even upon a question of unlacing one's doublet or blowing one's nose, I agree.'

'Very well,' said the Prince of Savoy.

*

Save for a few late-stayers, the great hall was almost empty. Rigo Leone, as he had announced, had mounted horse and was on his way back to the cruder delights of Pistrola, and to his cannon. Leonardo, his hair tousled, was sitting in an inglenook by the huge hearth, charcoal and notebook in hand. Others yawned in corners or, in some cases, lay beneath tables asleep or drunk before being aroused by attendants and valets, but he seemed as wide awake as ever. He pulled several loose sheets from beneath his thigh, where he had thrust them for security, and held them out to Bianca Maria Visconti.

'And for how long have you been working thus?' she asked. 'Six hours? Seven? I despair of you, sir. I had hoped for your company.'

'That you are welcome to at any time,' Leonardo said.

'And must I sit by you in this grimy fireplace in order to have it? How gallant of you! And in any case I should have been forced to push my way through a press of stupid women, or so I observed; and I did not care to do so.'

'Very wise of you,' said Leonardo. 'However, do not imagine that this throng of beautiful ladies was fascinated by myself.'

'I am sure they were not.'

'It is simply that a man who appears to be doing something, no matter what it may be, is a powerful attraction for those who are doing nothing whatever.'

'Of course. And now that they have all gone elsewhere, may I ask you to accompany me and speak with my guardian?' Bianca asked.

'I shall be happy to accompany you anywhere, and for any purpose. Where is he?'

'In the archery range. I warn you that he is very powerful, and does not approve of you. He believes that you have been leading me astray, though I have assured him that it was far from being true. But he will not bite you.'

'Then I will try not to be nervous,' Leonardo said.

'And brush the soot from your sleeve.'

'It is honourably acquired soot, and Milan is a city of smoking foundries. *Il Moro* will not object to a little honest dirt.'

'And do not address my guardian as *Il Moro*, in his hearing. Come with me, then, if you please.'

*

'Cousin,' said Lodovico Sforza a quarter of an hour later, 'it is time you were abed. I thank you for bringing Messer Leonardo da Vinci to me; for the present, may I ask you to retire?'

If Bianca seemed prepared to offer some argument to this, her guardian's manner brooked none. When she had gone, he addressed himself to Leonardo, wasting no time upon ceremony.

'Castelmonte,' he said.

'What of it, my lord?'

'I do not believe Florence can take it,' said the Regent of Milan. 'Am I correct?'

'My lord,' said Leonardo carefully, 'my duty is at present to Lorenzo de' Medici, as I think you must be aware.'

Sforza eyed him for several moments, as though in calculation.

Then: 'I am aware of it,' he said, 'and perhaps we misunderstand one another. I am not asking you to be indiscreet. Let me begin anew. Milan and Naples are considering an alliance with Florence; an alliance which, without consulting your patron, you must perceive that he needs. Do I offend your sensibilities thus far?'

'No. Milan would make Florence a valuable ally.'

'Good. You are an engineer, you tell me, and hence think objectively. Were you in my place, Messer Leonardo, would you think such an alliance of advantage?'

'Beyond doubt,' replied Leonardo promptly.

'You speak without hesitation, I notice.'

'I have already considered Milan's position, with some care.'

'Have you, by Hades? Then persuade me, since you appear to be surer of your ground, and Milan's, than I am.'

'Persuasion should not be necessary. Naples I discount, as being of little importance to Rome. It is the Republics which His Holiness wishes to swallow.'

Lodovico Sforza fingered the silk of the pavilion beneath whose shelter they stood. The archery range was bare and white; the musicians had long since retired. Snow sifted into the footprints that dotted the lawn, obliterating them.

'Milan,' he said brusquely, 'is a Duchy, not a republic. Where is your argument?'

'Milan, with great respect, is a Duchy in name only. In all other respects it is as much a republic as Florence, Genoa or Venice. The essence of a republic is that it is ruled by those who are strong enough to rule it, whether by popular acclaim or through seizure. Let us look at Milan in this light. Your brother, Gian-Galeazzo, is Duke. Does he rule Milan? No. You rule it, my lord; and my argument stands.'

'I still do not altogether follow it, though I may grant your premise. What of Rome, then?'

'Rome's ruler,' said Leonardo, 'holds office through means other than purely temporal power.'

'He holds it through the grace and will of Almighty God. Well? Surely, a power stronger than . . . let us say my own?'

'I would be more impressed if the Almighty did not, apparently, find it an advantage to work through the College of Cardinals,' said Leonardo.

Lodovico Sforza blinked. 'Why,' he said cheerfully, 'you are a damned heretic. But proceed with your heresy.'

'It is plain enough. His Holiness, not content with the authority of his spiritual office, seeks temporal power as well. More: he seeks gold, the fount of all temporal power. From whom will he wrest it? From those whom he perceives as controlling it, which is to say the republics; they are golden plums, my lord, from which His Holiness will squeeze what juice he can, if they are foolish enough to let him.' Leonardo held up his left hand, and folded his fingers down one by one. 'Florence first,' he said. 'Then Siena, Genoa. Mantua, it may be. Then Milan. After that, Venice, Savoy, and the kingdoms of France. Therefore he must be stopped now; and therefore, my lord, it follows that you should make your alliance as soon as possible.'

'And provoke Rome thereby?' said Sforza. 'I wonder.'

'Rome will not wait to be provoked. She will, as always, divide and conquer. Make your alliance; there is nothing to be gained by waiting.'

'I thank you for your counsel, engineer. But I think I will at least await the outcome of Lorenzo's fight for Castelmonte. Which brings me back to my starting-point. Your guns cannot take it.'

'I would not feel too sure of that.'

'They have failed thus far.'

'I admit it. None the less I will make you a prophecy, if it will ease your mind, and Milan's. The guns of Florence will take Castelmonte for Florence next spring.'

'We shall see,' said Lodovico Sforza. 'We shall see. Meanwhile, I bid you farewell, Messer Leonardo.'

He strode away, the newly fallen snow spraying from his boots as he crossed the lawn. Leonardo sat on the steps of the belvedere and plucked idly at the strings of a discarded lute. On the face of it, he thought, his prophecy seemed mere bravado, and doubtless the Regent of Milan had taken it thus. What did he, Leonardo, artist turned engineer, truly know of gunnery? The calculation of angles and trajectories was one thing; practice was another. What made him so certain, then—and certain before he knew how he would set about it—that he could succeed where Rigo Leone, Florence's Master-Gunner, had failed?

Yet certain he was, as he had often been. Ideas swam in the

reaches of his mind like fish in the sea, pale and fugitive, as they did when he conceived a picture, seeing its essence before he could perceive its form, yet knowing that form to exist in some way he could not define. As it was with artistic discovery, so it was with science; his solution existed, and it remained only to grasp it.

He laid down the lute and walked from beneath the pavilion's eaves, following in Sforza's footsteps.

He had barely passed through the archway that gave onto the middle courtyard when his passage was barred by three figures.

'A moment, if you please, good fellow,' said Silvio Grimiani di Torino. He stood easily, his feet slightly apart. At a discreet four paces behind him, Francesco Pazzi lounged in simulated conversation with Bernardo Bandini, who was propped against a torch-standard, hand on hip. Leonardo halted.

'Why, good morrow, my lord,' he said. 'Is there something I can do for you?'

'Nothing,' Silvio said. 'That is to say, the merest trifle. I have a question to put to you.'

'It could, perhaps, wait until daylight?' said Leonardo mildly.

'I think not. It will not detain us long. It is simply that I have observed that you spend overmuch of your time in the company of the lady Bianca Visconti, a circumstance which I find odd and, on the whole, offensive. My question, then, is this: why does a man such as yourself—a mere artist and the bastard, I believe, of a notary gotten upon some serving-wench—presume to thrust his company upon a lady so far above his station? I am sure that you can offer me a short and simple explanation, and we need then keep you no further.'

Leonardo frowned slightly. Behind the Prince of Savoy he saw that Pazzi and Bandini had turned their faces expectantly in his direction.

'Ah,' he said. 'I perceive, my lord, that I have been remiss. I confess that I had not considered the matter in the light which you now cast upon it. I am bound to say, however, that had I done so I doubt whether it would have disturbed me unduly.'

'It disturbs me,' said Silvio.

'I can see,' said Leonardo with the greatest courtesy, 'that it might do so, though I am not sure why.'

'Well, and then?' inquired Silvio. 'It is not necessary for you to know why. One sees that you have no sword, though we have noticed you strutting with one upon occasion. One assumes, then, that you know how to use it; and for the present either of my friends here will be glad to lend you one. Between gentlemen, these matters are quickly settled.'

'I am sure you are right,' Leonardo replied. 'However, I must point out a flaw in your reasoning. For here we have but three gentlemen upon the one hand; and upon the other, myself, the bastard son of a serving-wench, as you have rightly described me. In general I am at your service; but as regards your proposal, I am afraid that I find myself with better things to occupy me than to brawl with slighted princes. I suggest you return to your cups and your toys, and leave me to what concerns me.' He laid a hand gently on Silvio's sword-arm, as one pats a fractious child, and moved him aside. Passing between the two men a few paces farther on, he nodded to each of them, and was gone.

*

Dawn found him in the company of Lorenzo de' Medici. As on a previous occasion, the two men sat in Lorenzo's private and monastic retiring-room, beyond whose window the sky promised sunshine after the night's snowfall.

'When do you wish to leave?' Lorenzo asked.

'As soon after Christmas as I may.'

'Well. By then you will, I expect, have attended to the roasting of my geese and my capons, if I understand your drawings of mechanisms for my fireplace aright, so that we shall be able to spare you.' He smiled thinly. 'It is unnecessary for me to point out that in going to Rome you cannot assume our protection.'

'I do not seek it,' said Leonardo. 'I hope that Rome is unaware, as yet, of the nature of my employment with you. I go not as Florence's engineer, but as a humble seeker after truth.'

'A dangerous commodity,' said Lorenzo de' Medici. 'If you should come across it in any quantity, then have a care.' He drummed his fingers on the table-top. 'I confess I am uneasy,' he continued. 'Will you not tell me what it is that you seek? Our libraries here are extensive, and it may be that your journey can be avoided.'

'With respect, sir, I doubt it. The archives of the Church are a source of information I must examine now, since it is certain that I shall not be allowed to do so later. My mind runs upon the subject of gunpowder; a substance which your Captain-Gunner tells me is made in quite different fashion by different men, and whose properties differ according to its maker. These differences are vital to both Captain Leone and myself. Since the making of gunpowder is an ancient art, I must consult ancient records; which in turn means that I must consult Rome.'

Lorenzo rose and crossed to the window.

'Very well,' he said. 'I did not appoint you my military adviser in order to question your judgement. You have my leave to go.'

CHAPTER NINE

On a morning in early January, 1478, in a spacious and sunlit upper-floor room of the Lateran Palace, Cardinal Domenico della Palla sat behind his writing-desk and surveyed his visitor with tranquil and inquiring eyes, his fingertips tented and resting on his lips.

It was probable that no more than two men—one of whom was himself—were aware that the Apostolic Chancellor was the most powerful personage in Rome. Certainly his appearance gave no hint of the fact. Precise, calm and careworn, Cardinal della Palla at fifty looked like the teacher he had once been.

His power was of a peculiar kind; so peculiar that it had not even existed before he had invented it. Its source and mechanism lay beneath his feet and those of his guest, and occupied, in terms of space, more than a third of the entire building. Its nature was both simple and, at the same time, complex. Della Palla's stock-in-trade was knowledge.

He had, in his youth, been handsome, and still kept the fair hair and piercing blue eyes of his northern ancestry. Over the treacherous years his mouth had firmed with the need to conceal those secrets his mind had acquired, and a vertical furrow had eaten its way into the centre of his brow; a furrow which deepened each time he listened, intently, to a message whose import lay not in the words that composed it but in the unspoken hints betrayed by a tone of voice, a moment's hesitation, a sudden blandness of expression on the part of its bearer. If he smiled seldom, and laughed never, it was because he found little in the state of the Church to provoke amusement, still less joy. Daily his two hundred clerks received and transcribed accounts of venery, fraud, treason, banishment, and murder; and even the news of a marriage or of a birth of a son gave rise not to good cheer, but to the calculation of a shift in advantage between one family and the next. The road of truth which the Cardinal had chosen to tread was severe, and thorny. It had begun almost a quarter of a century previously.

When the Spaniard Alonso de Borja had assumed, at the *habemus pontificem* of April 8th, 1455, the title of Callistus III—thereby inaugurating a control of the Papacy, directly or through nominees, by the Borgia family that was to last through fifty years and six Pontiffs—his first act was to promote his nephew Rodrigo, a student at Bologna, to the office of Apostolic Notary. The fact that the young man did not at the time possess a degree in Canon Law, he felt, was but a small disadvantage and one speedily rectified; he sent Rodrigo back to Bologna to obtain his Doctorate. Unsurprisingly, Rodrigo passed his examinations a year later with high honours, presenting his teachers and his examiners with caps and gloves of the finest leather to mark his appreciation of their wisdom.

If there were those who felt—but were careful not to say—that the three hours each day which the young Rodrigo Borgia had felt able to steal from his hunting to devote to his studies in Canon Law were perhaps insufficient to have justified his Doctorate, one man disagreed with them. Domenico della Palla, albeit acidly and with a certain dry wit, wrote to Callistus III and informed His Holiness that his nephew, when persuaded to discuss matters as dull as jurisprudence, showed a surprising grasp of his material and might—or so his tutor felt— eventually fill his position at Rome's Chancery with distinction in fact as well as in name.

Since neither Rodrigo nor his uncle intended that he should do anything so mundane, this letter from the twenty-six-year-old della Palla gave them some quiet mirth; but, ironically yet with gratitude for an opinion he perceived as honest, Callistus summoned his nephew's tutor to Rome and offered him a position as secretary to his former pupil.

Della Palla, with equal irony, accepted.

Over the years which followed, the relationship between Rodrigo Borgia—now Cardinal—and his mentor blossomed, if slowly. At first it was assumed as a matter of course that Domenico della Palla would play at politics with the same fervour as did the Borgias. He did nothing of the kind. His allegiances, it was discovered with surprise, were three: to God, to truth, and to the Church. The Supreme Pontiff, his family, and his supporters regarded this first as an affront, then as an amusing curiosity, and finally, in the roaring tumult of warfare with Aragon and the Turks, as an asset. Bribes without number were offered, including even the Bishopric of Valencia, once held by Callistus himself. Della Palla declined them all, graciously.

Seldom moving from the confines of the Lateran Palace, he seemed to do little but increase his staff of clerks and under-secretaries, and the Borgias were on the whole content that he should do so. His advice before the sea-battle off Mytilene gave Rome victory. His insistence that Venice would shortly conclude a trade agreement with the Ottoman Empire and could not, therefore, be expected to contribute to the Pontiff's proclaimed crusade against the unbelievers proved embarrassingly correct; and his unauthorized diversion of funds to Janos Hunyadi, the Hungarian *condottiere*, and his military adviser Cardinal Carvajal, ensured the defeat of Mohammed II at the gates of Belgrade. Slowly but surely, then, while tramping the dusty corridors of the Lateran, Cardinal Borgia's secretary forged himself an empire; founded upon the pens of his scriveners, existing only in rank upon rank of specially constructed cabinets filled with a tide of documents, its range and power would eventually have surpassed the belief of those who in fact refused, through lack of understanding, to admit its existence.

As he had foreseen, he became indispensable. More than this, he remained neutral. Upon the death of Callistus III, the Borgias decided to elect the former satirical playwright and humanist, Aeneas Piccolomino. They did so. Pius II, as he had amusingly styled himself, proceeded to the Lateran Palace on a rainy autumn morning in 1459, was shown its bulging cellars, and retreated in awed haste before the evidence of so much industry; two months later, for reasons he himself only dimly comprehended, he appointed Domenico della Palla to the Cardinalate of Santa Lucia da Vignola. His successor Paul II, who had been expecting opposition to his Pontificate from the new Cardinal on the grounds that he, too, was an openly political Borgia appointee, was pleasantly surprised to find that della Palla gave not a fig for the mechanics of succession, and rewarded him with the position which the latter had been seeking for years; that of Apostolic Chancellor.

Cardinal Rodrigo Borgia, maker of Popes, was the only man in Rome who was less than intimidated by the paper empire in the Lateran Palace. He visited his former tutor and secretary often, complimented him without flattery, drank wine while laughing good-naturedly at della Palla's water-carafe, and tried to make a friend of the Chancellor. He failed in this, as all men failed, but their relationship was none the less comfortable. Della Palla, as always, had written only the truth in commending Rodrigo's intelligence to his uncle, Callistus III. Therefore, Cardinal Borgia prospered; he listened, as few did, to what the Apostolic Chancellor had to say, and acted upon it.

Thus it was that when Francesco della Rovere became Pope Sixtus IV and ostensibly the most powerful figure in Rome, two men and two men alone could have told him (but did not) that Rome's true power lay elsewhere; to wit, in the Piazza di San Giovanni in Laterano. Rodrigo Borgia did not tell him so, because he intended to become Supreme Pontiff himself in due course; and Cardinal Domenico della Palla, that quiet and withdrawn man who wore truth as a breastplate and carried knowledge as his only sword, would not have considered telling him anyway.

*

On this January morning, then, della Palla sat, conscious as always of the industrious army beneath him digesting the state of the world and thereby extending his reach, and watched the young Florentine who stood at the far side of his table with a leather-covered notebook under one arm. Before the Cardinal lay a letter. Since he knew its contents by heart, he had no need to consult it, preferring instead to study its author.

'Messer Leonardo da Vinci?' he said.

'Myself,' his visitor replied, 'and at the service of Your Eminence.'

'Please sit down, my son. And then tell me, if you will, in what precise way you hope that we may be able to assist you.'

Leonardo sat in the chair the Cardinal indicated, transferring his portfolio to his knees. 'My hope is, Your Eminence,' he said, 'to discover in the archives of the Church some learned works upon the making of gunpowder.'

Della Palla drove the tips of his fingers against his lower lip thoughtfully. He was accustomed to concealing surprise.

'Gunpowder,' he said. 'Yes. If I may say so, an odd preoccupation for an artist. May I say that I have admired your portrait of Donna Ginevra Benci? I will not, therefore, pretend that you are

115

unknown to me.' Leonardo inclined his head in acknowledgement. 'Gunpowder, then,' the Cardinal continued in a brisker tone. 'I assume that this letter of yours is ironic in flavour, and that you regard warfare as the highest art form? An intriguing position. Why should you suppose the Church to have any material that might help you?'

'It is an assumption on my part, I agree,' Leonardo said. 'But I already know of the treatise by Albertus Magnus, the *Kriegsbuch Bellifortis*, and of course the *Epistola de secretis operibus Artis* of Brother Bacon, all of which your libraries possess. I was hoping to find the original *Liber Ignium* of Marcus Graecus, though I believe the only copy to be at Nuremberg; but there may be other sources.'

'Your scholarship is impressive,' said the Cardinal, 'and I thank you for making it clear to me that you are far from wasting my time. Or yours, of course. May I ask what exactly your interest is in gunpowder?'

'It is philosophical,' replied Leonardo.

'A careful answer. I accept it, for the present, though there are others who may not. Well, Messer Leonardo, I will make some search of my own for anything I believe may interest you. Philosophical? I approve of that. From what aspect?'

'Specifically, then, Your Eminence, upon the vexed question of how the power arrives in the gunpowder during the making of it. For consider that charcoal, sulphur and saltpeter separately possess no power of explosion; how, then, does a mixture of all three come to have its force?'

The Cardinal's face remained as neutral as ever, though a subtle and observant man might have perceived that he was pleased by this.

'An excellent point,' he said. 'I shall ponder it while I am about your errand. Meanwhile, I have an errand of my own to inflict upon you, if I may. I should say rather that it is a request from my colleague Cardinal Borgia. Since it will in any case take me until tomorrow to search for your philosophical material, I am instructed to ask you to attend at the Papal Palaces for an audience with Count Girolamo Riario of Imola. Have you any objection?'

'None whatever. Have I not said that I am at the service of Your Eminence?'

'Then this afternoon will be suitable. Have you met the Count?'

'I have not had that pleasure. I have heard of him, of course; who has not?'

Cardinal della Palla studied the artist's face closely. 'Messer Leonardo,' he said finally, 'it may be that we shall become better acquainted, through God's grace. I hope so. If things should fall out thus, it is also my hope that we shall, in time, learn to be candid with one another. In this spirit, then, I believe I must tell you that the Count of Imola has already seen *you*.'

'Has he, indeed?' said Leonardo. 'I thank your Eminence. I must consider where he may have done so.'

'Yes,' said Cardinal della Palla drily. 'In view of your philosophical interest in gunpowder, it might be worth considering the matter very carefully indeed. I expect to see you here tomorrow at this hour.'

*

As he walked along the bank of the Tiber beneath the buried mausoleum of Hadrian, now Castel Sant' Angelo, Leonardo found his thoughts running not on the man he was about to see but upon the Cardinal who had interviewed him that morning. Since what had passed between them had been merely the courteous fencing which Leonardo himself enjoyed and regularly indulged in, he was at a loss to explain a certain curious mental excitement which he had felt when talking to della Palla, and still felt even now. It was true that the Cardinal was a man of massive learning; his position alone guaranteed the fact. Compared with the Cardinal's mind, the mind of the venerable Dr Cino di Lapo Mazzone was that of a buzzing and importunate gnat. Yet there was more to Cardinal della Palla, the artist considered, than learning; more even than wisdom, a quality so rare that one might spend a lifetime without meeting more than one or two men who possessed it. Perhaps, Leonardo thought, he was being over-imaginative. Was there something, however tenuous, in the mind of Cardinal della Palla which called to his own? If so, he was aware that he had not, as yet, answered the call.

He walked on, the river boiling past him; the walls of the Leonine City rose at his left, and he turned aside.

Arrived in the Borgia apartments, his destination, he was obliged to wait for almost an hour in a salon overlooking the San Damaso courtyard. At the end of this period he was relieved of his sword by an impassive Swiss mercenary, and ushered into a small room whose windows were all but obscured by heavy drapes. In one corner, seated in an oaken-sided stall, was Count Girolamo Riario.

Leonardo remembered with distaste what he knew of the man —and what he himself had seen from the gunners' ridge in the Arno valley—and shuddered internally, despite himself. Today, however, the Count was relaxed and charming. His legs, clad in parti-coloured hose, were crossed, and he held a small grey cat on his raised knee. He stroked it as he greeted the artist.

'Welcome,' he said. 'Welcome to Rome, to whom all roads lead sooner or later.'

Leonardo bowed.

'And my thanks,' the Count went on, 'for allowing me some portion of your time here, which I am sure is very valuable. My good friend, Cardinal Borgia, tells me you are here on some academic mission of deep importance, and I hesitate to keep you from it overlong. Stand forward in the centre of the room, please, so that I may see you. Yes. I knew my memory did not fail me. Last November . . . was it last November? Yes. You were beneath my wall, were you not?'

'I was,' replied Leonardo.

'My dear sir, think nothing of it. I wished but to see you to assure myself of the fact. I apologize for my somewhat hasty greeting to you at the time; I did not know who you were, and my men discharged a few crossbow-bolts in your directions, from which I perceive you took no harm. Had I known then what I know about you now, I would have been . . . less ungracious. I refer of course to your standing as an artist. Tell me,' Riario said conversationally, 'what were you doing there? I dare say you were upon some artistic pursuit.'

'Quite so,' said Leonardo. 'I am at present painting an allegorical scene of battle for the monastery of Santa Cecilia, and to that end was making some studies in the field.'

'But how admirable!' exclaimed the Count. 'What industry! What devotion to your craft! To risk life and limb in the pursuit of excellence deserves the highest praise. Why, as I recall matters, you were even feeling the texture of my somewhat battered wall, were you not?'

'I had not thought that you observed me so closely, my lord.'

Riario lifted his hand from the animal on his knee and waved it airily. 'It was but for a short few instants,' he said. 'And in any case, it is all long past now. A scene of battle; you must allow me to see it when it is finished, though I am no artist. And you undertake . . . studies of this kind for every subject you paint?'

'Most surely. To set down the truth of things it is necessary to understand them fully. One then shows not only the surface appearance, but the reality.'

The Count nodded.

'For example,' Leonardo continued, 'let us take yourself. You wear your armour-jacket, even now. You sit in a corner of a room with drawn curtains. Seeing you thus, another man might say that you were withdrawn, reserved, that you sought to enclose yourself as do those crabs which live in discarded shells. Yet such is not my perception.'

'This is presumption,' said Girolamo Riario, frowning.

'Artistic presumption only.'

'And what, then, do you see?'

For reply, Leonardo crossed to the window and threw back the curtains, flooding the small room with light. He unfolded the cover of his notebook and returned to the middle of the floor. Intrigued despite himself, Riario rose from his chair and dropped the cat beside him. As Leonardo began rapidly to sketch, he came and stood behind the artist's shoulder.

'If I were to depict you,' said Leonardo, his hand moving the while, 'it would be thus. Not enclosed; not in the corner of some darkened room; but so—and so . . .'

Watching the flying charcoal in da Vinci's fingers, Riario with amazement saw himself emerging from the paper as a figure standing on the top of a hill, air and space all around; and dressed no longer in armour, but in loose and flowing robes, as though inviting the very winds to caress him. He was, momentarily, stunned; and in that moment felt obscurely drawn by something akin to gratitude towards the artist, a man who—almost as though by wizardry—had perceived something of that inward nature he had so firmly thrust aside for all his lifetime.

The moment passed, and he fingered his collar, his hands writhing. Freedom, his mind shouted at him, meant openness to attack, and had he not long since agreed with himself to barter freedom for security? And what right had this Florentine, Rome's enemy and his own, to recognize his childhood bargain and mock him with it? A trap had been set for him, he now saw; and he had nearly fallen into it.

He reached across and tore the uppermost sheet away from the notebook, unfinished. In unreasoning fury he was about to crumple it, when he saw a brief irony in the artist's eyes and controlled himself. He walked back to his chair, holding the sketch as though studying it, his eyes and his mind rejecting its message the while. By the time he had seated himself once more, he was able to speak calmly.

'An interesting demonstration,' he said. 'I will keep your drawing, if I may; it shows that talent which all of us know you possess. Well, well. I thank you once again for your time, Messer Leonardo, and will keep you no longer. I hope your researches in Rome prove fruitful.'

*

'I am happy to be able to tell you,' said Cardinal Domenico della Palla in the Lateran Palace next morning, 'that I have the answer to your question. It is contained in a treatise written by Fra Sfabalmaccio di Pisa in 1428, in which he clearly attributes the force of gunpowder to the accumulation of '*vis naturae*' or natural energy. He appends twenty-three different recipes for its manufacture. I am having the relevant passages copied out by my clerks and will give them to you when they are finished. A most fascinating problem, and one which I am grateful to you for having brought to my attention.'

Leonardo, who had risen from behind a small side-table at the Cardinal's entry, now sat down again.

'I thank Your Eminence,' he said. 'It was good of you to put yourself to so much trouble on my account. May I see the manuscript for myself?'

The Cardinal walked to his own desk.

'There would be no particular objection, of course,' he said, as though in faint surprise. 'But why?'

'Because,' Leonardo replied, 'I should like to satisfy myself as to the extent of the learned friar's expertise in the matter of gunpowder. Is he reliable?'

Cardinal della Palla raised an eyebrow.

'I am not sure what you mean by that, Messer Leonardo. His

thesis bears the Church's *imprimatur*, which means that he is the acknowledged authority on the subject; therefore, your question answers itself.'

'None the less,' Leonardo persisted, 'I should very much like to read his opinions.'

'By all means, then.'

The Cardinal rose and left the room, to return a few minutes later with a sheaf of parchment tied with a ribbon. He placed this on the table before Leonardo, who thanked him for it.

'I will leave you to peruse it for an hour or so,' the Cardinal said. 'If my room here suits you, please feel free to stay here while you do so; I have in any case to confer with my chaplain. Will an hour be sufficient?'

'It will be more than enough, Your Eminence.'

'Kindly keep the sheets in their proper order. I have somewhat of an obsession with these things,' the Cardinal said. He nodded, and withdrew.

It was almost noon when he came back. Leonardo, intent upon the final page of the manuscript, did not notice him until the Cardinal had coughed discreetly; then, carefully squaring the edges of the parchment sheets, he rose.

'Well?' inquired della Palla.

'I owe Your Eminence more than I can say for your indulgence,' replied Leonardo. 'None the less, I must tell you that the conclusions reached by Fra Sfabalmaccio are inadequate. In fact, they are barely worth the paper they are written on.'

'I am afraid that once again I fail to understand you,' the Cardinal said.

'I have put it thus bluntly because Your Eminence was kind enough to suggest, the last time we met, that we should learn to be candid with one another.'

'I did. Candour is one thing. I did not invite you to be sacrilegious.'

'I intend no irreverence,' said Leonardo. 'But if I may give you an example of your friar's lack of knowledge, he nowhere implies that gunpowder made according to one or another of his twenty-three recipes will vary in strength according to its ingredients. From my own knowledge, not to mention that of my friend Captain Roderigo Leone—a gunner of great experience—I can assure you that such is the case. I must therefore assume

Fra Sfabalmaccio to have been as ignorant as he is wordy. However,' Leonardo went on good-heartedly, 'I am fortunately, as you see, engaged upon a study of gunpowder myself, and will thus be able to report the true facts to you when I am finished. Your records may accordingly be set straight.'

Cardinal della Palla, during this cavalier recitation, crossed once more to his writing-table, where he fiddled with various objects before seating himself.

'It is hard for me to know where to begin,' he said finally. 'The Church is already satisfied that she has the true facts. They are set down, with authority, in what you have before you; that is what the *imprimatur* means—and, I assume, why you came to Rome in the first place.'

'But suppose,' said Leonardo gently, 'that the Church is wrong?'

'Be careful.'

'Of what? I fear that it is my turn to fail in understanding,' pursued Leonardo blithely. 'Why should the Church, in a practical matter of some importance, rely upon the opinions of a verbose and ignorant friar who says nothing except by way of retailing nonsense concerning '*vis naturae*'—a concept which is totally meaningless, as Your Eminence must perceive—when there is better information available to her?'

'*Your* information?' said the Cardinal.

'My information, naturally.'

'Be very careful, my son.'

'Does the Church, then, believe that she can influence facts by denying them, or by accepting unsound views upon them? This is not some learned and scholastic question, such as that of how many angels may dance upon the point of a needle. Nature is nature, and will not be gainsaid. If His Holiness announces, like Joshua of old, that the sun shall stop in its course, will it heed him and do so?'

'Be very careful indeed,' warned the Cardinal once more. 'I beg you to say nothing—even by way of philosophical argument—from the consequences of which not even I could save you. Your outlook, Messer Leonardo, is heretical. Heretical, and thus extremely dangerous; therefore say no more, I pray you.'

Across the width of the room the two men exchanged an unblinking and steadfast gaze.

'My lord Cardinal,' said Leonardo, 'the time for sword-play in words is past, and has been so since I parted from you yesterday. We have provoked each other into argument, and have known that we were doing so. You believe in the work of your Fra Sfabalmaccio no more than I do; you produced his treatise for me in order to try my mettle, and I have but replied in kind. The *imprimatur* of the Church gives him no more authority than would the cawing of rooks in an April tree-top, and this too you know as well as I. As for danger, Your Eminence has pointed out to me what I already know, which is that I have accepted bodily risk in the very act of setting foot in Rome; and if my soul lies in peril, I look to Almighty God to save it. For what is God, my lord, if He is not truth?'

Cardinal della Palla held out his hand to receive the stacked sheets of parchment, and Leonardo gave them to him.

'Then go with God, my son,' the Cardinal said.

*

'My dear Chancellor,' said Cardinal Borgia after a late supper in his apartment, 'Riario tells me that this man is military engineer to the Medici in Florence. Were you aware of that?'

'Yes, I am aware of it,' della Palla replied.

Cardinal Borgia consumed a grape. 'The Count's suggestion,' he said, 'is that Leonardo da Vinci be assassinated before he can leave Rome, thus saving us all a great deal of trouble. I don't know how much merit there may be in his point of view?'

'The Count of Imola lacks patience,' said della Palla, 'unlike yourself. Given his very limited vision, I am not in the least amazed by his suggestion. It might, certainly, save trouble. And yet Rome is, and Rome will be, when you and I are dead; and therefore haste is inappropriate. Furthermore, upon the short discussion I have had with Messer Leonardo, he appears—albeit somewhat impertinently—to have a greater grasp of the subject of gunpowder than our own published authorities. A slight matter, I realize, but in the long term it should also be considered, do you not think?'

'I see. You are, as always, a model of restraint. Would you recommend protecting him, then?'

'No.'

'You would not? I am a trifle surprised, I confess.'

'He is in the hands of God,' pointed out della Palla. 'I am far from certain that we can offer him better protection.'

*

Leonardo da Vinci saw the slight movement of shadows farther down the street, and paused.

He was walking through a narrow alley in the Trastevere, on his way to the suburban inn where he had stabled his horse. The night air was wet and bone-chilling and the cobblestones slippery with ice, but neither darkness nor weather had so far dampened his spirits. If he had discovered little about gunpowder, and therefore his journey to Rome must be accounted a failure, his meetings with Cardinal della Palla had left him with a feeling of well-being which he still found exhilarating. No word of friendship had passed between them, and he knew that upon reflection the Cardinal might decide that his direct attacks upon the authority of the Church were threatening; and yet, in a curious way, this seemed to matter very little. What mattered was that they had recognized each other, for good or for ill, across the gulf of twenty-five years and more which separated their ages and the greater gulf between the Cardinal's temper as a cleric and his own as a free-thinker; and the recognition of a mind akin to his own sang in Leonardo's blood.

Therefore he smiled at the shadows that awaited him, and walked on, loosening his cape about his shoulders.

At the foot of the slope the alleyway emerged into a tiny square. As he approached this, the sound of sliding steel reached his ears, and his smile widened. Rome, wisely, was abed, and the piazza deserted; the gutters, marbled with frozen snow, shone in the fitful glare of dying torches and the pale silver light of a quarter-moon.

Of the three men who stepped into his path, Leonardo recognized only one. Francesco Pazzi, in padded gambeson and velvet breeches, advanced towards him with drawn sword; to right and left of him, his unknown accomplices moved outwards until they blocked the alley's mouth. Their ambush was well-placed; their victim, with a steep and icy slope at his back, could not turn and flee them, and they were confident of success. Death shimmered on their blades, and Leonardo's smile became one of pure delight.

'Well met, my friends,' he said softly.

Francesco Pazzi made no reply, but instead launched himself

124

forward, his face twisted into a silent grimace of effort as he lunged. He had little need of finesse, and employed none. The murder of one man by three opponents was, as he saw it, a simple matter, and rendered still easier by the fact that his target had not yet drawn sword.

Disobligingly, Leonardo stepped backward a pace, and the sword-point flickered in the air a handsbreadth from the front of his doublet. Before Francesco could regain his lost balance, the artist swept the cape from around his neck with his left hand and swung it, entangling Francesco's head and sword-arm in its folds and temporarily unsighting him. He staggered aside, losing his footing on the treacherous cobbles in a wild and unsuccessful struggle to free himself from the wet and clinging camlet.

Leonardo dropped to one knee, drawing his rapier as he did so. Rolling, he removed himself from the reach of Francesco's blindly sweeping blade. The man on Francesco's right, leaping forward in his support, skewered himself an eyeblink later on the tip of Leonardo's upthrust weapon, which rose from ground level into the pit of his unguarded belly. His breath whistled, and he collapsed, carrying the sword-point which pierced him downwards and losing Leonardo an essential second or two in freeing it from his body.

Seizing this advantage, the third assassin crossed in front of the flailing Francesco and hacked swiftly and clumsily at Leonardo's head. He missed his mark, but his edge bit deeply into Leonardo's right arm near the shoulder as the latter, continuing his acrobatic roll sideways and gathering his feet beneath him, disengaged his point from the fallen and mortally wounded man on the flags. A warm gush of blood darkened Leonardo's sleeve. His third attacker saw this and, in the certainty that his victim was now disarmed and helpless, moved in triumphantly for the kill.

It was a fatal mistake. Transferring his rapier from his right hand to his left, Leonardo swept it, razor-like, across the backs of his opponent's legs, hamstringing him instantly. As he fell, the artist reversed his weapon and drove the pommel with a terrible and anatomical accuracy at his temple. There was a soft crunch of breaking bone, and the assassin tumbled and lay with staring eyes beside his fellow.

Leonardo got to his feet, pressing the side of his sword-bearing left hand against his torn and dripping sleeve. A vein had been severed, he knew, but his touch informed him that the artery was intact. Satisfied, he turned his attention to Francesco Pazzi, observing with slight surprise that, having been tripped by the second of his companions while the latter was pushing past him to the attack, he was still on his knees and cursing sulphurously at the layers of cloth which hampered him. Leonardo placed a foot firmly in his chest and toppled him. As his face finally emerged, therefore, he was greeted by a rapier-point six inches from the end of his nose; a point from which sinister and dusky drops slid and fell, one by one.

'Get you gone, Francesco,' said Leonardo genially. 'The streets of Rome are dangerous enough at night, in all conscience, and even a serving-maid's bastard may, like the scorpion, prove fatal if provoked too far. Look about you, and think twice before you annoy me again. Good night.'

CHAPTER TEN

Three days after this regrettable occurrence, Leonardo reined in his horse at the head of that high Arno valley from whose floor soared the bastions of the town-citadel, Castelmonte. It was late, and Florence still stood thirty miles distant. His right arm was recovering strength, and he disregarded its ache as he looked with appreciative eye down the stretch of road that wound ahead of him. The hills were snow-covered and glowing in the Tuscan light which, as though filtered through golden silk, bathed the evening. Before the stronghold men moved like ants, gathering firewood and repairing their grim wall against the spring; but the autumn's battlefield itself now lay innocent beneath the same delicate mantle which had softened the crags about him and smoothed the gunners' churned ridge below.

He started, automatically, to raise his notebook in an impulse to set down the peaceful scene. Reminded by an immediate twinge that he was, for the present, in no condition for sketching, he let it fall to the end of its short chain with amusement, and instead pulled his horse's head aside to ride down the narrow track which led to Pistrola.

He arrived in the village at sunset, and found warm activity all around. Blacksmiths, farriers, metal-workers in all trades had gathered from miles around to service Captain Rigo Leone's cannon; up and down the length of the street the dull glow of forges shone through open doorways and from beneath rude shelters, and the two great guns themselves stood at the centre of the village square, figures swarming over them amid the chink of hammers and the dull rasp of files. To his immediate right a mammoth wheel was propped against a wall, the iron tyre stripped from its rim; beyond it, three carpenters were working on a dismantled trunnion-block. Leonardo dismounted before the inn, tied his horse, and walked to meet Rigo, who was advancing upon him with outstretched hand.

'Welcome, Sir Scholar,' the Master-Gunner said. 'From whence do you ride?'

'From Rome. Where else? I see you keep warm for January, Rigo.'

'To be sure we do,' Rigo said, his face gleaming in reflected firelight. 'And you? I see you are wounded. Did I not foretell that you would find Rome inhospitable?'

'It is nothing. A slight political disagreement.'

'You amaze me. I trust, at all events, that you left His Holiness in worse condition than you found him.'

'I did not see His Holiness,' said Leonardo, grinning. 'How should I, being but a poor scholar and seeker after truth? None the less, my time there was not entirely wasted. I come to ask you to ride with me to Florence, Rigo. Will you come?'

'And leave my guns again?' said Rigo. 'No. For how long?'

'A month, at least, and perhaps two.'

'No.'

'Rigo, my esteemed friend, your devotion to your guns is beginning to pass beyond reason. Let Agnolo Fulvio and your baby-faced Tesoro see to them, in God's name; they will not shatter into fragments because you are not there every minute of the day to watch over them. Things stir in my mind, Rigo. I need your help, if only to douse my head with cold water.'

'A service I shall render you with pleasure, but not in Florence. What things?'

'Things more important than your two cannon here.'

'Heresy, damned and outright. My ears are closed,' said Rigo.

'How if I were to make you the most famous gunner in all Italy?'

'A foolish and most inadequate temptation,' said Rigo promptly. 'I am already the best gunner in Italy, and fame will therefore follow in due course, without your help.'

'The most famous gunner in history, then.'

'History begins when I am dead,' replied Rigo, 'and is thus of no concern to me. History will not drag me from my cannon.'

'What will, then?'

'I do not know,' Rigo confessed. 'Whatever it may be, you have not yet hit upon it.'

'Knowledge,' offered Leonardo. 'I will undertake to teach you things about gunnery of which you have no conception.'

'Shrewd, but unbelievable.'

'Unbelievable, yet true none the less.'

Rigo considered him. 'Your heresy begins to tempt me,' he said. 'What can you teach me of gunnery that I do not know already?'

'That is easy,' said Leonardo. 'I can teach you what it is that you have been doing these past twenty years and more, and why it is now time to stop doing it. Come, Rigo. Enough is enough. I am not here to buy you, or bargain with you. I ask you to come with me, as a friend.'

'More folly,' said Rigo. 'The height and extreme of folly. Go to Florence, Sir Scholar, and I will join you there four days from now.'

*

'Sir,' said the Medici surgeon, bending over the newly cleaned wound and examining it closely, 'it will mend of itself, but things will go better and more swiftly if I sew the margins together.'

'Then do so, by all means,' said Leonardo. 'First, however, stand aside and allow the lady Bianca to see what we are about, if you please.'

'My lady has no right to be here,' said the surgeon, a stolid and competent man who was not in the habit of deferring to rank. 'Madam, will you not return to your room?'

'Certainly not,' said Bianca.

'There you are,' said Leonardo. 'Few of us have the opportunity to see what lies beneath the skin, except on the field of battle. Allow her to observe and learn, I pray you.'

The surgeon, raising his eyes towards heaven, stood away. Leonardo, who was at present seated on a divan in his room at the Medici Palace, offered his arm to Bianca's gaze.

'It is deep,' she said. 'And what are those things that look like the ends of severed cords, buried in the flesh?'

'Vessels,' Leonardo said. 'They carry the blood. Observe that they have sealed themselves, as part of the healing process.'

'It must have hurt terribly.'

'I was in no position to notice at the time,' said Leonardo, 'which is fortunately often the case. Have you seen enough?'

'Thank you, yes.'

'And do you not feel faint?'

'No,' said Bianca. 'Should I?'

'Many people do. I confess that I have not yet discovered the reason for it. Sir, I apologize for delaying you; please proceed with your stitching.'

'I usually advise my patients to drink wine,' the surgeon said. 'Can I not persuade you to take a little?'

'No, I thank you. I have an admirable faith in your delicacy of touch, and the lady Bianca will distract me, I have no doubt.' The surgeon rummaged in his bag for instruments, and Leonardo asked Bianca how her lessons were going.

'Badly. It is exactly as you warned me,' she said. 'All my tutors bore me, and especially Fra Sigismondo. You cannot argue with them, for as soon as it looks as though you have the right of it they become angry and take refuge in books and easy phrases. I detest them.'

Leonardo laughed, gritting his teeth an instant later as the surgeon went to work on his arm. 'Did I not tell you to be polite to them?' he went on. 'This is always the way of the foolishly learned, and they cannot help themselves. I found something of the same attitude in Rome, as I expected. And yet, not entirely; I may have discovered one wise man, for which it is worth travelling five hundred miles or a thousand, as you will also find out.' He grunted involuntarily.

'I think you should drink some wine,' said Bianca, looking at him. 'If you imagine that you are impressing me with this show of determination you are quite wrong.'

'Unkindly spoken,' said Leonardo, 'and far from just. Tell me, have you noticed any change in our friend Giuliano of late?'

'If you mean that he now walks and rides without looking where he is going,' said Bianca, 'of course I have. The explanation is simple, I assure you; he is madly in love with Constanza, and she is behaving in exactly the same manner. I think it very charming, though I am bound to say it makes them both a little dull; Constanza passed three paces away from me this morning and did not notice I was there. Poor things. I am afraid they are both due for a sad let-down, though I would not dream of telling them so.'

'Indeed?'

'Yes. Lorenzo will never let them marry.'

'Will he not? May I ask, with the greatest respect, how you come to know so much?'

'By listening,' replied Bianca tartly. 'I have become a very good listener since meeting you. Lorenzo, I gather, wants Constanza to marry someone else. I consider it despicable, but there is nothing to be done about it. At least . . .'

'Go on.'

'Nothing. I do not really see how anything can be done.'

Bianca fell silent, and remained so until the surgeon, having set two layers of stitches in Leonardo's arm, had sponged the last trace of blood from the skin and bound the wound. He bowed to Leonardo's thanks, and left the room. Leonardo prodded the bandage gingerly, and shifted the arm to test its mobility.

'A skilled craftsman,' he said. 'And now . . . let me see. I think we should not despair so easily, Bianca. You were going to make a suggestion concerning the plight of Giuliano and Constanza, were you not?'

'I *have* an idea,' Bianca admitted, 'but I don't think I shall tell you what it is.'

'Come now,' Leonardo said. 'In matters of high policy such as this, discussion is always valuable; two minds are better than one. Perhaps not always, now that I come to think about it; but in this case . . .'

Bianca smiled. 'Very well,' she said. 'Here is what I think.'

*

Summoned by Lorenzo's page, Giuliano and Constanza found the ruler of Florence waiting at the door to the library, one arm outstretched, bidding them enter. Giuliano considered him to be suspiciously affable.

'Good morning, my lady. Good morning, brother. I thank you both for attending me.' Lorenzo's voice was silken and gracious, and Giuliano raised an admonitory finger at the sound of it.

'Hearken, Constanza,' he said. 'My brother is using his policy-voice this morning, which means that he wants something of us.'

Constanza, who had been chattering gaily all the while they had climbed the stairs, was unconvinced. 'Let us wait and see, Giuliano,' she said. She led the way into the quiet room and took her seat at the table. 'I will confess, Magnifico,' she continued, 'that I have been hoping for some time that you might wish to speak with us both. Do I guess aright, sir? Are we meeting to discuss our wedding plans with you?'

'We are indeed,' said Lorenzo, 'in a fashion.'

Giuliano said nothing. He was looking attentively at Lorenzo's face, and did not appear to like what he found there.

'Has it been decided, then,' Constanza went on, 'that we need no longer wait for two more years?'

'My lady,' said Lorenzo, 'you know that I take most seriously my pledge to your father to serve as your guardian and to protect your interests in all things. You will also know that, before he died, your father gave to me all those powers which a guardian must have in order to satisfy Florentine law and custom.'

'I know all this, sir,' said Constanza.

'None the less, while thinking of you, my lady, my duty is also to think of Florence.'

Constanza looked towards Giuliano with inquiry and misgiving, but the latter remained silent.

'It grieved me deeply, as it grieved us all,' went on Lorenzo, 'when your sister Carla was taken by the Pope's bastard general and slain so foully. I know you understand this. I have now to remind you that your sister's hand was pledged to the eldest son of the Duke of Ferrara. Shortly after Christmas I received a letter from the Duke, who now requests your hand in Carla's stead. I called you here this morning to inform you of this fact.'

Constanza's hands gripped the arms of her chair, though when she spoke her voice was low and controlled.

'I see.'

'I will not conceal from you that your marriage to the young Count will bring certain . . . advantages to the Republic. But it is also in your own best interests, since you will thereby eventually become Duchess of Ferrara. Weighing all this up, therefore, I have dispatched my courier to the Duke approving your alliance with his house in principle, though much remains to be discussed. I am not sure that this will be to your liking now, my lady—or to yours, brother—but you will see the wisdom in it as time passes. That is all.'

Lorenzo rose, as though to signify that their meeting was at an end, and Giuliano rose with him. From her seat Constanza looked up at both of them, her eyes brimming with tears.

'What kind of men are the Medici?' she breathed. 'Have I no word in this? Am I a piece of merchandise to be offered first to this one, then taken away when that one offers more? Under your protection, my lords, my sister Carla is dead. Never mind! Here sits another d'Avalos sister. She is all but betrothed to a Medici, but never mind that either! The Medici will give her up, so long as it benefits the Republic of the Medici!' She rose then, and ran to the door. 'You deal with my body too freely, my lords,' she said, 'and it makes me feel a whore. Pray excuse me.' She whirled, and was gone.

Lorenzo walked to the door and closed it quietly.

'The lady Constanza speaks her mind,' he said. 'Not that I expected otherwise.'

Giuliano nodded.

'You, in contrast,' Lorenzo continued, 'have had very little to say thus far.'

'True.'

'Am I to hear no argument from you, then?'

'Would my arguments persuade you?' Giuliano asked.

'Probably not. But I had thought to hear a question or two.'

'I have none to which I do not already know the answers,' Giuliano said with asperity. 'I know them because I know you. Ferrara wants the d'Avalos dowry rather than Constanza. Is it one hundred thousand florins? I forget. Possibly, now that Carla is dead, her marriage portion is added to Constanza's? It's a nice point.' Sudden rage flooded his face. 'And what will these florins buy you, Lorenzo? Ferrara himself, it goes without saying. Your own men in Ferrara's guilds, banks, and courts? One imagines so. Trade concessions, I have no doubt. Control of his army?'

'Very necessary,' agreed Lorenzo calmly. 'Did I not say that I must think for Florence? Within a few years Florence will be fighting for her very life, Giuliano. You know this, and I cannot stand idly by even if I wished to do so. I need allies. With Naples, Milan, and Genoa I can deal in other ways. With Venice I may not be able to deal at all. To obtain Ferrara I must also bargain, and it happens that what I have to offer him is Constanza d'Avalos—or rather, as you justly observe, her dowry. Come, Giuliano; you are no child. Are you angered?'

Giuliano was silent for a while.

'Have I said so?' he asked finally.

'You have not. But as you know me, so do I know you. It is unlike you to fence with me, for one thing.'

'And if I were angered—and I do not admit it—what reason would I have, think you?'

Lorenzo studied him. 'It has crossed my mind, brother, since I am not entirely blind, that you have grown to care for this young woman since her sister's death, and think to keep her. I am not considering marriage contracts, but your feelings.'

'Very observant of you,' said Giuliano shortly. He got up again and headed for the library door. 'However,' he said, 'I would remind you that I have not yet opposed the interest of Florence, or yourself. Good day, Lorenzo.'

*

He found Constanza in the middle garden, wearing her great cape of blue velvet. As he approached she turned her head from him, and he laid his hand upon her arm.

'Well?' she demanded. 'Why did you say nothing?'

'I had nothing to say. I know my brother better than you do, Constanza. How many days and nights of planning has it taken him thus to untie the strands of our marriage-compact, think you? Had he consulted me earlier perhaps I might have deflected him from his purpose, but I have seldom known Lorenzo to consult any man. This being true, what hope was there of altering the case with a few well-chosen words?'

'But . . . to make no protest at all, Giuliano?'

'Protest? He had already answered Ferrara. Only the weak protest after the fact. I am not weak, and neither are you.'

'Ferrara!' She spat the name out, like a curse. 'I will never marry that fat little princeling, I promise you!'

'Nor will I let you, my heart. Have we come so far together, to be overset by a Duke's policy? But it is not angry words we need now. We need the means to convince my brother, or to defy him, and neither will be easy. It will, I think, take time—as he has taken time.' He held her arm, gently yet insistently, and she turned towards him.

'You have the Medici blood and mind, Giuliano,' she said. 'Tell me what we must do, and I will do it. I trust you, since I have learned to do so; and it is too late for me to unlearn.'

Her voice was firm and full, and Giuliano's throat tightened as he looked at her. A delight to the eye, he thought. Black hair, smooth and shining and roped now with tiny seed-pearls; her skin olive-dark and soft, and those dark eyes, long-lashed. A generous face, animate and strong-willed. He knew he must go forward, but of a sudden could not find the words to do so.

'It is bitter cold this morning,' he said. 'Do you not find it so? And sunlight is never as sweet for kissing as the moon; yet let us kiss now, Constanza.'

'And why not? I know of no better way to say that we love each other. I am sorry I spoke angrily to you, Giuliano, a while ago.' And, minutes later: 'I would that it were moonlight now,' she said. 'And that we were alone together, in some warm and secret place.'

He drew his head back and smiled at her.

'A bed, perhaps?' he said.

'It might serve,' she replied, looking at him steadily.

Despite himself, he was taken aback. He let her go. A suspicion, insistently merry, was beginning to form in his mind. He drew her to a stone bench and sat down beside her.

'I . . .' he began.

'Yes, my lord?'

'Well. To put it straightly, my dearest heart . . .'

'Yes? I had not thought to find you tongue-tied, Giuliano, at such a moment,' she said gravely. 'Indeed, quite otherwise, or so I have been told.'

'I have been speaking, then, with Leonardo,' he said.

'Have you, indeed?'

'His suggestion, you see . . .'

'Ah. More good advice from Leonardo. Well?'

'This is not exactly as I pictured things,' said Giuliano with a touch of desperation. 'It is true that I used to have some skill in affairs such as this which seems to have deserted me now, but then,' he added hastily, 'I was never in love before this, as I am with you. As you know. And thus—'

'Giuliano,' said Constanza dangerously. 'If I wait to hear much more of this I am very likely to freeze to death. If you cannot find the correct words for the occasion, let me help you. If we have a child, Lorenzo will be put out of countenance. You see? It is hardly complicated at all.'

'I perceive that you also, Constanza, have been talking with Leonardo,' Giuliano said as soon as he could regain some small part of his composure.

'With Leonardo? Certainly not. That would be most improper

of me,' said Constanza indignantly. She gave way to mirth. 'Oh, if you could only see how you look, Giuliano! Tell me, have I given way over-easily, do you suppose? I should not like you to think my virtue too swiftly won, but it cannot be helped. Naturally,' she added in a meditative tone, 'I understand that one cannot always hope to succeed in such things at the first attempt, or even at the twentieth. Or am I wrong about that?'

'To whom have you been talking?' demanded Giuliano, his face crimson.

'Oh. To Bianca Visconti, of course. We discuss everything together; did you not know?'

'The little vixen. I see. Since I am, then, outnumbered three to one—'

'Outnumbered? That is hardly gallant of you!'

'Supported, then. What you will.' He embraced her; held her lovingly, laughing with her the while. 'Just the same,' he said, 'Lorenzo will be far from happy.'

'Let him be unhappy, then. If he can play at politics, so can we. And I may say,' Constanza finished, 'that I had never until this moment imagined that politics could be so joyfully played. One can learn something new every day, as Bianca is always telling me.'

CHAPTER ELEVEN

'And how did your researches go?' Lorenzo asked.

'Very well.'

'You discovered what you were searching for?'

'Hardly. At least, not in Rome. But the ride there and back cleared my head.'

'I must attempt the exercise myself sometime,' said Lorenzo drily. He pinched the bridge of his nose. 'Well?' he asked. 'What now? Their wall is in better condition than it was last September, so Giuliano tells me. How are we to proceed?'

'From theory to practice, as always, sir. I need the use of your archery-range again. May I have it?'

'You may. Though I had hoped you might have finished your games there by now.'

'By no means. I have a great deal of work to do, and little time to do it in,' said Leonardo. 'And I have yet another request.'

'Make it.'

'You have a pair of small cannon on the roof of your eastern wing. May I borrow them?'

Lorenzo shifted impatiently in his chair. 'For what purpose?' he asked. 'They are toys, to be fired upon occasions of rejoicing or proclamation, that is all. I do not see what use they can be to you.'

'I am aware of their present function,' said Leonardo. 'None the less, I have examined them carefully. They were given to your father by no less a person than the great Milanese gun-maker Bertolo Bracci, and bear his name engraved upon them. Toys they may be, sir, but Ser Bertolo was the most renowned man of his time in his craft, and they are excellently made. Their bores are accurate to within a hair's-breadth, and they are accordingly just what I need; it is no matter to me that their carriages are silver-chased and their barrels somewhat over-ornate for my taste.'

'Very well. Have your toys. I take it that you intend to perform more of your experiments with them?'

'I do. I need to know, for instance, a great deal more about gunpowder than I do already—a subject about which I found little in Rome to enlighten me, and must therefore examine upon my own account. There are other matters too. I will not hide from you that I am on the point of forming a new concept in my mind, of great interest and far-reaching consequences.'

'These are large words,' said Lorenzo de' Medici discontentedly.

'Nay, I do not mock you; but *my* interest lies in Castelmonte, and in Castelmonte alone. I trust you will remember that during the course of your experiments. And now tell me how you came to be wounded.'

'It was a private matter, I believe,' Leonardo told him. 'A scrape with some friends of the Prince of Savoy, who seems—for what reason I know not—to have taken something of a dislike to me.' He recounted the incident, Lorenzo de' Medici listening attentively while he did so.

'Perhaps you are right,' Lorenzo said when he had finished. 'And then again, perhaps there is more in it than you suppose.'

'I hope not.'

'Such is my hope too. At all events, I thank you for telling me the details of the affair. Even small and seemingly unimportant scraps of information are valuable to those who have to govern. We have little common ground between us, Messer Leonardo, and yet sometimes I think that in this we resemble one another; you are a man who attends to what others consider trivial, extracting kernels of knowledge from the shells of circumstance, and so also—though for quite other purposes—do I. Perhaps, therefore, we are not as unlike each other as one might suppose.'

'Perhaps,' said Leonardo.

'Well, then. Use my archery-range as you see fit. Borrow my toy signal cannon, if that is your wish. Try to avoid killing any of my courtiers with your experiments; though it is possible that I might be persuaded to turn a blind eye should some unfortunate mishap occur to the Prince of Savoy. But above all remember that your experiments are of no consequence beside the fall of Castelmonte; the achievement of this end alone is the whole of your duty towards me. You understand this?'

'I am of one mind with you,' Leonardo replied. 'There is one more thing. I need the advice and assistance of Captain Roderigo Leone.'

'My Captain-Gunner? He is at work on his guns.'

'He is willing to leave them, sir.'

'Then you had better know what you are about,' said Lorenzo bleakly. 'Should spring come, and I find my cannon in no fit condition for their appointed task because you have diverted Captain Leone from his duties upon some fruitless quest, then I warn you that your case will be hard indeed. You may go, Messer Leonardo.'

*

Rigo, arriving in Florence upon the day he had promised, paid his respects to the Medici Chamberlain and proceeded at once to the archery-range. The snow had melted from the lawn, and he found Leonardo squatting by a contrivance somewhat similar to the framework he had been using to study the flight of arrows, save that this version was stronger and more compact, its angles bound with strips of brass.

He stood in the archway and took in the scene. The belvedere, he saw, was now stacked with powder-kegs, and the former target had been replaced by a wooden box, open-fronted and filled with coarse bags of sand. The artist himself was at present adjusting the barrel of a small decorative cannon, which was in turn clamped to the framework with its muzzle pointing towards the distant butt. A burning slow-match was clipped beside the gun's breech. Oblivious to Rigo's presence, Leonardo reached for this and stood upright, examining the lay of the cannon critically with the smoking match poised above it.

Alarmed—as his profession demanded he should be—by his display of amateur gunnery, Rigo shouted and strode forward.

'And what the devil do you imagine you are about?' he demanded, upon reaching the artist.

'Rigo! A welcome sight indeed!' Leonardo said. He transferred the slow-match to his right hand, which he was still using with caution, and held out his left to the gunner. 'This confounded arm has had me fumbling for two days now; I am delighted to see you, my friend.'

'The fiend take your pleasantries,' said Rigo, taking his hand none the less, if briefly. 'What are you doing with this damned pea-shooter, I should like to know?'

'Discovering its accuracy of aim, naturally, as I did with my mechanical crossbow last year. It is a superb piece of work, I find;

139

though since its maker was Bertolo Bracci, I am unsurprised. Watch.'

'Watch? I do not care if it was made by Vulcan and St Michael acting in concert,' said Rigo. 'It is an unproven gun, and only a fool—or a scholar—would fire it.'

'Not so,' said Leonardo. 'Bracci's proof-marks are inscribed alongside the pan. See for yourself.'

'And keep that pox-ridden match away,' persisted Rigo, unheeding. 'I have no wish to lose my head, even if you have.' He examined the breech, sweeping away traces of loose powder with his fingertip. 'Very well,' he admitted grudgingly. 'It is marked, which means very little. How many times have you discharged it?'

'Thrice. A beautiful weapon. Stand away, and observe.'

Before Rigo could offer further argument, he applied the match to the powder on top of the breech. Rigo backed away. The touchhole having little depth, there was a bare instant between the first fire-spurt and the clanging detonation which followed it, rocking the framework askew and surrounding the gun with a cloud of acrid smoke. When this cleared, both men could see that the barrel had burst open for a full hand-span along its length. The ball was still whining invisibly after chipping the top of the range-wall when Rigo, feelingly and with a string of oaths, spoke his mind.

'Most marvellous,' he concluded his diatribe. 'Marvellous indeed. Where are you hurt?'

'Nowhere, I thank you,' said Leonardo.

'A great pity. A wedge of bronze, properly lodged in your skull, might have served to let some of your science out and a little common sense in. So much for your proof-marks. Now show me your powder.'

'It is by your foot.'

Rigo kicked at the small keg, rolling it with his toe until the letters burned into its side were uppermost. 'Mining-powder,' he said succinctly.

'I know that.'

'Then why use it in a gun? Have I not already explained to you that powders differ? This kind explodes sharply, and is therefore used only for rending rock.'

'It was but a trial,' Leonardo pointed out to him. 'Though with unfortunate results, perhaps. I knew both from what you told me and from what I have read that powders differ in strength; accordingly, their effect on the shot must differ also; but I confess that until now I had not realized that some were strong enough to split a gun-barrel.'

'I can see that you need me here after all, or your learning is likely to cost you your life. Except, of course, that you now have no gun to play with.'

'Not so,' said Leonardo. 'I have the second of the pair yonder, in the belvedere. Be kind enough to bring it here.'

When Rigo came back, he was carrying the little cannon—it was no longer than his arm—in one hand. 'Let us put an end to this foolishness,' he said confidently. 'I conceive that you wish to study the principles of gunnery, a notion which has its merits. Now in Pontassieve there is an excellent cannon for your purpose, cast by Ghiberti, in length about four ells—'

'No,' said Leonardo.

'And why not? What can you learn from this plaything here? The Ghiberti is quite a tolerable weapon, and will throw you a ball for two thousand paces and better as prettily as you please. I have been thinking of hauling it over to supplement my own two guns in the spring—'

'No,' Leonardo said again. 'Save yourself the trouble. We shall not be using your guns in the spring, my friend.'

The Master-Gunner laid the toy he was holding down on top of the still-canted framework between them.

'I cannot have heard you correctly,' he said. 'Repeat that, if you will.'

'You heard me well enough. Listen. Your guns are inadequate to the task in hand. Let me list their deficiencies for you. Firstly, they are heavy.'

'They have need to be.'

'Doubtless. But because they are heavy, they lack military flexibility. You cannot move them.'

'They are not supposed to be moved. How would I bring them to their point of aim, were I to shift them every hour?'

'Precisely. Also, being heavy, they sink in mire, a fact of which you are sufficiently aware, I imagine. Secondly, they are large, and cannot be hidden.'

'And why in the devil's name should I wish to hide them?' Rigo demanded. 'Will my enemy fly away with them in the middle of the night? Your arguments are ridiculous.'

Leonardo tapped him on the breast. 'Open your mind,' he said. 'We are not done with the tale yet. Thirdly, then, they are costly; fourthly, inaccurate—'

'They are not.'

'Damnably inaccurate,' continued Leonardo calmly. 'Finally and in sum, they are ineffective; you have not yet knocked down Castelmonte's wall with them, nor will you in the spring. Come now, Rigo: loving them as I know full well you do, will you yet refuse to acknowledge the truth in all this?'

'There may be some particle of truth there,' Rigo said. 'But these disadvantages you mention are but the normal facts of an artilleryman's life.'

'Not all the facts,' said Leonardo. 'Not all of them.'

*

In the library some five days later, Leonardo sat beside Lorenzo de' Medici and listed his requirements. The ruler of Florence, nodding to his clerk at each item, heard him out with impatience.

'Six cannon,' Leonardo said. 'I have the specifications here.'

'Give them to Messer Arnolfo when we are done,' Lorenzo said. 'They are details.'

'Two hundred rounds of shot, cast and polished.'

'Very well.'

'Forty kegs of powder from the factory of Nencio Migliorini, the making of it to be supervised by myself.'

'Ser Nencio is not likely to take kindly to your supervision; but proceed.'

'Sundry other small items in metal of a mechanical nature, to be made here in the city at a probable cost of two hundred florins. Here is the list.'

'Give it to Messer Arnolfo. What else?'

'The hardest of all, sir. I need fifty men of Captain Leone's choosing, beginning not later than the first day of March and for two months thereafter.'

Lorenzo knitted his brow. 'Gunners?' he inquired.

'The best of our gunners.'

'When I must take Castelmonte as soon as the ground is firm enough to hold their siege-cannon?'

'I know the gravity of my request,' Leonardo said. 'But I must have them. There are one hundred and ten men in Pistrola at this moment, many of them skilled.'

'As craftsmen. Not gunners.'

'Some of those we shall leave there will be gunners, though we shall take the cream,' Leonardo said. 'I cannot accept any man for my purpose who is not in the front rank of his profession; but the less skilled will serve to move your siege-guns from Pistrola to their firing position when the time comes to do so.'

'Upon your head be it, then,' Lorenzo said. 'I will not hinder you. My task is to select men, not to obstruct them when selected, and I judge them—as I have told you—by the results they produce for me. You know the scale in which I intend to weigh your performance, Messer Leonardo. You may have your fifty men, though the giving of them bleeds my artillery force dry. If Florence is crippled because you have led them on a wild-goose chase, then God help you.'

CHAPTER TWELVE

From Leonardo da Vinci, artist, to the Most Eminent Cardinal Domenico della Palla, Apostolic Chancellor at Rome: Greetings.

My Lord,

Ever mindful of your kindness toward me at our last meeting, and of my undertaking to communicate to Your Eminence such result as I might achieve in my study of the composition and effects of Gunpowder; I here submit to the regard of Your Eminence those conclusions which I have thus far been able to reach:

i: the effect of powder varies notably as the proportions of its three components, viz: Sulphur, Charcoal and Saltpeter.

ii: that powder burns the most vehemently which consists of, 1 part of sublimed sulphur, 2 parts of willow charcoal, and 6 parts of redissolved saltpeter.

iii: those powders are the more suited for use in cannon which have their grains corned, which is to say, in particles of the bigness of one-quarter of a grain of barley; and this is achieved by the mixing of water with the powder and milling it.

iv: of the effects of powder upon shot there remains so great a field of ungathered knowledge as cannot be reaped in many months, nay, I had rather say years.

Therefore it is folly in the Holy Church Our Mother to place reliance upon the work of Fra Sfabalmaccio di Pisa in these matters.

Given by my hand the 28th Day of January, in Florence.

'Impudently heretical,' said Cardinal Rodrigo Borgia. 'My dear Chancellor, if this is all your case, then I am bound to say that I favour the leaving of this young man to the tender mercies of Girolamo Riario.'

'He is somewhat careless in both his speech and his writing,' conceded Cardinal della Palla. 'But I do not yet perceive heresy here. Has he not communicated these matters to us, thereby proving himself a good son of the Church?'

'I do not object to his information, but to his attitude and style of thought,' said Cardinal Borgia. 'Let me restate the case. I have here'—he lifted a piece of paper—'a letter from an informant of Riario's in Florence; we need not mention his name. This informant confirms that Leonardo da Vinci is military engineer to Lorenzo de' Medici, a fact of which we were already aware; but he goes on to claim that da Vinci is now indulging in activities which our informant says are highly dangerous to Rome's cause. I admit that these activities, whatever they may be, are not described, since the writer clearly does not understand them; but—if we accept his view—then Riario is certainly correct in pressing for the . . . elimination of da Vinci. Since I knew you to have an interest in the young man, I saw it as only courteous to consult you.'

'A kindly thought,' murmured della Palla.

'In his defence you have produced for me a letter from da Vinci himself, which you believe proves his possible future value to us. This I allow. Yet this same letter shows a disrespect for established authority which, if encouraged, will lead him one day to the stake; and your contention that he shows his good-will towards the Church in no wise diminishes his present threat to Rome. My conclusion is that we may as well allow Riario to have his way, thereby saving the Church the trouble and expense of burning him in a few years' time. You see?'

'He may yet be saved from heresy,' said Cardinal della Palla.

'By yourself?'

'Or by Almighty God.'

'Upon which chance you propose to visit Florence and persuade him to see the light of reason?'

'If you have no objection.'

'My dear Chancellor, I have not said that I object. All I have pointed out is that your letter from him makes no real case in his favour.'

'And I suppose that it would be foolish of me to suggest that Your Eminence has little moral right to dispose of a human life in such a cavalier fashion?'

'Purely for the sake of argument,' said Borgia with a faint smile, 'may I remind you that I intend to do nothing whatever about him. The question lies in whether or not one should restrain Girolamo Riario from taking matters into his own hands.'

'It was merely an idle thought,' said della Palla. 'The more idle since it seems that the Count has already attempted to murder him.'

'Ah. There, your ground is stronger.'

'I thought it might be.'

'Although two dead men found in a gutter on the night of Messer Leonardo's departure from Rome hardly constitutes proof of such an attempt.'

'I am not seeking proof,' said Cardinal della Palla blandly. 'I presume that your knowledge of the matter is adequate.'

Cardinal Borgia looked out of the window of his apartment at the wheeling pigeons.

'A most extraordinary occurrence,' he said. 'Here we have an artist, untrained—or so we may guess—in such affairs as swordsmanship; and he kills two highly skilled assailants and routs a third, single-handed? I do not, I think, believe it.'

'By which you mean that you do not believe it happened?'

'I know that it happened, though the man who remained alive has left Rome without telling his story. I am forced to conclude that Messer Leonardo was helped. And yet, so far as you know, he came to Rome alone?'

'Quite alone.'

'Therefore,' said Cardinal Borgia, 'we have Medici agents in our city, upon whom he called for aid.'

'Possibly. Probably, in fact.'

'I meant, of course, agents of whom I am unaware. I would not have left such an incident without investigation, and have thus accounted for known Medici supporters. Well. The idea irritates me, and therefore I would take it as a favour, my dear Chancellor, were you indeed to follow your own inclination and have a few words with Leonardo da Vinci. By whom was he assisted? And what, exactly, is he doing that makes Count Girolamo's correspondent so nervous? Your visit might prove well worth while.'

'Then I will do what I can,' Cardinal della Palla said.

'Excellent. I am delighted to find that, once again, we understand each other. Meanwhile, I shall endeavour to keep Girolamo leashed.'

*

Cardinal della Palla set out for Florence on a morning of warm rain, accompanied by a small entourage containing his Chaplain-confessor, his secretary, and eight men-at-arms. He arrived at his destination in mid February, and was received there with distant courtesy, a circumstance which troubled the Cardinal but little, since he hardly expected to be *persona grata* in the Republic. Indeed, his ostensible purpose being the fruitless one of attempting to persuade Florence to accept the installation of Archbishop Francesco Salviati in the See of Pisa—an errand which had been pursued with total lack of success by previous Papal emissaries—he was somewhat surprised to find the citizens of Florence confining themselves to hostile glances whenever he passed through its streets.

As ecclesiastical custom and duty demanded, one of the first persons that the Cardinal visited in his rooms was Fra Sigismondo Carregi. He found the latter, after a few minutes' encouragement, so inflamed and vituperative concerning Leonardo da Vinci's free-thinking habits and the manner in which—so Fra Sigismondo contended—he was engaged upon the spiritual corruption of Bianca Visconti, that the Cardinal invited him to unburden himself freely.

'It has, Your Eminence, become impossible to teach her,' Fra Sigismondo complained bitterly.

'This is regrettable indeed. And are you sure that it is the influence of Messer Leonardo upon her which is the true cause?'

'Beyond doubt, Your Eminence. She defies all authority, in the pretence that he has taught her to think for herself . . .'

'And does she?'

'I beg your pardon, my Lord?'

'I said, does she think for herself?' asked the Cardinal.

'How would that be possible? She is a child.'

'I see. How old is she?'

'She is fourteen years of age, Your Eminence.'

'And has Messer Leonardo, then, a powerful intellect?'

'By no means,' said Fra Sigismondo. 'His philosophy is negligible, as Your Eminence may confirm by speaking with Dr Cino di Lapo Mazzone, my colleague. He postures and plays, seeking thereby to impress those around him. Mentally he is a butterfly.'

'Most regrettable,' said Cardinal della Palla. 'Fra Sigismondo, I wonder if you would oblige me by writing down the substance of your complaints against Leonardo da Vinci, so that I may better consider them upon my return to Rome?'

'With the greatest pleasure, Your Eminence.'

The Cardinal blessed him, and left Fra Sigismondo a gratified man.

*

It was the afternoon of Sunday, February 22nd, when he finally sought out Leonardo da Vinci, finding him in a spaciously untidy attic beneath the roof-beams of the eastern wing of the *palazzo*. The room was bare, well-lit, and dusty, being littered with small lengths of timber, stained chairs, many-hued rags, and pottery jars filled with oils and turpentine. On an easel rested a half-finished painting of a Madonna holding a striped cat; Leonardo himself stood framed in a window against a pewter sky, brush in hand.

'My Lord Cardinal,' he said as della Palla entered, alone. 'This is a visitation which does my heart good! I have seen you from time to time as I laboured, but I hardly dared to hope that you would find time to speak with me.'

'It was to speak with you that I journeyed hither from Rome,' said the Cardinal. 'May I sit down?'

'By all means, if I can find you something that will not soil your robes.'

'My robes are nothing. This will serve.' So saying, Cardinal della Palla seated himself on the nearest chair, nodding towards the easel. 'An interesting picture,' he said.

'It is but a quarter done. Less. And uncommissioned,' Leonardo said. 'Today being Sunday, it would be inappropriate of me to continue my studies of warlike instruments, and I am thus able to please myself.'

'A very proper spirit. Will you not also be seated, my son? There are things I must discuss with you.'

'Of course.' Leonardo sat down on a packing-case, and crossed his legs. 'What is it that you wish to speak of, my lord?'

'I came here,' said the Cardinal surprisingly, 'to ask you if there were anything you needed to confess.'

Leonardo smiled. 'My lord,' he said, 'I am a poor churchgoer, and it is a long while since I felt the need for confession.'

'Indeed?'

'Moreover, my sins are of a peculiar nature, and not to be found in any calendar. Being a sinner, as all men are, I therefore take my sins to God, since He will not misunderstand them.'

'The sin of pride is easily understood and in all calendars,' said Cardinal della Palla with some asperity. 'Do not speak so glibly.'

'My lord, I am frequently guilty of pride, I admit,' Leonardo said. 'But to look at the stars is to cure all pride; and when I most lack humility God seizes me by the neck and directs my gaze heavenward, thereby both correcting and absolving me.'

'I see. You are stubborn, my son. What, then, of murder?'

'Murder?'

'Did you not kill two men, as you left Rome?'

'They would have killed me first, Your Eminence. I have asked God's forgiveness for it, but it was no murder.'

'Then you did kill them?'

'I did.'

'And you were wounded by them?'

'It is better now.'

'I was not expressing sympathy. Were you wounded before killing both of them?'

'Yes. I am afraid that they had not been told that I fight equally well with either hand.'

'So much for murder, then,' said della Palla. He swivelled on the seat of his chair, robes in hand. 'This painting,' he went on.

'Yes?'

'A Madonna?'

'Yes, my lord.'

'But with no Holy Infant.'

'I intend later to paint the Infant in place of the cat. False starts are a part of . . . I do not know how to put this, my lord. It is hard to explain. The cat arrived there by accident.'

A curious half-smile lit the Cardinal's face for an instant, though when he spoke his voice was as severe as before.

'It will not, in any case, serve for a Madonna,' he said. 'I advise you to leave the cat where it is, since—if my perception is not at fault—we have here another of your uncalendred sins.'

'And what sin is that?'

'Carnality. No man, seeing this painting, is likely to be led by it into a state of grace. Far otherwise, I would say. The appearance of your model, if I may be blunt, is sexually suggestive to the point of concupiscence. Who is she, by the way?'

'No model sat for me, Your Eminence.'

'You are fencing with me again. The face is that of the lady Bianca Visconti. Well?'

'It may be.'

'It is. Must I wring confession from you as one wrings a cloth? Are your feelings towards this child carnal, my son?'

'If they are,' said Leonardo carefully, 'is that a sin? I doubt it. Were I to indulge in the passions of the flesh with her, the case might be different; but my thoughts are between myself and God, since they harm no one.'

The Cardinal swung towards him once more.

'It seems,' he said, 'that there is a great deal which lies between yourself and God, Messer Leonardo.'

'That, too, is possible.'

'To the exclusion of the Church. God's bride and mediator, if I may remind you of the fact.'

'The fact? This is not a fact, as I understand facts,' said Leonardo.

'Your contempt for the Church knows no bounds.'

Leonardo rose, and took a step towards the Cardinal in momentary passion.

'You are wrong, my lord,' he said hotly. 'Quite wrong, and I marvel that you have not seen it yet. My chief concern is for the Church, however foolish, ambitious, and venal she may appear to me. Why should I labour to correct her, if not from love? If the Church is indeed prepared to accept her own *imprimatur* as the sole guarantee of truth, why should I care, unless from love?'

'We are back to Fra Sfabalmaccio again, I see,' the Cardinal said.

'And shall return again. I have a vision, my lord, which troubles me from time to time. It is a vision of the future; of a day which neither you nor I will see, but which will come none the less. In it I see a Pope in Rome, claiming before all his children that if God had meant men to fly, he would have given us wings; and therefore that flight is impossible to us; and all the while he stands and claims this to be so, I see an impudent and heretical man with wings in the sky above his head, proving him to be speaking nonsense. On that day, my Lord Cardinal, the world will see the Church for the foolish creature I now perceive her to be; and I will not let it happen, if I have to shake her as a terrier shakes a rat and force her to recognize truth when it lies before her.'

'Sit down,' the Cardinal said gently. 'My son, you have—or so I believe—some regard for me.'

'I have.'

'Then attend to me in the light of that regard. What happens to those who presume to drag the Church towards a truth of their own?'

'They are burned,' said Leonardo promptly. '*Ecclesia non novit sanguinem*; the Church sheds no blood, being hypocritical, and therefore burns those who displease her. If you came here but to threaten me with fire—'

'I did not. I came to ask you to come with me to Rome,' said Cardinal della Palla. 'Your talents will be appreciated there; you may win fame and position; and more than all this, your passion for what you call facts can be guided, thus keeping your body from the flames and your soul from perdition.'

Leonardo laughed. 'What is the difference between being burned by the Church and being burned on the battlefield?' he asked. 'It is the same death, to which we all come but once.'

'It is a death which can be better avoided in Rome.'

'If you mean, my lord, that Rome will be at war with Florence in the spring, and that Rome is the safer choice of sides,' said Leonardo, still laughing, 'then I thank Your Eminence, but must disagree. Florence, to mention but one thing, has myself.'

'You rate yourself highly.'

'As do all thinking men.'

'I warn you again. You are walking a knife-edge.'

'Then so be it,' replied Leonardo. 'All paths are dangerous in this world. If I displease Lorenzo de' Medici, he may have me killed tomorrow. Rome may have me killed next year. A score of days ago I was almost dispatched by a bursting cannon; therefore I put my trust in God.'

The Cardinal got up, sighing. 'So be it, then,' he echoed. 'We are not yet friends, but neither are we enemies. I wish you well.' Almost abruptly, he turned and left. As he passed out of the room and into the long corridor that ended at the narrow attic stairway, he was suddenly conscious of age, and did not know why.

Half way to the stair-head he stopped. He remembered, with an odd surprise, that he had been asked for no blessing, nor had he given one. His impulse was to keep walking. A man of the artist's nature and beliefs would not seek something which he must, in logic, regard either as a courtesy or else as a meaningless gesture; and yet della Palla knew that his duty was to bless, as always, to stand as a tree stands in the middle of a plain so that the lightning of God's grace might strike through him if it would, whether sought-after or not and whether the speaker invested the words with meaning or with none.

He also owed the man in the room behind him a lesser duty. He had failed to warn Leonardo directly of the immediate danger by which he was surrounded, of sudden death at the hands of Count Girolamo Riario or of whatever human tool the latter might choose. That Leonardo had already escaped murder once did not alter the case; Rome might conveniently wish him dead, but it did not follow that Cardinal della Palla must acquiesce in that wish.

He turned and went quietly back to the attic. What he saw there stopped him on the threshold, amazed.

At the far end of the room Leonardo da Vinci, humming softly to himself, had returned to work upon his too-worldly Madonna. With his right hand he was oil-colouring what appeared to be a section of blue sky, seen through a corbelled arch; which would have been unremarkable save for the fact that with his left hand he was, at one and the same time, swiftly over-blocking the outlines of the cat and transforming it into the figure of the Infant.

His eyes travelled easily between charcoal-stick and brush, his head tilting slightly from moment to moment as he changed his viewpoint. The palette from which he selected his sky-colours was clipped to the upper corner of the easel, and he would occasionally stop his drawing for an instant while he gave attention to the choice of a hue from it; but for the most part both hands moved simultaneously, yet upon different tasks and in different directions, each stroke commencing near the picture's centre and finishing towards its edge, to right or to left.

He stopped humming, and turned.

'My lord,' he said to the advancing Cardinal. 'I did not hear you return.'

His mind in a whirl, the Cardinal questioned him.

'Do you always work thus?' he asked.

'Only in private, of late,' replied Leonardo. 'I have done so since childhood whenever I wished; but my master Verrocchio having described it as a mountebank's trick, and finding that it made my fellow apprentices uneasy, I desisted from it.'

'But does it come naturally to you? To work thus, with both hands together?'

'Yes. God gave me the ability when I was born, I suppose, though I do not know why.' He put down his brush and took up his notebook, laying it upon the seat of a chair and squatting in front of it. Baring its topmost sheet, he wrote on it with his left hand, the letters of the script running from right to left and as though seen in a mirror. Changing hands quickly, he wrote a second line beneath the first, right-handed; the script this time was normal. Then, picking up a second charcoal stick in his left hand, he wrote two lines simultaneously, each one running in the opposite sense to the other.

'But this is astounding,' Cardinal della Palla said. 'A miracle.' He picked up the notebook and examined it closely. 'And is there no difference, in ease or difficulty, between one hand and the other?'

'There is,' Leonardo replied, 'and it is another matter which I find hard to explain. I work best with my right hand when I do so carefully and with deliberation, upon tasks whose nature I have decided before I commence them. When I am caught unawares by an idea—be it a swift glimpse of a picture or a half-formed principle in science—it is with the left hand that I set it down. Indeed, I do better with it when I am not attending to it too closely, and allow it to move as it wills; hence, when I use both hands together, as you might have seen me doing upon this painting just now, it is upon the right that I concentrate my mind.' He held his fingers out. 'One might say that they are two different persons, these hands of mine,' he said reflectively; and then, breaking off: 'May I ask why you returned, my lord?'

Cardinal della Palla set down the notebook again.

'For a reason which I now think of smaller importance than I did some moments ago,' he said. 'I came back to warn you that the Count of Imola wishes you dead.'

'Girolamo Riario,' said Leonardo, still thoughtfully. 'An unhappy man, and evil; he lives, I conjecture, in a coffin of his own

153

making. The notion if his ill-will costs me little sleep, Your Eminence, though I thank you for your warning.'

'Even so,' said the Cardinal. 'Sleep in peace. For I see that God has blessed you with peculiar gifts and for some purpose of His own, and will therefore protect you.' He raised his hand. 'Walk, then, with God, my son.'

CHAPTER THIRTEEN

... It is evident that the chief among qualities in cannon is accuracy. For a small shot, in flying rapidly, has the like effect to a larger shot travelling more slowly; so that the effect of the shot is as the weight of it multiplied by its speed in flight. Thus a small cannon, in placing its shot according to prediction, may have the like effect to a heavy siege weapon, if its accuracy be but improved.

... and the accuracy of a cannon resides in the following: one, the fineness of the bore: two, the speed with which the shot is projected from the muzzle; and three (as I discover) by the imparting of rotation to the ball by means of grooves in the interior of the bore. And the shot itself must be polished to hold its course by reason of its smoothness.

From the Notebooks of Leonardo da Vinci

Rigo Leone, who was patching the rectangular wooden target in the meadow with thin timber and bone-glue, discovered once again that his feet were freezing inside his boots, and swore. Leonardo, warming his hands at the brazier upon which the glue-boiler rested, looked up in time to intercept a glare which would have dropped a more sensitive man in his tracks, and grinned.

'Suffer in silence,' he advised. 'I gave the same counsel to Matteo Barletta when he was, like yourself, undergoing privations in the cause of science.'

'I wish him here now,' Rigo said. 'This playing of games was well enough inside the palace walls, where it was at least sheltered. Out here it is a different matter, and your bowman may have my job for the asking.'

'He would not take it. He has but a low opinion of gunnery, and of gunners. Heart up, my friend. Six more shots, and we can retire for the evening.'

'Making a total of some two hundred and fifty thus far,' Rigo said. 'And for what? I still do not understand what you are trying to achieve.' He removed his palm from the last wooden patch and brought the glue-pot across to the fire. 'I am beginning to think that my mind is ill-suited to this science of yours, which is but mystery under another name.'

'Remove the thought from your head. There is nothing mysterious in it. Science is the study of what is possible; and what is possible may be seen by all men who have not lost the mother-wit they possessed as children. Let me see if I can advance you any further, then. What do you think of our toy cannon here?'

'It is a very adequate little gun. Where does that get us?'

'It throws a little to the left, I fancy,' said Leonardo.

'I agree. All guns have their peculiarities.'

'And throws, perhaps, a trifle more to the left with one powder than with another?'

'As I told you it would. We are agreed by now, I trust, that powders differ.'

Leonardo pointed at the target, now patchworked with small plugs where the scattered shot-holes in it had been repaired.

'And yet,' he continued, 'when one has settled on a particular powder and weight of ball, there is very little spread between the impact of one shot and the next.'

'I have already admitted that it is a well-made weapon,' Rigo said. 'I appreciate a true gun as well as any man, if not better. Allowing for its shorter range, it may even be the equal of my own two beauties in Pistrola—which is high praise indeed.'

'Good. Now tell me, once again, how you would proceed with your siege-cannon in the spring, were you to use them.'

Rigo sighed. 'Nothing I have seen here persuades me that I shall *not* be using them,' he said. 'Very well. I shall haul my guns over to that damned ridge, though I shall choose a different position this time. I am not going to pound at a newly strengthened piece of wall, being no fool. I shall ask Agnolo how far we stand from whatever portion of the wall I select as target—'

'He is a good judge of distance?'

'The best. Better even than myself.'

'Go on.'

'Why, then the matter is straightforward. I shall aim my guns roughly and fire some ten or twenty shots from each, adjusting them as I perceive them to strike, until both are delivering their shots in the same place. After that I shall repeat last autumn's performance, though—God willing—with more success.'

Leonardo stirred the glue idly with a piece of stick.

'But suppose,' he said, 'that you could predict, in advance of firing any shot at all, where your guns would strike? What then?'

'I would see no value in it,' Rigo said, scratching his chin. 'It would be interesting, I dare say, and of course I can already do so by guess; one does not want to spend hours in heaving one's cannon to and fro to bring them to the correct point of aim. I do not see where this leads us, however. How many shots did I fire last year? Two thousand, and more. Five, ten, or twenty shots spent in bringing my guns to bear are a small price to pay, with so much time at hand.'

'And how if time were not available?'

'It always is. Time is what siege-gunnery is all about. Time, and patience.' Rigo glanced over Leonardo's shoulder, and nodded. 'Yonder stands your light-o'-love, at the other side of the stream,' he said.

Leonardo turned. Seeing Bianca Visconti, he raised a hand in salute. 'And watch your tongue, gunner,' he admonished without rancour.

'Surely,' said Rigo. 'No doubt I am mistaken, and she comes here not for love of your company but merely to freeze while watching us fire shots at a board. It is possible, I suppose. Well, call her over.'

'Not I,' said Leonardo. 'If she wishes to come hither, she will; and otherwise, she will not. I am not her master.'

'She may stay away for all of me. Gunnery is no business for women, and she puts me in a terror lest I utter some mild and well-deserved curse in her presence,' said Rigo.

It appeared, however, that the Lady Bianca had on this occasion no intention of crossing the brook. Instead, she beckoned imperiously, walking along the far bank towards the footbridge. After some indecision, and with a frown at the look of amusement on Rigo's face, Leonardo went to meet her.

'And what brings you here, my lady?' he asked.

Bianca advanced one foot onto the planks of the bridge and leaned against the rail. 'Nay, do not trouble to put on that stern look for me,' she said, offering him a small bundle wrapped and tied in a silken kerchief. 'I have brought you something to eat, that is all, and have no wish to distract you.'

'Then I thank you, and apologize for my lack of grace,' Leonardo said. He took the kerchief from her. 'Will you not come and share it with us?'

'No. Captain Leone will only glare at me, as he always does. With the bribe of a pastry—you have two there—I hope to soften his heart somewhat, so that next time I come he may abate some of his ferocity. In any case, it is nearly sundown, and very cold.'

Smiling, she laid a hand briefly on his arm, turned, and was gone. Leonardo carried the kerchief back to the brazier, unwrapping it as he walked.

'Observe,' he said, 'that there are rewards in teaching the young, particularly young ladies.'

'Is that what you are doing? Teaching?' asked Rigo. Then, as Leonardo made to withdraw his hand and its proffered burden, he added hastily, 'Not that I would ever dream of doubting you; and, as for my lady, may heaven forgive me if I have ever harboured an unkind thought towards her. A shrewd girl.'

'And kind of heart,' said Leonardo.

*

Bianca returned slowly along the path that led from the foot-bridge to the side-gate of the palace, her fur-collared cape drawn closely about her neck. Following vespers, she was to have a lesson in logic from Dr Mazzone; it was one of her more unpleasant weekly trials, and she was happily conscious that by dawdling she might succeed in missing both service and lesson.

Dusk was therefore closing in by the time she reached the shallow and broken steps that climbed from the water-meadows to the gateway, winding between skeletal winter hedges and among stands of evergreen. At each turn in its familiar ascent the rough stairway broadened into a circular bay, enclosing the base of a statue and surrounded by balustrades. As a friendless child, delivered into Medici care by her cousin-guardian Lodovico Sforza, she had learned her Latin not from the school-books of her new tutors but from the inscriptions beneath these stone figures; nondescript though most of them were, she had named them all, and now greeted them silently like old acquaintances.

158

She was therefore rudely surprised when, from behind an image of the Emperor Diocletian, the Prince of Savoy stepped into her path and detained her.

'An unseemly hour for strolling in damp fields, Bianca,' he said. 'I disapprove of this passion of yours for spying upon Messer Leonardo da Vinci and his gunner colleague; you indulge it too frequently.'

The note of peevish malice in his voice took her aback for a moment, and she answered without thought.

'I am spying on nobody,' she said.

'No? Perhaps not. In which case you are too familiar with them, and I disapprove of that still more.'

'Then it is a mercy that I care little for your approval,' said Bianca. 'Let me pass, if you please.'

'Nor would Lorenzo approve of it, if he knew,' suggested Silvio.

'You are more privy to Lorenzo's mind than one would have thought,' said Bianca. 'Let me pass, sir. It is no business of yours how I choose to spend my evenings.'

'There you are wrong,' Silvio replied. 'It is very much my business, since your continued attentions to this sweaty artisan are observed by all, and thereby make me a laughing-stock. We are not yet betrothed, my lady, but we shall be; such is Lodovico Sforza's intention, and all at Court know it.' He gripped both her arms now, pinching her flesh in deliberate spite. 'For five days out of six, and over more weeks than I care to consider, you have trotted at the heels of Leonardo da Vinci. Fra Sigismondo, who is supposed to be your instructor in matters of decency, may countenance it if he wishes to. I will not. Do you understand me?'

'You speak, sir, as though you owned me,' said Bianca coolly, 'which you do not.'

'Evidently. It is, or so it appears, this artist who does so.'

'He does nothing of the kind. Nor would he think of it, being possessed of a mind quite unlike yours. He is my teacher.' She made no move to free herself from his grasp.

'Aye,' agreed Silvio Grimiani. 'And the whole palace wonders what exactly he teaches you; which is entertaining for them, but mocks me. Well, madam, I can suggest better teachers for you, if that is your bent. Myself, for example. In but a short year or two from now, Bianca, you shall wear the saddle of Savoy; and I am a

rider with many tricks to teach you. Study, then, to please me. If
you do well, you will not find me unkind.'

'Now,' said Bianca, still without moving, 'this is sweet courtship indeed! First I am a spy, and then something between a
stable-mare and a common whore. What charm! No doubt this is
how love and marriage are viewed in the pigsties of Savoy, which
alone is reason enough for me to stay away from them. Release
me.'

'I find you beautiful, my lady, but lacking in respect. I am not
done with you yet.'

'Prince,' said Bianca sweetly, 'I have had other teachers besides
Leonardo. My Sforza cousins were rough company as boys,
though they have grown out of it, as you have not. I learned early
from fighting with them that the shortest way to discourage any
man is to kick him between the legs. Therefore release me, or you
will walk like an old man for the space of an hour or so.'

Silvio let her go as though stung.

'What fashion of talk is this?' he demanded.

'Courtship, after the Savoy manner,' said Bianca promptly.
'Thus it is conducted; you may speak of riding me like a stallion,
and I may kick you where I please. Farewell, Prince.'

She left him open-mouthed, and walked away—a little faster,
perhaps, than she had intended, despite her assumed nonchalance
—until she reached the gateway at the head of the path. Once
safely inside the walls of the *palazzo*, she closed the wicket and
leaned against it, her mind busy. The crudities of Silvio Grimiani
as proposed lover or future husband were not, surprisingly, her
chief concern. Another and sinister suspicion about the Prince of
Savoy had arisen to trouble her, for men who speak in haste or in
passion reveal—so she saw—more than they intend.

*

She told Leonardo of her conjectures two days later. It was shortly
after dawn, and he was engaged in inspecting the powder-barrels
which were still stored in the belvedere, as a protection against
both weather and prowlers. Finding him thus occupied, she sat by
him on one of the kegs, and spoke without preamble.

'I think the Prince of Savoy is spying on you,' she announced.

Leonardo paused in his work, spitting a few grains of powder from between his teeth. He was learning to test the qualities of different batches through feel and taste, though he was aware that he had some way to go before he would be Rigo's equal at the task.

'Why do you suppose that?' he asked.

'He was lying in wait for me the other night, near the top of the side-path. Among all those statues, you know?'

Leonardo nodded.

'He seized me as I passed, and tried to detain me. He was angry,' Bianca went on.

'What was the cause of his rage?'

'Nothing. Some nonsense which doesn't matter,' said Bianca hurriedly. 'Among other things he accused me of spying on you. I hardly paid attention when he said it, but a little later I began to wonder why he'd used the word, when I had obviously been doing nothing of the sort. Do you see? And then he had been watching me for a long time—at least that is what he said—because he knew how often I had come down to the meadow . . .'

'I assume, then, that it was your liking for our lowly company which annoyed him?' Leonardo said.

'Well, yes.'

'Speaking for myself, I find it well worth braving the displeasure of the Prince of Savoy,' Leonardo said gravely. 'He had some few words to say to me on the subject, around Christmas, but we cannot all run our lives to suit Silvio's wishes. Go on.'

'Perhaps I am being silly over this,' Bianca said, 'but I thought it a little odd that he should have been skulking in the bushes—or wherever he was—evening after evening, just to see how many times I was coming to make myself a nuisance to yourself and Captain Leone. Perhaps his jealousy kept him warm. He is that kind of person. But I thought it more likely that it was you he had been watching, to see what you were doing with that little cannon. Don't you think so?'

'It is possible. In which case, who would he be spying for?'

'I worked that out too. He has always been as thick as thieves with the Pazzi family, because he wants them to offer him a partnership in their bank. And the Pazzis have worked for Rome ever since Lorenzo lost a good deal of business to them a few years ago. So I think—'

'One moment,' interrupted Leonardo. 'How is it, little

Madonna, that you know so much about the affairs of the Medici?'

'Oh, that is easy. Lorenzo has always favoured me, ever since I came to Florence. He was furious for weeks, I remember. Naturally he didn't say why, but I could tell; and I found out all about it by asking Donna Francesca, who thought I wouldn't understand what she was explaining to me.'

'Formidable,' said Leonardo. 'It seems to me that you must have been a scant eleven years old at the time. Florence's commercial secrets will be at risk for many a year with your sharp ears listening to them.'

He spoke lightly, but was considering the facts as he did so. A great deal of what she suggested was possible, and more than possible; his experience in Rome supported it. He had argued to Lorenzo de' Medici that his fight with Francesco Pazzi was of a personal nature, a supposition which neither Lorenzo nor himself believed; but it was Lorenzo's concern rather than his own if another view were to be taken of the affair, and both of them had let it pass. There was now no doubt in his mind that Cardinal della Palla was correct and that Girolamo Riario had been ultimately responsible for the attempt on his life, but it was difficult to regard the Prince of Savoy in any serious way as an agent of the Count. And yet, if Bianca's sense were not at fault, it might be so. Money greased many hinges, and a share in the Pazzi banking concerns . . . He became aware that Bianca was addressing him again.

'And do not patronize me,' she said imperiously. Her face, upturned towards him, seemed angry. 'I am no child, though I am sure that to you I must seem one.'

'True. Though I spoke thoughtlessly, and meant you no offence.'

'If that is how you find me, there are others who do not,' said Bianca. 'Silvio Grimiani, for one,' she added as a wry afterthought.

'And which approach do you prefer?'

'Oh, you think that you are now going to reason with me, very coldly and logically, and crush me because you are better at debate than I am; and so you may, but it will prove nothing,' Bianca cried. 'Do you tell me you have no feeling towards me? None, I suppose. And much I care.'

'I have said nothing of my feelings,' Leonardo pointed out.

'No. And I expect you will wear a long white beard before you arrive at doing so.'

Despite himself, Leonardo burst out laughing. 'And you will be a matron, past middle age, I suppose?' he said. 'Come now, Bianca.'

'Do not say it!'

'You are—'

'If you tell me how old I am,' said Bianca, far more calmly, 'I promise you I shall scream. And there is another thing. Since you know me for a good listener, shall I tell you what rumour says of you? That you prefer boys to women. What have you to answer to that?'

'I have heard the rumour myself,' he replied judicially.

'Oh! And is that all?'

'Except to point out what you already know. What are sexual pastimes at the Medici court—or any other, I dare say—but an excuse for strutting display and the cackling of idiots? Love is a toy for idle and rich people who are also, as it happens, notoriously stupid and lack all occupation which might otherwise bring meaning to their lives. You know this to be true. Fetch me a pretty woman or a pretty boy, both equally stupid, and I will send both away. Do you suppose nobody scratches at my door of nights? Since I am known to have no mistress, naturally they say I am a taker of catamites. It is said, in particular, by those ladies who might otherwise fancy themselves in my bed.'

'Your conceit,' Bianca said, 'is astounding.'

'Whether I am conceited or not has nothing whatever to do with the case. Do you deny anything that I have said?'

'No. But you are beginning to debate again. You were doing much better a few moments ago.'

Leonardo sat down on the steps of the belvedere by her feet.

'My lady,' he said, 'this is neither debate nor quarrel. If love is to be a mere plaything for the wealthy and vicious, then it is worth neither my time nor yours. I will play no such games with you. You claim that I treat you like a child; perhaps I do so because it is, for the present, better that I should. Do you understand me?'

Bianca surveyed him, her chin in her fists.

'Perhaps I do,' she said. 'Give me your hand.'

He reached up to her from where he was sitting, and they remained companionably silent for a time.

'Tell me, then,' said Bianca.

'What?'

'When they scratch at your door, do you never open it?'

'Never,' said Leonardo.

'Your nights must be somewhat dull.' Her eyes were shining with amusement, if nothing more. 'How do you spend them?'

'In reading books, or star-gazing. What else is there to do?'

'Giuliano returns from Milan today,' said Bianca, 'and therefore I imagine that Constanza might return me a different answer. However, I am content.'

*

Constanza slipped along the quiet and moonlit gallery like a shadow. At the door to Giuliano's chambers she halted, stealing one last look to right and left. The *palazzo* slept. Lifting the latch and opening the door just wide enough to admit her, she entered.

'Giuliano?' she whispered. 'Giuliano? Where are you?'

Silence. 'Giuliano?' she called softly, once again, and crossed the marble floor of the dressing-room to stand in the arched doorway to the bedchamber beyond it. There, illuminated by the gentle glow of candles, stood the great canopied bed, and she contemplated its crimson expanse, her hand on the rough stone of the pillar at her side. Room enough and more for the two of us, she thought, no matter how we may sprawl. She smiled to herself at that, and her heart quieted. She felt, suddenly, the warmth of a thousand mornings to come when she and Giuliano would awaken to the new day, bodies fitted in the sleep of a good marriage, replenished by a thousand nights of love given and received.

She sat on the edge of the bed, palms caressing the velvet texture of the spread. This will cover us on cold nights and we shall talk of the Court and of our children, she told herself, and we will plan visits to my aunt in Modena and my friends in Ravenna and speak of the new dresses that I shall wear and a thousand things besides.

The fat candles gleamed steadily, and were reflected in an oval mirror that hung upon the wall opposite her. I shall dress by that mirror, there, she thought. Giuliano will watch me, and I, knowing it, will watch him. She rose and went to the glass, studying her face with a small and critical smile of greeting.

This will be your first time, she said to her reflection silently. The first. Let me remember every moment of it for ever. It will hurt, they say. But the pain passes and the pleasure comes soon; and will I also remember how I shiver now? I feel so full. Her thighs tightened, informing her of what she barely understood as yet, and she felt a kind of heat, as though from some internal and secret midsummer, flood her. She lifted her hands to cup her breasts, and her face, returning her gaze from the dark mirror, seemed to swim out of focus for an instant.

Then the door of the outer room clicked softly and she turned. Giuliano came through the arch into the bedroom; the draught of his entry stirred the candle-flames and sent shadows dancing across the tapestries. Within his embrace she murmured, 'Where have you been, my lord? Almost I had begun to wonder if you had suffered a change of heart.'

'Nay, my Constanza. I have but been to my strong-box, which is in the library. I went there for this.' He opened the fingers of his cupped right hand to show her a ring; a heavy gold band crowned by a perfect oval ruby with an encircling fence of diamonds. 'Our wedding ceremony will come in God's time, my heart,' he said. 'But we are wed this night, and this shall be your marriage-ring, though none know it but ourselves. I brought it with me from Milan.'

'Where you have tarried too long for my comfort, Giuliano.'

'And too long for mine. I suspect that Lorenzo sent me there in order to cool my passion. He reckoned poorly, if so. Not an hour has passed without my thinking of you, and of this moment.'

'As I have thought of you, my lord. Though I have no ring to give you, which shames me.'

'No matter. You have captured a far-sighted husband. I chose one for myself as well. Look.' In his other hand he held a pair of miniature golden serpents, twined together in perfect symmetry and with eyes of ruby to match the stone he had given her. 'The emblems of wisdom,' he said. 'Wisdom of the heart, not of the mind.'

Constanza laughed happily and slipped the ring onto his finger. Impulsively she bent to his hand, and felt his answering lips on her hair.

'Let us to bed, Giuliano,' she said, 'since that is what we are here for. I am immodest, I know; and yet I care not.'

Wordlessly, he guided her to the bed. She watched his face while, confidently, he undressed her until she stood naked, and as softly white as shadowed ivory. When he left her side to quench the candles, she reached out and touched his arm.

'Leave them alight,' she bade him. 'Have I not said that I am immodest? I want to see you. I must learn, and shall learn less in darkness.' She began to unlace the points of his doublet, her hands as confident as his own had been. He looked at her, and felt passion rising within him. The artless grace of her body as she moved fired him, and he wove his fingers into the tumbled and midnight strands of her unbound hair. 'Yes,' she breathed. 'This is what I need to remember, every time I see you so. How much a man you are, and how I feel when I see that you want me.' She stood close to him, tracing her fingers slowly down his chest. 'I have never touched a man before, as you know. You must teach me, since I am a virgin and hence unskilled. I pray that I may please you, Giuliano.'

He took her face in his hands and kissed her. 'There is little need for me to teach you anything, Constanza, my bride,' he said. 'All that a loving woman should know, you know already; it is, as love is, within you for the finding. And as you pray to please me, so I pray to please you, though I may cause you pain in doing so. Be prepared for this, in the knowledge that I mean you no hurt.'

'I am prepared for it, and welcome it. Teach me.'

For a long while she let herself drift, surging now and again with the touch of his hand and his mouth; and when it occurred to her, as he had foretold, to please him in all the ways he had shown her she felt him respond so that when the pain came at last her body arched to meet it, and him, in a softly exhaled cry that turned the sharpness at once into the promised joy. For a while they lay still and still connected, breathing in unison, the rhythm of loving echoed in the slow rise and fall of their breasts. She spoke into his ear.

'How long will it be before we can do this again, Giuliano?' she asked. 'Will it be soon, or must our bodies rest now?'

Startled, he raised his head. 'There is something, after all, that I can teach you,' he said. 'You did not know? That we can do this again, tonight? Now, if you are not tired.'

166

She leaned up and bit him softly on the lips. 'No, I did not know,' she replied. 'You see? I am no virgin now, it is true, but it seems that I am still no wife either. Will you then teach me more, my husband?'

CHAPTER FOURTEEN

... received of Maestro Gian Giacomo Portinari of Arezzo 6 cannon, these being for the new artillery and very fine, in weight 280 pounds each one and bound with iron straps. Remember to speak with Maestro Gian Giacomo concerning his means of slowly cooling metals after casting them ... and from Ser Nencio 300 lbs of powder, milled and corned according to our speech together ... the spikes to hold the wheels to the carriages must be in bronze or in marine alloy, since iron will rust and is sometimes friable under pressure ...

Show that the effect of the shot in going forwards must be equal to the effect of the cannon in recoiling, and that the backward travel of the cannon must be unhindered, which is contrary to the practice of our gunners. Is it possible to propel a cart by ejecting fire or stones from behind?

... I shall have to cut the screws for myself. Scarpellino is a good workman but cannot understand them ... and those parts of the carriage in which they work must likewise be made of bronze ...

From the notebooks of Leonardo da Vinci

'*Quid vobis videtur?*' Pope Sixtus IV asked. 'I borrow here the language of the Consistory, since the question is one of some importance. Something must be determined, and quickly.'

'I see no reason for haste, Your Holiness,' said Cardinal della Palla. 'A man's life is at stake.'

'We are aware of the views of Your Eminence,' said the Pontiff. 'However, they are but one factor among many. We must beg you to confine yourself to military reality, since your colleagues will undoubtedly do so.'

'I have learned to be a realist,' replied della Palla. 'Your Holiness need have no fears on that score. I had rather be here to argue the case than elsewhere. My question remains; why must a decision be taken now? I seek only for information.'

'For reasons of war,' said Girolamo Riario, at his left.

Della Palla turned his mild blue eyes towards the Captain-General's face, dwelling briefly upon what he seemed to see there.

'Nothing else?' he inquired.

'We shall, as His Holiness points out, be discussing only matters of war here,' Cardinal Rodrigo Borgia said. Della Palla looked at him in turn.

'Very well,' he said. 'Would it be improper to ask what your position is?'

'I take no position,' said Borgia comfortably. 'You should surely be aware of that by now, my dear Chancellor.'

Sixtus recalled them to order.

'What, then, of Leonardo da Vinci?' he asked, apparently of the room at large. 'He has refused the Most Eminent Cardinal della Palla's invitation to bring his talents and lay them at Rome's feet. This argues to us that he is indeed working directly for the Medici, as claimed by the Count of Imola and confirmed by His Eminence Cardinal Borgia. More than this: he represents Florentine thought at its worst and most reprehensible: neoplatonist, heretical and humanistic. Do I hear any dissent from this?'

'None,' said della Palla. 'Except that I had thought, with respect, that we were confining ourselves to things military, in which case his style of thought is irrelevant.'

'Not if it shows antagonism towards Rome,' said the Pontiff. 'Riario?'

'He will prove a thorn in our side at Castelmonte,' said Riario shortly. 'Kill him, and have done with it.'

'Borgia?'

'There is a good deal to be said for the Captain-General's point of view,' answered Cardinal Borgia. 'None the less, I will hear the opinion of the Apostolic Chancellor. All human life is precious in the sight of God, and only God may call a man to final judgement.'

'Enemies are killed in war,' said Riario impatiently, 'and he is a fool who hesitates overlong in thoughts of final judgement. Rome is at war. Leonardo da Vinci is Rome's enemy. The conclusion speaks for itself.'

Sixtus fingered the lobe of his ear.

'Defend him,' he suggested to Cardinal della Palla.

The latter leaned back in his chair. 'Leonardo da Vinci,' he pointed out, 'is hardly likely to take Castelmonte single-handed.

We were informed that he was studying the art of gunnery, and so he is. He came here openly seeking information on gunpowder, and—equally openly, if tactlessly—transmitted some of his own conclusions on the subject to me; in this, at least, he has shown himself a good son of the Church. I see no danger here. I have watched his gunnery studies myself; the weapon he is using is no longer than my arm, and is in point of fact an ornamental cannon used chiefly for firing salutes. I assure you that its effect on Castelmonte's walls would be non-existent, and I see no danger here either. He is an artist, a philosopher, a somewhat conceited young man, and a butterfly.'

'Who says so?' asked Borgia.

'That he is a butterfly? It is the opinion of those around him,' said della Palla innocently. 'Notably, of one Fra Sigismondo Carregi, who is tutor to the lady Bianca Maria Visconti and himself a theologian of renown in Florence. Most fortunately I have a letter from Fra Sigismondo, amply confirming this view. He denounces Leonardo da Vinci bitterly, but as a danger to nobody except the lady Bianca, with whom—according to Fra Sigismondo—he flirts continually, his experiments being aimed largely at impressing this young lady, and the Court at large, with his own brilliance. Well. I see no terrible danger to Rome here, and no reason for seeking the hasty death of a man who may, when all is said and done, be of service to God one day through his undoubted talent as an artist.'

'That is all very well,' said Riario, 'but my correspondent—'

'Your correspondent in Florence?' said della Palla. 'The Prince of Savoy, if I am not mistaken? My dear Captain-General, if Leonardo da Vinci is paying court to the lady Bianca Visconti, he is without doubt also annoying the prince, who intends to marry her one day. I hardly think that Silvio Grimiani's opinions are free from bias.'

Sixtus IV cogitated in silence, while Cardinal della Palla offered up a brief prayer for absolution; his own testimony, he was aware, having carried bias almost to the point of distortion. Finally the Pontiff delivered himself of judgement.

'We have decided,' he announced, 'to proceed as follows. Cardinal Borgia will send a letter to Florence forthwith, commanding—not requesting—this young man to come to Rome and place his artistic talents at the service of the Church. He is to obey immediately. If he does so, then we may regard His Eminence Cardinal della Palla's assessment as correct, and need trouble ourselves no further. If he does not comply, whether it be of his own free will or because our errant son Lorenzo de' Medici will not release him from service, then we shall accept the position of the Captain-General, who will at once proceed as he sees fit. My Lord and Your Eminences, I thank you.'

*

Relentlessly, and at last, March shouldered February aside and the springtime of the year 1478 began to fulfil its annual promise. Snows softened and melted; meadows and bottom-lands were soggy with new water, and everywhere brooks ran full to their banks. Only in the higher peaks and in the deep slashes on mountainsides did the winter snow persist, doomed but still stubborn.

With spring hastened Rome's messenger to Florence; His Grace the Bishop Manfredo Romolo-Paro, Apostolic Prothonotary and Nuncio Extraordinary, member of the Curia, and aide to His Eminence Cardinal Rodrigo Borgia.

Lorenzo received this prelate, and the pontifical decree he bore, with courtesy. 'We shall send for Messer Leonardo at once,' he said, 'and the command of His Holiness shall be that of Florence.'

*

So, a bare hour after the withdrawal of His Grace to prayer in a chapel of the cathedral of Santa Maria del Fiori, Lorenzo de' Medici and Leonardo faced each other across the table in the library. The ruler of Florence extended the papal summons.

'It seems,' he said, 'that Rome has urgent need of your services. Read.'

Leonardo scanned the ornate scroll rapidly.

'Evidently,' he said. 'I am here commanded by God, by His Church, by the Supreme Pontiff—twice—and by Cardinal Borgia; and also, your assent being presumed, by yourself. These are a great many commands to one poor Florentine artist, and almost overwhelming in their weight. Well, though it pains me, I cannot go.'

'Naturally,' said Lorenzo. 'But allow me to point out the difficulties. If I do not relinquish you to Rome, then I defy Sixtus and the Church. Since I am already doing so in the archbishopric of Pisa and at Castelmonte, this is a small matter for me. But if you defy Sixtus your position may be dangerous; both he and the Count of Imola have long arms and claws of iron. Let yourself be gripped by those claws, my friend, and your days of experiment are over.'

'They are over in any case, sir. At least for your purposes.'

'Say you so? With what result?'

'If my studies are now confirmed by trial in the field, then I have invented a new warfare,' said Leonardo simply. 'And one which has never before been contemplated in man's history.'

'Hum,' said Lorenzo, looking at him closely. 'And how is this warfare waged?'

'With cannon. You cannot have supposed differently, after all that I have been doing in your meadow and your archery-range. I have designed new cannon for the Medici; that is the long and the short of it.'

'Which you need to test in the field?'

'Exactly.'

'Will they give me Castelmonte?'

'By God's grace, sir, they will.'

'Then test them. Where had you thought of doing so?'

'In the marshes outside the city.'

'That will no longer serve. And you are now going to demand from me your fifty gunners, I have no doubt. In March, you said; and it is March now.'

'I am grateful for the excellence of your memory.'

Lorenzo motioned impatiently with his hand. 'It will be necessary for you to disappear,' he said. 'You, and your new cannon, their powder and shot, and my fifty gunners, and Captain Roderigo Leone. Let me think. Have you any objection to mountain terrain?'

'None whatever, provided I can have a practice range of some three thousand paces,' Leonardo said.

'Then I have an answer. There is a hunting-lodge of mine in the mountains between here and San Marino, unused these many years. Behind it—I will give you a map of the region—you will see a notched ridge, with a path that climbs steeply to the notch; and beyond the ridge is a valley where I used to play as a boy. Few know of its existence save for Giuliano and myself; yet it lies less than thirty miles from this room. You will be safe from prying eyes there. Take your men, and go. I suggest that they travel in small groups, gathering only at the lodge.'

'I can arrange it. The idea is admirable, and we are ready to leave at once.'

'You had better leave sooner than that,' said Lorenzo with an ironic smile. 'By which I mean that you have already left, since I propose to inform Rome's nuncio that such is the case. Moreover, since you are close friends with my brother, I am sure he will lend you both his horse and a cloak. Do you follow me?'

'Perfectly,' Leonardo replied. 'I have vanished even now.'

'Good. The ground in the Arno valley will harden within some eight or ten weeks. Whether your trials have been crowned with success or not, you will return at once to Florence whenever I send for you. At once; you understand? Castelmonte . . .'

'I know. Sir, we have here not one paradox, but two. For though I stand here in your library, I have left Florence; and, though we seem to be doing nothing, yet the siege of Castelmonte has already begun. Therefore trust in me, and in God's will.'

*

'You should not be here, my lady.'

'I know that. The tally of my sins grows longer every day.' She took her seat in the window. 'However, since you are no longer in Florence, having left for I know not where some hours since, there can be little harm in my entering your apartments. They are empty, are they not?'

'And who informed you of all this?'

'Constanza.'

'And who told her?'

'Giuliano, of course. He has lent you his cloak, I see. How long will you be away?'

'I do not know, Madonna.'

'Well. At least I do not need to ask you for what purpose you are leaving, since I already know that much.'

'With respect, Madonna, I doubt that you do, since nobody is aware of my purpose save myself.'

'More conceit. You have devised a means of aiming guns not by trial and error, as hitherto, but by mathematics. I admit that I do not understand precisely how.'

'My lady,' said Leonardo, 'every day you amaze me, since you perceive what has entirely escaped such learned men as your tutor and the worthy Dr Mazzone. Lorenzo would have been well advised to ask you to guard your tongue long before this. I ask you to do so now.'

'You have no need to ask it, Leonardo *mio*. And as for my perception, how could it fail to be better than that of others?' Bianca said. 'I have had, you see, an excellent teacher.'

'And I an admirable pupil.'

'That is understood. Nevertheless . . .'

'Yes, Madonna?'

'Will you not kiss me, before you go?'

*

To the Count of Bosco and Imola, Captain-General of the Armies of the Church at Rome, from Silvio Grimiani di Torino, Prince of Savoy: Greetings.

Most Excellent and Noble Count:

No matter what may have been told you by my Lord Bishop Manfredo Romolo-Paro, you may believe me: Leonardo da Vinci has left Florence, and this after the arrival of my Lord Bishop rather than before. Therefore Lorenzo de' Medici and Leonardo da Vinci, severally or in concert, it matters not, are guilty of grave disobedience towards the commands of His Holiness. It follows that the opinion which I have been urging upon you, and upon Rome, is correct: and accordingly, I am taking such pains to rid you of the nuisance caused by this most impertinent and malicious enemy as will, I hope, satisfy Rome and His Holiness of that devotion with which I have always served their cause. And since you are aware, my Lord, that Rome lies already in my debt over the matter of the lady d'Avalos, I trust in her generosity and yours to assist me in the attainment of those mercantile ambitions of mine whose nature you have long known.

Given by my hand the sixth day of March, at Florence.

CHAPTER FIFTEEN

... Now the means by which we perceive objects to be far from us, or nearer, are these. First, by their colour, distant objects being the more azure. Second, by reason of one thing standing before another so that the second thing cannot wholly be seen. Third, by their size. Fourth, because in moving a little way from one place to another we see things appear to move also, the nearer moving more than the farther. And fifth, because the eyes being set a little apart in a man's head, each eye sees things differently, as may be perceived by closing first the one eye and then the other; and these two views fusing with each other and being seen as one, enable us to judge the distance of things. ...

... And if it be doubted, whether matters of art and of science are one and the same, I shall show it to be the case. For consider, that the eyes being set at a space from each other of but the tenth part of an ell, how much more readily the distance of things might be perceived were they to be set apart for a greater space, even two ells: for thereby the views seen would be the more different as between one eye and the other, and the task made easier. And this can be achieved mechanically, as I shall show: and by it cannon may be aimed over great distances ...

From the Notebooks of Leonardo da Vinci

It was strange, Leonardo thought, how poorly men's childhood memories served them, particularly in matters of size. He sat outside the smaller of the two caves, his back resting against the side of a gun-carriage, and surveyed the pocket-valley which sloped gently away from him. A narrow rill of snow-water meandered along its floor, to vanish where the stony path entered it between two pillars of rock. Lorenzo, he recalled, had assured him that it was at least three thousand paces from end to end, and in fact it was barely a quarter of that length. Well, it would serve. A thousand paces was the maximum range he intended to work at, when the time came to do so, and they could achieve eight hundred or so here by siting the guns carefully.

What he needed this morning was a gesture; something to dispel the air of scepticism—if not of incipient mutiny—which the fifty men about him almost palpably exuded. He could hardly blame them. Urged blasphemously onward by Rigo, they had taken an entire day and the better part of last night to wrestle the six guns up the steep and zigzag path from the lodge in the foothills below, with no knowledge of why they were engaged upon such a back-breaking exercise. They had sought enlightenment, of course, both continually and colourfully. They had been given none. To each question Rigo had offered the advice that their breath might be better saved for climbing, and their scabrous suggestions for the alternative disposal of their burdens had been met by invitations to fall out of line and be beaten to a pulp by their Captain in person.

They had gained the valley-head, and the caves which they now occupied, well after midnight. The detritus of their prompt collapse lay all about Leonardo this morning; bags of flour and salt-fish, lanterns, canvas and rope for bivouacs, boxes of candles, mallets, spikes, a small anvil, sacks of charcoal, three barrels of last season's apples, and a single discarded boot, hurled into the darkness by young Tesoro di Veluti, whose head upon arrival had been as sore as his feet. Leonardo noted, however, that the powder-kegs, shot and other appurtenances of the cannon had been care-fully stowed within the larger cave. Rain or snow might be allowed to soak all else, but their professional equipment would receive greater care, under Rigo's command, than would the gunners themselves.

'Good morrow, friend engineer,' said Rigo, arriving at that moment with a platter of bread, cheese, and olives, which he handed to Leonardo. 'Tell me how you wish us to proceed. We shall be ready for your instructions in an hour or so, after I have broken a few heads in reducing the disorder here.'

'Exactly as I outlined to you,' Leonardo replied. 'The first four or five days are to be spent in learning to dismantle the guns and reassemble them, neither procedure to take longer than a slow count of ten. Eight men to each gun, with two as runners or replacements. Four men in each team to carry the barrel; three more for the carriage and its wheels, the wheels to be removed from the axles or not as occasion and terrain demand; one man to carry the powder, the shot, the sponge-staves, and the slow-matches. They must learn to move fast and silently, bearing these things.'

'Before firing a shot?' said Rigo. 'That will come hard, Leonardo.'

'It will come harder yet if they enter battle while they are still falling over each other's feet,' Leonardo pointed out.

'Quite true. None the less, if you will accept some advice from me, I would in your place show them some purpose in sweating off their winter wine-bellies,' Rigo said. 'You have succeeded in convincing me. *They* remain unconvinced, and therefore surly, and I had rather they saw the light. We have grown to understand each other somewhat, you and I, so forgive my bluntness. We are not now dealing with machines and mathematics, but with men.'

'So we are,' said Leonardo. 'Let us, then, give them some theatre.'

*

By ten in the forenoon the ground was unlittered, and three storage-tents had been raised. The gunners, in a silent group, were gathered about one of the small cannon at the valley's head, between the mouths of their caves and the stream. Five hundred accurate paces away, a wooden target was propped against a rough triangular base of poles. It was, in point of fact, the door to an abandoned hut, stolen opportunely from behind the hunting-lodge at the commencement of their climb to the high basin they were now in.

Leonardo da Vinci was pouring gunpowder into a small brass measure. He tapped the side of the cup, settling the grains.

'One of these measures goes with each gun,' he told the assembled men, 'and each to its own. Do not confuse them, for they differ slightly in amount; by half the weight of a hazel-nut, it may be—but they differ.' Several of the gunners nodded, among them Agnolo Fulvio and Scudo. Care in measuring powder was a concept they already knew.

Leonardo now moved to the cannon. Save for its smaller size—it was a bare four and a half feet long, and weighed perhaps one-hundredth as much as the guns they were used to—its appearance was familiar. The trunnions at either side of its barrel rested in notches, so that cannon and carriage could be quickly parted, and the wheels were spiked to the axles with removable pins. Aside from these features, its sole peculiarity lay in the fact that its breech rested on a curved block which could be raised or lowered by means of a screw, this screw being part of the carriage itself. A pointer on the screw-block moved, as the thread turned, past a series of marks engraved on the carriage, thus showing the degree of elevation of the barrel; and by tilting both screw and block backwards the gun's breech could be disengaged from them, allowing it to fall and rest on the oaken carriage-tree so that the muzzle—as Leonardo now demonstrated—pointed steeply skyward for loading purposes.

He tipped the measured powder into the barrel, following it with a leather patch and then with the four-pound polished iron ball. Then, reaching into the front of his tunic, he produced a narrow brown cylinder, about the length and thickness of a goose-quill. It was tapered at either end.

'This is your fuse,' he said, showing it to them. 'It is merely powder, twisted into a roll of paper and sealed with gum of Arabia. You will have little time to fill the breech-hole with loose powder to serve as a train, as you are used to doing; the same end may be achieved with this, and more quickly . . . thus.' He inserted one end of the quill into the touch-hole, pushing it home until only an inch or two of it protruded. Lifting the breech and lowering the muzzle, he swung the range-screw forward once more, and then allowed the breech to settle itself in the curved upper surface of the travelling block.

'Ready,' he said.

Turning his head, he looked down the valley at the far rectangle of wood. From this distance, it appeared no larger than a man's thumb-nail. He knelt behind the cannon and shifted the carriage fractionally, aligning the barrel so that it pointed neither to one side nor the other of this diminutive mark.

'Who will undertake to strike us yonder board?' he asked, still kneeling.

Agnolo Fulvio at once stood forward and crouched beside him. Looking along the top of the barrel, the gunner-lieutenant saw two filed notches, one at the swell of the breech and one cut into the rim of the muzzle. Sitting in these notches, as an acorn sits in its cup, was the distant target.

'I have seen these sighting-marks before,' said Agnolo, 'upon Turkish cannon. How many shots will you give me?'

'One,' said Leonardo.

'With an untried gun?'

'The gun will shoot as truly as any you have handled,' said Leonardo, smiling, 'and better. You have my word on it.'

'That may be. I still do not know how it carries,' Agnolo said. There was a murmur of agreement from his colleagues. 'What is the range, do you say?'

'Five hundred paces.'

'Give me three attempts, then, and I will do it.'

'One,' said Leonardo remorselessly.

'An impossible task,' Agnolo said. 'No man can do it. My first shot, look you, must either strike short or else fly above and beyond the mark, unless I have the luck of Satan. My second will serve to determine by how much I must raise or lower the barrel in order to increase or shorten the range by a given number of paces. Once I know this, I am in a fair way to have my third shot strike home. Eh, Scudo?' He looked at the big gunner for confirmation.

'He is right,' agreed the latter. 'That is the way of it.'

'Stand aside, then,' said Leonardo, 'and observe how mathematics may replace both your first shot and your second.'

'It will be a pleasure.'

Agnolo rose to his feet. Rapidly, Leonardo turned the range-screw until the pointer attached to the block rested upon the mark corresponding to five hundred paces. He got up, dusting his knees.

'Give me a short space of time,' he said, 'and then fire. One shot is all that is needed.'

'How much time?' demanded Agnolo. 'And for what purpose?'

'Why,' Leonardo replied, 'so that I may check upon my calculations.' He turned to Rigo. 'Perhaps you will accompany me?' he asked.

'Where to?'

'Down to the target, of course. In the cause of science.'

Rigo, who had opened his mouth in order to deliver himself of some comment, shut it again as the artist strode away.

'Fire when I raise my hand,' he bade Agnolo Fulvio. 'And

remove that look from your face, or I might mistake it for impertinence.'

Agnolo bowed deeply. 'To command, Captain,' he said. 'He is your friend, and doubtless you know what you are doing.'

Several minutes later, Leonardo and the Captain-Gunner were standing at either side of the propped door. A short distance from them, the brook pattered its way between snow-patches and over sunlit pebbles, heeded by neither of them.

'Closer,' suggested Leonardo.

'Why not directly in front of it?' Rigo snarled. 'Theatre is all very well, but I had not imagined being asked to lay my head on a block.'

'Take courage,' Leonardo advised him. 'Though I admit that I have less to lose than you do. If this should fail, your gunners will probably tear me limb from limb, and hence I may as well be decapitated before they are given the chance to do so. Give the signal.'

Rigo raised his hand.

A puff of white smoke bloomed from the centre of the group of men clustered at the top of the valley. The whipcrack of the cannon's detonation reached their ears almost at once; they caught a glimpse of the shining ball in mid-trajectory an eyeblink before the target between them shattered into matchwood. Splinters flew, one of them driving deep into the fabric of Rigo's sleeve; he plucked it out with a grunt of relief, his eyes following the ball which, spent and misshapen now, was rolling away in the direction of the stream. The men were beginning to pour downhill towards them, some waving their caps.

'Well, Sir Gunner,' Rigo said, 'I like a confident man, to be sure. The next time you take it into your head to make a point, however, I shall be glad if it chances that I am elsewhere.'

*

At dawn a day later and some twenty miles away, Silvio Grimiani di Torino allowed his great black horse to pick its way through the rubble-strewn courtyard of a ruined abbey. Below him the roofs of Fiesole glistened damply in the grey light of the day's coming; farther away, the river Arno made its presence known in the drifting banks of mist which the bitter night had breathed upon its surface. Indifferent to the cold, Silvio watched the wooded trail that slanted up the hillside from the sleeping town. Close to the old and broken wall he was invisible he knew. His charger snorted, steam curling from its nostrils, and the reins in his hand slapped gently against its neck.

Four of us, he said to himself. Three, if the truth were told. Paolo Pazzi would be worthless; so much was already clear. He had spent too many hours hunched over his figures; a clerk, not an assassin. His brother Francesco would have been better for an undertaking such as this one, even taking into account his failure in Rome, but old Jacopo had insisted that Paolo should accompany them, thereby learning—as his father ironically put it—some of those aspects of commerce which were not to be found in ledgers and bills of lading. Besides, Francesco was elsewhere.

Well, there was likely to be little for Paolo to upset. Benno Foscari, and his stiletto, would be worth two men; so would Mario Bandini, who was vouched for by his more notorious elder brother Bernardo—the latter, like Francesco Pazzi, having other fish to fry. Two professionals, a scrivener, and himself, then, Silvio thought; it was enough.

He had spent three days in scouring the countryside for news of Leonardo da Vinci's whereabouts. Roderigo Leone was said to be with him. Tales of mysterious night-time comings and goings abounded; Silvio supposed that such was the way with rustics, who had—God knew—little enough to excite them. He had learned nothing specific until his arrival at the Medici hunting-lodge. The place was crumbling, but was still occupied by an aged caretaker and his wife, to whom Silvio had offered a simple choice; speech or death. The old woman had cursed him, but her husband had proved less stubborn. He had taken the Prince of Savoy outside, pointing up the steep and hidden trail to the notched ridge that commanded the house. Messer Leonardo da Vinci, he averred, was even now up there upon some errand. Had he a thickset man for companion? Yes, he had. The caretaker had thereupon lapsed into mumbled and incoherent pleas for mercy, and Silvio, satisfied, had allowed him to rejoin his toothless wife.

He would doubtless have been less complacent had the ancient retainer—who was less terror-stricken than appeared to be the case, since he had served as a foot-soldier under Cosimo de' Medici, Lorenzo's grandfather—informed him that the artist and the Captain-Gunner were accompanied by fifty armed men. Since this intelligence had not been sought by the Prince, however, the caretaker had seen no reason for adding it by way of afterthought.

In the ruined courtyard above Fiesole, Silvio strained his ears, hearing the sound of approaching hooves. He blew into his cupped hands and awaited, with caution and a growing anticipation, the arrival of his accomplices.

*

'I see a difficulty,' Rigo said.

'There are several,' admitted Leonardo cheerfully. 'What is yours?' He was tossing a handful of pebbles, one by one, from where he sat onto the path beneath them. It was late afternoon, and the weather was fine. The gunners were preparing their evening meal outside the caves at the upper end of the valley; Rigo and Leonardo had taken a stroll, and were now perched on the summit of one of the rock pillars which guarded the entrance to the glen from the head of the track outside. The hunting-lodge lay, minuscule, seven hundred feet below them; from its door a wider road descended, across foothills streaked with snow, towards the distant plain.

'It concerns the measurement of range,' said Rigo, rubbing his neck. 'Your piece of theatre this morning was admirable in its effect, but for all of that Agnolo made a telling point. We are not troubled overmuch by estimating the distance of our targets, since hitherto we have done so by guesswork and by means of our sighting-shots. Your new method does not allow this, if I am correct in my reasoning.'

'You are.'

'And you were careful to pace out the distance between your cannon and its target before you fired. You had need to do so, since otherwise your approach could not have succeeded. Am I also correct in this?'

'Quite correct.'

'Then how,' asked Rigo, 'do you proceed when you do not know your range beforehand? That is my difficulty.'

'Rigo, my friend,' said Leonardo, 'your perception is acute, and your point crucial; the more so since we shall eventually be firing our cannon at night.'

'At night! This grows harder to fathom by the minute. How in the devil's name can we do that?'

'By means, once again, of mathematics, together with a device I have constructed for the purpose. Sit closer, and let me show you.'

Leonardo unfolded the cover of his notebook, took charcoal in hand, and began to draw.

'Let us suppose,' he went on, 'that we take a long staff, and lay it on the ground before us with its ends to left and right. So. Now upon either end of this staff, let us mount two notched strips of brass, like the arm of a pelorus, or like the sighting-notches which you saw filed upon the barrel of our cannon up there. We first set our eye to this one, here at the right, and align its notches upon the target . . . thus. Without moving the staff, we proceed to its left-hand end, and do likewise with the notched arm there. Both arms are now pointing at our target. Do you understand?'

'Yes. It is as though we had aimed two small guns at the same mark.'

'Exactly so. Now you may readily perceive that although both arms are aimed at the same place, yet they point in slightly different directions, since they are set apart by the length of our staff. In fact, they point inward towards each other, though to but a small degree. Very well. The nearer the target, the greater will be their inclination towards each other, thus. And by measuring this inclination inward, which I can do by means of a graduated wheel mounted beneath one of the arms . . . thus, and thus . . . I can compute the distance of the target from where my staff lies. Once you perceive the nature of the device, it is easily done.'

'And you have built it?' asked Rigo. 'Now that you have drawn it for me, I can indeed see that it might work.'

'I have built it, and it works with sufficient accuracy for our purpose.'

'And at night? What then?'

'That also I have considered . . . what is it?'

Rigo, interrupting him, laid a hand on his shoulder and pointed.

'Look,' he said. 'Below us. There, by the side of the lodge. Riders.'

Leonardo stared downward through the tops of the pines. 'Four,' he agreed. 'And they are coming this way, by their direction.' He lowered himself, slowly, until he was lying prone on the rock's surface; Rigo had already done so.

'Here is trouble, then,' said Rigo. 'It is too far to see who they may be, and they will be among the trees soon. Friend or foe? What think you?'

Leonardo, reaching into a leather pouch that was chained alongside his notebook at his waist, brought out a small cylindrical object and held it to his eye. 'The Prince of Savoy,' he announced matter-of-factly. 'And Paolo Pazzi. The other two I do not recognize, but your question is answered.'

'Now, by the Passion,' cried Rigo, 'what is this? I took you for long-sighted at Castelmonte last year, but this passes all belief! Show me what you have there.'

Leonardo handed the metal cylinder to him. It was the thickness of two fingers, and a little longer than it was broad. 'You have seen eyeglasses before, have you not?' he inquired mildly.

'Not of this sort. Eyeglasses are flat, and worn by old men and lawyers. How is this thing made?'

'With two glasses, at a short space from each other, as you see,' replied Leonardo, 'the rear one being ground in the opposite sense to the one in front. I hit upon the principle by accident when playing with a pair of such lenses, and mounted them myself.'

'A miracle,' Rigo proclaimed, peering through the tube. 'They are gone,' he added. 'But they must be climbing towards us; I can even see their tracks. My friend, this will make you a rich man. I would pay—'

'You need pay nothing,' Leonardo said. 'Accept it, as a gift from one artilleryman to another. Only be so good as to keep it concealed; let others think, as you thought of me, that you have keen sight and no more.'

'I thank you. What am I saying? I cannot thank you sufficiently.'

'In God's name,' said Leonardo with a smile, 'let us have less turmoil over a piece of trumpery through which to gaze at the moon. It will take me but a few days to make another. Meanwhile, if you will drag your attention back to more immediate matters, shall we decide what to do about Silvio and his friends? I own that I am beginning to tire of them.'

'Of course. Well, it will take them a half-hour and more to reach the head of this track.'

'Then I will await them here,' said Leonardo, 'and do you collect together a small group of such as may feel the need for exercise; and then let us see what they are about.'

*

It was Benno Foscari who saw him first. He signalled the others to silence with upraised arm. There was no need for him to point at their prey. Two hundred paces ahead of them, and clearly visible through the pine-trunks which flanked the final curve of the trail's ascent, Leonardo was sitting on a log in the centre of the path, his back to them. He appeared to be sketching; evidently, he was making use of the last of the daylight.

Silvio reined in beside Foscari.

'An easy matter,' he whispered. 'But where is the gunner?'

'Either behind us, or else around yonder bend where those twin rocks hold the path,' Foscari replied softly. 'For I see no horses. Is that the entrance to the valley you spoke of?'

'I imagine so.'

'Then they are encamped in it,' Foscari said. 'You may depend upon it.' His horse pranced, but there was sufficient wind in the trees to hide any small noise they might be making; they would be seen before they were heard, if they were reasonably quiet. 'How important is the gunner in this affair?' Foscari asked.

'A side-dish. If he appears, kill him. If he does not, well and good.' The Prince of Savoy beckoned to the two riders behind him. 'Paolo,' he said, 'keep our rear. Cry warning if you see Captain Leone; otherwise, do nothing. Is it understood?'

Paolo Pazzi nodded, hoping that his relief was not making him shamefaced. He had little stomach for what he knew was about to happen, whether fighting or simple murder, and he was grateful for the proffered chance of returning to Florence in neither triumph nor disgrace.

Even as rearguard, he was incapable of fulfilling his duties, though this mattered but little in the circumstances. Pulling his horse aside, he kept his eyes not on the trail below him, but upon Silvio Grimiani, who—flanked by Benno Foscari and Mario Bandini—now advanced up the last stretch of the path towards the still-unsuspecting artist's back.

By the time they had halved the distance to their intended prey, Mario was conscious of faint unease. Was the man deaf? Breeze or no, he should have become aware of their deadly purpose by now? He had heard that painters often became immersed in their work to the exclusion of all else, and certainly it seemed true of this one. Surveying the scene from a professional point of view, Mario Bandini could find nothing amiss. Twenty paces beyond the seated artist the track turned sharply to the right, presumably entering the upper valley. There was nowhere for him to run except away from them; and if he did so, it would be a simple matter to ride him down, and his companion with him, should the latter be anywhere about.

At thirty paces from his back, Silvio Grimiani halted. He drew steel, his teeth set in remembrance of past slights, both real and fancied.

'Artist,' he called menacingly.

Leonardo da Vinci turned, rising to his feet in a single fluid movement. There was a look of dangerous amusement on his face. At the same instant, as though signalled by Silvio's rapier, men appeared from all about the Prince and his companions. From behind boulders and trunks of trees they arose, and from around the corner where the track vanished between its guardian rock pillars; dark, leather-clad men, their skins powder-grained, bearing daggers, iron spikes, clubs and short-swords.

Benno Foscari, his stiletto already in his hand, saw his defeat at once and spurred his horse desperately. The animal reared and then plunged forward for a step or two. Rigo Leone seized its bridle, sweeping his thigh against its forefeet and heaving simultaneously at the leather. Foscari, badly seated, had a second to marvel at the gunner's enormous strength as the horse toppled, whinnying; then, after a brief moment of soaring flight, he crashed into the side of a rock. Rigo, a gutter-brawler by nature, promptly and unceremoniously kicked the side of his skull in.

Paolo Pazzi, terror-stricken, watched the first instants of this ambush from his distant station among the pines. In offering himself as bait for their trap, Leonardo had ordered the gunners—much to Rigo's disgust—to refrain from violence until Silvio Grimiani had made his intentions clear, and moreover no time had been available to cut off their opponents' retreat by closing the trail farther down the mountainside. Their chief concern, in any case, was to prevent penetration of the valley. Pulling his horse's head around, therefore, Paolo was able to see Mario Ban-

186

dini wrenched from his saddle by the gigantic Scudo, who clamped the crook of an arm about his neck and bent the assassin's head inexorably forward until his spine snapped like a rotten twig. Then, incontinently, he spurred his horse into tumbling flight, and was gone.

The Prince of Savoy cast a glance in the direction of his rear-guard's retreating figure, and twisted his face into a sneer. Ringed by men and blades, he still sat his charger, whose bit was held by Leonardo da Vinci.

Rigo Leone, idly casting Benno Foscari's stiletto into the air and catching it again, came towards the group and grinned carnivorously at the artist.

'What say you?' he asked, gesturing at the Prince with the weapon he held. 'From ear to ear?'

Leonardo shook his head and retrieved the rapier which Silvio had thrown to the ground in surrender.

'We gain little by silencing him,' he pointed out. 'His friend is already lost to us, and news of our whereabouts must therefore reach Rome's ears before long. Well, it was bound to happen sooner or later, and matters little. Let him live.'

'This is folly, Leonardo,' Rigo said. 'Leave aside, if you will, the fact that this princeling would have slain you unarmed, and that nothing stands in the way of our doing likewise to him. Our whereabouts may no longer be a secret, but outside this valley nothing appears of our purpose. Would you hold him prisoner?'

'Yes. For Lorenzo's mercy.'

'Then you risk a great deal, for there is more that he will see. Let us cut his throat like the dog he is, and hurl him down yonder cliff.'

'No,' said Leonardo. 'For one thing, there is a matter I have to discuss with him.' He addressed Silvio Grimiani. 'Prince,' he said, 'will you give us your word to seek no escape? It is that, or death.'

'I give it,' said Silvio. 'Keep your peasants from me.'

'Then dismount,' Leonardo told him, 'and keep a civil tongue.'

*

They housed him—under continued and vehement protest from Rigo Leone—in the smaller of the two caves. There, after the evening meal, Leonardo visited him. He found the Prince in ill-humour.

'These are no conditions for a prisoner,' the latter said at once.

'They are the same as our own. Better, in fact, since you have privacy,' Leonardo said.

'Your swinish companions may live as they choose,' said Silvio, 'and you also. I am of different breeding.'

'I would be the last to deny it. Have a care, prince; I may throw you to them yet.'

'You would not dare,' said Silvio. 'Not if you hope for mercy from Rome, whose cause I serve.'

Leonardo, who had brought with him a low stool, set this down and sat upon it. He trimmed the candle which was their only light, and moved it until it stood equidistant between them.

'Oddly enough, I do not walk in constant fear of Rome,' he said, 'though I am pleased to hear you declare your allegiance at last. Let us, then, discuss the nature of your service to Rome. In particular, let us talk about a certain *camisado* which took place in the autumn of last year.'

'I do not comprehend you,' said the Prince.

'I think you do,' Leonardo said gently, studying his face in the glow of the candle. 'I think you do. I mean the foray in which the Lady Carla d'Avalos was taken from your custody by the defenders of Castelmonte, thereafter to die most foully at the hands of the Count of Imola. You recall it?'

'I do. What of it?'

'I have been wondering, these last five months,' said Leonardo, still conversationally, 'how much you were offered by the Count for betraying her?'

'What is this talk of betrayal? I betrayed nobody,' said Silvio. 'Giuliano de' Medici himself can testify that I fulfilled my duties as escort as well as could be expected, numbers being against us. Your suggestion is infamous.'

'No,' replied Leonardo. 'No, I am afraid that will not answer. Giuliano told me, certainly, that you were fighting with their rearguard when he arrived upon the scene. He also believed that the attack had been part of a chance foray, perhaps by a party from Castelmonte breaking siege in search of supplies. This notion was never challenged, and Giuliano, of course, was too distressed to draw the correct inference from what he had seen. It was, he said, a *camisado*; and men do not wear shirts over their armour unless their sally is of deliberate purpose, and one which involves recognition by friends in the darkness of night. Had their encounter with your party been accidental, as was claimed, they would have been plainly dressed. It follows that it was not by accident, but by design, that they came upon you. By whose design? By yours. It was you who insisted that the lady Carla and her companions should leave Pistrola at midnight, rather than wait for Giuliano's escort the next day. It was you who led them past Castelmonte, rather than by the longer and safer route through the hills. Therefore, you betrayed them, and sent Carla d'Avalos to her death. Did you suppose,' he continued, his voice still soft, yet terrible now, 'that I had spared you as prisoner for Lorenzo's justice in the trivial matter of my own attempted murder? I did not. It is for the life of Carla d'Avalos—a woman helpless, and no part of your miserable contrivings for Rome and against Florence—that you will answer, to Florence and to God. You may keep the candle by you, prince; it would be a needless cruelty in me to consign a man with your craven soul to darkness.'

He left the Prince of Savoy white-faced, and found his way out of the cave. Rigo joined him by the side of the stream.

'A snake, Leonardo,' he said. 'Tread on him swiftly, my friend, lest he bite your heel, for I see from your appearance that you know him to be evil. Meantime, I will set a guard over him.'

'He has given his word,' said Leonardo. 'Let him keep it, if he hopes to take one small step towards salvation.'

'I would not give you a pinch of dust for his word.'

'Nor I,' said Leonardo grimly. 'Therefore set your guard, but not too closely. He cannot outrun you, when all is said.'

'There, by God, you speak truly,' said Rigo. 'Get some sleep, engineer, and I will order things as I see fit.'

*

Shortly after midnight Giunta di Lenzo, who had drawn the unwelcome task of sitting outside the cave which housed the Prince of Savoy, heard him groaning within it. He got up.

'What ails you?' he demanded.

'Bring me a candle, as you are an honest man,' said Silvio. 'Mine has expired.'

'Then sleep,' said Giunta. 'I am not your servant.'

'Nay, good fellow,' Silvio said. 'I cannot sleep, since I must pray for my soul. Do not leave me without light, I beg you.'

'A pest on your soul,' the gunner replied. None the less, he fetched a candle from the nearest store-tent, which was a bare ten paces away. Returning with it, he incautiously entered the cave, his hand outstretched. The Prince, who was stationed immediately inside the entrance, struck him on the head with a stone and stepped over his unconscious body into the open air. Flattened against the granite, he waited for five long minutes; then, satisfied that the remainder of his captors were asleep, he dropped to his knees and began to crawl.

Half way down the valley, he rose to his feet again. The night sky was covered by clouds, and he walked swiftly towards the rocks at the valley's exit, secure in the knowledge that he could not be seen and that, even should the alarm now be raised behind him, he could be lost among the trees outside before any pursuit could reach him.

They heard him coming while he was still a hundred paces away from them.

Kneeling in the damp grass beyond the twin rocks he was approaching, Rigo grinned invisibly and blew on the end of his match, shielding its tiny glow with cupped palms. His four companions, crouched by their cannon, held their breath in alert anticipation. The cannon itself, standing on the surface of the outer trail and loaded with small-shot, was pointing into the valley, its muzzle exactly covering the gap between the natural pillars at either side of the path.

Silvio Grimiani dropped lightly from the bank he had been following into the track, his feet sliding almost inaudibly on the loose stones of its surface. He recovered his balance, peered into the blackness that surrounded him, and then walked confidently into the gateway which led to freedom.

Twenty paces away, Rigo touched the match-end to the fuse.

The shower of sparks startled the Prince of Savoy, bewildering him for an alarmed instant or two before he realized its import. He half turned, screaming; his shout, merging with the brief thunder of the gun, was torn asunder with the rags of his body, fading amid the crashing echoes from the nearby rocks into a dreadful patter of unseen fragments of cloth, metal, bone, and flesh.

Rigo Leone fanned smoke away from his face with his cap.

'Say a Hail Mary over the pieces,' he suggested to nobody in particular. 'We cannot hope to collect them all. Tomorrow we shall build a dam and divert our stream down this pathway. I am, as all men know, fastidious, and I do not care to live with carrion scattered about my doorstep.'

CHAPTER SIXTEEN

Francesco della Rovere, Pope Sixtus IV, in robes trimmed with purple, sat before a sunlit window in nervous discontent. His state of mind was occasioned neither by robes nor sunshine, but they formed a subtle part of it. For his dress was Lenten, and Lent was drawing to a close; the fine weather announced the arrival of spring in earnest, and with spring must come decision.

His Holiness was unprepared for decision as yet, and therefore he fretted, the more so since his nephew the Captain-General and Count of Imola had requested an audience. He would arrive soon, and would—so Sixtus knew—press for an immediate opening of the season's campaign. To this, Sixtus had no objection, having laid his purely military plans well in advance. The Count would also press, however, upon other matters; matters more tenuous, more liable to go awry, of dubious ethical standing and, worst of all, of questionable utility. The trouble with Riario, Sixtus reflected, was that as a weapon he resembled a hand-cannon—noisy, potentially terrifying, yet liable to backfire.

Somewhere, a bell chimed softly. His chaplain rose from a table and crossed to the door of the suite. He returned, to the Pontiff's faint surprise, with Cardinal Rodrigo Borgia.

'We are delighted to see Your Eminence,' said Sixtus after the formalities of greeting, 'but unfortunately we are shortly expecting our beloved nephew. At noon, perhaps . . .'

'The Count of Imola has been called elsewhere upon military matters, and asks your forgiveness,' said Cardinal Borgia. 'If Your Holiness will graciously pardon his absence, I am come in his place and upon his errand.'

'Then please be seated,' Sixtus smiled. 'We confess to some relief, and welcome Your Eminence unreservedly. Along with our relief, we confess to both curiosity and, if you will accept it in a spirit of charity, a little suspicion. Your Eminence is notably more persuasive than the Count, and we take it that your errand is one of persuasion.'

'To the very slightest extent,' said Cardinal Borgia. 'I will not conceal from Your Holiness that it was thought that mine would be a more delicate touch.'

'So I feared. But proceed.'

The Cardinal settled himself. 'May I summarize for Your Holiness?' he said. 'Leonardo da Vinci, upon the orders of Lorenzo de' Medici, is in the Apennine mountains. An attempt—the second attempt—upon his life has miscarried; the Prince of Savoy is believed to be dead and two of his companions certainly are. The one man who escaped this affair reports that Leonardo da Vinci is accompanied by Captain Roderigo Leone and a large force of gunners. All this confirms what we have long presumed to be the case; that Lorenzo de' Medici plans to resume the siege of Castelmonte as soon as may be, and that da Vinci is for this purpose devising new weaponry.'

'Of what nature?' asked Sixtus.

'That is the difficulty. Since none of us possesses the mind of Messer Leonardo, and since the escaped man did not see what he was doing, his work remains an unknown factor. We may guess that he has built a larger and more formidable cannon with which to pound Castelmonte's walls, Florence's guns having proved inadequate to the task last year.'

'It is very likely,' said the Pontiff. 'Go on.'

'The point is,' said Borgia, 'that whatever is being planned clearly concerns gunnery, and must therefore take time to deploy. None the less, your Captain-General is anxious that no surprise be sprung upon himself, the Count della Rovere of Castelmonte, or the Duke Federigo da Montefeltro in—let us say—six weeks from now. They have allowed for a preliminary bombardment of two months' duration—as was the case last autumn. They do not wish to find themselves suddenly faced with a gun which, because of its size and power, could reduce their wall within—again, let us say—one month. Since his task is to hold the Arno valley until Rome's armies need to pass through it, this is a reasonable attitude upon Riario's part.'

'We accept it as such. Well?'

'Riario feels that Florence's designs, of whatever nature, should be flushed into the open as soon as possible, so that he may lay his plans accordingly. Therefore, he proposes to force their hand.'

The Pontiff's eyes immediately narrowed in caution.

'By what means?' he demanded.

'We have with us in Rome,' said Borgia, obliquely and carefully, 'the man who escaped Leonardo da Vinci's ambush. He is Paolo Pazzi.' The Cardinal paused.

'We know what is proposed by the Pazzi family,' said Sixtus IV at once. 'We cannot be a party to it. An attempt on the life of Lorenzo de' Medici himself—'

'Your Holiness does not need to be a party to it,' said Cardinal Borgia. 'That is why I am here, and not the Count of Imola.'

Sixtus perceived the force of this argument. Had Girolamo Riario been sitting before him now, their discourse would undoubtedly have been unpleasantly direct.

'Then let us state it in terms,' he said. 'In no circumstances will we countenance what is planned by the Pazzi family, useful though it would certainly be in the present context. Is that clear?'

'Perfectly. Save for one thing, Your Holiness need trouble yourself no further.'

'What thing?'

'A trifle,' said the Cardinal. 'As . . . let me consider how best to put it . . . as a token that Rome's displeasure, should anything untoward occur that might force Florence to reveal her plans, will not be extreme, the Count of Imola requests that the young Cardinal Rafaello Sansoni-Riario, his nephew, be sent to Florence from Pisa to attend High Mass upon Easter Sunday. That is all.'

'Thereby ensuring that we do, in fact, lend countenance to violence? By no means. We must refuse.'

'Your Holiness speaks too hastily, which is perhaps understandable. By sending the Cardinal to Florence the Church will, on the contrary, demonstrate her innocence of any design upon the persons of the Medici. The Cardinal,' added Borgia reflectively, 'is but seventeen years of age, and a youth of admirable purity.'

Pontiff and Cardinal regarded one another for a long while. Sixtus perceived his dilemma only too clearly. If he refused to agree, Borgia would proceed to set out the details of whatever conspiracy was being planned in Florence against Medici, and invite him openly to forbid it. Should he then do so, it would follow that any failure in the spring campaign could be laid directly at his own feet. The Cardinal, expertly as always, had left him only one possible course. He took it.

'For the protection of the Church, and as a sign of our continuing love towards the ruling family of Florence, no matter how far they may have strayed in our esteem, we shall so ordain. Take care, Your Eminence, that no harm befalls the Cardinal Sansoni-Riario,' Sixtus said, 'who is as dear to us as he must be to the Count of Imola, his uncle.'

*

'And what of my word?' asked Lorenzo de' Medici coldly. He was furious, as they could all see plainly; even Bianca, who had endured his rage more frequently than her companions and had learned to survive it without harm, was somewhat paler than usual. Lorenzo's temper, however, was more than matched by that of his brother.

Giuliano released Constanza's hand and stepped forward.

'What of it?' he demanded in reply. 'Has anything been signed between the Ferrara and the Medici? I doubt it. Let the Duke find another woman to marry his son.'

'You speak like a child,' said Lorenzo. 'Doubtless he will do so; how does that assist me, or Florence?' He turned to Constanza. 'Let me hear it plainly from you, my lady. You are with child?'

'I am, my lord.'

'By Giuliano?'

'My lord,' said Constanza, 'I will allow you a certain displeasure in the news, but do not insult me. If you have made promises, so have I. No doubt you believe yours to be the more important, but do not expect me to share your opinion.'

Lorenzo put his palms on the table and pushed himself to his feet.

'Displeasure?' he said. 'Take care, my lady, that I do not visit my displeasure upon you. I do not take kindly to being thwarted.'

'Then I suggest you quarrel with me,' Giuliano said, 'since the offence was mine. It is time that you and I came to a reckoning, Lorenzo. You have my loyalty and my service, because you are best fitted to rule and I to follow. When they have plotted against you, I have taken your enemies as my own. If you have the interests of Florence at heart, so do I. But the love which I bear for the lady Constanza is not at the disposal of your contracts and seals. If that is not plain enough for you, then I know not how to make myself better understood.'

195

The two men glared at each other across the width of the table.

'Come now,' said Giuliano with less animosity, 'will you admit that half your anger is caused not by what you must tell Ferrara, but by your having been cozened by us? We have defied you, yet we took the only path that was open.'

'They are right,' said Bianca. 'They—'

'Will you be silent?' thundered Lorenzo. 'I perceive your hand in this, madam, in any case. And were I to look farther, I dare say I could lay some portion of blame with another, by which I mean Messer Leonardo da Vinci. None of which, I may say, finds favour in my sight. Well.' He rubbed his jaw.

'Not everything which happens here is Leonardo's doing,' said Bianca, correctly observing that the worst of the storm was now over.

'I commanded you to be silent.'

'I am very sorry.'

'As for the two of you,' said Lorenzo to Constanza d'Avalos and his brother, 'I would be within my rights were I to banish you from Florence. It has been done before. However, what is done is done, and Ferrara is unlikely to rejoice at having a Medici bastard wished upon him.'

'Sir, your style of speech is offensive,' Constanza said.

'Possibly. Do not assume that because my forgiveness seems likely, I have become soft. I have not.'

Constanza laughed. 'We are to be forgiven, then?'

'In time,' said Lorenzo. 'For now, give me your hands, both of you.'

'I will do better,' said Constanza. She came around the table and kissed him heartily. Giuliano extended his hand.

'Touching upon this question of bastardy,' he said, 'may we now announce our betrothal?'

'You had better.'

'And your blessing?'

'Unwillingly wrung from me, but that also,' said Lorenzo, relaxing at last into a smile. 'Easter approaches; a suitable time for rejoicing, I think. However, we had better first seek the approval of the lady Bianca, without whom it is clearly impossible to move in matters such as this. Come here, little one. It is seldom these days that I have the opportunity of being embraced by two ladies of beauty and determination at once; I had better seize it, so that I may later remind myself that my authority is not always as powerful as I fancy it to be.'

*

On Easter Sunday, the twenty-sixth of April, the city of Florence awoke to a warm and cleansing thunder-shower which left the streets and squares sparkling in the later sunshine of mid morning. Through these precincts, in bannered guild processions or as informal groups of relatives and friends, the Florentines walked in cheerful concourse; made joyful by the close of the Lenten fast, and in costumes which matched their gaiety of spirit, they greeted one another on their way to church to give thanks both for the Risen Christ and for the official commencement of spring. Children splashed in the remaining puddles, to be cuffed without rancour by their elders; soldiers swaggered beneath arcades in scarlet doublets, their harness burnished to a fine gleam for the benefit of the passing ladies; clerics bustled by in twos and threes, with robes gathered, towards whatever ecclesiastical duties awaited them.

There were those, however, who saw this Sunday with different eyes. For them, it was to be a day of fulfilment, the climax of a plot so foul in its impiety that one of the original parties to it—the disaffected mercenary Gian Batista da Montesecco—had found it too strong for his stomach and had withdrawn. He was not known to be squeamish; its aim, which was the dual assassination of both Lorenzo and Giuliano de' Medici, troubled him not at all. What he recoiled from were its intended time and place of execution.

Others were not so delicate. Paolo, Francesco and Ippolito Pazzi, together with their father and the killer Bernardo Bandini —who now sought vengeance for his brother's death in the Apennines—found nothing objectionable in staining the marble of the cathedral itself with Medici blood. Nor did Archbishop Salviati, still smarting from the continued denial to him of the See of Pisa. Indeed, so thorough was his approval that he had at once found replacements for Montesecco in the persons of two priests from his own *entourage*, Stefano di Bagnone and Antonio Maffei di Volterra; grimly humorous, he had already pointed out that should the Medici die in church, their souls would be so much closer to heaven.

Young Cardinal Rafaello Sansoni-Riario, innocent of all part in this scheme of cowardice and sacrilege, rode to the Cathedral of Santa Maria del Fiori on a white palfrey. He had been told by prelates older and wiser than himself that Florence held little love for the Church he represented, and had begun his ride from the Villa dei Pazzi in a fit of nerves. He was surprised to find himself welcomed on every hand. His downcast eyes were seen by the Florentines as evidence of a pleasing humility, and they were far from vindictive. Confronted with a Legate-Extraordinary who, far from showing the conceit common to princes of Rome, seemed on the contrary to have nothing whatever to say upon any subject, the nobility had taken him to their hearts, and the townspeople followed suit. He had, moreover, been given a rose by the lady Constanza d'Avalos at the steps of the Medici Palace, a gesture which left him scarlet with embarrassment. Not knowing what to do with this offering, he bore it through the streets in one hand, the reins of his pony in the other, and the picture of simplicity he thus presented won him smiles wherever he went.

He was greeted at the cathedral by Lorenzo, whose groom led his mount away, and by Giuliano, who asked the blessing of His Eminence upon the forthcoming union between the lady Constanza and himself. Archbishop Salviati watched this amiable scene with satisfaction, observing that the practical purpose of the young Cardinal's visit had been served no less than the symbolic; both Medici brothers were attending Mass in recognition of his presence.

Some half an hour later, towards the end of the first portion of the service, the Archbishop was seen to rise, genuflect, and leave the cathedral. His departure caused a brief stir of whispered comment. Those nearest to him drew the conclusion, from the pallor of his face, that he had been taken ill.

That they were wrong became plain almost immediately.

For the signal to proceed with their violent plan, the conspirators had chosen one of the most solemn moments of the Mass; the elevation of the Host before the eyes of the faithful. Tactically, if in no other sense, their timing was admirable. As the officiating priest raised his hands with their sacred burden, he held the attention of every person present. From high above him sounded the single chime of a bell.

At once Francesco Pazzi and Bernardo Bandini, thrusting aside those who stood between their victim and themselves, attacked Giuliano de' Medici. With daggers produced in haste from beneath their cloaks, they stabbed him repeatedly and viciously; so viciously indeed that Francesco, aiming his fourth downward stroke at the reeling man in an insensate ecstasy of rage, missed him and drove his blade deeply into his own thigh.

In the same instant the two priests from Archbishop Salviati's train hurled themselves at Lorenzo. Their assault was hurried, nervous, and pathetic. Stefano di Bagnone, jostled by his accomplice, achieved an ill-aimed stab-wound in the muscles of Lorenzo's neck before the latter, who had turned his head in the other direction at the sound of Francesco Pazzi's first shout of passion, realized the full import of what was occurring. The nearest of Lorenzo's friends, the poet Angelo Poliziano, pulled him backwards and sprang between him and his assailants, warding off their blades with a cloaked arm and drawing his rapier. At once the priests dropped their weapons and fled, amid the cries of the now alarmed congregation.

Of these, only those closest to the short-lived drama had more than an inkling of its actual nature. Panic spread among the rest, borne like an infection upon the rising clamour. Many of the worshippers towards the back of the crowd became seized by the notion that the great cupola of Brunelleschi's Duomo itself was about to fall in upon them, and within moments the nave was a maelstrom of surging and fear-stricken humanity.

With blood gushing from his neck, Lorenzo was being hustled by his supporters towards the sacristy. He fought with them like a tiger, trying desperately to reach his younger brother; but Giuliano de' Medici, his body torn by a dozen wounds and more, had dragged himself some fifty paces away and already lay sprawled and lifeless at the end of a hideous trail of red. Beyond him, at the foot of the altar steps, could be seen the figure of Cardinal Sansoni-Riario. He had stumbled in the course of an appalled flight for sanctuary and, with his gorgeous robes twisted about his knees, was now huddled and sobbing in terrified outrage.

Thus, in the space of time between one breath and the next, were altered irretrievably both the course of the war between Florence and Rome, and the fortunes of those who were caught up in it.

For the Pazzi family and their associates the alteration was immediately disastrous, since their conspiracy was as inept politically as it was vile.

Archbishop Salviati, at the head of two hundred armed men, was sweeping towards the Palazzo della Signoria, the city's council-chamber, as the confused exodus from the cathedral began. Buoyed by an optimism the source of which was known only to himself and God, his intention was to take Florence's centre of power without further ado.

In this ill-considered task he failed. The Signoria's defenders, under the leadership of the Gonfaloniere della Giustizia, beat his attacking force back with rocks cast from the windows and with swords deployed upon the stairways. Within minutes they found themselves surrounded by swarming and enraged Florentines, into whose heads the news of their favourite's assassination had now penetrated. Before his rebellion was fairly under way the Archbishop was hanging, partially dismembered and writhing, from a window of the very building he had hoped to capture and occupy; and by the time he was joined in his death agony by Francesco Pazzi, similarly mutilated, nothing remained of their *coup d'état* save for the screams of their followers as these succumbed to the vengeance of the mob.

Jacopo Pazzi, together with his sons Paolo and Ippolito, fared no better. Alerted by the single chime which had announced the death of Giuliano, they rode from their mansion at the head of a demi-squadron of horse, raising a shout for liberty from the Medici yoke. They misjudged badly, as Archbishop Salviati had done, the temper of Florence, and they paid dearly for doing so. They were met, in the Piazza San Giovanni, by the spectacle of Archbishop Salviati's men in attempted flight from a crowd which outnumbered them by ten to one and had no thought at all of seeking liberty from a ruling family which, far from being tyrannous, was universally held to be just, competent and benign.

Barely half of their cavalry escaped to the countryside, the rest being pulled from their saddles and slain on the spot. Paolo and Ippolito Pazzi rode for Castelmonte and safety with the Count Giovio della Rovere. Their father was captured during the afternoon; he was dragged back to the city, tortured, and—at the close of a smoking and bloodthirsty evening—executed. Days later, his mouldering body was dug from its rough grave by

Florentine urchins and pulled through the streets at the end of a rope before being thrown into the Arno.

*

Constanza d'Avalos stood, motionless, as she had been standing for five hours. Giuliano's body, covered in a cloth of purple and gold, rested upon a table strewn with spring flowers between her still figure and the altar of the Medici chapel. Fra Sigismondo had come, and gone.

'My lady,' said Lorenzo de' Medici, 'I do not pretend that we are close, nor that we have been brought closer by this terrible thing. Let others feign such sentiments; we cannot serve each other thus. I offer you what is mine to offer: revenge.'

He was behind her, nursing his shoulder. She did not turn.

'I care nothing for your revenge, my lord,' she said.

'I did not suppose that you would,' Lorenzo said. 'Not now. You are as you are, and I am likewise myself; a harsh man, as befits my calling in this world. Think upon it, none the less. You may come to desire it, as I do.'

He left her, and mounted the stairway to his suite. Exhausted both from his wound and from a fury which he could control only by the exercise of an iron will, he called his secretary to him as soon as his doctors had left the room. The message he dictated was brief and to the point, and a travel-stained messenger brought him his reply towards nightfall on the following day. '*Set your siege,*' Leonardo da Vinci had written. '*I follow your courier within the hour. Both justice and warfare now demand the fall of Castelmonte; I promise you that the taking of it shall be swift.*'

CHAPTER SEVENTEEN

. . . Powers are converging, and will soon meet. To the twin forces of gunpowder and human anger has now been added that further force of which I have written: the force of the mind. Therefore the first arrow loosed in the gardens of the Medici bore in its flight the seed of Castelmonte's doom, for its shaft was the shaft of thought.

From the Notebooks of Leonardo da Vinci

From the city's easternmost turret the view across the valley was clear, and menacing.

Federigo da Montefeltro, Duke of Urbino and commander of Castelmonte's defenders under Rome's Captain-General, stood with the Captain of his wall, Guido Falcone di Riccomano, and surveyed the panorama spread out before them. Except that the golden light of last autumn was now replaced by the fresh sunshine of an early spring, the scene was a familiar one. On the summit of the ridge immediately opposite them, the two great Florentine siege-cannon stood again in their positions of the previous year, having appeared there overnight; men were gathered about them, hauling them into final alignment. Again the tents of Toscanelli's infantry had sprung up along the lower slopes of the ridge, while upon their right flank the picket lines of the Medici cavalry stretched away into the middle distance.

Montefeltro turned his gaze skyward, eyeing the clouds that drifted in convoy overhead.

'What is your assessment?' he asked.

Guido Falcone considered his words before replying. He was a tall, squarely built man whose aquiline nose befitted his name. Like his superior, he was a professional soldier, born of a line of distinguished mercenaries; his mother had been Swiss, and her ancestry was displayed in his skin and his fair hair, now thinning at the temples. When summer came, his face would redden and peel.

'Firstly,' he said, 'Roderigo Leone is not with them.'

'I agree,' Montefeltro said. 'But let me hear your reasoning.'

'Their guns are resting on grass,' said Falcone. 'That is their primary error. Captain Leone would have spent several days in laying a foundation of rock and timber; the ground is still far too soft for them to hold any degree of accuracy. I will grant them twenty shots, at the most, before they are forced to move. What puzzles me further is that their point of aim appears to be exactly the same as it was last year, and they can hardly fail to be aware that we have strengthened our wall. It is a hasty piece of work, however you look at it. Therefore, it is not Captain Leone's.'

'Then he is still in the mountains,' said Montefeltro, 'perfecting this new weapon of which we have heard so many rumours.'

'I dare say.' Captain Falcone pursed his lips, and expelled air from between them explosively. 'It will be a bombard,' he announced. 'You may depend upon it. They mean to throw their missiles high, thus clearing our wall and damaging our inner defences. I know these so-called engineers; Martini thought always of mortars and the lobbing of rocks over the perimeter walls of his opponents. A pointless exercise. At Rapallo he tried to use missiles that were stuffed with powder and burst at the end of their flight, though it seems to me that he killed more of his own gunners than of the enemy in doing so.' He tapped the side of his head. 'They are always too clever, and this da Vinci will be no different.'

Montefeltro smiled. 'Your opinion of military engineers, then, is on the whole a poor one?' he said.

'Sir,' replied Falcone, 'when I hear that my opponent has an engineer in his employment, I rejoice at the news. Why? Because I know, of a certainty, that he will spend months in the building of escarpments, counter-escarpments, redoubts, towers, tunnels, bridges and similar pieces of foolery. When he finally makes his assault—which is to say, when his engineer and his military commander have all but come to blows with one another—his men are worn out from shifting earth and stones and are easy meat for the defence. Your engineer, sir, is well enough employed while he sits with quill and paper; in warfare he perceives a God-given opportunity for inflicting his fantasies upon others, to the detriment of their purses and their backs. You have spoken with the Count of Imola. When does he say that Rome will march this way?'

'Next week.'

'Then, sir, I care not what our friends opposite are doing, nor what new weapons they bring. If Rome's army marches next week, it must be here within ten days from now; and if our wall cannot withstand Florence until then, we may as well jump from the top of it here and now.'

*

'Set your siege,' said Leonardo.

'So you advised in your message. I have already done so. Where are my gunners?'

'They are on their way.'

'On their way? Why are they not here with you?'

'Because they are marching directly to Castelmonte. They will reach it tomorrow night.'

'I see. Very well.'

Lorenzo de' Medici, his neck bandaged, sat behind the small table in his private and cell-like conference chamber overlooking the *palazzo* gardens. His wound would have kept a lesser man confined to bed, but the ruler of Florence, driven by a rage for vengeance, would no more have received his adviser there than he would have considered appearing publicly in his nightshirt. He was dressed for campaigning in soft leather tunic, breeches, and boots. He could turn his head only with difficulty, and his face was sallow. Leonardo studied him.

'Sir,' he said, 'your neck is poorly bound. May I suggest—'

'I did not summon you to act the physician,' put in Lorenzo.

'By no means. None the less, I see that you intend to ride your horse,' said Leonardo. 'Is this so?'

'Very likely it is. What of it?'

'Then, sir, your head must be braced so that it will not easily move, or you will tear open your wound anew. I can design a support of armature-wire that will achieve this for you, if you will allow me to do so.'

'I thank you for your solicitude, Messer Leonardo, but you distract me. Did my gunners leave the mountains at the same time as yourself?'

'Perhaps some few hours later.'

'They are the same distance from Castelmonte as from Florence,' said Lorenzo. 'That being the case, why will it take them until tomorrow night to reach their destination, since you are here now?'

'Because,' Leonardo said, 'they are carrying your guns—the Medici Guns—with them. They will have requisitioned wagons, but even so their progress must be slower than my own.'

'A moment,' said Lorenzo, raising his hand. 'Let me understand you aright. These guns you speak of are the same six that you took with you to the valley?'

'They are.'

Lorenzo, his eyes hard, pushed his chair fractionally backwards.

'I would not care to suppose you were jesting with me,' he said. 'I have read your original specifications. These cannon weigh, as I recall, some two hundred and eighty pounds each?'

'That is correct,' said Leonardo calmly.

'And were designed only for purposes of experiment and practice? We seem to be at odds here, Messer Leonardo.'

'They were designed for practice,' Leonardo replied, 'but hardly for that alone. Our practice is done, and we shall now wage war with them. Did you suppose differently?'

'*With small cannon?*'

'Even so.'

'I cannot believe you. I had supposed, indeed, that by your science and with the help of the knowledge you had gained from your trials with them, you would be able to use my big siege-guns to better effect. Do you tell me I was wrong in this? In God's name, what nonsense have we here? What damage can a four-pound ball inflict upon such a wall as Castelmonte's?'

'Sir,' said Leonardo, 'I pray you, for the sake of your own ease of mind, suspend your disbelief. With the coming of these small cannon, as you term them, your great guns are surpassed; and the nature of warfare from this day onward is changed entirely for all the centuries to come.'

Lorenzo de' Medici laughed shortly. 'I care nothing for the centuries to come,' he said, 'and therefore let us have this straightly. Will they give me justice, for Giuliano and for Carla d'Avalos? Will they give me Castelmonte, that foul city?'

'They will. And when they do so, shall it be—as we agreed—the full and final discharge of our bargain together?'

'*If* they do so. In how long?'

'In one day from the time of their arrival there.'

Lorenzo laughed again, mirthlessly. 'I agree to your terms,' he said. 'Also, I will watch your guns—and you.'

'In that case,' said Leonardo, 'you had better permit me to construct you a neck-brace, and save yourself discomfort.'

*

During the afternoon of the following day, the two heavy guns on the ridge bellowed their first challenge to the citadel across the river. It was a loud challenge, but—in the absence of Florence's Captain-Gunner—ineffective.

Lorenzo de' Medici and Leonardo, on horseback, examined the terrain from a smaller ridge, opposite the postern-gate and a quarter of a mile upriver from the point where the road crossed and led to the main portal of the city. In the shallow basin beneath them, Guido Toscanelli was attending to his supply-lines. Barely a tenth of his mercenary force was present, as yet, together with some two hundred Florentines; there was, after all, little need for urgency, since several weeks of bombardment must follow before any large force of field-troops would be needed for an assault. He had invested Castelmonte, and could hold his siege with what men he already had. More to the point, his main force was encamped twenty miles to the south, awaiting the appearance of the army of the Church of Rome.

Lorenzo, silent, was fretting, though his neck and shoulders seemed more comfortable than before. Leonardo followed his glance.

'Have no fear,' he said. 'One hundred men, at most, will be all you require.'

Lorenzo made no reply to this. Leonardo dismounted, and began to unfasten from his saddle-roll a curious contrivance of wooden poles, hinged in three parts. Allowing his horse to graze quietly, he set up his rangefinder and lay on the ground behind each arm in turn, adjusting these with great care. Then he sat up, opened his notebook, and began to write figures in it.

His calculations showed that the distance from where he sat to the postern-gate was three hundred and sixty paces.

He turned over the top two sheets of the notebook, consulting some previous drawings and comparing them with what he could see now. Beyond the gate lay the defile, he knew; beyond this again, the vineyard where Toscanelli's assault-force had perished last autumn, and then the inner gate which gave onto the alley-ways of the city itself.

This inner gate, he noted, was invisible from the ridge they now occupied, since it lay in dead ground behind the outer wall. While this added to his difficulties, he had made allowance for the fact in his plans and was undismayed by the problem it presented.

'I wish to dismount,' said Lorenzo. 'Assist me, if you please.'

Leonardo rose to his feet and, forming a step with his interlaced fingers, enabled his patron to descend painfully from his saddle.

'I thank you,' said Lorenzo. 'And now show me your purpose.'

Leonardo held out the notebook for his inspection, pointing away to the left.

'Yonder stands the main gate,' he said. 'We cannot see it from here, since it faces north-west and is beyond the angle of the wall. For the same reason your siege-guns cannot bombard it, nor is there any position from which they could succeed in doing so. We knew this, of course, last year.'

'Well?'

'Inside that gate,' Leonardo went on, 'there is a small open space, and then a covered lane which leads to the square.' He added a rapid sketch. 'This lane is angled at its centre, so as to provide neither a clear line of fire between the gate itself and the square nor a straight path for skirmishers. This is a common and sensible arrangement, as you are aware. Behind the square the streets climb steeply, thus, to the top of the hill; at the summit stand the inner keep, the *palazzo*, and then the building which you can see beside them, which is the monastery of San Piero Maggiore. All of these we can ignore, together with the hill-top and its immediate surroundings, if the main gates be opened and we succeed in taking the square.'

'I will agree,' said Lorenzo.

'Very well,' said Leonardo. 'Our scheme is a simple one, and ancient in conception. We propose to take the postern, make our way to the square, and hold it; then we shall open the main gates from inside, and admit your attacking force.'

'Excellent thinking,' said Lorenzo ironically, 'but a possibility foreseen by those who built Castelmonte. You cannot take the postern. You know what lies beyond it, and its name?'

'Of course. Its supposed invulnerability forms part of our plan.'

'And how will you take it?'

'With the Medici Guns.'

'I will concede that you may, after some time, be able to breach the outer postern,' said Lorenzo. 'What then?'

'We shall then take the vineyard, and the inner gate.'

'You propose to take your cannon *inside* the citadel?'

'Yes. Did I not tell you yesterday that the nature of warfare was about to be changed for ever? Guns, sir, are no longer immobile and unwieldy. Therein lies my entire strategy.'

Lorenzo scratched irritably at the bandage where it emerged from the collar of his tunic.

'I do not know with what speed you can carry your guns,' he said, 'and I must, perforce, believe that you are no fool. However, your gunners will be cut to pieces in the vineyard.'

'With respect, sir, nothing of the kind will occur.'

Behind them and to their left, one of the two great siege-guns roared again. Lorenzo half-turned, and swore.

'A diversion,' said Leonardo. 'Let us by all means continue with the obvious, if only to keep the minds of Federigo da Montefeltro and the Count of Imola occupied. I presume that Rome's Captain-General is within the city?'

'He is. He has been there since before my brother's murder, in which I know his to have been the guiding hand. Were I forced to choose between Girolamo Riario and the Pazzi, I would take him.' Lorenzo raised his fingers to his shoulder again. 'God grant that I may be given him,' he said softly. 'God grant it so.'

CHAPTER EIGHTEEN

By the third hour past midnight, Lorenzo's impatience was ill-concealed. Earlier, a foot-soldier had brought two plates of fish from the camp below; Lorenzo had declined the meal, and Leonardo da Vinci had eaten both. Hour by hour twilight had faded into darkness, and now a quarter-moon illuminated the river and the city, from which little sign of life had been seen since early evening when the trumpet had sounded and the guards posted in each turret had changed duty. Through the long night Lorenzo's eyes strayed, ever and again, towards the tethered lines of dozing horses at their right; Leonardo knew that he was thinking of Giuliano, who should have been moving among the pickets exchanging greetings with knight and farrier, and would do so no more. If he wished to offer comfort, the artist also knew that he had none to give that would turn the scales by a hair against the service he was about to render his commander-in-chief, and therefore kept silent. Only the wind in the grass, the clink of the bits in the horses' mouths, and the occasional call of one man to another in the valley broke the night's stillness, until a sudden axle-creak on the track that climbed behind them to the ridge-top caused both men to stare, alerted, into the blackness.

The gunners, led by Rigo Leone, were barely thirty paces away when they became visible; fifty men, in dark clothes and with their faces smeared with mud, and beyond them two open carts. The Captain-Gunner saluted Lorenzo, who lifted a hand in acknowledgment, and then turned to Leonardo.

'We rested at Pistrola,' he said.

'Good. I trust that you left your wagons hidden outside the village,' Leonardo replied.

'We did. Nor were we dressed as you see us now. We gave out that we were but returning to our duties on the ridge over there, though few troubled to ask us. Why should they?'

'Why indeed?' replied Leonardo. 'Well, I see no reason for delay, if you are ready. Whose guns remain here?'

'Those of Marco di Carona and Giunta di Lenzo,' said Rigo.

'And Balestraccio has broken a bone in his foot. He has changed places with Piccio Berignalli of Marco's team, since he can still load for you. Otherwise, we are in good order.'

'Then let us commence,' said Leornado.

Rigo spoke into the night. 'Move,' he said. 'One.'

There was an instant stir about the wagons. Sacks were thrown aside, revealing the dull barrels of the Medici Guns.

'Two,' said Rigo.

Wheels and carriages were grasped and lifted to the ground.

'Three.'

Men seized sponge-staves, powder-kegs, shot.

'Four,' Rigo said. 'Five.'

The cannon slid towards the wagon-sides, tilted, and were lowered. The carriage-bearers were already in position, six paces between each team.

'Six. Seven. Eight.'

The teams stood partially ready. Two of them were assembling their weapons, fitting the barrels to the wheels and carriages; pins dropped into place, range screws were swung forward.

'Nine.' Rigo said.

Forty of the men rested easily, their drill complete. The remaining ten had unhitched the horses from one of the wagons, and were pushing it steadily towards the ridge-top. They positioned it on the right flank of their formation, and rejoined their comrades.

'Well,' Rigo said, 'I suppose it will serve.' He grinned at Leonardo. 'Marco and Giunta have already loaded, so that in fact we are somewhat slower than I would like. What is your first range?'

'Three hundred and sixty.'

'Then they are yours. I retain command of the assault crews. Is it acknowledged?'

'By all means.'

Lorenzo de' Medici cleared his throat.

'I congratulate you,' he said, 'upon your demonstration. Your men are well trained indeed, and it does all of you credit. And now, if you will help me to horse, I shall go and take some sleep before the morrow. Good night.'

Leonardo detained him gently.

'Sir,' he said, 'it appears that we misunderstand each other yet again. This is no mere demonstration of skill with which to seek your approval. Spring is somewhat advanced, and dawn comes early these days. We take the city before it does so.'

Lorenzo turned, moving his head and shoulders carefully.

'You intend gunnery at night?' he asked. His voice contained less surprise than it had done of late. 'Perhaps you will be shooting at the moon, since it is the only target to be seen?'

'We shall have our target shortly,' said Leonardo. 'It is true that you cannot make out the postern-gate from where we stand, but that is a small matter. We can strike it.'

'Can you? And how will you know whether you have succeeded in doing so or not?'

'We do not need to see where our shots strike,' replied Leonardo, 'and were we now in the darkest pit of Hades, your gunners could still fight. All we await are your instructions to proceed.'

Lorenzo de' Medici looked from side to side, striving to pick out men and weapons he could barely perceive; only their outlines, and a faint shine of moonlight upon scoured metal, told him of their presence. Abruptly, he slapped his glove against his thigh.

'Give me my city,' he said. 'And God go with you all.'

Leonardo walked over to where the two assembled guns stood, their crews at the ready. He knelt behind each in turn, and set the range-screws to three hundred and sixty paces. Rigo strode in the opposite direction, joining the four teams that were to make the assault. They carried the parts and accessories of their weapons, eight men to a crew, as they had been trained to do. When he saw Leonardo stand up once more, silhouetted against the starlight, the Captain-Gunner signalled to the two men who belonged to no team, and who now stepped forward. Each of them carried, in a waterproof pouch, flint, steel, and a length of slow-match. A knowledgeable observer would have called these slow-matches peculiar, since each was fully two inches thick and made from heavy rope soaked in a solution of nitre.

'Go,' said Rigo. He slapped them on the back in farewell, and they set off down the face of the ridge towards the river. Within ten paces they had melted into the darkness and disappeared.

'And what now?' asked Lorenzo.

'Our target team is fording the river,' said Leonardo. 'Can you not see them there, against the moon's reflection?'

'I believe I can. What is their function?'

'To provide a target, as their title implies.'

'You intend to shoot at them?'

'If they do not stand aside quickly enough when their task is done,' rejoined Leonardo, 'we shall do exactly that. Fortunately, they are aware that such is the case, so that I have no great fears for their safety.'

*

Across the stream the two advance-gunners, unseen and soaking wet, pressed themselves close beneath the arch of the postern-gate. The overhang hid them from the guardhouse above.

Both unwrapped their small burdens, finding them dry. One man nodded, therefore, and struck flint against steel, while the other pulled from his belt a fine metal spike, testing its sharpness with his thumb. A spark caught amid the loose strands at the end of one of the matches, and was quickly blown to a spitting redness, soon turning the entire width of the rope into a brightly glowing ember. Its bearer centred himself carefully in the doorway and positioned it against the planks; his fellow drove the spike through the strands of cord, working the point well into the grain of the wood with repeated twists of his fingers. They would have liked to make sure of it by giving it a few blows with some improvised hammer, but they dared not do so; even the struck flint had sounded, to their nervous ears, like the clash of cymbals.

When he was satisfied that the spike would hold, the gunner who had driven it tapped his companion's arm and stepped with him from beneath the doorway. One upon either side, they slid around the side-columns of the arch, hunched themselves into what protection they could find, and looked back across the river. They could see nothing against the blackness of the ridge.

In silence, they awaited the shattering of the night.

Leonardo saw the glowing head of the fuse as it was fairly alight, but said nothing; it vanished almost at once, screened from him by the body of the man who held it. A minute later it reappeared, pinned in the centre of the invisible archway as though hanging, disembodied, in the void. To right and left of him Marco di Carona and Giunta di Lenzo were already swinging their guns to the point of aim, and once again he knelt briefly behind each barrel in turn, seating the tiny and distant spot of fire exactly in the muzzle-notches.

'Ready,' he told them. 'Rigo?'

The Captain-Gunner, standing with two assault teams at either side of him, raised his left arm. In his right hand he held, as several of his companions did, the weapon of his choice for fighting at close quarters; Rigo favoured for this purpose a six-foot length of stout chain, the bulk of which was wrapped around his forearm. He looked towards the wagon at his extreme right. One man—the powder-carrier—from each crew had left his fellows in order to push this vehicle, whose flat bed accordingly bore, for the moment, the powder-bags, sponge-staves, and shot.

'Go,' said Rigo.

The wagon, propelled by strong arms at each wheel, began to roll down the slope. It gathered speed, and was followed by the charging assault-teams; seconds later, its hurtling splash into the river announced the making of an improvised bridge for their crossing. The powder-men hastily unlashed their burdens, and were clear of the boards as Agnolo Fulvio reached its nearer end, carrying a pair of wheels and with boots pounding. No shout had as yet broken the stillness, and the wash of the cart's entry into the water could be heard plainly from the top of the ridge.

Rigo crossed himself, lifted a hand again at Leonardo in unseen salute, and ran downhill after his men.

'Fire,' said Leonardo.

*

Agnolo Fulvio reached the postern-gate some five paces in front of his fellows. The grass of the bank was trampled, and his foot slid on a loosened piece of turf. He stretched down a hand to preserve his balance, and it seemed to him that in the instant of lowering his head, the door in front of him exploded into fragments. The twin cannon-cracks from beyond the river and behind him rang as one; he imagined that he had seen the flash of the balls, passing within inches of his head, but was uncertain. Half of the postern-door, torn from its hinges, fell slantwise across the mouth of the arch, and a rebounding timber struck him heavily on the shoulder. He regained his footing, took another two steps, and kicked the obstructing door-section inwards to clear his path as the four men who carried the barrel of his gun arrived at his back, their breath rasping in their throats. His powder-man clapped him on the arm to signal his presence, and Agnolo threw himself forward into the hollow blackness of the tunnel's mouth.

*

Cipriano di Ser Giacomo Giachetti di Lucca, the last man to cross the wagon-bridge save for Rigo himself, threw the wheels of the gun he commanded onto the bank and followed them, stepping delicately and without apparent hurry. He was held by his companions to be a dandy, which meant that he washed himself twice daily; they also called him a cold-blooded fish. They had called him other things in the past, since his family were haberdashers and inclined to give themselves airs; he had once been handsome, but now displayed a broken nose in witness of the battles he had fought for acceptance.

His present task, a dangerous one, allowed him several seconds of grace as compared with the other three assault-crews, and he took advantage of these by refraining from working himself into a sweat. Rigo overtook him, two steps from the shore, in a flying leap whose momentum carried the Captain-Gunner a quarter of the way up the bank; Cipriano climbed after him, reaching the small flat area outside the postern in good order and scarcely out of breath.

Three of the crews had vanished into the mouth of the defile beyond the shattered door. Cipriano's two carriage-bearers raised their load, and he fitted the wheels to it, pegging them securely in place with the metal spikes he also carried. The four men who held the barrel lowered it into position, its trunnions slotting into the tops of the carriage-wings, and Cipriano swung forward the range-screw and block. The gun was already charged with powder and his loader now tipped a double handful of small-shot into the muzzle, following this with a patch and then ramming the handle of the sponge-stave home to seat the olive-sized missiles in the breech.

The screw was set at point-blank range, the duty of Cipriano's crew being to cover the defile beneath the guardhouse from outside.

Since, in order to do this, they were forced to remain unprotected below the guardhouse windows, and hence were sitting targets for both the defenders immediately above them and those

214

who might man the wall-top at either side, Cipriano's icy calm was a necessary ingredient in their task. His crew watched him as he took the match from his loader; his face, briefly lit by its glow, was impassive, and he made a small and nonchalant sucking noise with his lips and teeth. Around and above them, a confused uproar was beginning to swell. Cipriano di Ser Giacomo Giachetti di Lucca paid it not the slightest attention as he blew, gently and without haste, on the end of his match.

Three hundred and sixty yards away, on top of the ridge, Leonardo saw his fiery target disappear, blown inwards with the shards of the postern-door, and grunted with satisfaction. He could make out nothing else; in the deep shadow at the wall's foot, the attacking gunners were but deeper shadows still. His guns had recoiled, and he had thus no guarantee that they were aiming as before, but for the moment it mattered little. He reset the range-screws, elevating both barrels slightly so that they would now rake the face of the guardhouse, and told his crews to reload. In a short while he would need to fire another precision volley; until his target for this was presented, he would meanwhile give the outside assault-group what covering fire he could.

*

Inside the gatehouse confusion reigned.

The watch-commander, Ridolfo Peruzzi, had been alerted by the splash of the wagon as it plunged into the stream, but had from that point onward been able to make no sense of what he saw. Dark figures had crossed the river, using the wagon as a bridge. They were heavily laden, but the nature of what they carried was unclear. While he strained to see what was happening the flash and roar of cannon had come, not from the northern ridge, but from directly opposite him, to be echoed at once in the rending of what he knew—though he could hardly believe it— must be the oaken door beneath his feet.

'At night?' he exclaimed. 'In God's name, it cannot be possible!' He rallied himself. Whether he could credit his eyes and ears or not, he was under attack; so much, at least, was plain. 'You, and you,' he ordered, 'to the roof, with arbalests! Nofri, Alessandro! Find Captain Falcone; tell him we are assaulted, and have lost our gate to cannon-fire. Say also that we have dropped our portcullis.' He turned, as more of his men thrust into the room

215

from their sleeping-quarters behind it, and gestured towards the supporting ropes that slung the heavy iron grille from the roof-beams. 'Lower it!' he snapped.

Feet were clattering along the passage below him. He counted his men. With the departure of his messengers and crossbowmen, fourteen were left to him. He watched the foot of the portcullis being fitted into its slot between the floor-timbers, heard the rasp of its massive and swift descent and the crash as it met the stone surface of the tunnel.

His defences secured for the moment, he crossed again to the window of the room and leaned out. It was his last action in life. A four-pound ball, travelling six hundred and fifty feet in each second of its flight, tore a section of masonry from the wall beside his head, half-decapitating him instantly and bloodily. Chips of flying stone filled the air, and his body, hurled backwards like that of a doll, collapsed across a bench amid breaking crockery and the shafts of tumbling pikes.

Aghast, his men looked at one another. The walls shook under the impact of yet another ball from Leonardo's guns; oil dripped from a swinging lamp, and a helmet fell clangorously. From the defile below, no further sound could be heard.

'They have taken the vineyard, then,' said Guaspare di Piombino, the dead Ridolfo's second-in-command. 'Down, and counter-attack!'

'And the guns?' he was answered.

'They are not our concern,' said Guaspare. 'Our task is to hold the gate, as always. Lanterns, and follow me.'

He ran down the winding stairway that emerged into the defile. His detachment followed, stumbling out into the passage as though bewildered; which, indeed, they were. At their right, their upheld and flaring lights revealed the portcullis, and beyond it, barely perceived, the deadly circle of a cannon's mouth. Hardly one of them recognized it for what it was, in the terrible instant before Cipriano addressed them from the shadows.

'Farewell,' he said, and held match to fuse.

The gun's enclosed bellow turned the passage into a reeking and smoke-filled charnel-house. Every man in it died, mercifully, at once. As they strained their backs to raise the iron grid which barred their progress, propping it with the fallen door-bolt, and stopped to haul their cannon beneath its lower edge, even the most hardened among Cipriano's crew were thankful that there remained no light to show them what nameless things they strode through—and kicked aside—before they gained the open air of the vineyard.

*

Leonardo, informed by the muzzle-flash of Cipriano's gun that their immediate task had been completed and that they were accordingly on their way to join their fellows, tapped Giunta and Marco on the shoulder.

'Rest,' he said. 'And load with care for your next shot.'

Lorenzo spoke from behind him.

'What progress do they make?' he asked. 'I confess that I can see nothing whatever.'

'They have won the Serpent's Mouth, sir. All four cannon are now within the wall. Next they must take the inner postern at the far side of the vineyard, which we shall break for them as we did the outer. It will be a difficult shot, since even in daylight the inner gate cannot be seen from here; but I dare not rely upon Captain Leone to shatter it himself, since he must use his guns for close-fighting. It can be done from here, by calculation, once they provide me with a range-mark.'

'By calculation?'

'Sir,' Leonardo said, 'when you and I are long dead, the time will come when men shall fire guns by calculation only at targets which they never see, knowing only their position. There is nothing marvellous in it, I assure you.'

'I am becoming accustomed to marvels,' said Lorenzo. 'Meanwhile, these guns of yours . . .'

'They are yours, sir. What of them?'

'Nothing. I find myself,' Lorenzo said, 'at a loss for words.'

CHAPTER NINETEEN

Captain Guido Falcone, sitting in the small room overlooking Castelmonte's main gate which served him as command-post, was in ill-humour. As Ridolfo Peruzzi had been, he was unable for the moment to comprehend the events he had just observed; and he had been further annoyed by the hasty reports of these same events delivered by various of his subordinates, no two of which agreed in content or interpretation.

The two soldiers dispatched from the postern-gate, and now standing uneasily before him, were proving to be of no greater assistance.

'It was a gun,' Nofri said.

'Sir,' dissented Alessandro Gambacorte, 'this is not so. There was—'

'Silence!' Falcone roared at them. 'You have brought, I take it, a message from your commander?'

'Yes, sir,' said Alessandro.

'Then deliver it, and nothing else.'

'Yes, sir. Sir, we are to report that the postern is under attack, and that the outer door is broken by cannon-fire. A party has forced the tunnel, and is now in the vineyard. The portcullis has been lowered. That is all, sir.'

'Thank you,' said Captain Falcone. 'Dismiss.'

'Sir,' said Nofri again, desperately, 'I will swear that they had a cannon with them, beneath the very gatehouse itself. I looked back over the parapet as we left to report to you.'

'Dismiss,' repeated his captain.

The two soldiers saluted and went out. Reaching for his burganet, Captain Falcone could hear Alessandro remonstrating with his companion in the corridor, and smiled to himself. He left the room by another door, and crossed above the gateway to its counterpart in the right-hand turret. Here he found Federigo da Montefeltro staring from a window. The Duke turned to greet him.

'Well, Guido?' he demanded. 'Six shots, and they have now ceased fire. Seven, perhaps, though I have seen but six muzzle-flashes. What news of the postern?'

Falcone repeated the contents of the message he had received, and then hesitated.

'And?' prompted the Duke of Urbino.

'One of the men who brought me this report, sir, believes that he saw another cannon on this side of the river.'

'Unlikely,' said Montefeltro. 'In God's name, for what purpose?'

'Precisely, sir. May I offer my views?'

'Please do so.'

'Then, sir, I do not think we need cudgel our brains overmuch in order to make sense of the situation. They have fired six shots, as you say, from the ridge at our left. In addition, there has been an explosion at the postern itself. Now it is true that I have never, until now, seen artillery used at night, but it is quite certain that they can be achieving no accuracy with it. I suggest that they are harassing our parapet, more or less at random, in order to give cover to an attacking party; and that this party has destroyed our outer postern-door by means of a mine set directly against it. This accounts for the seventh detonation which you heard. It is this mining-party and their equipment which the gatehouse messenger saw. His conclusion was false, but understandable.'

Montefeltro considered this for a while. Then:

'I accept your conclusion,' he said. 'A mine seems likely. It would seem, then, that we have here an engineer who is not wasting his time.'

'I admit it,' said Falcone. 'I will go further; their assault is damnably well planned, coming well before we might reasonably have expected it.'

'And our answer?'

'Why, sir, I see no reason for proceeding beyond the ordinary. It is evident that their attacking force has penetrated as far as the vineyard, having taken the gatehouse by surprise, but the portcullis is now down. With this in place, it is obvious that three men alone could hold the passage against any further assault; and those who have already entered can be dealt with in the usual fashion. I shall send reinforcements both to the postern and to the inner gateway, and that will be the end of the matter, since they cannot escape. As for this talk of cannon having been brought across the river, it is moon-madness, and nothing more.'

*

From the inner mouth of the defile, a fairly steep and uneven path led across the vineyard and upwards, to end at the inner gateway at its farther side. To right and left of this path, the gun-crews of Agnolo Fulvio and Scudo had deployed, and their weapons were now assembled and ready to fire. Cipriano di Ser Giacomo Giachetti had emerged from the tunnel to join his fellow, Guccio Berotti, who was in command of the third assault-group. Guccio's cannon was already charged with small-shot, and Cipriano's loader was sponging out his barrel before doing likewise.

None of them had been troubled overmuch by the arbalestiers who had gathered on the gatehouse roof and the top of the wall to either side of it. The moon had disappeared behind a cloud, and the vineyard was therefore a black arena against which neither the clothing nor the faces of the gunners were visible. Their movements could be heard, to be sure, and a single stray bolt had whanged metallically off the barrel of Scudo's gun, cutting open his cheek; but since they were not even on the path, whose position could be guessed, the crossbowmen behind them could loose only haphazardly, and did so with poor success.

As soon, therefore, as Cipriano's crew had reloaded, both his gun and Guccio's moved forward and up the path. The creaking of their boots provoked a brief rain of crossbow-bolts, none of which took effect. Passing between the teams of Scudo and Agnolo Fulvio, they took station at the sides of the track and about twenty paces from the inner gatehouse, turning their muzzles slightly inward so as to cover the gate itself.

The two men who had formed the advance target-party for Leonardo's guns on the ridge now prepared to repeat their task, with a slight difference. They approached the wall to the right of the inner postern with lines and grapnels, and were followed by the loader from Guccio's crew, who carried a sponge-stave with its tip soaked in oil. With them, also, came one man from each of the rearmost guns. They were to give the target-bearers what support they could during the vital minutes it would take them to perform their dangerous function.

220

A murmur was now arising from within the turret above the gateway. The six guards inside it, whose look-out duties were as a rule negligible, were peering cautiously from their embrasures and conversing with each other in low tones, trying to make some assessment of their position.

Their first instinct, upon hearing the tumult at the outer postern, had been to emerge from their post in a body. In this they had been restrained by their leader, whose orders were plain. The gateway itself was to be held in case of assault, since behind it lay the streets and alleys of the city itself; and the fact that within living memory no enemy had survived the vineyard to attack it made—in his view—no difference whatever. The destruction of the outer postern had told them nothing useful, save that the vineyard was probably occupied by the foe. Therefore, they must remain where they were until instructed to the contrary and, more particularly, until reinforcements arrived.

They did not hear the soft clink of the grapnels at their flank, and by the time they became fully aware of Rigo's target-bearers and their supporters, events had overtaken them. Thankful that some positive line of action had at last presented itself, they now rushed from the gatehouse onto the parapet, armed with swords and halberds. The clouds had drifted clear of the narrow moon, but two men, unseen, were already on the roof above their heads. The remaining three were crouched—for what reason, the defenders could not fathom—behind the low curtain-wall that faced the vineyard.

Reason enough burst upon them at once, though only one of them survived the moment of knowledge.

One of the crouched men shouted. From half way across the vineyard below, Agnolo and Scudo swept the parapet with a murderous hail of small-shot, killing five of the guards instantly. The sixth, who was partially screened by the breastwork, staggered to the open rear of the wall and fell, screaming, twelve feet into the alley at its foot, one ball in his shoulder and another lodged by his ribs.

The attackers rose. Two of them kicked open the door to the gatehouse, but found it empty. The third man, jumping nimbly to the top of the curtain-wall, passed the oil-soaked sponge on its eight-foot stave to the pair on the roof. Taking flint and steel in hand again, one of the latter ignited a pinch of tinder, blew it into flame, and held it to the sponge, which flared into a brightly blazing torch. The second target-bearer stationed himself in the centre of the roof, took the flaming stave from his fellow, and held it at arm's length above his head.

'There is my second target,' said Leonardo.

He was already lying prone behind one swivelling arm of the range-finder, which lay, as before, upon the grass some little way from the guns. As the distant torch rose into view above the top of the outer wall, wavered, and then steadied, he took his sight on it and then rolled swiftly to the other end of his device to set the second arm.

'A light,' he called, and sat up. After reading the marks at the base of either arm and working his brief calculations beneath a lantern held by Giunta di Lenzo: 'A little more than five hundred paces,' he announced. 'Set your guns, therefore, to four hundred and ten paces.'

Giunta moved away.

'I understand—if but dimly—the nature of your contrivance,' said Lorenzo de' Medici. 'But why four hundred and ten paces, rather than the true distance?'

'That is easily answered,' Leonardo said. 'My sight was taken upon the flame of yonder torch, but it is not the torch I wish to strike. Since I could not see the inner postern-gate itself, I asked one of your gunners to stand on the roof above it and hold a burning sponge as high as he could reach. He is doing so now, as you see. But the centre of the door must lie some five *braccia* beneath his feet, and hence ten *braccia* below the flame. Do you see?'

'Yes.'

'Very well. My experiments have taught me that towards the end of its flight, a ball from one of these cannon will fall in height by one *braccia* in every nine paces. Accordingly, in order to strike ten *braccia* beneath the flame, I must shorten my range by ninety paces, which gives me four hundred and ten.'

'And you believe this firmly in your science?' asked Lorenzo.

'Sir,' replied Leonardo, getting to his feet, 'science will stand of its own accord, whether I offer it the prop of my belief or no; and what was a fact yesterday will remain a fact today.'

'Ready,' said Giunta.

'And now forgive me,' Leonardo said. 'I must not keep my

torch-bearer standing thus exposed any longer than is necessary.' He walked past Lorenzo to the guns.

*

'Sir,' said Guccio Berotti to Rigo, who was standing by him, 'why do I not take out this door myself? At ten paces it is a simple matter, even with small-shot.'

Rigo ignored him. 'Agnolo,' he called. 'Scudo?'

From the middle of the vineyard behind him his gunners, who had now reloaded, apprised him of this. At the far side of the inner gateway, hammering footsteps and the clash of carried weapons told of the arrival of a party of reinforcements from the city.

'How many?' Rigo asked his men on the parapet.

'Twenty,' replied a voice from the night above. 'Perhaps more.'

Rigo turned back to Guccio.

'There is your answer,' he said shortly. 'Hold your tongue, then, in patience.'

*

Before his eyes the torch-flame, blown by the softest of nightwinds, danced in the muzzle-notch of the cannon. Leonardo patted its breech and rose, releasing the pent-up breath from his lungs.

'Fire,' he said.

Tesoro di Veluti, his hand on a wheel-rim of Cipriano's gun, was looking over his shoulder and saw the glinting arc of the shot in their flight overhead. 'One,' he counted, as the sound of the volley reached his ears. 'Two.'

The door burst asunder, one leaf of it ripped from its supporting post, the other slamming backwards into the archway and re-bounding from the wall. Unseen voices yelled their dismay.

'Fire,' said Rigo.

From either side of him the guns of Cipriano and Guccio belched forth torrential death. Scudo and Agnolo gained the head of the vineyard path, their cannon loaded but disassembled; they were running awkwardly, since each of their teams was still a man short. Rigo addressed the other two crews.

'Leave your guns,' he said, 'and fight.' He charged the now-broken entrance to the city, unwrapping the chain from his fore-arm.

Not all of the reinforcement party had been killed or crippled

223

by the cannon's blast, though the archway echoed with the shrieks of those who, entering it with the intention of holding the doors, had been thrown back by their inward disintegration and then immediately decimated by ten pounds of scattered and hurtling death from thirty feet away. The gunners who had just fired their broadside fell on the remainder, who were milling about the small *piazza* behind the gateway in disarray, stunned by the sudden descent upon them of the incredible. Rigo Leone accounted for three of them within as many seconds, flailing them to the cobbles with the chain he swung. Back-alley fighters to a man, his companions joined him, opposing sword and halberd gleefully with fists, boots and iron bars. Into the midst of this mêlée, a few moments later, came the crews of Agnolo Fulvio and Scudo; they assembled their guns with what haste they could, and then looked eagerly about them for opponents. They found few, their comrades having beaten down all the defenders except for two fleeing and terrified crossbowmen. One of these, brought to the ground by a sponge-stave accurately thrown between his feet, impaled himself upon the point of a bolt he was carelessly holding; Scudo felled the other with a cannon-ball, tossed as though it were a pebble from a distance of fifteen paces.

*

Upon the roof of the gatehouse, Tomasello Cennini drew his palm away from the quarrel in his shoulder and wiped blood across the front of his shirt. His fallen and still-flaming torch lay beside him; in a sense, he accounted himself fortunate, since he had accepted realistically the risk of sudden death in standing, as he had done, immobile and unflinching for what had seemed to him like hours. His companion knelt by him.

'How bad?'

'Bad enough,' said Tomasello. 'Wave the torch.'

'What?'

'Pick up the plague-blasted torch,' said Tomasello pleasantly, 'and wave it in the air, misbegotten and stinking son of a pig. I had no time to give the signal.'

His friend complied, raising the flaring sponge above his head and swinging it to and fro in a wide arc.

'Thank you,' Tomasello said.

'And what of you?' demanded the other, lowering the stave once more. 'We cannot leave you here.'

'And why not? Even your worm-infested mind must perceive that no dog of Castelmonte is likely to find me up here,' replied the wounded man ungratefully. 'Go to the devil.'

*

Across the river, Leonardo da Vinci had seen the fall of the torch and had guessed that its bearer was now wounded or, possibly, dead. It was a hazard that he had been forced to accept, but it left him in ignorance concerning the success or failure of his volley. He was relieved, therefore, to see it rise once more into view and move steadily from side to side in the prearranged signal which told him that the inner postern had, indeed, been destroyed. Giunta and Marco, seeing it also, cheered wildly; gunners and engineer embraced, slapping each other on the back.

'By God,' said Marco di Carona, 'I swear that until this minute I had not believed it possible! At five hundred paces, and in the dark? It is a thing to tell one's grandchildren, and they will not believe it either.'

'None the less it is true,' said Leonardo, 'and I thank you, my friends, for your patience.' He disengaged himself with some difficulty, and went over to where Lorenzo de' Medici stood by his horse.

'It would appear,' said the latter, 'that you have earned your hire, Messer Leonardo.'

'Not yet,' Leonardo said, 'but I will agree that the Medici Guns, at least, have proved worthy of further study. Sir, you should now collect what force you may require; God being willing, we enter Castelmonte at first light.'

CHAPTER TWENTY

Rigo Leone looked about him, ignoring the huddled and silent bodies. The *piazza* was roughly semicircular in shape, and alleyways radiated from it like the spokes of a wheel. He counted, and found nine of them, though half he could immediately discount; they led either to the right or straight ahead of him, and therefore away from his objective.

The four men who had been on top of the wall came out of the archway at his rear, having descended the gatehouse stair.

'Tomasello?' he inquired.

'Wounded. He will live,' came the laconic reply.

'Well enough,' said Rigo. 'From which of these streets did the reinforcements come?'

Scudo's loader pointed. 'From that one,' he said. It was the alley that ran closest to the back of the wall itself. Rigo nodded.

'Good,' he said. 'We will take it, then, since it seems likely to lead us most speedily to our goal. Number your crews.'

'All present,' Agnolo said.

'Present,' said Scudo.

'Present,' said Guccio, 'but Stefano has a cut in the arm.'

'How is it, Stefano?'

'It is dead, sir, but it is my left. By God's grace, I can still carry my share.'

'Very well. Cipriano?'

'In order, sir.'

'Then move out,' Rigo said. 'Wheel your guns, unless we come across a stairway. You are reloaded, Cipriano?'

'With ball, sir.'

'Take the rear.'

Quietly, save for the chatter of their wheels over the cobblestones, the gunners rolled forward.

A hundred and fifty paces farther on, Rigo raised his hand; they stopped, and at once heard the sound of footsteps on the top of the wall that lay close at their left hand. Motionless and in deep shadow, they waited. A body of men went by overhead at a run, heading for the gatehouse. When they had passed, Rigo motioned again, setting a faster pace. The quarter seemed deserted; doubtless, the Captain-Gunner concluded, because the defenders had taken the opportunity presented by the winter truce to rid the city—at least temporarily—of its civil population. A mistake on their part, as things had turned out, thought Rigo; he remembered the legend of the geese which had raised the alarm and saved Rome, centuries ago, and grinned to himself as he strode past the unlit doorways.

*

The second reinforcement party, whose arrival at the inner postern had been delayed by the fact that they had reached it along the wall-top rather than by the streets of the town, searched the gatehouse and its surroundings with some care. They found little to enlighten them; to his good fortune, they missed the wounded Florentine on the roof, who held his breath in fervent prayer when the head of an archer appeared briefly in an embrasure a mere armlength from where he was lying.

Their leader, one Mariano di Gaddo, turned over a body which was crumpled against the curtain-wall of the parapet and frowned.

'How is one to make sense of it?' he said. 'They have been torn to pieces.' He crossed to the rear of the wall and spoke into the darkness of the *piazza*. 'What of the others down there?'

'A hand-to-hand fight,' one of his men called up to him. 'And those beneath the archway have been killed by cannon-fire.'

He came down the stairway. 'What nonsense is this?' he demanded. 'Cannon-fire?'

'Most certainly,' replied his subordinate, extending a hand towards him, palm upwards. 'I know small-shot when I see it, and if we cast about I will wager we find the ball that has shattered this door. Did not Nofri speak of a cannon, back there at the main gate?'

'Nofri is a drunkard,' muttered di Gaddo.

'Perhaps. But in this he was right.'

'And where is this cannon now?'

'How the devil should I know? I draw my conclusions from what I see, and that is all.'

Di Gaddo cleared his throat and spat.

'Back,' he decided. 'There is nothing to be done here.' Being no fool where immediate tactics were concerned, he told the two archers in his party to string their bows and walk the alley; then he climbed the stairs again, collected the rest of his men, and set off on the return journey along the wall.

*

He overtook the gunners, as luck would have it, at the point where the wall turned sharply to the left and then ran westward to join the outer battlements. The alley forked here, one arm continuing behind the wall and the other proceeding directly ahead. Estimating that this latter route would take them to the main square, Rigo Leone had chosen it for his assault force; three of his gun-crews had already rolled beyond the corner, and were thus out of sight when Mariano di Gaddo gained the small turret which straddled the angle of the wall.

Cipriano's team, however, had paused at the fork. They would not, according to plan, follow their colleagues until the gun in front of them had safely passed the next cross-alley, some eighty paces ahead. Cipriano heard the footfalls overhead while they were still some distance from him, and would have moved forward in order to avoid detection had matters been left to his discretion. His instructions, none the less, were plain, and he therefore waved his crew to silence and hoped for the best. The approaching defenders were not, he considered, troubling to conceal their presence, and there was thus a chance that they were merely retracing their path to headquarters rather than seeking opposition.

A moment later, clapping his hand to his side, he knew that his hope had been ill-founded. Softly treading and unseen, di Gaddo's archers had advanced in parallel with their fellows on the wall; and now, transfixed by an arrow whose point had glanced along his ribs and was protruding beneath his arm, Cipriano had time only to utter a single hoarse shout of warning before the halberdiers above were leaping down among his men.

Instant confusion prevailed. The eight gunners, outnumbered, accepted the odds with brutal enjoyment; it is to be doubted, indeed, whether they noticed any disparity. For one thing, the weapons and perspiring faces of their attackers enabled them to be seen, if fitfully, while their own blackened skins remained invisible. For another, di Gaddo's pikes, although excellent in a formal charge, were clumsy at close quarters such as these and impeded their holders from the moment their feet touched ground. Landing clumsily and thus burdened, several of the soldiers were smashed into insensibility by the short iron billets of their adversaries before they could regain their footing; discipline and training were, in these surroundings, no match for crude instinct. Cipriano, after snapping off the head of the arrow that impaled his chest in order to withdraw the shaft from the other end of the wound, found himself assailed with drawn sword by Mariano di Gaddo; with cold precision he took the latter's descending blade in his leather-clad upper arm and drove the barbed point he was gripping ferociously upward into the pit of his opponent's stomach. Di Gaddo's breath whistled as he fell, and Cipriano dropped a knee across his throat before wheeling aside to seat himself against the wall. He was in the act of grasping the feathers which still projected from his back when his loader collapsed across him, a pike between his shoulders and blood gushing from his mouth. By the time he had heaved the dead gunner off him, the fight was nearing its end. Tesoro di Veluti stooped over him.

'The archers?' he said.

'Good lad,' said Cipriano. 'They must not escape.' He pointed down the alley towards the inner postern-gate.

'I see nothing,' said Tesoro, 'but no matter for that.'

He ran back to the cannon. All around him men were struggling in the darkness, but he paid them no attention. Swinging back the range-screw, he allowed the muzzle to rise; then, finding the bag which contained the small-shot, he crammed a fistful of these down the barrel on top of the single ball he knew was already resting there. He vaulted nimbly back to the breech, tilted the barrel back to the horizontal, and wrestled the entire gun about until it was pointing down the alleyway. The slow-match, its end burning, was clipped to the side of the carriage; as the last of the swaying combatants cleared from before the cannon, he touched off the fuse, praying that none of his comrades would stumble unwittingly in front of him within the next few seconds.

The gun's fiery explosion seemed to rock the walls at either side of the narrow street, its muzzle-flash freezing the figures around him in a momentary and unreal tableau which vanished at once in the billowing smoke of its discharge. Ignoring the enraged curses of his fellow-gunners, Tesoro sprinted down the alley. He discovered two mutilated corpses, both sprawled in a doorway; there seemed to be no more, and he was certain, after examining them briefly and by touch, that nobody had survived his ill-prepared but lethal shot. He returned to the cannon, to find the surrounding stones littered with prostrate soldiers and four gunners left on their feet.

Cipriano called to him from the angle of the wall.

'It was well done, child,' said his crew-leader painfully. 'The gun is yours. How many are we?'

Tesoro reported the facts.

'Pray, then,' said Cipriano, 'that you come across no stairs. Five of you will be enough to roll it on the level.'

'Perhaps Guccio will give us one of his men.'

'If Captain Leone agrees. You had better not rely on it. Go with God, boy.'

*

Muttering to himself, Noldo Pellegrini surfaced like a mole at the head of his cellar-stairway three streets away. He was a shoe-maker by trade. He was also toothless and—according to his former neighbours—three parts mad. These same neighbours were now dispersed throughout the Tuscan countryside, while Noldo Pellegrini remained undisputed (though solitary) king of the artisans' quarter. When the soldiers had come to drive out the inhabitants of the district shortly after Christmas, he had concealed himself among his flour-bins, mouthing unheard obscenities and clutching a bradawl to his scarecrow chest. Now, hauled from uneasy slumber by the dull concussion of gunfire, he shuffled downhill to determine the cause of his awakening.

In the alley beneath the vineyard wall, he stumbled almost at once over the body of an archer. Cawing in outrage, he bent to prod the obstruction and brought his fingers away sticky with congealing blood. He wiped them on his rags.

A little farther on he detected the sound of breathing, and moved warily towards the noise. He squatted by a fallen pike.

'What passes?' he asked.

Between rattling exhalations, the dying soldier told him.

*

Cipriano di Ser Giacomo Giachetti di Lucca watched Noldo's cackling departure for the inner postern in the first premonitory light of dawn, and sheathed the dagger he had drawn. The effort needed to overtake him would be small, but it was more, upon reflection, than the wounded gunner felt like expending.

*

Girolamo Riario stood at a high window overlooking Castelmonte's main square.

'Cecco,' he said.

His secretary rose nervously and came to him.

'Yes, my lord?'

'Fetch Stoldo, Buonaccorso and Serpe hither. Then go to the Count Giovio della Rovere, and tell him to make ready to meet me. He knows where.'

'Yes, sir. My lord, what does this . . . what does your lordship think is happening out there?'

Riario turned sharply and struck him full in the face with the back of his hand.

'What I think is no concern of yours,' he said. 'Begone.'

*

In his room above the massive north-western portal Captain Guido Falcone, in addition to his other and more pressing troubles, was being forced to reassure Paolo and Ippolito Pazzi, both of whom were clearly panic-stricken.

'I have spoken with those outside,' said Ippolito. 'Falcone, they are saying that we . . . that the postern-door . . . in short, that we are taken. I do not know what the truth of it may be. But I—'

'Sirs,' said Falcone heavily, 'calm yourselves, I pray you.'

'That is all very well,' said Paolo Pazzi. 'But this is no time for calm, or for delay. We must hold at all costs! What are your dispositions? If we are taken in the rear, how will you answer it? And they are mining us!'

'Be silent,' Falcone ordered, more brusquely. 'By God, I find this unseemly. I understand well enough that you are fearful for your skins; but I must tell you plainly, sirs, that I am here to defend a city and not to play wet-nurse to a pair of assassins. Get you hence, and at once! You have swords, have you not? Use them, then, if we come to it.'

Silencing their protests, he ushered them through the doorway and started in search of his commander. In the passageway outside, however, he was detained by a guard, who held the arm of a filthy and ragged greybeard.

'I cannot understand him properly,' said the sentry, 'since he is obviously a lunatic. But I think he is saying that he has seen a dead man in the street, blown to pieces by a cannon.'

*

Federigo da Montefeltro was studying the far bank of the river, where a company of men and horse was gathering beneath the paling sky.

'At all events,' said Guido Falcone, 'it seems plain that there is an assault-party within our wall, however it may have come there. It follows that their objective must be the gate under our feet.'

Montefeltro took his captain's arm and drew him to the embrasure. He pointed.

'And there is the proof of it,' he said. 'Well, now. Would you care to hazard a guess at the size of this assault-party, Guido?'

Captain Falcone rubbed his eyes, grimacing wearily. 'Thirty, or thereabouts,' he said. 'They mined the postern, as you said, but they also killed Peruzzi and his detachment. And di Gaddo has not returned; his party was fifteen strong. They are in force, then, but more than thirty would be unwieldy for a surprise attack.'

'And the inner gate?'

'Mined again, I would think.'

'Or they are still in the vineyard.'

'No,' said Falcone.

'No,' agreed Montefeltro. 'No, they have won the inner gate. Blood of Christ, but we need some knowledge of what has taken place down there!'

'I have sent a reconnaissance party, now that there is light to see by.'

'Their information, I fear, will come too late. Well. We have a town to hold, and hold it we shall, Guido my friend. Where is Rome's Captain-General?'

'I neither know, nor do I care,' said Falcone. 'What of this cannon, sir?'

'I will believe in it when I see it, and not before,' said Montefeltro. The two men looked at each other. 'Let me be honest,

Guido, since we have seen many things together, you and I. A mine I am prepared to accept. If I am wrong, and they have taken the postern with a cannon, then the rest may be true as well. And if they can fire artillery in the black of night, and that with an accuracy unheard of even by daylight . . . why, then, Guido, you are but an old hound, and I another, and we had best seek our place by the fire to warm ourselves and twitch in our dreams.'

*

The Medici Gunners—thirty-one men strong now, and with their four light artillery-pieces—rolled into the main square and at once crossed it, diagonally, to gain the inner mouth of the covered and sharply angled lane which led from it to the city gates. After Cipriano's skirmish in the alley, they had met with no further opposition; nor indeed could they see any sign of life here, though a buzz of turmoil was to be heard at the lane's farther end, invisible to them because of the defensive bend at its central point.

The square itself lay deserted in the half-light. On all sides the façades of the surrounding buildings rose like the grey walls of a canyon, seeming to press inwards upon the space they enclosed. In an upper window, a solitary lantern burned; everywhere else, the shutters were closed and barred, as though the town had turned her back on civil life and now looked only outward, over tower and parapet, towards the hostile world beyond her guardian river.

Guccio Berotti, in the lead, reached the corner by the lane's entry and swung his gun briskly about to cover the square. Behind him came Tesoro di Veluti, his depleted team restored somewhat by the addition to it of the remaining target-man, who was presently acting as replacement loader. Pausing only to allow this worthy to drop his leather bag of solid-shot at Guccio's feet, Tesoro's crew wheeled onward beneath the timbered roof of the lane, to be followed by Agnolo and Scudo, who similarly deposited a bag each with Guccio as they passed him.

Rigo waved at the empty square.

'Keep it as you see it now,' he said. 'I have no wish to be interrupted by a score or so of pikemen at my back.'

'Attend your own business,' said Guccio disrespectfully, 'and leave me to mine. I am beginning to get the feel of this pea-gunnery.'

233

Rigo nodded and followed his other three cannon.

'Lay to the left of that corner opposite us,' said Guccio promptly to his crew, 'and set the range at seventy paces.' He sat on his heels behind the gun. 'Good,' he said. 'Fire.'

The four-pound shot, its impact velocity barely less than that with which it had left the muzzle a split instant earlier, tore a whole section from the corner-pillar of a colonnade as a man might chew out the middle of a carrot. The unsupported upper portion of the column fell from its architrave and toppled into the gutter. Before the smoke had cleared from before the barrel, Guccio's loader was ramming home the wad on top of another measure of powder.

'Now the next,' said Guccio, 'and stop moving as old women do.' He checked the cannon's aim once more. 'Fire,' he said.

A second column collapsed, spurting dust.

'Again,' Guccio said. 'Fire.'

With the removal from beneath it of a third column, the entire corner of the colonnade, together with thirty feet of the face of the building which rested upon it, cracked outwards.

'Fire,' said Guccio.

A quarter of the building shuddered, split, and fell rumbling across the far corner of the square, blocking two access streets with five hundred tons of masonry and timber.

'Excellent,' said Guccio, 'but we have not all day at our disposal. Take the corner to our right, and start with the third pillar from the end. It is a very fair little weapon we have here, all things considered. Fire.'

*

Below Riario's feet, the house shook.

He stared, immobile and in fascination, at the drifting powder-smoke and the half-glimpsed barrel of the gun by the lane.

'Mother of God,' said his aide Buonaccorso from the doorway behind him. 'They will reduce Castelmonte to a heap of rubble!'

'Perhaps,' said Riario. 'Where is Serpe?'

'Downstairs, my lord.'

'Stoldo?'

'By the courtyard gate, sir.'

'It is time for us to leave,' Riario said. 'Find them, and go to the Cappella dei Morti in the Via San Marco, as I told you earlier.

234

Wait there until I arrive, and beware of any treachery on the part of della Rovere and his men.'

*

Tesoro di Veluti, his back against the wall of the lane, checked that his gun could be swivelled quickly and without obstruction so as to point along either arm of it.

His task was twofold. Should the defence overcome Guccio in the square, he must prevent them from storming the lane and taking Rigo's rear; and, if need should arise, he was to give support to Agnolo and Scudo when they emerged into the *piazza* behind the main gate itself. Until called upon to perform either of these duties, he would remain where he was.

Like his comrades about him, he stood easily and with his mouth partly open, a trait which all gunners acquired early and which often gave them the appearance of being half-witted. To stand next to a discharging cannon with jaw set, however, was to invite a ruptured eardrum, the more so in the confined space of the tunnel whose centre he now occupied.

Fifteen paces away from him, Agnolo and Scudo trained their weapons on the farther mouth of the lane. Rigo stood between his lieutenants; knowing that they had, perhaps, three or four pulse beats before their final battle commenced, he pounded each of them on the shoulder in turn as the first of Guccio's shots broke the morning's silence. Dearly though he would have liked to employ these moments, and the sharp edge of surprise they represented, in assessing what lay in the open air ahead, he would be throwing away a badly needed advantage if he did so, and had elected to begin his last assault from where he was.

'After the first volley,' he told them, 'fire as you will. If there are steps, take them. And, for your lives, recharge your guns speedily.'

The dim rectangle of the lane's exit was suddenly filled with oncoming figures. They knew nothing of what they faced, Rigo thought with grim compassion, but they would hardly have been human had they not charged at the sound of Guccio opening fire. The latter's second round thundered from beyond Tesoro di Veluti, and was answered without pause by the overpowering twin percussions to the Captain-Gunner's right and left.

Reloading, his crews advanced, through swirling fumes and

235

over the fallen bodies of the dead and dying, into the *piazza* which was their ultimate objective.

Directly in front of them and some fifty paces away, the huge gates dominated the courtyard, their leaves secured by a bolt half as thick again as a man's body and twenty feet from side to side. Above them the archway supported a narrow and castellated bridge, spanning the gap between a pair of looming turrets. From these, broad stairways led downwards and towards the gunners, forming the chief routes of access to the top of the mighty wall that stretched away until it disappeared from sight behind the houses to east and west of the *piazza*.

In and around this arena there were, Rigo estimated, a hundred men or more. Down the right-hand stairway a party of crossbow-men was running, closely followed by a ragged stream of halber-diers and men with swords. A group of horsemen was clattering away from him into the alley which followed the base of the western wall; presumably, he thought, they intended to retake the main square from one of its flanks. In the gateway itself a some-what indecisive throng of knights and men-at-arms, their faces turned in alarm towards the mouth of the lane, was milling back and forth. He glanced upward, and saw more arbalestiers on the roof-tops; bolts sang, and two of his gunners fell.

His cannon roared again, and the crowd in front of him withered like grass before a scythe. Scudo, first to make ready again, mowed down the defenders on the stairway, and an instant late Agnolo's gun filled an arcade on their left with writhing bodies. Both crews, reloading, dismantled their weapons and fought up the stairways with them, one at each side of the gate, hacking with their boots at those who, wounded, still tried to contest their passage.

Rigo retreated beneath the roof of the lane.

'Tesoro!' he shouted.

'Sir?'

'To me, infant! We have them!'

His third gun rolled to the lane's mouth, thus giving him three sides of the *piazza*. On the bridge above the gates he now saw Federigo da Montefeltro, who had emerged from the turret at the right. Rejoicing inwardly, and heedless of the crossbow-bolts that still hummed about his ears, he advanced to the middle of the square.

'My lord Duke!' he called.

From the tower opposite, Captain Guido Falcone appeared, to stand beside his commander. Both men took in the scene that confronted them. Montefeltro stepped towards the parapet's rearmost edge, looking down at Rigo.

'Surrender,' said the Captain-Gunner. 'I hold you in the palm of my hand, as you see; therefore give up, and save further carnage.'

Montefeltro, undecided, turned to the west, where a detachment was rushing towards him along the battlements. Their charge was suicidal. Almost unable to appreciate what was happening, he saw Agnolo Fulvio's crew set down their gun-carriage at the stair-head, drop the barrel into position, seat the breech, and fire, sweeping the wall-top clear of men as a gale scatters chaff. Behind him he could hear the steady approach of Lorenzo de' Medici at the head of a column of cavalry and foot-soldiers; in the doorway of the turret at his right, Paolo and Ippolito Pazzi stood with craven faces. Of his force in the *piazza* below, more than half were already dead or wounded.

He made up his mind, as a *condottiero* must; his mercenaries, or those of them that were left alive, would fight like men if he ordered them to do so, but what he saw about him now was a chicken-slaughter rather than a battle. Defeat stared him in the face, but defeat could be survived in the world of the *condotta*, whereas massacre could not; and fighting to the last drop of blood was the mark not of a soldier, but of a fool.

He raised his hand.

*

Thus it was that when Lorenzo de' Medici, riding stiffly with Leonardo da Vinci at his right and Toscanelli at his left, arrived before the city gates of Castelmonte, he found them—as Leonardo had foretold—open to greet him. So easy did his victory seem, indeed, that he would almost have suspected a trap, had it not been for the sight of his gunners waving from the battlements overhead.

The *piazza*, when he entered it, was crowded. Immediately opposite him were the guns of Guccio Berotti and Tesoro di Veluti, their crews grime-caked and cheerful. Rigo Leone, his single concession to the formality of the occasion being the discarding of the chain from around his arm, now held Montefeltro's sword and was talking to him, as one professional to another, by Guccio's cannon. The dead were already being dragged aside, and the wounded were limping, or being carried by their fellows, into the shot-scarred buildings at either side.

Toscanelli and Leonardo fell back a little, the latter dismounting and giving his reins to the Florentine mercenary. Lorenzo de' Medici halted a few steps ahead of them, and was approached by Federigo da Montefeltro.

'My lord,' said the *condottiero* simply, 'your guns have taken us. Therefore we surrender this city, and all within it, to the mercy and justice of Florence.'

Lorenzo gazed coldly past him, his eyes searching. A half-minute and more passed in silence before he spoke.

'Give me the Pazzi,' he said.

'They are held, sir, at your pleasure.'

'It is well for you that they are,' said Lorenzo, looking at him for the first time. 'Show them to me.'

*

Among those who watched this scene, there was one at least who did so with cynical indifference. He was seen by few and recognized by none, since he was wearing the cowl and habit of a friar. He had walked unhurriedly through the covered lane, and now stood some distance past the bend at its centre, satisfying himself that the course of action he had chosen was both necessary and correct. Having done so, he turned, and was about to retrace his steps when he was addressed from the ground beside him.

'Bless me, father,' said the mortally wounded soldier who lay against the wall, 'for I have sinned.'

'As have all men,' said Girolamo Riario. 'Farewell.'

At this the dying pikeman cried out in rage and desperation. In the lane's mouth, a gunner turned at the sound. Though it was yet dark beneath the roof-beams of the tunnel, and despite robes and cowl, Tesoro di Veluti recognized the man he sought as though by instinct.

He would have shouted his hatred and defiance, but restrained himself. The Count of Imola was his meat, and his alone. In the dust, a few paces from him, lay a discarded and bloody rapier; he bent swiftly, snatched it up, and ran into the lane like a hare. His

238

sudden departure caused a stir only among those who had been nearest to him. Of these, two men alone instantly perceived the reason for it.

Leonardo gripped Rigo Leone's arm and pointed.

'We are not yet done with Castelmonte,' he said.

They detached themselves from the gunners around them, made their way inconspicuously to the lane's entrance, and then broke into a run.

By the time they gained its inner end, only Tesoro's back was in sight. He was scrambling over a bank of rubble at the corner to their right, and dropped from view beyond it as they changed their direction to pursue him. Skirting the broken pillars and spills of stucco which were all that remained of the arcade and house-fronts along this side of the main square, Leonardo reached the pile of ruined masonry ahead of the Captain-Gunner, and reached back to pull him to its summit. Ahead of them the street lay empty, the first drifts of an early morning mist wreathing its cobbles and gathering at door-sills. They heard the diminishing sound of footsteps in the shadows farther down it, and then nothing more. Rigo, who was still holding Federigo da Montefeltro's sword, gestured uncertainly with its tip.

'We cannot leave the boy to his own devices,' he said. 'Both of us know what he is about.'

*

Tesoro di Veluti took the stairway which led up to the porch of the Cappella dei Morti in three strides and burst open the door with his shoulder, heedless of what he might come upon behind it. For all he cared, he might be entering the very portals of hell itself, so long as he found revenge there for the hideous death of his brother Andrea.

The room in which he found himself was walled in black marble, and filled—or so it seemed to him—with men clad, as his enemy had been, in robes gathered at the waist with knotted cords. At one side of the chapel, for such it clearly was, stood a coffin on a litter. This contained no corpse, but rather a quantity of gold and silver coins, over which two of the seeming friars were in the act of folding a soft cloth.

He understood at once the preparations for flight which he had interrupted. They were not his concern; what enraged him was

239

that he could not distinguish his foe among the fifteen or more similarly dressed figures who now turned menacingly towards him in the gloom. He charged through them, cutting and thrusting with his sword in a white heat of frustration and turning his eyes to this side and that in quest of the murderer he had come to destroy. The sheer fury of his progress carried him to the far end of the nave; and here he found, not indeed the reward he longed for, but another. At the foot of the chancel steps a man was standing, his arms grasping a massive stone candlestick as though he were trying to lift it from its pedestal. His head jerked around, dislodging the cowl from his face. It was the face of the Count Giovio della Rovere, ruler of Castelmonte.

'Dog!' shouted Tesoro di Veluti, and hurled himself forward with thrusting blade. Della Rovere, hampered by the marble cylinder he was trying to support, had no time to draw his sword from beneath his robes. Had he been able to do so, the outcome would have been no different, so violent and uncaring was the young gunner's onslaught. The latter's point ran straight through his body from side to side, tearing open arteries and transfixing his liver; he rolled his eyes, staggered, and collapsed, the mighty candlestick toppling with him.

Across his lifeless body spilled a dazzling tide of emeralds, rubies, and diamonds, hidden within the pillar's core and now scattering, as from a cornucopia, about the polished flags; but Tesoro di Veluti, obsessive still in his lust for vengeance, paid them no attention. As he struggled wildly to free his sword, he was barely aware of those who now fell upon him and beat him, senseless, to the floor.

*

Leonardo and Rigo heard his cry of rage from the street and, crossing it, climbed the stairway to the mortuary-chapel in unison. Since they were not driven by the careless and all-consuming passion that held di Veluti in its grip, they might well have been daunted by the scene that greeted them beyond the doorway; but their approach had been noiseless, and they accordingly had the advantage of those inside, if not in numbers.

Most of their opponents were clustered around the fallen gunner, and those who were nearer to the door were impeded by their monkish costume. Two were already dead, having been slain by Tesoro in his rush towards the altar. They disposed of another pair within moments of their entry, but the odds against them were still heavy.

Upon surveying these odds, Rigo Leone at once seized a lamp from a low cabinet beside him, poised it for an instant, and then hurled it at the group by the chancel steps. It burst among them, spreading flame and striking many-coloured glints from the gems that lay unheeded all about the marble floor of the nave. Three men, their oil-soaked robes afire, struggled vainly to strip themselves of these; Rigo charged into the remainder, chopping right and left unskilfully but with overpowering strength, and won his way to the choir-stalls beyond them, from which vantage-point he was able to overturn the second of the gigantic candlesticks upon those who sought to reach him, and thus gained himself a breathing-space.

Leonardo, choosing for the moment to stay where he was in order to divide the opposition, found himself assailed by a tall fellow with a stiletto, upon whose heels followed two more with drawn blades. He picked his spot with care, ran the dagger-bearer through the stomach, and plucked the weapon from his nerveless fingers as he fell. Left-handed, and without pause, he flung this with chilling accuracy at the first of the men who came behind, sinking it to the hilt in his chest, and dropped his fellow a second later with an upward flick of his rapier that took him in the throat.

There being no more to do at this end of the chapel, he ran the length of the nave to Rigo's assistance. The gunner, who was standing on a choir-bench, had placed the sole of his foot squarely and without ceremony in the face of the nearest and most determined of his attackers, and now straightened his leg with the force of a piston, catapulting his victim backwards with a velocity that raised the latter's heels from the ground and spread his arms wildly as though in flight. He was dead even before he landed at the foot of the chancel-steps, with the pommel of Leonardo's rapier jammed hard against the small of his back and two feet of its blade jutting forward from his breastbone. His hurtling weight tore the grip from Leonardo's hand; off-balance, the artist stepped aside, and lost his footing on one of the treacherously rolling jewels that littered the ground. He stumbled gracelessly, fighting for poise, and heard Rigo laugh. His hand, seeking a purchase, alighted upon what he recognized as the fallen body of Giovio della Rovere. Being now unarmed, he placed his knee against the side of the corpse for purchase and heaved the sword from its rib-cage, regaining his feet as two of the burned men dashed at him. Their assault lacked both skill and conviction; he cut one of them down contemptuously and, whirling aside from the charge of the other, seized him about the neck with a vice-like grip and ran his skull into the base of the pulpit.

Breathing a little rapidly, he turned once more, his back against the choir-screen, only to find that with the collapse of Rigo's last opponents there was nobody left to fight with.

In a corner beneath the lectern, he saw Tesoro di Veluti begin to stir. Rigo came heavily down the steps into the nave, blood dripping from his sleeve and a grin on his face.

'Riario?' asked Leonardo briefly.

'Nay,' said the Captain-Gunner, 'you must have killed him yourself. Things have been somewhat hectic these past minutes, but I believe I would have noticed had I done so.'

They looked at one another and began, systematically and as though of one mind, to turn over the bodies that were sprawled around them. It was Tesoro di Veluti, regaining his senses and perceiving what they were about, who enlightened them.

'He ran,' said the young gunner, clutching his head. 'It was while I was in the act of killing della Rovere.'

'He did not come through the door, then,' Rigo said, 'or he would have passed us.'

'No,' said Tesoro, pointing. 'He went towards the altar, I think.'

Leonardo and Rigo climbed the steps to the choir with sinking hearts. Beyond the stalls, a tapestry moved slightly, and was still. They wrenched it aside, and revealed a narrow archway and a flight of stairs, from whose foot a cold and gentle breeze was blowing, its touch upon their faces an empty and ironic caress.

*

The Florentine guards at the postern-gate watched, incuriously, the progress of the friar who was making his way across the vineyard, stooping ever and again over the dead as though in blessing. He arrived without haste beneath the outer gatehouse, and raised a hand in grave salute.

'*Pax vobiscum,*' he said.

'*Et tecum, pax,*' replied one of the posted men, mechanically. 'Here is labour in plenty for you.'

'It is ever thus, in war,' agreed the friar, 'and there are more outside that have gone to meet their Creator. Have I your leave to pass?'

'Of course.'

'I thank you for your courtesy,' said the Count of Imola. '*Benedicamus Domine*, now and always.'

'Amen,' the guard said, and stood aside.

CHAPTER TWENTY-ONE

'He held against us last year,' said Guido Toscanelli. 'It is something, sir, to be considered.'

'That was last year,' said Lorenzo de' Medici. He was sitting at the head of the table in his library, and turned his head and shoulders towards Leonardo, who was at his right. 'Things are different now.'

'His *condotta*, none the less, is famed,' insisted Toscanelli. 'The very name of Federigo da Montefeltro—'

'Has been diminished somewhat since yesterday morning,' commented Lorenzo drily. 'He has paid us a fine of sixty thousand florins. Are you now suggesting that I should give it back to him in hire?'

'By no means,' said Toscanelli. 'He will come with us for less, since he knows Rome cannot march this way. Offer him his keep, and that of his men, for nine months, and let him hold Castelmonte for Florence instead.'

'I will consider it,' said Lorenzo. 'More to the point is the question of Rome's next move. Sixtus cannot now attack us directly, and will seek an alliance with Lucca or Siena; and we cannot afford to stand still while he does so. Captain Leone, your task for the present is clear enough, I think. We have all summer before us, and you will want to perfect the use of your new guns. Messer Leonardo, how many more should we acquire? Our coffers are full.'

'That decision is yours, sir,' Leonardo said.

'Naturally,' said Lorenzo, 'but I am seeking your advice as their inventor and my engineer.'

'With respect, sir, I must point out that our bargain is fulfilled.'

'So it is. I had not forgotten. What terms do you ask for a further period in my service?'

Leonardo leant forward. 'Sir, I owe you my thanks for your forbearance during a time when my intentions cannot have been clear to you. May I ask for it again? I leave Florence at the start of next week.'

'I would persuade you otherwise if I could. Where do you go?'

'I have not yet decided. Perhaps northward, to Milan. Perhaps not.'

He rose from the table, bowed, and left the room. They watched him depart.

'An agile mind,' said Toscanelli. 'But a devious one.'

'I am not so certain that it is devious,' said Lorenzo de' Medici. 'Something else, perhaps. None the less, I would give a great deal to know what his intentions are. Do you have an urge to see Milan, Captain Leone?'

'I had not thought about it, sir,' said Rigo in some surprise.

'Do so,' Lorenzo told him. 'The Milanese are excellent gun-makers, and in any case it would be no disadvantage to Florence should Sforza—happening, it may be, to hear the tale of the fall of Castelmonte—decide to join us because of our skill in cannonry.

*

'They say,' announced Bianca Visconti from the balcony, 'that you are a hero. Were we in ancient Rome, they would have given you a triumphal procession. What does it feel like to be a hero?'

'Very pleasant, for an hour or two,' Leonardo told her. 'After that, one begins to wonder whether it is true, and a day later one concludes that it is not.'

'That is what you would conclude, of course.'

'I am not sure what you mean by that.'

'I mean that there are a thousand other men who would conclude nothing of the kind. Silvio Grimiani, for instance.'

'He is dead,' said Leonardo. 'And I remain alive, which is all that matters.' He came to the window and stood behind her.

'True,' said Bianca. 'You are right, as ever. Giuliano is dead, too, and Constanza weeps; you are here, and if I weep, it is for her grief and my own happiness. What will become of her?'

'I have written on her behalf to Cardinal della Palla.'

'So that he may find her a convent?'

'It is what she wishes,' said Leonardo.

'I know. I would not choose the life of a nun, were I in her place,' Bianca said. 'But then, I am not in her place. And she may change her mind when the baby comes . . . No, she will not; I know her too well. She will send it to her aunts. Why Cardinal della Palla?'

Leonardo considered this.

'Because,' he said, 'he is the nearest I have to a friend, now that Giuliano is gone.'

'You have Rigo Leone.'

'Not yet,' said Leonardo. 'Eventually, perhaps, but not yet.'

Bianca turned to face him.

'And myself.' She put her arms about his neck, and he kissed her. 'Friend,' she said. 'Pupil, always. Lover, if you wish it so.' She laid a finger against his lips. 'And do not start to argue with me, Leonardo, as you always do. You may say yes, or no; but I will not listen to your reasons, since love itself is unreasonable.'

'Madonna,' said Leonardo gently, 'in a few days from now I am leaving Florence.'

'I know that too. What has it to do with anything? Giuliano is dead, and Constanza will spend her life in a convent; and already you are speaking of tomorrow. I will give you anything you ask of me, but tomorrow is not mine to give. If we meet again, we shall rejoice in it, and if we do not, how will reason help us? Therefore choose now, and for both of us; yes or no?'

'And how do you know that I love you, Bianca?'

'Oh, as to that,' Bianca replied, 'I have known it for much longer than you, since I have no need to reason, or consider, or conclude. Sometimes I feel quite sorry for you. Well?'

'Yes,' Leonardo said.

CHAPTER TWENTY-TWO

Ahead of them the road led southward into summer. His companion seemed ill at ease, and finally spoke.

'I have a confession to make,' he said. 'Lorenzo—'

'It is made,' said Leonardo, 'and therefore let us talk of other matters, such as the possible defences against mobile artillery.'

Rigo Leone made no reply to this, and they rode on in silence. After another mile had passed:

'This is not the road to Milan,' the gunner said.

'I am not going to Milan,' said Leonardo, 'but to Malta.'

'Malta! In God's name, why?'

'For good reasons, or bad. Life is full of surprises, if we but allow them to come to us.'

'I had thought . . .' Rigo began. 'That is . . .'

Leonardo leaned forward and patted his horse's neck. He was laughing.

'I know what you thought,' he said, 'and what Lorenzo thought. But let us ride together anyway.'

A Site of big guns on main ridge: as the contours indicate, these cannot be
   sited so as to fire directly at main gateway of Castelmonte
B Site from which final assault commences and from which Leonardo shoots
   out the outer and inner postern-gates
C Outer postern ('The Serpent's Mouth')
D Vineyard
E Inner postern with small square behind it
F Main Square (shot to bits by Gunners)
G Angled and covered lane between gate-square and main square
H Gate-square, with stairways leading up to wall and turrets
 I Main gateway
J Cappella dei Morti
K Castle and monastery on top of Castelmonte's peak: access road zigzags
   up steep approach

Main wall of Castelmonte

Roadway from Rome to Florence

River

Rough tracks for gun-haulage

Route taken by Medici Gunners in final assault

THE STORMING OF CASTELMONTE

The Principal Characters

*

THE FLORENTINE COURT

*Lorenzo de' Medici	Ruler of the Republic of Florence
*Giuliano de' Medici	Brother to Lorenzo de' Medici
Guido Toscanelli	*Condottiero* in the employ of Florence
Bianca Maria Visconti	Ward of Lorenzo de' Medici; Cousin to Lodovico Sforza, Regent of the Duchy of Milan
Constanza d'Avalos	Ward of Lorenzo de' Medici, betrothed to Giuliano de' Medici
Carla d'Avalos	Sister to Constanza d'Avalos
Silvio Grimiani di Torino	Prince of Savoy
*Andrea del Verrocchio	Artist
Dr Cino di Lapo Mazzone	Scholar
Fra Sigismondo Carregi	Cleric
Matteo Barletta	Archer

THE MEDICI GUNNERS

Roderigo Leone	Captain-Gunner, the Army of Florence
Scudo	Lieutenant-Gunner
Agnolo Fulvio	Lieutenant-Gunner
Cipriano di Lucca	Gunner
Tesoro di Veluti	Gunner
Andrea di Veluti	Gunner
Marco di Carona	Gunner
Piccio Berignalli	Gunner
Balestraccio	Gunner
Guccio Berotti	Gunner
Tomasello Cennini	Gunner
Giunta di Lenzo	Gunner

THE DEFENDERS OF CASTELMONTE

Giovio della Rovere	Governor of Castelmonte
Bona della Rovere	His wife
*Federigo da Montefeltro	*Condottiero*, Duke of Urbino
Guido Falcone di Riccomano	Captain
Ridolfo Peruzzi	Watch Commander
Guaspare di Piombino	His second-in-command
Nofri	Soldier
Alessandro Gambacorte	Soldier
Mariano di Gaddo	Soldier
Noldo Pellegrini	Shoemaker

THE PAPAL COURT

*Sixtus IV, Francesco della Rovere	Pope
*Rodrigo Borgia	Cardinal
Domenico della Palla	Cardinal, Apostolic Chancellor
*Girolamo Riario	Count of Imola, Captain-General to the Armies of the Holy Roman Church
*Rafaello Sansoni-Riario	Cardinal
Manfredo Romolo-Paro	Bishop

THE CONSPIRATORS

*Jacopo Pazzi	Banker of Florence
*Francesco Pazzi	His son
Paolo Pazzi	His son
Ippolito Pazzi	His son
Benno Foscari	Assassin
*Bernardo Bandini	Assassin
Mario Bandini	Assassin
*Francesco Salviati	Archbishop-Designate to Pisa

THE INVENTOR OF THE MEDICI GUNS

*LEONARDO DA VINCI   Seeker of truth

*These characters lived in history.

Pistrola and Castelmonte, although quite typical of the many fortified hill-towns and villages of Tuscany, exist only in our imagination.

M.W.
R.R.